THE ROOMS WE HIDE

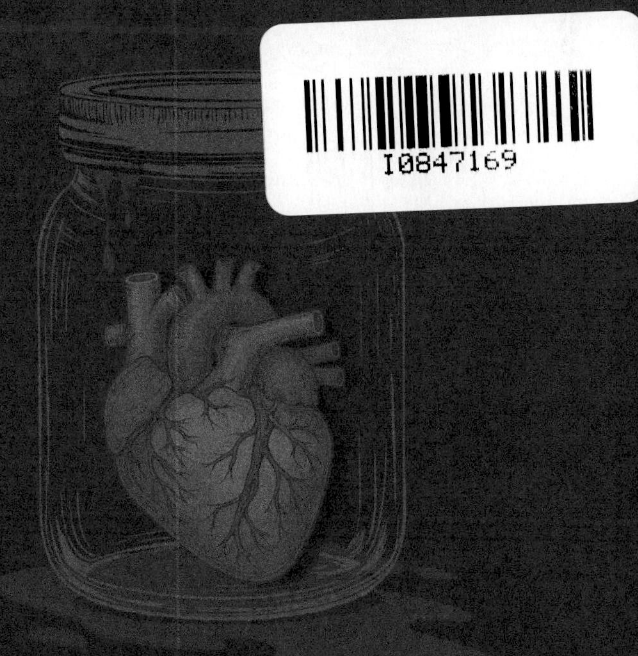

J.S. MERCIER

Dedication

While there are so many people to thank and dedicate this book to, I have to narrow it down a bit.

First, to my friends and family who supported me on this journey, especially those of you who will still speak to me after you read this and realize that there is more wrong with me than you ever knew. I tried to warn you.

Second, to Kim, Boda, and Peaches, my alpha readers. You bitches rock my world. Thank you for being such a big part of this ride from the very beginning - this story wouldn't be what it was without your help!

Third (and last but not least), to my baby sisters. While I don't recommend that you follow the actions in this book, let it act as a reminder that there is no need to endure some limpdicked fuckboy with delusions of grandeur. Call me, I'll help hide the bodies.

Also, please don't tell Mom and Dad if you read this. I'm too old to be grounded.

Interested in listening along with the mucis that helped inspire the story? Check out the Spotify playlist for this story and all my others!

Content Warning

This book is a mixture of humor and darkness - I truly believe life isn't worth living without both.

The goal is to make you laugh, cry, and yearn for revenge along with Jenevive. There is betrayal, torture, murder, revenge, references to previous physical assault, and plenty of spice. Please be mindful of your own limitations and triggers as you read.

Chapter 1

H e's dead.

I trained for this. Dad made sure I have the skills, and it's not like I haven't planned it out a thousand times already... so why shouldn't I? I know I can get away with it, and this is the last straw. I can lure him to the cabin, slip something in his drink, and then take him out to the barn to destroy the evidence.

Easy peasy.

I'll make it quick since we have so much history. Painless enough he won't even be aware of what's happening. He's been my best friend for ten years. My ride or die. Does that cut him some slack, though? I could take him out while he's unconscious instead of drawing his death out like I really want to for putting me through this.

I could... wait.

"I'm sorry, but... what?" I couldn't have heard him right.

"One hundred and seventeen!" He repeats, his beady little eyes lit up with a holy zeal. "All different, most hand made and one of a kind. I buy a lot of them off Etsy and from specialized dealers. I set up custom shelving and glass cabinets with dedicated lighting to showcase my best pieces. It's quite the collection." He smiles at me like he thinks his collection prowess equals sex prowess.

Hint: It does not.

"You own... one hundred and seventeen dragon statues?"

Surely not. This man is 27 years old. This grown ass man cannot seriously be talking about a collection of dragon statues. The excitement shining through his baby face makes him seem more like he's a 14-year-old boy seeing his first pair of tits than a dude talking about dragon statues.

"Absolutely! I've been collecting them since I was 17. They're just so majestic, don't you think?"

Um, ok. "I guess I never really thought about it. I'm more of a shifter girl when it comes to fantasy."

He glares at me like I offended his ancestors. "Dragons aren't fantasy! There is an incredible amount of documentation from many cultures throughout history that proves dragons were real. If these cultures had no way of contacting each other still believed in and depicted the same creatures in their literature and art, it is definitive evidence they truly existed! Just because you've never seen one yourself doesn't mean they didn't exist. You've never seen a woolly mammoth walk down the street, but you believe they existed, right? What about a Dodo bird? Ever seen one of those in a pet store? Just because they're not still around now doesn't mean they weren't around at some point in time. On top of that, new theory and research shows the T-Rex may have been a dragon in its own right. Everyone was always so confused about why they had such small arms, right?"

"Um, I guess?" Are dragon arms something people think about?

"Well, their arms have now been compared to that of an ostrich, and they are remarkably similar in design. Many researchers now believe the T-Rex didn't have arms, they had wings! Whether they breathed fire is debatable, but it is entirely possible the" and here, he uses finger quotes because obviously he buys this, "'arm bones' are actually the base of their wings. The length of the wings isn't with their remains because they were cartilage and therefore decomposed with the rest of the body. It's quite probable some species survived and evolved and were seen by primitive societies."

All I can picture now is the meme of the guy from TV with the crazy hair saying "I'm not saying it's aliens, but it's aliens" superimposed over this weirdo's face. I wonder if he would let me mess up his hair so he could better look the part? Probably not. It's too short anyway, he wouldn't be able to achieve that lovely volume and lift. Shame.

"Current popular theory is if we can find the right set of bones and obtain DNA, scientists can figure out how they breathed fire and can help humans do the same." The gleam in his eye is zealous as he talks about it. Because humans breathing fire is right up there in importance with, say, curing cancer. Solving world hunger. Literally anything else.

"That is so interesting, I never thought of it like that, but I can understand your point." I fake a smile and then give a real wince, "Can you excuse me for a second? I need to run to the restroom."

"Of course, I'll wait right here."

Because he would wait somewhere else? I cannot leave this table fast enough. What was Brandon thinking, setting me up with this guy? I understand I need to get out more, but I would rather turn into a 67-year-old spinster with one hundred and seventeen cats than end up with someone like Dragon Boy and his precious figurines.

As I lock myself in a stall and pull out my phone to send my soon-to-be-deceased best friend an SOS text, I take a few deep breaths to ensure I don't start screaming and frighten the middle-aged woman who had walked out of the stall to my left and started picking at her teeth in the bathroom mirror with her fingernail. Without washing her hands first.

Gross. Does she want dysentery? Because I'm pretty sure that's how you get dysentery.

> **Me:** 911. 5 minutes or you're DEAD to me.

> **Bran:** What's wrong? I thought you'd like this guy!

> **Me:** Brandon I WILL SET YOU ON FIRE.

Heh. Get it?

> **Bran:** Oooook. 5 minutes.

After a few moments of continued deep breathing (sadly, sans fire), I pull myself together enough to go back to the table. I haven't heard the door open since I entered the stall, so I flush the toilet to make it appear like I had a reason to be in here for as long as I was and... yep. The tooth picker is still at the mirror. No floss, just two inches long acrylic nails and damn is she getting deep in there.

I wash my hands thoroughly to waste a little more time while she continues to dig for gold, briefly considering offering her one of the floss picks I keep in my purse, but decide to refrain since she has such dedication working for her. I finally head back to what will hopefully be my last few minutes with my most recent dating failure. Arriving back at our table I allow myself to indulge in a few more homicidal fantasies. Does he deserve a quick and painless death? Should I visit karmic justice on him and set him ablaze like the dragons that are the current bane of my existence? I could Blood Eagle him as punishment like the Vikings did. That plan has merit, so a small smile curves my lips as I take my seat across from the man I have now dubbed DB since I can't remember his actual name. Brett? Aaron?

"Do you want to see some photos?" DB questions with hope in his eyes. "I had some professionally done, and they're amazing!"

Jesus wept.

"Wow, professionally done, huh?" I take a deep breath to prepare myself for this insanity but I'm saved by the bell. Faking another wince when I check my caller ID, I say "Sorry, this is work."

He mumbles "no problem" while scrolling through his photos like they're of a cherished first child, and I suppress a shudder.

"Hello?"

"Hey Killer. This is me calling you with yet another excuse to leave yet another date with yet another guy you aren't giving a chance. Come on down to the store . We'll get drunk after I lock up."

Screwing my face into an Oscar worthy show of worry about a cherished co-worker and her crotch goblin, I gasp and say "Oh no! Of course, I can come in. Please tell Steph to let me know if she needs me to cover for her tomorrow too, and tell the rest of the staff I'll be there in 10." I hang up to the sound of Brandon chortling and give DB a rueful smile and apologetic wince. "I'm so sorry, my night shift manager got a call from her babysitter and had to rush home for an emergency with her youngest child. I need to go in, so I can close up the store for her, I'm the only other person available with the authority."

"Oh wow, how terrible. I can come with you though! I can browse while I wait and then you can come back to my place and see my collection and meet my iguana Steven. Maybe we can watch a movie or something, too." The hope on his face almost makes me feel guilty, but then I imagine trying to have a relationship with a man while constantly being supervised by a hoard of dragons and an iguana named Steven, and it evaporates much like his chances of ever getting laid did when he set up his first curio cabinet.

Barely suppressing my shudder, I try to be as polite as possible while declining. "Thanks, but no. I'm not into dragons." As I stand I drop a $20 bill to cover my meal and tip -- I hate having these failed dates pay for my meals. "You should check out the Dungeons and Dragons group that meets up in the store on Tuesday nights. There are a few single girls you may click with."

His face flashes with fury so quickly I can almost swear to myself I missed it. "Yeah, maybe. I'm not really into those kinds of girls, they can get a little obsessive about fantasy and lose track of reality."

Annnnnnd, that's my cue. Walking out like one of his precious dragons lit a fire under my ass, I call out "It was lovely meeting you!" and head to my car.

Never. Again.

Cat lady life, here I come.

CHAPTER 2

B efore I head to the store I run home to drop off my car and purse. Lucky for me, our apartment building is located in the same shopping center as the store where Brandon and I work, so I don't have to worry about getting home after a few drinks tonight. The sprawling center is only a few years old and filled with amazing shops, bars, and restaurants and is full of life almost 24 hours a day. I love it here. There are small grass covered spaces with picnic tables, gazebos, and fountains for people to gather and relax or enjoy a treat from one of the coffee or sweet shops scattered throughout the area, and they have festivals and concerts in the biggest plot throughout the year. Everything is kept tidy and free of trash and graffiti and the security staff that oversees the complex is made up of an awesome group of guys. I know a lot of them and always feel safe walking home at night thanks to them.

If I hadn't been on a date I wouldn't have carried a purse. I usually don't need to. My apartment building uses an app or codes instead of door keys and the store has a keypad entry, so for a while all I needed a key for was my car. A few months after my dad passed away, my beloved 1997 Honda CRV broke down on the side of the interstate and I finally admitted her time was over. I used some of my inheritance to buy a Hyundai Tucson, because it has a keyless open and start app and I became key free. Now, unless there's a reason for me to bring my purse I can head out with just my phone with the wallet case on it and my trusty Carmex. I don't go anywhere without at least one tube of Carmex.

I think about changing into some comfy clothes, but I made the effort to get dress up tonight for this date, and by God I am going to take advantage of that as long as possible. My black crop pants hug my curves and the cami under my royal blue three-quarter sleeve cardigan is low cut enough to give a decent hint of the girls while perfectly framing the turtle pendant on my favorite necklace, and the sweater's color sets off my highlights and tattoos nicely. My strappy sandals show off my fresh black and silver french pedicure. I can't believe I wasted this fine ass on a dude obsessed with dragons.

I drop my purse off at home and grab an empty tote bag with a picture of Shakespeare on it and reads "Oxford Dictionary in the streets, Urban Dictionary in the sheets -- Willy Shakes" so I can raid Brandon's apartment for liquor since my crappy mood is one hundred percent his fault tonight. Entering the code to gain entry to his apartment, I break in and pick through his stash until I find a new bottle of Honey Jack, toss it in my tote, and head to the store on a mission to get plastered. I have no idea what on Earth made him think DB and I would have a connection. Not only are dragons so not my thing (unless they're sexy alpha male dragon shifters), but he came to dinner wearing jorts.

JORTS, for fuck's sake.

Because ironed jean shorts creased and paired with a polo shirt, braided leather belt, and loafers is an attractive look on anyone.

I know Brandon is worried about me. I know he thinks I'm already well on my way to spinsterhood, that I need to get out more and sow my oats or whatever it is a normal 20-year-old does, but I'm not so desperate that I need to sacrifice my dignity yet. He thinks being a 20-year-old virgin is the worst thing that could ever happen, but I'm not this picky because I think I'm too good for anyone, or because I'm stuck up like a few of my coworkers think. I'm picky because I know what it feels like to connect with someone in a way that was just... right. I know how it feels to meet someone and know they're the one for you, to feel complete when you're with them. I had that once, and even though it was years ago I've never met anyone else who held a candle to him. Why settle for less than you know you deserve?

Besides, who needs men when you have battery operated boyfriends?

I love this store. On The Rebound is a second hand book and entertainment store that was opened by Brandon's mom when we were kids. Back then, it was in a much smaller location a few miles away and if I wasn't with my dad, at school, or hanging out with the guys, I was often there. Browsing the shelves for the newest treasures. Helping Mrs. C stock shelves and assist customers before she gave me a job. Creating displays for her, and chatting with her about one day taking over when she's ready to retire. My love of reading and music was developed and nurtured here, and to be honest, I think I got my ability to read people from seeing what people read, watch, and listen to as much as I did from training with my dad.

Since I started hanging, and eventually working, at the store, I've realized you can't always judge a book by its cover (pun completely intended). I cannot tell you how many uptight looking women come in looking for smutty books. The majority of them seem almost ashamed, which is sad to me because everyone should be able to let their freak flag fly. Once, I had a woman who had to be in her 80s come in looking for a hardback copy of Den of Vipers to add to her collection. She was about five feet tall with gray-blue hair pulled back in a sleek bun, and she wore an oversized dressing gown with sagging knee socks and loafers. When I told her we didn't have one in stock but I could check about getting one for her, she winked at me, cackled, and said "If I can't have my own Diesel, at least I can have a sexy book for my shelf! Talk about a dream guy!" She's since come back multiple times, and we always take a few minutes to swap book recommendations. That old bat is a trip and always outdoes me on the spice level of her picks, and I'm totally here for it. I've decided I want to be her when I grow up.

We moved the store over to the new shopping center about a year ago and Mrs. C decided once we were settled in at the new location she would back off and see how Brandon and I ran things. We're both working there while in school for business degrees, but while my ultimate goal is to buy the store from his mom, he wants something else. What, he's not sure yet, but he knows On The Rebound is my dream, not his. I have a feeling his ever-changing bed partners are a side effect of not knowing what he wants to do with his life and not feeling settled. I'm personally in no hurry, in either business or my personal life. I know the store will be mine eventually, and I'm in no rush to make it happen. It feels good to know I can learn the business without all the pressure on me to fail or succeed. I couldn't ask for a better mentor than Mrs. C, and since she didn't have any formal education we're both benefiting from mine. The same idea goes for my love life, or lack thereof. It will happen when it happens. There's no need to rush or pine for something I can't control. Whatever man I end up with will have a lot to live up to, both because my Dad raised me right, and because I read way too much.

I was shocked when Mrs. C took my advice and moved the store, but it has worked out so well. The new shopping center draws an insane amount of traffic and moving allowed us to expand which allowed us to add a cafe, meeting space, gaming areas, and reading nooks. Our cafe offers coffees, hot chocolates, smoothies, flavored teas, sandwiches, and pastries. We have groups reserve our meeting space for book and other club meetings, role-playing games, and sometimes birthday parties. I've even been able to schedule a few book signings and events for indie authors, which has been amazing. Our gaming area lets people play games together before they buy them, and once a month we have tournaments for prizes and money.

Since the store will transfer to me one day, Mrs. C had me help her design and set up the new location. The wooden floors and shelving are all stained a deep, rich brown and the walls are painted in a soothing shade of gray with a hint of purple. The reading nooks are comfortable places to relax and enjoy a book or magazine and hang out with friends. They all boast plush rugs, but depending on which nook you choose you will find either an armchair, couch, or bean bags to sit on. Each has an abundance of comfortable pillows, and some have a blanket for those who get cold. I often find myself hanging out in my favorite spot before or after my shifts, especially when one of my favorite authors releases a new book. My spot has a gas fireplace and is surrounded by floor pillows and bean bag chairs and I can lose myself there for hours. It doesn't hurt that it's in the view of the cafe and I can usually pout my way to having treats brought to me, which is awesome because I don't have to get up.

I'd say I don't understand how Brandon doesn't want to run this store for the rest of his life, but he has never loved it as much as I do. All the better for me though, because he won't stand in my way when his mom is ready to let go.

My walk is short and comfortable from the apartment to the store. It takes less than ten minutes, even with stopping next door for a half dozen specialty cupcakes and a Diet Coke. Making my way inside, I head to the front counter to check if my copy of Albany Walker's newest book is here yet and give Brandon my infamous death stare while he checks out a group of teenage boys who are cleaning us out of Dragonball Z figurines.

Jackpot! My beautiful new paperback is waiting for me in my cubby, and I snatch it up like I'm Gollum and the book is My Precious. Before I can head over to my favorite reading nook I head to the back and grab one of my favorite tumblers. It is coated in hot pink glitter and reads "All I want to do is pet cats and listen to metal," and Brandon got it for me for my 19th birthday. Filling it up with ice, I splash in a healthy portion of the Honey Jack and top it off with my Diet Coke. I don't care if everyone judges me for this drink, it's my jam, and with the way I make it, it often only takes one before I'm tipsy.

I hide the bottle of Jack in my desk drawer and stash the rest of my Diet Coke in the staff fridge before making my way back out front with my book, drink, and cupcakes. With about two hours left until we close, I intend to forget my shitty date by eating at least one red velvet cupcake and getting tipsy while losing myself in another of Albany's books.

Dropping down on to my oversized bean bag chair and taking a healthy sip of my drink, I settle in and crack my book. Ever since reading Friends with the Monsters, I've one clicked on anything she puts out. Brandon The Dead Best Friend comes by to try to chat with me, but I give him a cupcake and send him on his way. I may have said I'd come here to drink and hang with him, but the store is still open and I'm in the process of finding a new book boyfriend.

What seems like minutes later, but evidently has been a few hours by the dimmed store lighting, Brandon drags another bean bag over next to me, takes my tumbler to freshen up my drink and grabs my box of cupcakes. Plopping down on to his own beanbag he stretches out and tangles his legs up with mine while taking a huge bite of his strawberry and cream cupcake. "Spill," he demands through a mouthful of cake. "What was wrong with this one? I genuinely thought he was a nice guy."

"Are you fucking kidding me, dude? Nice is good and all, but what made you think I would fall for the master of dragons? In our more than fifteen year friendship, what made you think after all this time, dragons would be what finally gets to me?"

Brandon sputters and chokes on another huge mouthful of cupcake, and I'm hit in the face with a tiny chunk of cake. "Gross! What the hell!"

It takes him a minute to stop coughing up crumbs and icing, and by the time he's done his face has darkened about five shades of red. Once he's collected himself, he asks "What are you talking about? What do dragons have to do with anything?" Suspicious, I narrow my eyes at him. How can he not be aware of the dragon thing? Is this payback for swapping all his boxers for male g-strings last month? He said he wasn't even mad anymore after he realized how comfortable they are and then met the one crazy chick who was into them.

"Like you don't know. At this point, I don't even remember his name because I replaced it with Dragon Boy, or DB for short. The guy has one hundred and seventeen dragon figurines and an iguana named Steven. Granted, if the dragons weren't an issue I'd be fine with the iguana, but seriously! He talked about dragons like they're scientific fact and tried to show me pictures of them like they were his children. He asked me if I wanted to come over after I got off work and see them. And he was wearing jorts, Brandon!"

"What the fuck is a jort?" I'm not sure how he's hung up on that fact and not the dragon thing.

"Jean shorts. Like, knee-length tapered jean shorts that had been ironed with a crease down the center like they were a pair of khakis. With a tucked in polo, braided leather belt, and loafers with no socks. What part of me makes you think he would be a match for me?" I sigh and suck down half of my refilled drink, waiting for the alcohol to kick in and mellow me out. I'm a silly and sleepy drunk, and that sounds just about right tonight.

Brandon releases a sigh to match mine, and gives me a sheepish look. "I'm sorry Killer. I met him while out the other night, and he seemed cool. I swear, there was no talk of dragons, and he was chill. He wasn't dressed like a dork either, he had on khakis and a button down. The khakis didn't have creases, so I'm not sure what he was thinking." He snorts and continues by saying "Maybe he's like Date Michael Scott. He realizes he's on a date, so he gets all crazy and obnoxious because he thinks it's what he's supposed to do."

Narrowing my eyes, I scowl at him. "You set me up with someone you'd only met once? What the fuck Brandon? What if he was a serial killer or something?"

He deadpans me and then laughs. Shaking his head he apologizes. "I'm sorry. I don't know what else to say. He seemed like a cool guy and you never date. You never hang out with anyone other than me or Daniel, or sometimes someone from work. You don't go out, and you're still a virgin for God's sake! It's been four years, Jen. It's time to move on and live your life for you, not for a memory."

We've had this argument hundreds of times, and it's getting really, really old. "I've told you, I'm not waiting for him or putting my life on hold because of him. Why can't you understand I don't have the need to have sex with anyone with a pulse? I'm happy how things are in my life right now. I've waited this long, but I'm not waiting for Ryan, I'm just waiting for someone to make me feel something. If all I want to do is cum I can accomplish that myself. I'm just waiting for a connection. I deserve that. I want what my parents had, what your parents have now. I wish you would accept that and support me instead of making me feel like I'm abnormal."

"Shit, Killer. I'm not trying to make you feel abnormal. I'm sorry if I do. I want you to be happy, and I think you're holding yourself back from the possibility of something that could be good for you." He pauses and thinks over what he said. "I mean, holding back from the possibility of a relationship, not so much the sex. While I think a romp in the sack would do you some good, I think dating someone would be better. I know I'm an excellent companion, but even I can't give you everything you need. It would be like fucking my sister."

I snort and finish my drink. "I appreciate your concern, but you really don't need to worry about me. I'm not holding myself back. If I find someone worth my time and I'll see what happens. I don't think I'll find what my parents have and know it right away, but I also refuse to settle for someone who doesn't make me feel anything better than apathy. I certainly refuse to settle for anyone like

Dragon Boy. Do you think you can back off and let me deal with my love life on my own? I don't get involved in your revolving door of partners, so I think I've earned it." Brandon stares at me while chewing on his bottom lip, an obvious sign he's unsure. "Seriously B. I'm fine. Trust me?"

"Yeah, ok," he sighs. "I love you, you know? You're my sister in all ways but blood, and I just want you to be happy. Sometimes I think it's a shame we didn't fall for each other instead. It would have probably solved both of our relationship problems, huh?" He chuckles while I fake gagging.

"Um, I'll pass, thanks." My cup makes the sad little gurgle that means it's empty when I suck on my straw, and I pout at it. I think about getting another, but after this discussion I'm tired. "I think I'm going to head home and go to bed, it's been a long day. You coming? Or are you going to go out?"

"I'm coming. I got a new game today, so I'll probably put in a few hours on the PS5 before heading to bed myself." Standing, Brandon extends a hand to pull me to my feet and to him in a tight hug. "Let's go little sis. I'll protect you from all the dangers on the walk home like the badass big brother I am."

I hand him the unfinished box of cupcakes to carry for me, grab my empty cup and new book and link my arm through his for the short walk home. "Lead on, fine sir. My bed awaits!"

CHAPTER 3

Climbing into bed, I close my eyes and wish away the familiar hurt and longing that always hovers after talking about Ryan. Four years ago, the only person I've ever loved disappeared overnight after we shared our first kiss. I'd known him my whole life, we'd been friends for so long and I started falling for him around the time I turned thirteen. I suffered in silence for two long years until he told me he felt the same way I did. That was one of the best nights of my life. It was my first real kiss, and we talked about how things would change if we became a couple, especially in our friend group. We didn't care though, since we'd both been waiting so long for this. He was everything I ever wanted, and I finally had him for my own.

The next day at school, both he and his cousin, my other best friend Evan, were absent. We had planned to walk to homeroom together, but I ended up being late after waiting for him too long. Rumors started circulating that they were gone. There was a moving van at their house the night before, and no one could reach either of them on their phones or through emails or social media. No one knew where they went, they didn't tell anyone they were leaving, and they weren't responding to anyone. After school, I went to their house and when no one answered my knock, I looked in the window. The house was almost empty. There was trash all over, some small pieces of furniture strewn about, but otherwise everything had been cleared out overnight.

Ryan was gone. Evan too.

I finally, after two years, told him how I felt about him. He kissed me, and then he left me without a word. I'd like to think I have a reason to have some hesitation when it comes to dating. No one has lived up to the person he was, and no one has made me feel like it was worth wanting to risk my heart again.

THE WATCHER

Four Years Ago

The shards of the bathroom mirror reflect my face back to me in a dozen furious fragments, some of them tinged red with the blood that is slowly trickling down my fingers and making a puddle on the cheap laminate floor.

Drip. Drip.

They must think we're stupid. They say it's not about the kiss, that this is an opportunity to make a difference in a community that needs shepherding, but we both know they're full of Shit. I heard them talking when they weren't aware I was around, and they're lying about this "promotion." He's taking a pay cut to move to this podunk town, but they're willing to do it to take us away from her. They think she's trash, they think she's impure, and they think she's "not suitable wife material."

Fuck. That. Don't they see she's everything?

Drip. Drip. Drip.

Watching the puddle grow, I wait for the fury to ebb. I wait for the release of tension shedding blood usually fills me with. I wait for the calm that inevitably takes over as the thick crimson liquid flows. I wait for the void.

It doesn't come.

My heart races, hands shaking from a combination of anger, desperation, and hopelessness. They've already told us that part of the move to this new parish is a complete reset. No communication with our current friends will be allowed, not even friends from the church. This new parish is apparently more backwards and controlling than the current congregation, and they are using it as an excuse to control our lives more than they already do.

A pastor's children must be above reproach is something we hear every day. We're expected to have perfect grades. Speak with respect to our elders. Dress conservatively. Volunteer.

Behave.

Drip. Drip.

It's exhausting.

We came home from school today to learn they went through our rooms. They factory reset our computers and put parental controls on them to limit the websites we can visit. They took any photos, memory cards, USB drives, and mementos we had that were not related to the church and destroyed them. They used key logger software they had installed on our laptops to pull and change our passwords on email and social media, locking us out of all our accounts. Then they destroyed *our phones and provided us with new pay-by-the-minute flip phones that aren't internet capable. Where we're going is a closed community, where the internet is only available in the library and other monitored locations. Smartphones aren't permitted, and internet usage is extremely restricted.*

It doesn't sound cult-like at all.

They told us to pull out what we want to take with us and put it on our beds so they can check everything we are taking before we leave. We pull it, they pack it. They're even going to check our fucking pockets before we get in the car. I don't know why they're bothering, since they've already taken everything I had I could want to sneak with me. Everything that was ever important to me revolved around her, and they took it all.

We're leaving in an hour. I have one hour to pack everything I want to bring with me while under their watchful eyes. I can't get to her to say goodbye and tell her we're leaving. I can't talk to her to figure out how to stay in touch. I can't leave a note for her without them finding and destroying it. I can't see her beautiful face one last time, get one fucking picture with my new shitty flip phone camera, so I have something to keep me grounded in the new hell we're moving to. I can't kiss her goodbye and tell her I'm sorry I'm leaving her and that I would rather die than do this.

I can't tell her I was too chicken shit to tell her I love her. That I've loved her since I first saw her. That she's it for me, and always will be. I can't tell her I'll come back for her, no matter how long it takes.

They can't separate us like this forever. I will get back to her, and I will make it up to her.

And then I will make her mine.

CHAPTER 4

I'm startled awake by my phone the next morning. I feel like I haven't slept at all, but the clock on my nightstand reads 9:37am, so I got over ten hours. Since I'm comfortable I blindly search around for my cell until I can grab it and hide back under the covers with it. I don't recognize the number, so I force myself to sound awake when I answer. "Hello?"

"Hi, is this Jenevive Martin? I'm so sorry, did I wake you?"

Apparently I didn't sound as awake as I thought I did. Oh well. It's 9:37am on my day off, so he can deal with it. "Um, yeah. Sorry, this is Jenevive. Who is this?"

"My name is Andrew. I got your number from the game donation program. They told me you help out by butchering animals for them? I took my sons hunting this morning, and they both got a deer. We don't have room for the meat from both at home but I couldn't deny my second son after the first got one. I was hoping I could pay you to butcher one for us, and then take the other for donation. Are you available today?"

The game donation program is a charity local hunters can donate their kills to when they either don't want the meat or can't take it for some reason. People like me and my dad volunteer to butcher those animals and prepare the meat so it can be donated to hungry families in the area, so they have access to fresh meat. I'm not in the mood to drive out to the cabin and work today, but years ago when working with my dad I promised him I would continue helping them on my own, and I could use the extra money for the set of signed books some of my favorite Australian authors that are going up for sale soon. "Sure. I'm not at my cabin right now so it'll take me about an hour to get there. I can have the meat ready for you to pick up this evening, say around 7:00?" So much for a relaxing day of nothing.

"That's perfect, I really appreciate it. I'm sorry again for waking you."

I give him the address to the cabin and hang up, allowing myself three minutes to pout before slowly dragging myself out of bed. I'll wear my coveralls to do the butchering, so I don't have to worry about what I'm wearing other than to make sure I don't look like a total slob in front of a paying customer. Rifling through my closet, I decide today is a perfect day for my "Punch today in the face" t-shirt, so I pair it with some cropped yoga pants and sneakers. I skip makeup since I don't wear a lot of it anyway, throw my hair up in a messy bun, and brush my teeth, so I'm ready to go in less than ten minutes. Everything is clean, so I'm nailing the not-a-slob thing. The way I see it is if he expects his butcher to be glammed up that's a him problem, not a me problem.

As I walk to my car I scroll through my playlists to see what I'm in the mood for today. The weather should be comfortable, so I'll be able to make the drive out to the cabin with my windows down and radio up. I decide it's a rock kind of day, so I pull up my "Music to make sweet, sweet love to" playlist, which is anything but, and set it to shuffle. After my car starts, the opening tones of "Mein Teil" by Rammstein come through my speakers and I know it's going to be a good day. It'll take me about 30 minutes to make it out to the cabin at this time of the morning, so I stop at a fast food drive through and order a breakfast sandwich and the biggest Diet Coke available. Windows down, music blasting, and breakfast in my stomach, I sing along to some of my favorite songs as I head to meet Andrew.

Pulling up in front of my cabin, I can't ignore the slight twinge of sadness that always hits me when I come here. I love this place. I grew up here, but I moved out a year ago and my dad lived here alone until he died. The only reason I can come here now, other than the fact the happy memories far outweigh the bad, is that he wasn't killed here. I think if he'd have been murdered on the property I'd have to part with it even though it would devastate me.

My dad was amazing. After my mom died when I was young, he became everything to me. Both of my sets of grandparents were already gone at that point, and my parents were only children, so I didn't have any other mother figure family wise. He went to some of his friend's wives and had them teach him how to braid my hair and all the things he'd need to worry about as the dad of a girl. He encouraged me to have relationships with my friend's moms, so I'd have feminine influence, and I think that is one of the reasons I'm so close with Mrs. C, other than the fact that she's my best friend's mom. While he was trying to help me be the best girl I could, he also continued teaching me his trades. I can do my hair and makeup and give myself a mani/pedi, and then turn around and hunt, trap, and fish like one of the boys. He was a military man, some sort of highly trained specialist who did things he'd never talk to me about, and he taught me a lot of those skills too. I haven't trained with anyone other than him, but I can hold my own when it comes to fighting and self defense and I'm proficient with weapons, both for hunting and combat. He used to joke he was getting me ready for the apocalypse, but I think he was worried as the father of a daughter living in these crazy times. He wanted me to be able to protect myself no matter what, and that is a gift I could never thank him enough for.

Six months ago, he was meeting friends for dinner downtown when the police say he was mugged and something went wrong. He was shot in the stomach and left to bleed out in the parking lot, like his life didn't matter. His wallet, keys, and custom hunting knife were taken. His phone was shattered on the ground next to him and his truck was found a few hours later abandoned in an alley only a few blocks away wiped of prints. My dad's best friend, Detective Brian Dobbs, always tells me they're working on it, but he doesn't believe me when I tell him I don't think it was a mugging gone wrong.

The day my dad died he called me to check in, and while that wasn't unusual in itself, the conversation was odd.

"Hey Johnny, what are you up to?" my dad asked, sounding a little strained.

"Hey Dad. Just relaxing before I have to head to work in a few hours. You ok? You sound weird."

"Yeah, I'm ok," he said, sighing. "Just thinking about you and the fact I haven't seen you in a while. You got any free time coming up? Maybe you could come out to the cabin, and we can do dinner?"

That was weird, because he always preferred to meet at a restaurant for dinner, not stay in. "Sure. I have Saturday night off, would that work? Maybe around 5?"

"Perfect. I can grill something. Do you want to bring pasta salad?"

"Wow, you're actually cooking? I figured we'd order pizza or something. Sure, I'll bring pasta salad and some dessert. Are you sure you're ok?"

"I'm fine Johnny. Just a weird day. You know I love you right? I'm so damned proud of you. Your mom would be too."

"Ok dad, what the fuck is going on? Why are you being all weird and sappy?" He isn't a mushy person, and we don't talk about this stuff unless we're drunk.

He chuckles for a moment before sobering. "Nothing to worry about. Just a weird day, like I said. We'll talk more when you come Saturday, ok? Until then, have a good day at work. I've got dinner downtown with the guys tonight so if you need me send a text."

"Alright Dad. But you better be ready to talk about whatever is bothering you when I get there on Saturday, capiche?"

"Got it, kid" he laughed. "We'll talk, I promise. I'm ok though, nothing to worry about until then. I love you, kid."

"Love you too Dad. Have fun tonight. Don't do anything I wouldn't do!"

Five hours later, Brian showed up at my work to tell me the news. One of the detectives on the scene recognized my dad and had called him, and he asked to be the one to break the news to me.

Funny phrase, that. Break the news. It implies the news will be the thing breaking.

Not your heart.

Not your soul.

But those did break. My dad was the only family I had left in the world. He was my rock, my mentor, and my best friend. And because one asshole decided he had the right to take his life, he was taken from me, and I was alone.

After I pulled myself together as much as possible, I tried to tell Brian about the conversation I had with my dad earlier in the day. I tried to make him understand how weird it was. How he didn't sound right, how he said he had something to talk to me about. I didn't believe it was a robbery gone wrong then, and I don't believe it now. Brian wouldn't listen to me though. I got the "sometimes people are just in the wrong place at the wrong time" line, but he should know better. My dad wasn't someone easily taken by surprise, even if it was five guys who all had a gun. Some punkass street kid trying to make a couple of bucks would be no match for him. I truly believe it was someone he knew, and they took him by surprise. He would have been able to handle any situation thrown at him unless he'd let his guard down, and he's always vigilant unless he's with someone he trusts. Brian swears they're looking into it regardless. My friend Daniel is a police officer and is volunteering to help wherever he can but I don't think they're looking in the right direction, and it kills me to know my dad hasn't gotten justice.

I'm pulled out of my thoughts when I arrive at the cabin. It's about twenty minutes outside of town, and it has a lot of land for something so close to the city. Trees line the property at the road and follow the gravel driveway that is long and winding enough to ensure plenty of privacy. I guess it's not technically a cabin, but it's what we've always called it. It's a two story home made of dark gray stone and charcoal trim accents. The red door serves as a welcoming accent and always makes me smile when I think of begging my dad to let me choose the color.

My dad loved yard work and had a large garden to the side of the house he tended year around, but I have what he lovingly referred to as the "black thumb of death," so that has been removed since he died. I hate yard work, so I pay a local kid a hundred bucks a month to maintain the yard for me. He makes some money, uses my riding mower to make it easy, and I don't have to worry about it. Win-win.

There's a black GMC truck waiting for me at the end of the drive and I can see three people inside. The driver's door opens as I pull up and a middle-aged man covered in camo with a slight beer belly and a receding hairline drops to the ground and waves, a kind smile on his face.

Extending my hand to him as we meet, I say "Hi, you must be Andrew. I'm Jenevive."

"Yeah, hi. Thanks again for meeting me on such short notice. I really appreciate it."

"No problem. Let's see what you've got." I walk around to the bed of the truck, and he pops the cover so I can look at the deer. Two decent bucks are in the back, cleanly shot. "Wow, they did a great job with these!"

Andrew's eyes shine with pride as he inspects them. "They did. This one here was my youngest one's first deer," he says while pointing to the larger of the two, "so that's the one that we want to keep. I'd like to get the head mounted for him too if you can make sure we keep it."

"Sure thing. I'll charge $140 since there are two of them, and I'll handle both the disposal of what you don't want back and dropping off the donated meat. I prefer cash, but also accept Venmo, so whichever works for you is fine. Like I mentioned on the phone, it should be ready around 7:00pm, but I'll call if it will be any later than that."

"I can do $140. I'll make sure to hit the ATM before coming back. Do you want help taking them somewhere?"

"No, I'm good. If you don't mind waiting a minute I'll grab my UTV and load them up to transport them."

"Of course."

Heading over to the garage, I punch in the code to raise the automatic door and duck under. Grabbing the keys from the cabinet on the wall I hop in the UTV and start it up, pulling up perpendicular to the bed of Andrew's truck. Together, Andrew and I sling the deer across the back and I strap them down for the short journey to the barn.

"Do you need help unloading them?? I feel bad leaving them with you like this, they're pretty heavy."

Chuckling, I shake my head, pat the larger one on the rump, and say "I'm alright. I've handled bigger ones by myself before. I'll meet you back here at 7 unless I call to change the time."

I climb back in the UTV, start it up, and wave goodbye as I head down the two track path that leads from the driveway to the barn. On my right, behind the house is what I like to call Lake Martin. It's too large to be considered a pond, and too small to be considered a lake, but I like to feel fancy, so lake it is. A floating platform for swimmers to relax on bobs in the middle, and a few years ago my dad built a dock big enough to tie up a jon boat and have an area for some chairs. He even added places to strap down the poles for a pop-up tent, so I can hang out in the shade without worrying about it blowing away in the wind.

It takes a lot of work to maintain this porcelain pale skin, thank you very much.

Dad refurbished an aging barn at the back of the property, and we use it solely to butcher animals in. Putting it out there was done to try to keep any lurking predators away from our main living space, and causing it to take a few minutes to get there driving the UTV. The two track path weaves through the woods and I never rush through the trip, using the drive over to bask in nature and center myself for the work to come. While not mentally taxing, it does take skill, patience, and a decent amount of strength. The fact that I have two deer today makes me miss my dad a little more because he'd have called me to come help him out with them, so we could do it quicker together then use the fee to go out to dinner. After dinner if I didn't have to work in the morning I'd stay over, and we'd get hammered hanging out on the patio and catching up. He'd drink his own beer brew, and I'd drink whiskey since I think beer is disgusting -- something he always swore he would never forgive me for.

Dad was able to modernize the barn while keeping some of its old world charm. While it appears old on the outside, the barn is actually weather-tight and has a new tin roof. Hopping off the UTV, I unlock the padlock keeping the front doors shut and slide them open to the front room of the barn. This room is used to store the majority of my tools and bigger equipment. I grab the large stainless steel rolling cart used to transport the animals to the back, so I don't have to carry or drag them and roll it out to the UTV to load up and wheel them inside.

Locking the door back behind me, I push the cart up to the internal door to the cold room and key the code into the keypad and wait as the door unlocks. I tug the heavy door open and shiver as the cold air rushes out to meet me. Leaving the cart just inside the door, I head to the bathroom at the back of the room to change into my coveralls. The bathroom is utilitarian, all white subway tile on the walls and wider white tiles on the floor. A medium-sized shower stall with a glass door is flanked by a built-in wardrobe on one side and a toilet on the other, and a simple pedestal sink completes the space. Everything is simple and easy to hose down with the hose style shower head or wipe down with cleaning cloths since this is messy business.

I strip out of my clothes and fold them up to stow in the wardrobe before I pull the coveralls out and climb into them, zipping them up to my neck. Next, I pull out a pair of skull and crossbones covered fuzzy socks and a hot pink bandanna to keep my hair back and out of my face while I work. My rubber boots are sitting outside the bathroom door, and once I slip into them I'm ready to go.

"Alexa, play playlist Sleepytime Jams."

Pulling my gloves on, I head over to the cart as Spiritbox's "Holy Roller" starts playing through the surround sound system my dad installed for me a few years ago. Much like the bathroom, the entire room is stark white and easy to clean. The walls and floors are both painted white and covered in an epoxy coating to prevent staining and the floor dips slightly towards the middle where there are three drains throughout the room so fluids easily drain out instead of pooling and making it difficult to dry. My work table, standing cabinets, and utility sink are the only color in the room as they're stainless steel. Even the industrial cooler and freezer are white.

I bebop my way over to the cabinets to grab my tools while pretending I can work it like Courtney LaPlante (hint: I can't), and I prep my station before moving the first deer on to the work table and getting started.

It's going to be a long day.

CHAPTER 5

G ood lord, this one ended up being messy. I guess things happen when you have a surprise sneeze while you've got a knife inside an abdominal cavity. Fucking allergies. I'm covered in blood and gore, which is normal I guess, but even for me this is ridiculous. Sighing and thanking anyone who will listen for the fact that Dad put a full bathroom out here so I can shower when I'm done, I allow myself a second to pout and then pull up my metaphorical big girl panties. Time to bring out the Big Guns and get this mess handled.

"Alexa, play playlist 'Clean up, clean up.'"

Nothing pumps me up for a thorough cleaning like a perfect playlist, and this one always gets me in the right mood. The opening tones of "DONTTRUSTME" by 3oh!3 come on, and I hit my second wind as I boogie over to the cleaning supply cabinet. I hurry to grab my first items so that when the beat drops my ass can too. The perfect playlist can always put the pep back in my step.

The meat has been safely stored away in the walk-in cooler until it's time to take it to Andrew and the charity drop off, as is the head from the eight pointer for Andrew's son. The hide and requested bones have been bagged up to take to the taxidermist to sell to him, and the unusable parts have been stowed in the Biohazard trash bags for disposal at the landfill. With my tools in the utility sink waiting to be washed and the trash bags stowed in the front room, I pull my waders out of one of the cabinets and exchange them for my boots. All it takes is a few minutes with the hose and the room is wet, but clean. The three drains in the floor will ensure the whole room is dry by the time I'm done in here, and the waders keep me fairly dry even though the water sprays everywhere. After a quick wipe down of the hook and table, I switch to nitrile gloves and spray my work area and tools with CaviCide to ensure everything is clean. I never know what kind of nasty stuff the things I have on my table come to me with, so I always make sure I kill as many of their germs and diseases as possible.

I plan to either go out in a blaze of glory or be killed by someone I pissed off by what comes out of my mouth, not by some nasty disease I got from little Timmy's latest kill, ok?

Everything is clean, so I head back to the cleaning cabinet to swap my waders for my Crocs. I hate these things, but they were a gift from my friend Kenzie, so I use them here after working and before the floor dries out, so I don't slip and eat shit.

Again.

Learned that lesson real quick. They're black with cute little skull charms on them, but I can't bring myself to be caught wearing them in public, so I hide them here like a dirty little secret.

Sighing in relief that the day is over, I check the time and note it's 6:05pm. Andrew will be here in under an hour, so I have at least 30 minutes to clean myself up before heading back. I head to the bathroom to take a shower before changing back out of my coveralls. As comfortable as the bathroom here is, I always thought Dad should have done something more with it. The cleaning room is a perfect combination of form and function, and the man-cave-slash-trophy-room next to it (also now known as my She-Shed) is all comfort and relaxation. One day when I have the money I want to redo this bathroom and make it as much of a retreat as the rest of the barn is for me. I want one of those fancy two-button water saving toilets, a sink with a vanity that has storage in it, and a bigger shower with a bench. I'd like one of those steam showers with a fancy patterned tile so I can relax after butchering, and maybe a claw foot tub since I don't have one in my apartment. I'd lose a little space in the She-Shed, but I think it would be worth it to have that sort of escape in my safe place.

Freshly showered and back in my comfortable clothes, I wait for Andrew in the driveway in front of the cabin. I thought about staying the night and going home tomorrow, but I realized I forgot my new book at home, so I'll head back after dropping the donated meat off. After about ten minutes of waiting, I hear gravel crunching before headlights break through the trees. Since I'm anticipating a large truck, I'm surprised, and a little nervous, to identify a car coming towards me.

My nerves only last until I see the bubble lights on top, signaling it's the fact that it's a police car. My guess is it's my friend Daniel, but I have no idea why he would be here now. I haven't talked to him in a few days and I didn't tell him I'd be here. The car pulls to a stop at the side of the drive, and Daniel climbs out with a smile on his face. He's about 5'11", with crew cut dirty blonde hair and hazel eyes. His cheeks still have a small hint of baby fat, but his body is trim and toned in his uniform from working out.

"Hey Jen! I didn't know you'd be here, what's up?"

I raise a single eyebrow at him and answer "Shouldn't I be the one saying that?"

He blushes a little and rubs the back of his neck before shrugging and saying "Yeah, I guess so. I didn't tell you but I come out here every once in a while to check on the property, make sure no one is messing with it for you. You don't come down here too much and I just thought I'd keep an eye on it for you. I know you didn't ask me to, but I feel like I'd be letting your dad down if I didn't do what I could to help out."

He's struggling with the death of my dad too, I know. His mom is a single mother and my dad filled in the father spot for him a lot when we were growing up. Forcing a smile through my surprise moment of melancholy, I move to give him a hug. He holds on tight for a moment before releasing me with one last squeeze and stepping back. "Thanks, D. I do appreciate it. It sits out here alone since I'm not ready to move here full time yet. How often do you come out here?"

"As much as I can. Usually when I'm going by mom's house or I'm in the area for another reason. What are you doing out here tonight?"

"I got a call this morning from a hunter who wanted me to butcher his son's kills for him. I'm waiting for him to come pick up the meat before I can head out. I think he's here now." The sound of tires over gravel hits again and this time the expected truck rounds the corner into the drive. Andrew parks and climbs down with his brows furrowed in concern.

"Hey Jenevive. Is everything ok?"

"Hey Andrew, yeah everything's fine. This is my friend Daniel, he just stopped by to say hi since I was in the area. I've got everything ready for you. If you want to grab some, I'll help bring over the rest."

Andrew nods and steps up to Daniel to shake his hand before turning to follow me. "Thank you so much again. Ethan is so excited to have the meat for dinner tomorrow, we always have a celebration dinner after their first kill. He's already picked the spot in his room for the mount."

"I'm so glad! That's always such a special thing, thank you for letting me be a part of it."

Smiling, he closes the door on his truck and hands me some folded cash before climbing back up into the truck cab. "Have a great night you two! I'll be passing your information over to my friends if you'd be interested in that?"

"I'd appreciate it thank you. Call me any time if you need me again. Goodnight!"

With a wave, Andrew shuts his door and does a quick turn before heading back down the drive. Yawning, I cover my mouth and turn back to Daniel before giving him a tired smile. "What are you doing with the rest of your night? Are you off, or heading in?"

"Oh, I'm heading in. I had dinner with mom and was stopping by on my way in. What are you doing tonight? Any plans? I heard you had a date last night, how'd it go? Do you think you'll go out with him again?"

"Oh my God do not bring that up! Brandon is lucky I love him, or he would be spread out on my table like those deer after setting me up with that guy. I'm not going to lie, I fantasized about killing him to get me through that awful dinner. But no, I'm going to drop the donated meat off and then head home. Thank you for stopping by, it means a lot to me to have you checking the property for me while I'm gone. Don't go out of your way though, ok?"

Chuckling, he gives me an odd smile before nodding his head to agree. "Ok, like I said I usually just swing by when I'm near. Do you want me to check in with you when I do?"

"Only if you see something odd. Thanks D, let's talk to Brandon and hang out soon, ok?"

"Sounds good." He grabs me and picks me up with his hug, shaking me a little before putting me back down with a chuckle. "Text me when you're home, so I know you're safe, ok?"

Rolling my eyes at him, I agree before pinching his side and running to my car while cackling like a mad woman. He never learns.

Chapter 6

Morning comes again too soon, especially since I have to work a split shift. I'm closing, but Brandon had a doctor's appointment this morning, so I agreed to open for him. I texted Daniel when I got home last night, and he asked to plan dinner sometime soon, so I'll make sure I talk to Brandon and work that out once he comes in. We usually schedule these things for Sunday evenings since we close the store early.

My employees Steph and Caleb are waiting for me when I arrive, and we make quick work of getting the store set up and ready to open. We have a gaming tournament tonight, so I'll be making sure things are stocked and tidy throughout the store this morning between customers. After my break Brandon and I will set up the tournament area, leader boards, and refreshment area. I also have to prepare myself mentally, because although these Madden tournaments bring in business they also bring a fair number of douche bags. Normally, they accept no for an answer, but there are times when I have to turn down at least one guy who doesn't doesn't. I'm so used to it at this point it's almost unconscious, but he first few times I worried about offending the customer. After dealing with my 5,000th Chad, however, I no longer care. I've only had to have Brandon intervene once, and he handled it by throwing the guy out to protect him from the ass beating I was about to provide him with. It was magical and I made him a double batch of Christmas Crack as a thank you.

Time flies by between checking out customers and stocking shelves, and it isn't long before Brandon is in. "Hey B, which is it this time? Herpes? The clap? Maybe some new mutated disease that will force you to be taken by science and studied in labs?"

"Very funny, asshole. You know I get regular checks after that chick who claimed she had that weird cat disease and then left her hair in a bag on my doorstep."

I rush to cover my mouth when a snort escapes before I can hold it in. What he doesn't know is I also intercepted another of her gifts. She'd left him a painting one night that was of the two of them dressed as clowns and embracing like lovers. Not only was it creepy because they only went out one time, and she was still able to nail his facial features, but poor Brandon has been terrified of clowns since we went to the circus when we were kids. We saw two fist fighting over who got to drive the clown car, and he was traumatized. I grabbed it before he could find it, took plenty of pictures for proof, and then burned it the next time I was out at the cabin. I've never told him it existed. I'm saving it for a rainy day when he makes me mad.

Wait, he already did! He set me up with Dragon Boy without vetting him.

"Speaking of that chick, did you ever find any other gifts from her waiting for you at home?"

Furrowing his brows in thought, he asks "No, why?"

Grinning, I pull out my phone and start scrolling through them to find the photos. "Because I did."

"Wait, what? She left you a gift?"

I chuckle when I find the photo and hold it out to him saying, "Nope. But she left you one. I simply got rid of it for you before you saw it because I'm an amazing friend."

His face drains of color almost immediately and his Adam's apple bobs with his strong swallow. "Jen... what the fuck? When did she leave this? Why didn't you tell me? Why didn't you go to the police?"

"And tell them what? A girl you hit and quit is leaving you thoughtful gifts of beautiful artwork?" I laugh harder and continue saying "It was a few days after the hair. I got home before you and saw it, so I got rid of it for you. I was actually shocked at how realistic it was. She painted you perfectly! I wasn't going to show you unless I needed to have revenge on you for something. This is the perfect revenge for the hell you put me through the other night!"

Brandon narrows his eyes at me like he's angry, but drops his shoulders and sighs. "Yeah, I guess I deserved that. It's a shame she turned out so crazy, she was a tiger in bed."

I roll my eyes and stick my fingers in my ear. "I don't need to hear this, you dork. Keep it to yourself! Now, on to more important things. I saw Daniel last night at the cabin."

"What was he doing there? Why were you there?"

"I had a customer call me, so I went to butcher his kid's kills for him. I was waiting for the guy at the end of the driveway to pick everything up when Daniel showed up. He said he checks on the property for me every once in a while since my dad isn't there. He said he was heading to work from dinner with his mom. I appreciate it since I don't spend time there as often as I should."

"Weird," he hedges, "I thought he worked the day shift yesterday. Maybe he worked a double? " He shrugs and moves on. "What else is he up to?"

"He wants to have dinner soon. I was thinking tomorrow night unless you have plans."

"I'm free. Dinner at the cabin or do we want to go out?" He always lets me make the decision since it hasn't been very long since my dad died. Sometimes it's easier for me to be there than others.

"Let's go to dad's. We don't have to cook, but it's supposed to be decent out, and we can hang out by the lake." I really want to be able to spend time there as much as possible. If the guys are with me, it makes it a little easier to deal with the fact that the house is empty and my dad isn't there anymore.

"Sounds good. I'll pick up pizzas and drinks on the way out. I have to close, so I should be able to get there around 6."

I nod and shoot Daniel a text to be at my house at 6pm tomorrow for pizza. He responds with a thumbs up and says he'll be there and bring drinks. That taken care of, I give Brandon a saucy salute and head off for my break. It's going to be a late night, and I'm going to need a nap.

The tournament has been going on for a few hours at this point, and I've handed the controls over to Brandon because I'm tired of dealing with all the testosterone. Wandering the store, I straighten up what I can and make note of what needs to be restocked. I'm almost up to the front of the store when a twenty-something guy steps in front of me and smiles. He's tall, probably 6'2", with dark hair cut close on the sides and long enough on top to be slicked back. His black Lacoste t-shirt is paired with khaki shorts and flip-flops, and he very obviously thinks he's God's gift to many things.

"Hey, do you work here?" As if my giant name tag and the fact that I was reorganizing a display wasn't enough of a clue.

"Yes, what can I help you with?" Maybe it will be an easy answer and he'll move on. The level of smarm radiating from him hints I won't be that lucky though.

"I was wondering if you have any of the classic game consoles here? I went to GameStop and they didn't have anything. They recommended I come here."

"Oh, um, yeah I think we still have some. They should be over here." I gesture for him to follow me and lead him to a display in the front corner of the store by the windows overlooking the parking lot. "Yeah, here you go. These are the newer plug-and-play ones. If you're looking for actual classic consoles, We have a Super Nintendo and an Atari in stock right now. They've been checked for function and quality and we have a lot of games for both consoles."

"Damn, I'm surprised GameStop sent me over here. Why would I ever need to go back there when you seem to have more selection? Plus, the staff is vastly more pleasant."

Throwing my head back to laugh, it takes me a moment to respond to him. "You must have talked to Barry. He's kind of an asshole, but he's cool people. We have a terrific relationship with them and often refer customers to each other. Usually, if one of us doesn't have something the other does."

He grabs one of the classic consoles off the shelf and turns back to me to say "Well, you're certainly more attractive than he is. What time do you get off? We should go get some drinks."

Shaking my head I give him my manager smile, and say "I appreciate the offer, but no. I have other plans." He tilts his head and steps up close to me, reaching up and putting his filthy fucking fingers on my cheek, like he has any right to touch me.

"Come on sweetheart. I think we'd have fun together, I'm a good guy, you'll like me."

I jerk my face away from him and slap his hand away from me. "I don't like you now, and I doubt my impression of you would improve if I actually get to know you."

Eyes flashing with rage, he grabs my wrist and tries to pull me closer to him again.

No one puts their hands on me without my permission. With my blood boiling and my mind calling for blood, my body stills and I look him dead in the eyes, so he can understand I'm serious when I grit out my next words very quietly.

"Let. Me. fucking. Go."

His cocky smirk comes back, and he's about to say something else when Brandon rounds the corner. Brandon catches sight of it, but I give him a minimal shake of my head to tell him to leave it. Instead, he calls out "Hey Killer! I've been looking for you, we need to update the leader board but I'm needed for a return, can you help?"

"Of course! I'll be right there." Without another glance at the grabby douche canoe, I jerk my wrist free and head over to Brandon, linking my arm in his as we walk away together. Leaning into his shoulder, I keep my voice low and say

"Thank God you came when you did. I was about to beat the shit out of that little pissant. No means no!"

The years that passed dwindle to nothing the moment I catch sight of her again. The pictures I've been able to find online have served to help me keep my head straight and focused on my end goal, but seeing her in person?

It's the difference between the mild comfort a flashlight can bring you in the depths of night and the peace and safety that arrives with the new dawn.

She is my dawn. She is the light that burns off the heavy cloud of torment I've been surrounded with since I last saw her. Her soul shines through her every action and brings a peace to mine that before now I only ever knew at the moment my lips touched hers.

As beautiful as she was four years ago, she's stunning now. Her hair trails down her back in a riot of wild curls, something she used to lament as a curse, but I have always loved. Not only has she embraced the curl, but she's added some streaks of purple and hot pink to contrast against her natural dark brown, and each of the colors contrast beautifully with her pale skin and light dusting of freckles I know grace her cheeks and nose. She's grown a few inches, no longer the diminutive 5-foot pixie, she's probably topping out at about 5'3" since her beat up Converse aren't adding any height. Her thick thighs and luscious ass are deliciously hugged in a pair of skin tight jeans, and her hips, waist, and full breasts are showcased in a form fitting black t-shirt that is covered in bright flowers and an elegant script that reads "Death Metal" in the same pink as her hair. Her right arm seems to be covered in bright pinks, oranges, and yellows, while the left is covered in black, purple and blue. I can't make out what covers it from here, but whatever is there matches the aura of brightness radiating off of her.

Just like her shirt, she is a beautiful dichotomy. A stunning landscape of color and life that also blooms in the dark.

I watch as a young guy walks up to her and asks her a question. Smiling, she leads him over to a display closer to the window I watch her through and as much as I want her to see me, I know it's still not the right time. I'm not ready for that just yet.

Damn. The fucker must have said something funny because she throws her head back and laughs, her elegant throat elongating and making my mouth water. I've dreamed of that throat, imagined the places that I could kiss, lick, and bite her while I show her she's mine. The fucker smirks at her and leers at her body while she isn't paying attention. Grabbing something from the shelf, he turns to her and says something that causes her smile to fall a bit. She's still smiling professionally, but she shakes her head to indicate a negative response and tries to step back. She's lost the carefree smile she had only moments ago and obviously wants to leave. Cocking his head to the side, he takes a step closer to her and lifts his hand to run his fingers down her cheek, crowding her space. If I thought she was in real trouble, I'd step in faster than she could blink, but I know her. She doesn't need me to save her.

My fearless girl proves me right when she jerks her head away from his touch, swats his hands away, and loses the smile as she fires back at him with something that I can only assume is a scathing rejection. His face contorts into something resembling rage, and he grabs her wrist. Stilling, she clearly and calmly tells him "Let me fucking go."

The cocky smirk is back on his face, and he starts to say something else until Brandon walks around the corner and it forces him to let her go or be discovered manhandling her. Brandon waves her over to him and says hi to the customer, seeming to apologize for stealing her away. The customer stares after her with anger in his eyes, as if she owed him something.

I've got news for the spineless little fuck -- no one messes with my girl and lives. Never have, never will. He won't be bothering her again.

Chapter 7

S unday is my day off and no one called with a need for my services, so I was able to sleep in until 10:00am. I'm so warm in my nest of blankets I allow myself to doze in and out for about an hour before the need to pee forces me to get up and face the day. After taking care of business, I head to the living room and turn on the TV to reruns of Ren and Stimpy before making myself a huge bowl of Golden Grahams and allowing myself time to wake up. Last night was a late night, and no matter how well I feel like I handled myself, I'm always a bit twitchy after dealing with entitled assholes like the guy that grabbed me. It's not from fear as much as anger and irritation.

Why do people think it's ok to put their hands on someone else without consent? Why is "no" not a good enough answer? People like him should be locked up or put down. Not every female has my luck in that I had a father who taught me how to stand up and defend myself, but the worst part is that it is even necessary.

Refusing to let myself be dragged down into melancholy all day, I head to the kitchen with my empty bowl while singing along with the "Log" theme song. I'll clean my apartment so I don't have to worry about it later, then head out to the cabin to freshen things up there too. I do it about once a month so things aren't taken over by dust, but I'm considering hiring someone to come in and take care of it for me since it's a lot of house to clean by myself, especially after so long. I always tidy up before leaving when I come, but the house deserves better than what I'm capable of in my dad's absence.

It's been a while since I've stayed overnight there, and since the boys will be over we'll probably be up late, so I pack an overnight bag with everything I need to get ready for tonight and for work tomorrow. Other than my recent failed date, it's been a while since I've made an effort to get dolled up, so I think tonight I'll go for comfy/cute. A pair of high waisted jean shorts, black tank, emerald green cropped sweater, and black wedge sandals should do well enough paired with my turtle pendant necklace and a few silver layering necklaces and stud earrings. Work tomorrow will just need a t-shirt and jeans, so I throw those in my bag as well. I have everything else I need to get ready at the house since dad always made sure to be prepared for me to stay there at a moment's notice.

The house is a little musty when I arrive, so I open the windows that have screens in them to let the space air out. The bottom floor is an open floor plan with dark hardwood flooring throughout and a wall of windows to the back of the house facing the water. The living room and kitchen have a vaulted ceiling with wood beams stained to match the floors, allowing the wall of windows to stretch up two floors and let in an incredible amount of light, and the walls are painted a soft gray because my dad always hated a white wall. There are two caramel colored overstuffed couches and a recliner surrounding a plush cream rug and facing the large TV mounted over the fireplace, which is made of gray stone and stretches up to the vaulted ceiling. Built in bookshelves flank it on each side and are filled with books and trinkets my family has collected over generations. The kitchen is modern, but not incredibly sophisticated. Dad never cooked much, and neither do I, so while it has top of the line stainless steel appliances, it's not exactly a chef's kitchen. The cabinets are a shaker style and painted in gray with simple silver hardware, the back splash is a white honeycomb tile with grout that matches the cabinets, and the counters are a dark granite with flecks of silver throughout. Sometimes, when the light catches it just right, it sparkles like diamonds. A big island that can seat four people divides the space and contains the farm sink that is positioned so you have a view of the lake while washing dishes. Last year I was able to find bar stools that blended the grays of the kitchen with the caramel tone of the couch, so the rooms blend together seamlessly.

To the right of the living room and kitchen is the powder room, den, a guest bedroom with a bathroom, storage closet, and the 3 car garage. Upstairs is my bedroom with an attached bath, the master suite, my dad's office, his home gym, the laundry room, and another full bathroom. The master suite has a balcony sizable enough for a set of gliding Adirondack chairs and matching side table, and the view from there at sunset is breathtaking. One day, when I decide I want to move out here permanently I plan to redecorate the master bedroom in what I call "light Gothic" -- light colors with dark furniture and one accent wall covered in a skull damask wallpaper I found a few months ago. Until then, it can stay in the neutral scheme my dad chose. I set myself a goal to start going through his things and donating them in three months, hoping to have it done by a year after his death. I don't want to push myself to do it before I'm ready, but I don't want to allow myself to let it go forever either. My dad kept my mom's things for years after her death, and it just made it harder when he finally decided he had to let it all go.

All I really have to do today is dust, vacuum, and pull things out for dinner later. Brandon sometimes decides to jump in the water fully clothed, so I'll have a towel ready for him in case that happens too. Grabbing the vacuum and duster out of the storage closet, I tell Alexa to play my "Weird Stuff" playlist and "Bangarang (feat. Sirah)" by Skrillex starts pumping through the house's sound system. I sing and dance along with the music as I make my way through the house cleaning each room and making sure everything is in order. I've been saving my dad's rooms for last because they're the hardest, but I never let myself skip them because he deserved better. The gym and his office, though tough to enter, are clean quickly enough but by the time I make it to his bedroom I'm hesitant to go in.

Opening the door, I walk in and sit on the edge of his bed by his nightstand and pick up the photo of us from my eighteenth birthday. We have our arms wrapped together and are wearing coveralls dotted with paint from the paintball tournament we joined together. We beat the other 5 teams, and only had paint on us because we decided to go against each other after we won. Best out of five won and got to buy dinner that night. I won, but he still paid.

It's been almost exactly six months since he was killed, with no leads on who killed him. Staring down at the photo, I'm shocked when a streak of water slides down the glass. I reach up and touch my face and realize I'm crying. I haven't done it in so long, I'm surprised it's happening now. I pull the photo to my chest and hug it to me while I lay down and allow myself to truly grieve for the first time in a few months. I miss him so much it kills me some days. There are so many things we never got to do together. He'll never walk me down the aisle. He'll never hold his grandchild. I'll never hear him call me Johnny or tell me he loves me again. We'll never go hunting or fishing and I won't be able to help him with his special projects. When I finally meet someone, I won't be able to introduce them and have him give me his opinion. Growing up without my mother was hard enough, but now I have no one. Brandon and Daniel can't be everything for me, I need family and I have none.

My silent tears quickly turn to hiccuping sobs, and I let it out until I run out of energy. After I'm quiet for a few minutes I take a few deep breaths and check the time on my phone. It's only 1:00pm and I'm exhausted from my outburst, so I set an alarm for 3:00pm and pull the blanket from the bottom of the bed over me to try to take a nap. The pillow and blanket still smell faintly like my dad's cologne even though they've been washed, and I quickly fall asleep surrounded by the man that I loved most in this world.

At 5:00pm I'm in the process of towel drying my hair when I hear a text come in.

> **Bran:** Got caught up, will be a little late tonight. Going to order the pizza to be delivered since I'm not sure when I'll be there. Can't have you hangry.

> **Me:** Everything ok? Did something happen at the store?

> **Bran:** Everything is fine, just need to handle something. I'll be there later tonight.

It's weird that he didn't explain what happened, but I'm guessing it has something to do with someone he's seeing, so I'll let it go for now. I run gel through my hair and scrunch it to set my curls, draw a cat's eye with my liner, finish up with mascara, and call it a day. My cheeks will naturally pink up if I drink alcohol and I don't ever wear lipstick, so my routine is simple.

Letting my hair air dry, I check myself in my standing mirror and smile at my reflection. Thankfully, after a nap and shower you can't tell I was crying earlier. My shorts make my butt look fabulous and the tucked in tank gives definition to my narrow waist. The sleeves of my sweater hide my tattoos, but the color compliments my skin and hair. I pop in my earrings and pull on my necklaces. Like I have since the day I received it, I rub the belly of my turtle pendant with my thumb for luck before letting it go. I still have no idea where it came from, but it is one of my most precious possessions. The chain broke several years ago and I replaced it with a more sturdy white gold chain, but the pendant remains in perfect condition. I hope to one day solve the mystery of who left it for me, but until then I'm happy in the knowledge that someone cared enough for me to do something so thoughtful when I needed it most.

School was hard today. It is the fifth anniversary of my mom's death and I couldn't stay focused. My teachers all had to speak to me about my inattention, but even the threat of detention couldn't pull me out of my funk. My friends tried to encourage me to talk, to cheer me up, but nothing worked.

I miss her so much. I love my dad, he tries so hard to be everything I need, but sometimes I just need my mom. There are so many things I would kill to talk to her about -- especially about my feelings for Ryan. I think he likes me too, but I just don't know. I want to tell him, but I'm so afraid if I do, and he doesn't feel the same way our friendship will be ruined and everyone will hate me for ruining our friend group. I can't talk to my dad about it because he won't understand, plus he always tells me if I try to date before I'm 35 he'll shoot anyone that comes near me. He has the skill and the weapons, so I'm not sure if he's being serious or not.

I slowly make my way up the driveway with thoughts of my mom on my mind, plans to take a bath and go to bed early. Dad always disappears on this day until late, so he won't be home any time soon. As I walk up to the house, a small box and an envelope leaning against the top step to the front porch catches my attention. I peer around to see if there is anyone nearby but nothing is out of the ordinary, so I hesitantly make my way closer.

The envelope has my name written on it in neat block letters, the handwriting unfamiliar. I check again to make sure this isn't a joke but no one jumps out from the trees or bushes, so I cautiously pick it up. Breaking the seal, I pull the single note card out.

"For luck."

With a shaking hand, I reach down and pick up the small box. I pull off the simple brown paper and reveal a small white box. Slowly, I lift the lid and gasp. On a bed of foam is a silver necklace with a turtle pendant. I stare at it and my vision begins to blur as the tears come.

My mom loved turtles. She believed they were lucky and whenever we saw one by the pond behind the house we'd make sure to rub their shells in the hope that some luck would rub off on us. As we did it we'd say "for luck," and I still do it every time I see a turtle. I gently touch it and the limbs move independently of the shell. It's beautiful.

I snatch the card back up and flip it over to check if there is any indication of who it's from, but there's nothing. Not on the card, envelope, or in the box. Closing my eyes, I smile and kiss the pendant before putting the necklace on. I don't know who left it, but I will be forever grateful to them. They've given me a piece of my mom back, when I needed it most.

I rub the belly with my thumb, and with my eyes still closed I smile and whisper to my mom, "for luck."

Before Daniel arrives, I switch the music over to classic rock and sing along to Queen as I set out plates, cups, and napkins. At 6:00pm exactly my doorbell rings and I open the door to find Daniel smiling and holding two full grocery bags.

"Hey! Come on in. How are you? What the heck did you bring?"

He chuckles and follows me in and to the kitchen. Placing the bags on the counter he turns and picks me up in one of his trademark hugs, except this one lasts a few seconds longer than normal. "I brought drinks. I didn't know what you'd want, so I got you Diet Coke and those Jack Daniels cooler things you like, too." He shrugs and smiles sheepishly.

"Wow, officer! Providing alcohol to an underage woman? Scandalous!" I giggle and start unloading the bags so I can stow the drinks in the fridge. "Do you want something to drink now?"

He blushes again and admits "I won't tell if you won't. Besides, I figured if you drank I could convince you to stay here tonight. No driving involved so nothing to worry about. And no, I can wait, thanks."

"Oh, I already planned to stay tonight. I figured we might be hanging out late, so I'll crash here and go to work in the morning. Speaking of work, Brandon said he got caught up in something, so he'll be late tonight. He ordered the pizza to be delivered though."

I'm not sure, but I think I saw a flash of irritation, or disappointment In Daniel's eyes before he caught himself and smiled. "I didn't realize he was still coming. Is everything ok?"

Um, ok weird. Brandon is always here when we do dinner at the house, and he just told me he would be late. "Yeah, he said he had to take care of something first. He'll be here, but he's not sure when yet." A flash of light and color through the front window attracts my attention. "Pizza's here, give me a sec I'll grab it."

I pull a ten out of my pocket to tip the delivery driver and head to the door humming along with Steve Miller about jokers and smokers. Before he can push the doorbell I open the front door and smile at the older man holding a stack of five pizzas. What the hell? Why would Brandon order five pizzas for three people?

"Hi there! I have an order for Jenevive, is that you?"

My forehead creases in confusion and I tilt my head before I answer him. "Um, yeah. But are you sure it's all for me?"

He laughs and says "Yes ma'am. The man who ordered it said to tell you to just 'take the dang pizzas and stop judging him.'" Holding out the boxes, he smiles. "Enjoy! I say hide them from him if he's going to give you an attitude like that!"

Laughing, I hold out the ten for him, and we do an awkward hand off as he grabs the cash and I grab the boxes of pizza. "Have a good night sir! Thanks for coming all the way out here."

"You too miss! You have some lovely property out here, it's a pleasure to take in a pretty view every once in a while." He's looking at the water beyond the house as he walks to his car, so I know he's not being skeezy. How refreshing.

I walk back into the kitchen with the ridiculous amount of pizza, and Daniel jumps off his bar stool when he sees me with all the boxes. "Shit, Jen! Why didn't you call me to grab all this? What army are we feeding?" Before I can outmaneuver him, he grabs the boxes and places them on the stove.

Scowling at him, I roll my eyes and try not to punch him for his macho crap. "I am perfectly capable of carrying five large pizzas if I can carry a whole damn deer by myself thank you very much! And I have no idea. Brandon didn't tell me he was bringing anyone, and he told the delivery guy to tell me not to judge him. Maybe he's starving and wants leftovers? You know he loves cold pizza more than anyone should." I grab a plate and extend it to Daniel before checking the boxes. "Hmmm... pepperoni, BBQ chicken bacon, veggie, meat lovers, and extra cheese." I unashamedly slide three pieces of extra cheese on my own plate and grab the garlic sauce from the box before moving to the side. "Help yourself. What do you want to drink?"

"I'll have one of those cooler things you like. Are we eating in here or do you want to eat outside?" He grabs one slice of the BBQ chicken bacon and two meat lovers before grabbing the bottle from me.

"Let's eat on the patio. It's beautiful outside tonight and the bugs haven't been bad lately."

Sitting down at the table on the patio, we tuck in to the pizza and sit for a moment in companionable silence. "You look beautiful tonight, Jen. I meant to say it earlier."

I give him a big smile to show him a mouth full of half-chewed pizza and giggle when he cringes. After I swallow and say "Thanks, D. You look nice too. What were you up to today looking all fancy?" He's wearing a charcoal button down shirt with the sleeves rolled up to his elbows and khaki shorts with some boat shoes. He's handsome and it makes me wonder, not for the first time, why he's still single.

He blushes a little and rubs the back of his neck again. "I just worked on my house today. Getting some minor construction projects done. Did I tell you I'm thinking about finishing the attic and putting a game room up there?"

"No way! Are you talking like a pool table kind of game room, or video games? Are you doing it all yourself?"

"Probably video games, maybe a poker table. I think it would be hard to get a pool table up there, but you never know. I have always wanted one. I guess it'll depend on the amount of space I have up there when I'm done. I am doing it myself but I may ask Brandon for help with the sheet rock when it gets to that point."

Leaning back in my seat, I heave a contented sigh as I take a sip of my drink and gently rub my food baby. "I'm happy to help if you need me. I'm a miracle worker with a paintbrush."

"That'd be great, thanks. Hey, do you think..." the sound of his phone ringing breaks his train of thought, and he frowns as he checks the caller ID. "One sec. Hello? Um, yeah. ok. Hang on." Covering the phone with his hand he gives me a confused look and says "I need to take this. I'll be right back, ok?"

"Sure. I'm going to go down to the dock, come down there when you're done."

Half full bottle in hand, I head down to the dock to dip my feet in the water. The sun has gone down enough that the sky is lined in pinks and oranges, and the light breeze teases my hair as I walk. The birds are settling in the trees surrounding the property, and their chatter is soothing as I reach the end of the dock. Dropping to the floor I pull my sandals off and test the water temperature with my toes before submerging my feet. The water is still relatively warm, so I slowly kick my feet back and forth as I lean back on one arm and take a sip of my drink. I love sitting out here at the end of the day. The sky dances in a riot of colors and the serene surface of the water reflects it back and almost makes it seem like the world is on fire. I close my eyes and tilt my head back, basking in the warmth from the setting sun.

The sunlight halos her in pink and gold, bringing out the red undertones in her dark hair and setting the pink and purple strands alight. Leaning back against arms braced on the dock, her eyes are closed and her head is tilted back to embrace the dying light. Her long lashes lie against her pale skin in dark contrast and the small smile gracing her pink lips is breathtaking.

I have been waiting for this moment for four long years.

I'm alone for several minutes before I hear the first step on the dock behind me. Keeping my head back and eyes closed, I reach for my drink and take another sip before saying "Everything ok? The water is still warm, surprisingly enough. You should dip your feet in too."

The footsteps stop too far away and Daniel doesn't respond, so after a few seconds I open my eyes and turn around with a worried frown.

The second my eyes land on the person standing beyond me, my heart stops and I lose my grip on the bottle in my hand. In my shock, I don't even register that it hits the dock and rolls off into the water below.

The only thing I can see is a pair of blue eyes that I have been missing for four long years.

"Ryan?"

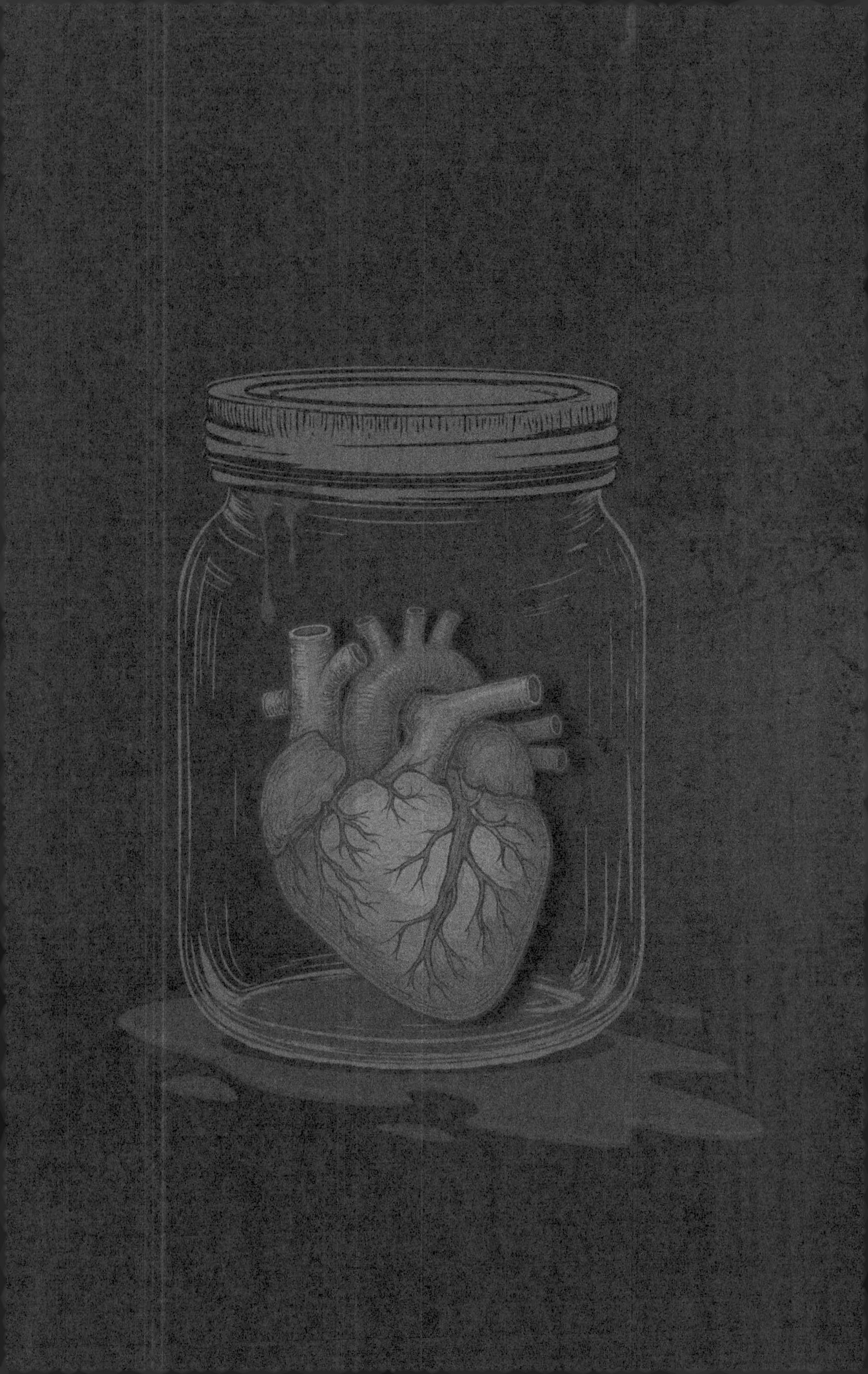

CHAPTER 8

I have been waiting for this moment for four years. Four long years when I switched from anger to depression to confusion. I wondered what I did wrong that would cause him to leave me without a word of goodbye. Hell, I wondered what I did to make both of them leave like that. But Ryan was my first love. He kissed me one day, and was gone the next.

Stunned, I sat there staring at him, and then jolted when his cousin Evan stepped up beside him too.

"Evan? Ryan? What the fuck? What are you doing here? How did you know I was here? WHERE THE FUCK HAVE YOU BEEN?"

I'm not stunned anymore, and when Ryan lets a smirk hit his lips and simply says "Hey, Jen," I decide then I want to murder him. Like, a lot. I've been worried about them for four fucking years, and that's his opening line?

Standing up and marching up to them, I poke him in the chest and glare at both of them. "Don't you fucking 'Hey Jen' me, you asshole! Where the fuck have you two been for the last four years? Were you somewhere with no phone or internet? You couldn't send me a damned letter to tell me you just didn't want to talk to me anymore? A goddamned smoke signal to tell me you were even alive?"

Evan gives me a small, sad smile and opens his mouth to say something before Brandon and Daniel walk on to the dock to join us. Brandon's face shows he's excited yet sheepish, and Daniel just looks as irritated as I am. Ryan was his best friend and he left him too. I shoot Brandon a glare promising punishment before looking at Evan and rolling my arm in an "out with it" gesture.

"Jen, we can explain, if you'll let us. We've both missed you all, and a lot happened that we had no control over. Can we please talk?" The sadness and hope in Evan's eyes is enough to sway me. He was always so sweet to me, the one I went to when I needed strength and support, and to see that pain in his eyes breaks my heart all over again. Looking at Ryan, his eyes don't give much away, but he's always held his feelings close to his chest, so I'm not surprised they don't show anything now. A lifetime of living with his parents would teach anyone to hide their emotions.

I check with Brandon and Daniel for their input, and while Brandon gives me a quick, short nod, Daniel observes Ryan and Evan with suspicion before giving me a reluctant nod too.

Sighing, I let my shoulders drop and shake my head in disbelief. "ok. You have one chance to explain things. Four years of no contact is a lot to explain. Come on."

We all head back to the house and I gesture for them to take a seat at the patio table. "Brandon, why don't you come with me to grab drinks."

Shoulders drooping in resignation, he follows me to the kitchen. Once the patio door is closed and we're in the kitchen, I spin on him and punch his arm hard enough to hurt. "What the actual fuck, Brandon? How long have you known they were here? Why didn't you tell me? Why would you bring them here like this?"

"Fuck, that hurt! I'm sorry ok? They literally showed up at the store right before closing today and I almost passed out when they walked in. I wanted to call you right away, but they wanted to tell you they were back themselves. They swore they could explain everything and wanted to do it when we were all together and begged me not to tell you before they could. I'm sorry Jen. I think seeing them after all this time messed with my head. I'm still kind of in shock, to be honest."

I can tell he's being honest because the tips of his ears turn red when he lies, and they're as ghostly pale as the rest of him. I grab him up in a tight hug and listen to his heart beating rapidly in his chest. Giving him a squeeze, I release him and walk over to the freezer to grab drinks. I hand him a few of the beers Daniel brought, and grab a few more of the Jack Daniels coolers for myself. They can suffer with the beer.

We share a look while we both take a deep breath. "I love you, you know?" I say with a sad smile. "I don't think I could stand to face them after all this time without you."

"I know Killer, me either. Let's find out what they have to say. We don't owe them anything, but I think you and I need this for closure, if nothing else." Releasing another deep sigh as he observes the guys through the windows, he continues. "I think Daniel is more angry than upset. He always did turn his upset into anger. Let's try to keep an eye on him too, ok?" I nod, and shoulder to shoulder we head back outside to find out what happened that caused the last four years of our lives to change so drastically.

The silence on the patio is deafening. Daniel is still looking over both men like he hasn't missed them as much as Brandon and I have. He's a cop, so the suspicion is part of his nature, but he missed them too. He was just as devastated as we were when they disappeared.

Unable to look at Ryan again yet, I sit across from Evan and take in how he's changed and search for anything that remains the same. He's grown out his dark brown hair so it's short on the sides and a few inches long on the top. It's the effortless style some men can pull off that looks like they just ran their fingers through it, or some woman just did, but it probably takes an hour in front of the mirror to perfect. He's grown a short beard that provides definition to his angular face, and when the light hits him just right, hints of red streak his hair and beard and adds warmth to his coloring he didn't have when he was younger. Down at the dock I noticed he's grown at least six inches since I last saw him, and he's bulked up enough to give him definition and width, but he's still lean. His gray t-shirt strains a bit across his chest and shoulders, and his jeans fit him well enough to accentuate his muscular legs.

His piercing forest green eyes are what prove to me, without a doubt, that the boy I cared about is still there. The pain that was always present is still there, but has transformed him into something beautiful. His features have sharpened, and they tell a story of a man who has lived through Hell and survived. We shared that pain as children, and I think we still do.

Screwing up my courage, I steel my heart and look next to Evan at Ryan. His dark blue eyes show nothing of what he's thinking, and while part of me is glad, the other part wants to strangle him to see if he feels that. His chocolate colored hair is cut similarly to Evans but it's meticulously styled back with product, and he has a five-o'clock shadow tinting his jawline. Taller than Evan by at least an inch, his bulk is that of a football player. His button down shirt is rolled up at the sleeves and unbuttoned at the top, the fit hinting at the muscles underneath, much like his slightly baggy jeans.

He simply stares back at me, seemingly waiting for me to start. Fuck that. He's the one that left me. They both left us, and this is on them to explain. Cocking one eyebrow, something that took me years of practice to perfect, I continue staring at him, not willing to break the silence. Brandon and Daniel are letting me take the lead, because neither says a word.

"I guess it's been a while, huh?"

I know that was not how he chose to start this conversation. Please tell me I misunderstood his "I'm so sorry Jen, I'm an asshole and I should have said goodbye when I left like a douche in the night," because that is the only appropriate opener in this situation. Evan must see the thoughts on my face before they spill out of my mouth, because he rushes to interrupt.

"Jen, we're sorry, ok? Please, please just listen. We can explain. Neither of us wanted to leave, and we definitely didn't want to leave without telling you. We didn't have a choice! You'll understand once you hear us out." He looks between me, Brandon, and Daniel with a desperate plea in his eyes.

I stare at both of them again while taking a sip of my drink and leaning back in my chair before slowly nodding at him to continue.

"The day we left, we weren't given a choice. Ryan's mom and dad took everything from us. They went through our stuff before we got home from school, wiped our computers and changed our passwords. Threw our stuff away, smashed our phones when we got home and gave us flip phones without internet capability. They packed for us and wouldn't let us contact anyone to say goodbye or find a way to keep in touch in the future." At this point, Brandon, Daniel, and I are all staring at them stunned. "They told us we were moving to a new parish" he continued, "and they were strict about contact with people outside of the church because they could influence members. We weren't even allowed contact with people we went to church with here because they talked to others outside of the congregation."

Evan pauses and takes a deep drink of his beer while works himself up to say something even bigger.

"They took us to a... a cult." He blurts it quickly, like he's ripping off a Band-aid, and I gasp and Ryan's head whips around to glare at Evan. "What, bro? They are and you know it. They go far past the normal teachings of Christianity, it's not normal there." Ryan is angry, but whether it's because he doesn't believe they're a cult, or he's admitting they were a part of one for so long, I can't tell.

Not wanting them to fall into an argument about cult semantics, I decide to interject. "But where have you been the last few years? Evan, you turned 18 not too long after you moved. Why did you stay if you're so against them? Ryan, why did you? And why are you back now?" I have about a thousand other questions but those seem to be the most pertinent at the moment.

Ryan shakes his head and sighs. "They aren't a cult, they're just... devout. My dad took on the roll of pastor there when we left here. I was so mad when they took us away and wouldn't let us say goodbye, but they were doing what they thought was right."

Evan scoffs and shakes his own head in disgust. "Fuck that man, they wanted to get us away from here because they didn't like the fact that we weren't perfect pastor's sons. This was about them, not us."

"Regardless of why they did it, we lost everything when we left. Any money we'd saved up on our own, they took to finance the move and never paid us back. We couldn't find jobs once we moved because no one would hire people from our compound. On top of that, my mom left about a year after we moved there. She ran away with another member of the church and my dad spiraled pretty bad. I had to work hard to keep him together."

Evan decided to take over at this point. "I tried to leave when I turned 18, but it was impossible without any money to live off of. I started working odd jobs for people in the community to make some money, and as I learned how to do things people from the neighboring area started hiring me too since I was willing to work for cheap. I tried to go to school online, but even if I got a student loan the internet was so closely monitored I wouldn't have been able to make it work. After three years of scraping together what I could, I had enough to lease a small apartment close to the compound and got a job as an apprentice at a construction company. I've been learning a trade and trying to get out of there ever since."

"But what about you Ryan? What have you been doing since you turned 18? And again, why are you both here now?"

"Dad is still the pastor there, but needed a lot of help otherwise. I've been taking care of him until recently when he married a widow in the community. She takes care of him now, so he doesn't need me anymore. We're here now because Grandma is sick. She called and asked us to come help her and said if we live with her and help her around the house she'll put us through college. I'm not sure what I want to do with my life, but I had to take the opportunity to come back when I had it." Finally, he smiles at me. It's small and strained, but it allows an emotion to show through his eyes, and that emotion is hope.

Brandon steps in with his own question. "Why didn't you try to get in touch with us sooner? Evan, why didn't you call when you moved out on your own? We're all on Facebook and Instagram using our real names. You could have found us at any time, but you didn't even bother, did you?" He's hiding it well, but I know him better than anyone. He's hurting, and he doesn't know what to think about what they've told us.

Join the club.

Evan scrubs his face with his hands before clasping them together on the table. "I thought about it. I really did. I actually looked you all up several times but I couldn't bring myself to contact you. I figured you hated us by now and wouldn't want to hear from me. The pictures I could see of you all looked so happy, I didn't want to ruin that for you by showing back up. Hell, Jen, I figured if I tried to contact you your dad would hunt me down and kill me."

My face drops and Brandon and Daniel both watch me with concern. I force a lopsided smile and say "Yeah, well. He, um... he died. Six months ago."

Evan's face pales and he gasps out an apology. Ryan, on the other hand, quietly says "I heard. I'm sorry, he was a good man."

Obviously, Evan had no idea because his head snaps around to glare at Ryan, fury etched across his face. "What the fuck, man! Why didn't you tell me?"

"My dad told me. He spoke with someone from the old church who told him. I thought he would have told you too."

"He fucking didn't, don't you think I would have said something? That's bullshit, dude. You should have told me."

"Ok boys. Enough. I've got enough to sort through in my mind tonight without the two of you adding your bickering." They both stop and give me sheepish expressions. Brandon and Daniel remain silent observers, but look are to step in if needed. "I'm going to ask one more time, and if I don't receive an answer you can both leave. You may be back here because your Grandmother invited you, but why are you here." I stab the table with my finger. "Why, after four fucking years are you at my house? What do you want?"

The two of them share a long look before Evan shrugs at Brandon. "We didn't know if we wanted to try to find you all since it had been so long. Like I said, we kind of figured you hated us by now for leaving like we did, and it would be totally justified. We were running errands for Gran today though, and Ryan happened to see the new store. I couldn't resist going in, and we bumped into Brandon while we were there. When he mentioned you and said he was seeing you tonight when we asked how you were, we couldn't pass up the opportunity to see you."

Finally, after four years I have the information I've been begging for and dreading all at once. I'm overwhelmed, confused, disappointed, and happy it wasn't something I did. I don't know what to think, and my brain is overloaded. I take one last sip and soak in the fact that my boys are together again at last after four long years apart. Brandon seems as confused as I am, and poor Daniel has shut down and is rocking his cop face.

"Ok."

"Ok?" Ryan asks. "What does that mean?"

"It means ok. I appreciate you coming out here to tell us this in person. The last four years have been... hard... without both of you. The three of us struggled with what could have happened. We worried, we got angry, and then we just got sad. This is a lot of information to work through. How long do you plan on staying in the area?"

Evan immediately responds. "Indefinitely. Grandma is sick but not terminal, and I've always liked it here. I think she would have asked us to come earlier if Uncle Patrick had let her do it sooner. My guess is he wanted Ryan out of the house, and us both out of the area, now that he's got a new wife." Ryan's jaw tenses like he's angry about the situation, but again, he's so hard to read I don't know what part he's angry about.

"Well, I guess we'll have time to catch up later if you want to, then. But it's getting late and I'm honestly a little overwhelmed, so I think it's time for me to go to bed."

Ryan and Evan both startle at my response, but after a moment are both resigned to the fact that this is as far as things will go tonight. They left us for four years. They don't get to slot right back into where they left because they come back when it's convenient for them and apologize. Ryan may be my first love, but I am not now, nor have I ever been, a doormat. If they want back in our lives, they'll have to work for it.

I stand and gather empty bottles and our pizza plates, and turn to head inside to clean up. I hear chairs scraping against the patio stones and the guys are talking softly among themselves as they file back inside. I'm so caught up in my own head I don't notice Ryan is behind me until I turn to put the plates in the dishwasher.

"Shit, Ryan! You scared me."

"I'm sorry, I didn't mean to. Can I have your number? I'd like to catch up properly once you've had some time to digest everything."

"Me too, I've missed you, Jen" Evan adds from the other side of the island.

After a slight hesitation, I agree. With only a slight amount of bitterness, I add "I'd tell you it hasn't changed since you left, but I guess you lost it." I recite my number for them, and after Ryan saves my number into his phone he reaches up and runs his fingers along my cheek, forcing a shiver through me when I realize it's the same place the creep from last night touched me. I swallow and step back. He gives me a slight frown as he drops his hand.

"Alright, I guess we'll head out, if you're sure?"

"Yeah, I think I need some time to work through everything." I give Ryan and Evan a strained smile as I walk them to the door.

Opening it before I can get there, Ryan turns and gives me the same cocky smirk that used to turn my knees to jello. "I'll text you tomorrow to check in." His eyes drop to my necklace and flash briefly with surprise before turns to walk to their car.

Evan steps up to the door and pauses, turning back to me. "Do you think I could text you tomorrow too? I don't want to push you too fast. If you need time, I understand." There's the Evan I knew, always so caring. Having that back would be so amazing, but I'm not sure if I'm ready to let them back in so quickly.

"Yeah, you can text me. I can't promise anything, but I think that would be nice." His smile makes my heart skip a beat with how genuine it is, and I know I made the right choice in agreeing.

"I have missed you Jen. So much. I'm sorry we never got to say goodbye. I'll do whatever I can to make it up to you. Maybe we can start over. Get to know each other as adults. I'll let you control the pace, but please know I am here no matter what you decide."

"Thanks Evan."

"Of course." He rubs the back of his neck and stares at my floor a moment before he meets my eyes. "I know I'm pushing my luck, but can I have a hug? It's been a few years since I've had one."

Shocked, I look at him like he's crazy. "Only from me, right? You're not saying that no one has hugged you in the past four years?"

Pink tinges his cheeks and the tips of his ears turn red with embarrassment. "No, I haven't hugged anyone. Our family isn't exactly touchy-feely, and it's frowned upon in the community unless you're related or married."

Uncaring of my own feelings, I jump forward and throw my arms around his neck and pull him in close. He wraps his arms around me and squeezes me tight, a slight tremor in his body making it evident that he's been without affection for a long time. My heart breaks for him, so I whisper "I am still hurting and angry, but I understand. Just give me some time to come to terms with everything, ok? We can start over tomorrow."

With a final squeeze, he releases me and steps back. "Whatever you need, it's yours. I'll send you a text tonight so you have my number, and then I'll text you later tomorrow to check in. I'm so happy to see you again, Jenny."

I roll my eyes at the stupid nickname he knows drives me nuts and give him a little push out the door. "Be safe driving home. I'll talk to you later." Closing the door on them, I turn and lean back against the door and close my eyes. Hearing two sets of feet come to join me, I keep my eyes closed as I say "Well, that was fucking weird."

Brandon's inelegant snort is the only response needed.

THE WATCHER
Small Victories

The anguish I saw in her beautiful green eyes when she saw us again nearly drove me to my knees. As much as I never want it to be directed at me, the fury that quickly replaced it lit a fire in me that will never extinguish. We deserve her anger, but I will prove to her that she can trust me again. It killed me to admit we could have reached out to her before today, but as desperate as I was to do so, I didn't feel like I deserve her yet and I will never lie to her. I couldn't come to her empty-handed, begging her to forgive me when I had nothing to offer her in return. She deserves an equal partner, and I wasn't able to be that for her yet.

Sitting across the table from her, looking into her eyes and hearing her voice was like a gift I never hoped to receive again. Touching her? It was like coming home.

Seeing her wearing the turtle necklace I left for her all those years ago made me feel a thousand feet tall, and watching her absentmindedly rub the belly when she was thinking? It's obvious she does it subconsciously and it gives her some kind of relief. To know she had a part of me with her this whole time fills me with a joy I don't deserve after what we put her through.

That turtle proves to me this is possible. That I can make her forgive me and earn another chance.

Tomorrow will be a new day. I'm a patient man. I'll do what it takes to make her believe she belongs with me, and then I'll never let her regret it, and I'll never let her go.

Chapter 9

The boys and I end up back outside on the dock, feet dangling in the water while we consider what happened in a comfortable silence. The night has cooled off to the point that I consider going in but the breeze and cricket sounds are helping center me, so instead I lay back on the dock and stare up at the night sky. Out here in the country we're far enough from the light pollution that I can clearly see some stars, and I distract myself for a while counting them.

After my mom died, my dad and I used to come out here at night and wait for shooting stars. I noticed that during those times in my life when I was struggling the most, those times when I missed her the most and wished I could talk to her and get her advice and a hug, those were the nights I'd see one. When I did see one it made me feel a little closer to her and gave me a sense of calm, like no matter what was happening everything would work out. Closing my eyes, I take a deep breath and send up a plea to my parents to let me know they're with me and that I'll get through this without another broken heart.

Seeing Ryan and Evan again was a blow I wasn't expecting. For four years I've been almost desperate to find out what happened to them. As happy as I was to see them, I'm struggling with the fact that they've been thinking about me but never tried to find me until now. I checked social media and searched the internet every few months trying to find them, worried something had happened to them. Looking for any mention of them to have confirmation they were at least ok. My heart hurts with the knowledge they didn't even bother to tell us that they were alive and well when they were able to, but after finding out what happened to them, I do understand it was a lot to deal with. We had been so close as kids, but people grow up and priorities change.

Evan had already been through so much in his life before he came to live with Ryan. He never knew his father and his mother, Pastor Holmes' sister, was an abusive, neglectful addict. She eventually took off with her new boyfriend slash drug dealer and Evan was left alone at fifteen years old. Being a pastor, Ryan's father felt obligated to take in Evan and "reform him," even though he had never been in trouble before. I think Pastor Holmes projected his disappointment in his sister onto Evan, and he ended up taking the brunt of his negative emotions. He was never good to Evan. He provided food and shelter but never love, approval, or simple kindness. Mrs. Holmes was indifferent to him, so he didn't receive any love from her either.

I think that was one of the reasons Evan and I bonded so fast once he moved here. We spent a lot of time together since he hung out with our friend group and I found both a kindred spirit in him, and someone who needed love but wasn't offered any. Both of us had lost our mothers, though it was in very different ways, and we shared some of the same pain. We leaned on each other during the times we struggled and having his support when I felt like I couldn't go to my dad without upsetting him was one of the few things that saved my sanity sometimes. Hearing he was all alone again after being taken away makes me ache for him, much like I do for Ryan after knowing his mother left him and his father was spiraling before essentially throwing him over for a new wife.

There is so much to think about. I wish my dad was here for me to be able to talk to him and ask for advice, but thinking of my dad just reminds me that Ryan knew he died. He knew his death would mean I was alone in the world, and he still stayed away. What am I supposed to think about that? He says he missed me, he wants to spend time with me, but when he heard my life was yet again turned upside down by the loss of my only remaining family member, he still stayed away. That is a hard idea to accept.

"Jen, look!" Brandon is pointing to the sky when my eyes shoot open. Sure enough, there's a shooting star up there and the vice grip around my heart loosens. Bittersweet tears fill my eyes and hope grows within me when I notice a second, larger shooting star follow the first. This has never happened before, and I can't help but believe it's my Mom and Dad giving me the sign that I asked for, telling me that they're here with me and everything will work out alright in the end.

"So," Brandon says, breaking the silence with hesitant words, "what are we thinking? Do we believe them?"

Daniel scoffs. "Their story is convenient, don't you think? Four years is an awful long time to be gone and then expect to be welcomed back with open arms. Besides, I don't think either of them really cared about seeing us, Brandon. They were mostly concerned with Jen."

"What is that supposed to mean?" I ask, defensive. "Are you saying they only came back for me? I don't believe that. I think I was just the one who was bitchy enough to demand answers instead of sitting back and waiting to find out what they had to say. Besides, Ryan kissed me and told me he loved me then disappeared. I think I deserved a little more from him than the two of you, unless there's something you neglected to tell me all these years."

Daniel rolls his eyes and Brandon chuckles. "As cute as they are, you know they were just as much my brothers as Daniel and you are my brother and sister. Sorry to burst your bubble Killer, but there is no MM in your future."

Faking a gag, I pick up my leg and plant my foot on Brandon's back and push him off the dock and into the cooling water. He pops up out of the water and glares at me while he sputters and wipes the water off his face. "What the fuck, Jen? What was that for?"

I'm laughing so hard at the shock on his face I don't notice he's after me until he grabs me up and holds me over the water. "Wait! No, Brandon! I'm sorry, ok? I'm sorry. I won't do it again! Please don't!"

"Hmm..." he hedges. "What will you give me?"

Daniel is standing on the dock watching this play out. "Come on man, don't dunk her. Give her to me and I'll help you out."

"I'll take a closing shift for you the next time you want to go on a date, no questions asked!"

Shoulders dropping, he agrees. "Ok, no bitching either, even if it means you work a double. Deal?"

"Deal!" Thank God. The water is warm enough to dip feet in, but I don't want to go swimming in it.

Brandon walks back to the dock and makes a move like he's going to hand me up to Daniel. "Oh, wait," he says thoughtfully. "You know what I just remembered?"

"What?" I ask, nervous.

"You punched me earlier. It's time for payback!" Without delay or telegraphing his intentions he spins and launches me away from the dock and into the water.

"Brandon!"

Luckily I remembered to take in a breath to hold before going under, because if I hadn't I would have inhaled a lungful of water from the shock of the cold. There's enough light from the moon to be able to see where he is standing in the water, so I swim over to him before coming up for air. Popping up behind him, I snake my arm around his throat and pull him backwards and back into the water. We get lost for a few minutes playing, both of us trying to get the upper hand and dunk the other. After the stress of the evening we both needed it, but I wish

Daniel would have joined us too. He's back to sitting on the edge of the dock with his feet in the water, chuckling as we mess around.

After a few minutes, I'm ready to warm up in a hot shower. We make our way to the dock ladder, and Daniel hands us both the towels I brought down earlier.

"Thanks, D. I don't know about you guys, but I'm beat. I need a hot shower and my bed. Are y'all going to stay tonight?"

"Can I take a shower and wash my clothes? I didn't bring spares. If you don't mind that I'll crash here."

Daniel considers me and nods his agreement that he's staying too.

"Alrighty, Brandon I think you've got clothes in my room still. Grab a change and give me your wet clothes to throw in the wash. Do you need anything D?"

"No, I've got a go-bag in my car. I'll grab it." He heads around the house to do just that, but pauses when Brandon calls out to him.

"You can take the guest room. I'll take the couch."

"Sounds good."

A few hours later I'm still laying in bed awake, thinking about the bombshells of the evening and the text Evan sent me while I was in the shower.

Evan: It's Evan. I'll text you tomorrow, but I just want to say again how sorry I am that it took us so long to contact you. I hope you'll give us another chance, because we missed you so much Jen.

Rolling over to my side and trying to pound my pillow into a comfortable shape, I jump when my door opens and a silhouette stands in the now open doorway.

"Hey, Killer, did I wake you?"

"No, I can't sleep. What's up?"

Brandon steps in and closes the door behind him. A crack between my blackout curtains allows in enough light to make out his shape moving through my room and to the other side of my king-sized bed. The reappearance of the guys must be doing a number on him if he's here, he only ever comes to sleep with me when he's really struggling with something. Pulling up the covers and sliding under, he scoots over until he's next to me and pulls me to him to spoon. Arms wrapped around me, he holds me to him for a few minutes while he gathers his thoughts. I stay quiet and let him work through it until he's ready.

"What are we going to do? We've gotten so used to it just being us but... I missed them, Jen. You are and always be my best friend, and Daniel is Daniel, but

Evan was like your male counterpart. You were number one, but he was a close second."

"I don't know B. I missed them too. I loved Ryan. Hell, I sometimes think part of me still does which is why I can't date anyone else. I felt the same way about Evan that you did." I sigh and sleepily burrow myself further into his warmth before continuing. "I think the only thing we can do is see how things pan out. We don't have to decide anything tonight. Let them prove to us whether they're sincere. I think more than anything, we'll regret it for ourselves if we don't."

He kisses my head and squeezes me tight. "Sounds like a plan. Let's get some sleep, ok? We can worry about all of this tomorrow."

"Ok. Nite Bran, love you."

"Love you too, Killer, so much. Get some sleep, it'll all still be here tomorrow"

His warmth and reassuring presence are enough to quiet my restless mind and allow me to relax enough to drift to sleep.

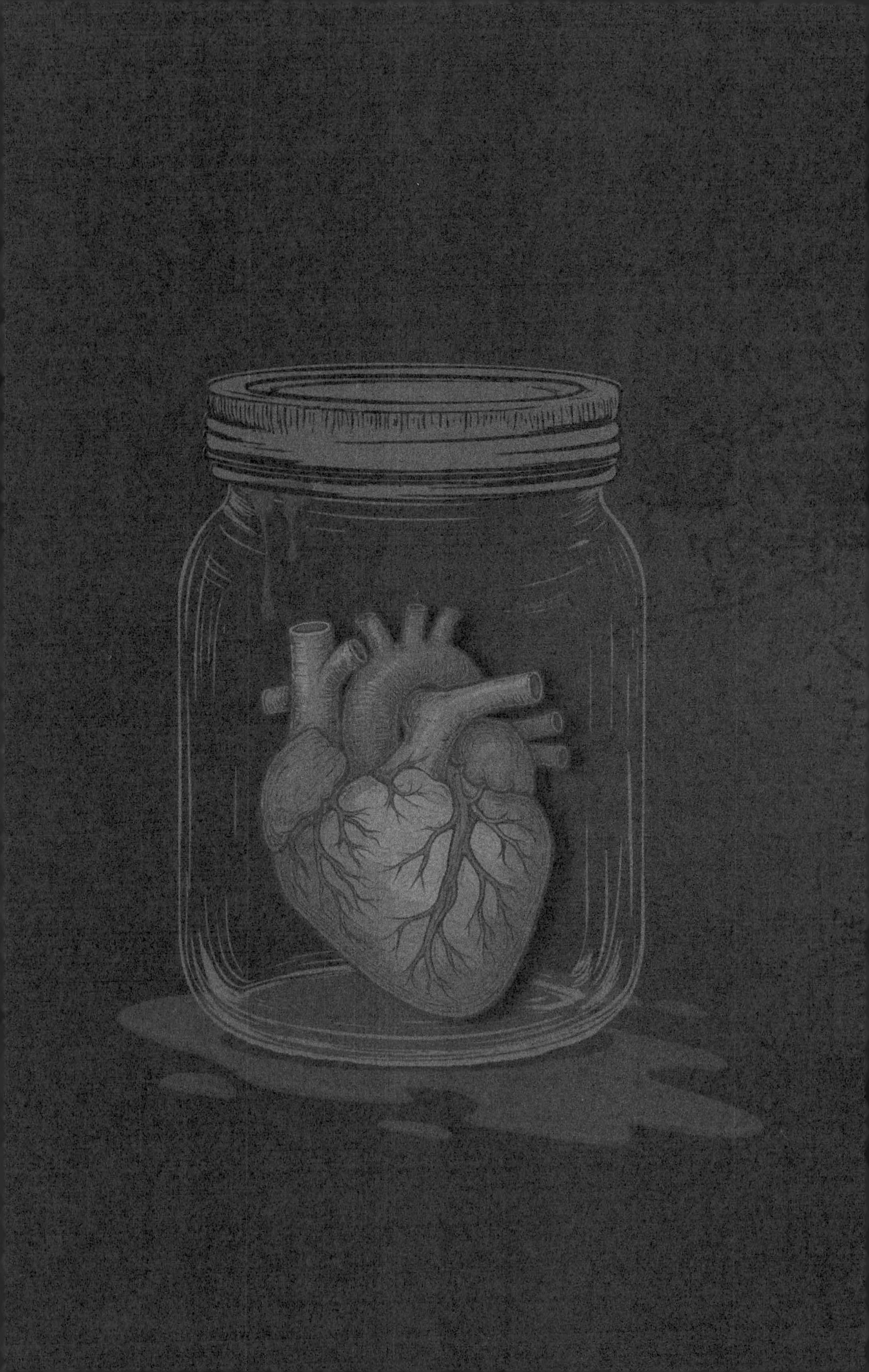

CHAPTER 10

I wake before Brandon and start the process of untangling myself from his octopus-like hold. He grunts in obvious irritation, but I'm having none of it. "Dude, if you don't let me go this instant I will pee on you."

I chuckle as he grumbles and switches from holding me tight to practically pushing me off the bed. I take care of my business and hop in the shower to prepare for the day. I work in a few hours, so I've got enough time to make breakfast for the boys, assuming Daniel is still here. Brandon will eat his portion if he's not so nothing will go to waste.

He's gone by the time I emerge from the bathroom, so I head to the laundry room and toss our washed clothes in the dryer before I make my way to the kitchen. Daniel is sitting at the island bar with a cup of coffee in front of him, scrolling on his phone. "Morning, you hungry?" I ask. Apparently he wasn't paying attention because he jumps and spins to face me, shutting off the screen on his phone and putting it face down on the counter.

"Shit, Jen! You about gave me a heart attack." He smiles and shakes his head in obvious embarrassment. "Yeah, I could eat. Brandon leave early? I didn't see him on the couch when I came down."

I move over to the fridge and pull out the things I need to make breakfast. I stopped at the store on the way over yesterday, figuring at least one of them would sleep over since they tend to when we drink too much. I don't often cook breakfast like this since I'm a cereal girl, but every once in a while I like to go all out and these mornings give me the excuse to do it.

"No, he's taking a shower. His clothes are in the dryer so unless he left in his pajamas he's here. He stayed in my room last night."

Daniel's face is priceless! His eyes are comically wide and his mouth is hanging open in shock. "He... slept with you?"

"Oh, gross D. Calm your tits, you know how he gets when he's upset. It wasn't like that and it never will be."

"Oh, uh, sorry. I didn't mean to assume. I think I'm still half asleep." His smile is sheepish before he hides it with his coffee mug. "Can I help?"

"Nah, I got it. Pancakes or waffles this morning?"

"Ohhhh, waffles! Do you have chocolate chips and whipped cream?"

Rolling my eyes at Brandon's dramatic entrance, I ask "Have I ever forgotten either?"

"Nope! That's why you're my best girl." Walking up to me he pulls me into a side hug and kisses the top of my head. "Give me two seconds to make some coffee then I'll work on the bacon and hash browns. Now, get to work on my waffles, woman!"

Once our food is ready we all sit at the island bar and dig in. This time Daniel breaks the silence, bringing us back to the conversation we put off finishing last night.

"So, what do you guys want to do? Do we accept their story and act like nothing happened? Do we ignore them and leave them in the dark like they left us? I have to admit, I barely slept at all last night trying to figure out what to do."

"I think we need to take things as they go. We don't have to let them back in with open arms, but we all missed them. If their story is true, I think we owe it to them, and to ourselves to find out if we can be friends again. They were a huge part of our lives and theirs were changed against their will. I have no doubt Ryan's parents pulled that shit, they were always crazy. At this point, my only problem is that they waited so long to get back in touch with us."

Grunting in agreement, Brandon finishes the bite of waffle he is chewing on before adding his thoughts. "Yeah, I wish they'd tried to contact us sooner, at least to let us know they were ok, or to ask for help, but we were kids. Four years is a long time, and if they went through the Hell we can imagine I'm not surprised we weren't their priority."

Daniel wipes his mouth with his napkin and nods. "Ok. I can see where you're coming from. I think, if you both agree, I'm going to run them to make sure there isn't anything they held back. Other than that, we'll go with the flow. We've all grown up, and it sounds like the last four years were very different for them. They could be the same guys we were friends with for so many years, or we may try to rekindle our relationships and realize we're too different now and it just doesn't work anymore."

"Don't do anything if it'll get you in trouble. I don't know what the rules are for that kind of thing." I warn him. "Regardless of what happens with them though, we still have each other. No matter what, you two are the most important to me. You've stayed by my side through the worst times in my life, and I'll stand by you both regardless of what happens. This has to be a group decision, so let's stay honest with each other, ok?"

Both of them nod their agreement, and we finish breakfast while discussing lighter topics. Daniel finishes his food first and after taking his plate to the sink he begins washing the dishes. After Brandon finishes his he joins Daniel at the sink and dries and puts everything away. They've spent enough time here over the years that they know where everything goes as well as I do. The level of comfort they bring takes me by surprise sometimes. Watching them take care of me and goof off together is like a salve on my frayed mind and nerves.

Regardless of my determination to see how things go, I can't help letting my mind drift. What would have happened if they hadn't left? Would Ryan and I be together even now? Instead of breakfast after a night of drinking too much, would it be Ryan and I cleaning up the kitchen after cooking breakfast together? Is that what I want? After seeing him again I realized Brandon really was right, even though I'll never admit it to him. I have been holding myself back from the possibility of intimacy with someone.

Brandon must notice my mind has drifted into potentially dangerous territory because he pulls me back to the present. "What's up Killer? What are you thinking?"

Not wanting to delve further into our situation again, I throw him a bright smile and an eyebrow waggle. "Oh, nothing much. Just thinking about how lovely it is to have you two hot young things cleaning my kitchen for me. It's a shame it would be icky because otherwise we'd be starting my own personal reverse harem up in this bitch."

Brandon throws his head back and laughs in delight before giving me an exaggerated wink and blowing me a kiss, while Daniel shakes his head and blushes. "You couldn't handle all of this, sweet thing," Brandon volleys back.

"Hmm... that bad huh? I guess it's just as well. We'd never work anyway, neither of you would be able to finance my reading habit." Both groan because they know it's the truth. As I turn to walk upstairs to brush my teeth, I yell over my shoulder "Alright, breakfast is over. You bitches need to get out of my house!"

I'm feeling better after our banter, but I still don't know what I'm going to do about Ryan. I'm going on the assumption that he wants to try to see if we can work together again, based on his words and actions.

The question now is, do I forgive him and see if we want to try again, or do I let him go and find out if I can move on?

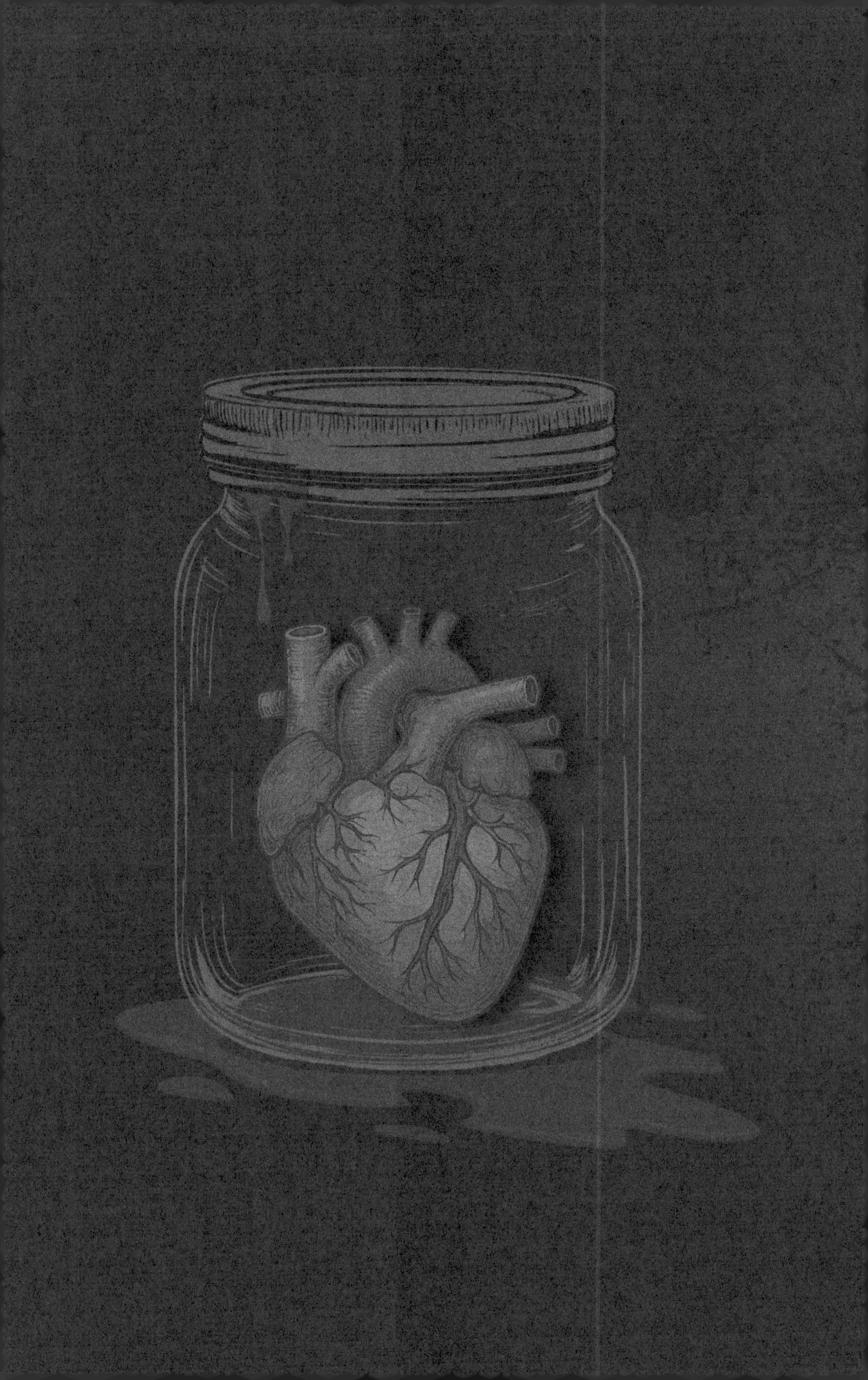

Chapter 11

My shift is flying by today because I've decided to set up a display celebrating my favorite reverse harem novels. My weird moment with the guys in my kitchen this morning gave me a little inspiration, so I pulled the books we have by my favorite indie authors and set up a display at the front of the store. Mrs. C was hesitant when I started doing displays of "dirty books" towards the front of the store, but she soon realized I was on the right track when they started flying off the tables. Our biggest customers were the moms who brought their kids in for their own books, toys, or games. Putting it at the front of the store would catch their attention when they came in, and they'd end up browsing and picking up a few books while their kids found their own things. It is so rewarding to see moms that would come in regularly finally getting something for themselves. Now, if we don't have a romance display set out when they come they often ask for recommendations. I love talking to these women because a lot of them don't take time for themselves otherwise, so if I can help give them a break I feel like I'm making a difference.

As I'm placing the final book on my display table, a notification plays on my phone telling me I have a text.

> **Unknown:** It's Ryan. Do you want to meet up today? I'd like to talk, just the two of us.

I give myself a moment to think while I save his number into my contacts. I'm not sure if I'm ready to be alone with him yet. He was the only person I've ever considered having sex with. I'm worried that if I let my guard down with him I'll make a decision I'll regret.

> **Me:** I'm working today, but I have a break in 30 minutes. Do you want to come by and get coffee or something?

> **Ryan:** Sure. Be there in 30.

Part of me wants to rush to the staff bathroom and make sure I look ok. My hair is up in a ponytail and I'm only wearing mascara because if I don't people think I'm tired or sick. My jeans are cropped and my long sleeved t-shirt reads "I still read fairy tales, they're just dirtier now." The other part of me is the part that doesn't care what he thinks of me, because I feel fantastic today. I don't need to impress him, or anyone else, as long as I'm confident in myself that is all that matters.

I used to be incredibly self-conscious. Growing up without a mother was hard when I hit those years when I was trying to find myself, my style, and my confidence. Mrs. C tried to help where she could, but we're so stylistically different it was difficult to connect with her that way. It didn't hurt that my friends were boys. I taught myself enough about makeup to accentuate my features but I will never be one of those girls who are able to transform their face with a brush and a few color palettes. On top of that, my naturally curly hair was always a source of embarrassment for me. If I wanted any sort of control over it I'd have to blow dry and straighten it, but after years of heat my hair was incredibly damaged. I finally did research and found the right combination of products for my hair and I will never go back to daily heat treating it.

My curls are a part of me, just like my thick thighs and hips. I used to lament that my bottom half was wider and bigger than the other girls but as I've aged I realized when in combination with my full chest and relatively small waist, I've been blessed with a sexy hourglass figure. I don't know if anyone else thinks it's sexy, and I don't care. I think it is, and that's all that matters.

At the end of the day you have to celebrate yourself. You have to celebrate what makes you uniquely you, and if no one else appreciates that then it's their loss, not yours.

Ryan arrives at the store as I finish checking out my favorite customer, Ms. Ruby. This time she's taken advantage of the reverse harem display and is leaving with every recommendation there she didn't already have, which isn't many. When I wave at Ryan and hold up my finger to indicate I'd be a minute, Ms. Ruby turns to figure out who I'm looking at. Facing me again with her eyes wide, she gives me a gummy grin (she forgot her dentures again) and wiggles her eyebrows at me. "Who is that hot piece of ass?" she asks me. "You hitting that, girl?"

Cheeks flaming, I dart a glance at Ryan to make sure he didn't hear her. "God Ms. Ruby, no! He's a friend. He's been out of town for a while and just got back, so we're catching up. Not everything has to be a sexual free-for-all."

Ms. Ruby cackles as she takes her bag from me. Reaching up to pat my cheek affectionately she leans in and says "Life is short, Jen. Take him out for a test drive before it's too late!" Then she turns, walks up to Ryan and tugs on his shirt sleeve until he bends his tall frame down, so she can whisper to him. His face drains of color as his eyes shoot to mine. Ms. Ruby releases him, takes another step further and swats him on his ass, sauntering her trouble making self out of the front door. He jumps and I can see horror in his eyes, then irritation as I laugh so hard I'm having to hold myself up on the counter.

"Who was that, Jen? What was that?" His cheeks are the cutest shade of pink and his ears are tipped red with his mortification.

"I'm so sorry!" Snicker. "That was Ms. Ruby. She's just a horny old lady who has no filter. She's harmless, I promise. Just a little feisty in her old age."

"Harmless? She told me if you didn't satisfy me sexually I could get her number from you and she'd rock my world. She's like 100 years old, shouldn't she be in a home or something?"

"She's only 82, and her bark is worse than her bite. Besides, she's happily married, so she was messing with you. Are you ready for some coffee? I've been told it's fantastic here."

As we walk over to the cafe, he questions "You've heard? You haven't tried it and you work here?"

"I don't drink coffee, I hate the taste of it. I'll drink hot chocolate in the winters, but it's the only hot drink I like. They keep Diet Coke on tap for me, so I'm happy."

Nick is manning the cafe today, so when he sees me walking over he grabs the tumbler I left there this morning and fills it with ice and Diet Coke. It's ready by the time we arrive at the counter, and he questions me with a raised eyebrow before acknowledging Ryan.

"Hey Nick, this is Ryan. He's our friend from when we were kids."

"Nice to meet you Ryan. What can I get you?" Nick is a few years older than me and gorgeous. He's fit and tall, with buzzed blonde hair and piercing blue eyes. He's intimidating as hell to look at if you don't know him, but he's one of the sweetest guys I've ever met. He's played my boyfriend on more than one occasion when a guy hasn't gotten the message that I wasn't interested, and I've joined him and his boyfriend Travis who is a guard for the shopping center for dinner many times. Last week he confided in me he was getting ready to propose to Travis and asked me to hold the ring for him so Travis wouldn't find it.

"Hey man. Um, I guess just a black coffee, thanks."

"Anything to eat, Jen? Ryan?" I point Ryan in the direction of the bakery cabinet before ordering.

"Do we have any red velvet cupcakes left? I've been craving one all day."

Noticing Ryan looking at him, he reaches under the counter and sets a plate with a giant red velvet cupcake on it next to my drink. With a wink, he coos "Saved this one for you, gorgeous," and I grin to show my appreciation. He leans forward over the counter and turns his face away while tapping his cheek in expectation. Laughing I lean forward, careful to avoid a stomach full of frosting, and smack a loud kiss on his cheek.

"My hero!" I cheer while batting my eyes at him.

"Nothing for me." Ryan's cold and harsh answer shocks me out of the moment with Nick, but his face is calm.

Drinks and cupcake in hand, we head over to the table farthest from the counter where we have a bit of privacy. I make sure to sit facing Nick, so he can't antagonize Ryan from a distance, and we stare at each other for a minute before I decide to wait him out and start on my treat. These cupcakes are so big I have to use a fork when I eat them or I'll be wearing it, but I don't care because they're totally worth it. My first bite has me closing my eyes in bliss and releasing a little moan, but they snap back open when I hear Ryan clear his throat and shift in his seat. My face flushes with embarrassment, but not because of my reaction. If you can eat a cupcake this delicious without some sort of similar reaction, I feel bad for you. This thing is positively sinful. My embarrassment stems from the fact that I forgot Ryan was there since we're not at the point in our relationship where I should be sharing my cake-gasms. In an effort to move things along, I lick my fork and say "So..."

His eyes are locked on my mouth, but find mine again when I speak. "Oh, yeah. So, um. I was hoping we could talk. You know, about us."

"Is there an 'us' Ryan? Has there really ever been? We had one afternoon where you kissed me and then you were gone. If you wanted there to be an us, why didn't you try to contact me when you turned 18? Your dad couldn't keep you from it then. The fact that you're here, now, only after your grandmother brought you here honestly makes me feel like a consolation prize. I wasn't important enough to you when it would have taken effort to talk to me, but now that it's easy you're here? It doesn't feel good, Ryan."

The frustration he's feeling is obvious. This is what I need to know if we're going to move forward though. I refuse to be with someone because it's easy for them. If they want me, they'll work for it -- I deserve nothing less.

"You don't understand Jen. You remember how difficult my father is, right?" At my nod, he continues. "After my mom left, he was kind of broken. I think it was more his pride than anything else, but he started drinking heavily and was a general mess. In his grief he went a little crazy for a while and threatened to disown me if I left him or went against his rules. I hadn't talked to Grandma for a few years at that point, and he had me convinced she wrote us off, so he was all I had left." He pauses to take a sip of his coffee. "Well, him and Evan. Evan was trying so hard to leave and I knew as soon as he did Dad would write him off too. I felt trapped, so I did what he asked of me. Dad started seeing Kathy after her husband died and I think she mellowed him out. When he told me about Grandma's offer I was surprised, but happy to go along with it because it meant I could come back and see you again."

"That's what I'm saying though. You're here now because your dad is happy with someone and doesn't need you." His jaw tenses at my statement, but I can't hold back to save his feelings. He didn't think about mine for the past four years so it's my turn to do what's right for me. "Are you telling me if he calls you back you won't leave without telling us again? I refuse to go through it again, Ryan. I deserve better."

Reaching out and grabbing my hand in his, he rubs the back of it with his thumb while he stares at it with a creased brow. "Can I promise you I'll never go back there? No, I can't. He's my father. I can promise you that he's agreed to let me decide what I want to do with my own life, and if I am ever called back there again I will not leave without letting you know." His eyes are full of a mixture of anguish and hope. "Do you think we could try again? Find out if what I've been dreaming about for the last several years is possible?"

"I'm not ready to jump back to where we were." His face falls, and he starts to pull back from me. I place my other hand on top of his to hold him in place. I understand wanting to determine where we could go, I really do. But can't he understand what I went through? I opened myself up to him, and he disappeared with no warning. Four years of wondering if I did something wrong. If he was alive. Four years of uncertainty and, if I'm honest, insecurity. I lost trust in him and a lot of others that day, and it's not easy to forget it and move on like the past four years didn't happen.

"Please understand that I'm not saying no. We've been apart for four years. I know I'm not the same person I used to be, are you? I think we should take it slow and get to know each other again. If you're here to stay, there's no rush, right?"

"You're right, of course. I'm not trying to pressure you, but I promised myself if I got another chance with you I'd take it and make things right with you."

I give his hand a squeeze and then release him so I can finish my cupcake. I only have 10 minutes left on my break and I won't go against my personal motto of "leave no cupcake behind" for any man.

"So are you going to make rounds with Brandon and Daniel too?" The surprise on his face tells me he wasn't planning on it better than any words could. "You do realize we're sort of a package deal, right?"

Ryan chokes on the sip of coffee he was taking when I spoke and his eyes are huge as he tries to cough it out. "Wh... what? Package deal?"

Realizing what he thought I meant I laugh loudly. "Not that kind of package deal. Gross!" I feign a dramatic shudder. "What I mean is that once you two left, the three of us banded together and got closer. It's not just me you have to win over."

"Ah. I get it. I'm glad they were there for you when I couldn't be. I'll never be able to express how sorry I am for how things happened. I'm just asking you to let me show you."

"I'm ok with that. You don't have to keep apologizing though. All I want from you is to be present and keep your word if you have to leave again and tell us. Other than that, we'll take things as they come."

"Deal. Though I can't say I'm not disappointed."

"Tough titties, dude. Consider it your penance." With an exaggerated smile I shove the last bite of cupcake in my mouth and chew it obnoxiously. Ryan grins and shakes his head at my antics.

"I see some things never change."

Chapter 12

The next morning, Ryan texts me again to ask if we can hang out.

> **Me:** I told you yesterday, I'm part of a package deal. If you want to spend time with me, you're going to need to spend time with them too.

> **Ryan:** Are you sure? I would rather catch up more with you.

> **Me:** Package. Deal. If you want to hang, you'll figure it out. Bran and I are both off tomorrow. Talk to him and figure it out.

> **Ryan:** When did you become so bossy?

> **Me:** Some time in the last 4 years. Text me later with details!

I'm not going to budge on this. If he wants to be back in my life, he's going to have to prove it. I take my time straightening my apartment and getting ready for work since I've got the closing shift tonight. About an hour after my last text with Ryan, he's texting me back with a plan update.

> **Ryan:** 6pm tomorrow. The arcade mini golf place. Want me to pick you up?

> **Me:** I'm sure Brandon and I will ride together. We'll meet you there!

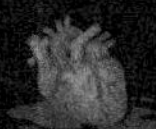

I haven't played mini golf in years. We used to come here at least once a month growing up, and I think Brandon, Daniel, and I stopped coming after the boys left because it was too hard. There's a full arcade, mini golf course, bumper boats, and batting cages, and we'd spend entire days here on weekends and during the summer. Surprisingly, everyone was able to make it tonight. Ryan, Evan, and Daniel are all waiting out front when Brandon and I arrive five minutes late thanks to his need to find the perfect outfit. I'm wearing some light denim jean shorts with a white cami and thin black zip up hoodie with my black low top converse. I've added a simple silver anklet and a dangling necklace with a silver pocket watch with my turtle pendant necklace. I've left my hair down so the natural curls cascade down my back in a wavy mass, and I'm only wearing mascara and Carmex.

All three men stare at me as we walk up to them and it feels a lot like I imagine being under a microscope would. It's obvious they're all trying to mask their feelings and it makes me curious about what's going on in their minds. Ryan is wearing a blue button down shirt that matches his eyes with the sleeves rolled up and shorts with boat shoes. While his facial expressions may not give anything away, his eyes do. He's looking at me like he's hungry and I'm a juicy steak. The look in his eyes makes me shiver, but not in an unpleasant way.

Evan is wearing a snug fitted navy blue t-shirt with dark wash jeans and heavy boots, and it makes me wonder if he wears those t-shirts on purpose, or if he is unaware of how they set off his wonderfully built body. Knowing him he has no idea, which is kind of sexy.

My mind once again wanders into fantasy land as I wonder if I could convince Evan and Ryan to hop on the #whychoose train. Not that Evan has ever said any-thing about wanting to be with me, but damn. They are two beautiful specimens and I would not mind being the filling in a Holmes sandwich.

I'm jogged out of my musings when Brandon says "Guess I'll just go fuck myself, then," with a chuckle under his breath before draping his arm over my shoulder and pulling me close.

"What?" I ask, looking up at him confused.

"Not one of them has looked at me, and I look fabulous today. Do they not realize how handsome I am? But nooooo. The three of them only have eyes for you." He's looking at me like I'm dense, but other than Ryan I can't figure out what he's seeing in them that I'm missing, so I shrug and let it go.

With a roll of my eyes, I elbow him in the stomach and mumble "Shut up you Shit stirrer," before we reach them. Daniel is the closest, and he's in his usual jeans and band t-shirt with Converse. I give him a quick hug, then make my way down the line giving Ryan and Evan hugs and saying hi to them too. Brandon does the handshake/hug/back slap combo with them, and I giggle at the weird look on Ryan's face.

"Alright guys, what's first? Have you eaten? We could hit the cafe then do mini golf?" They all agree with my plan, so we head over to the cafe. Nothing has changed in the years since we've been here, and it gives me a nostalgic, happy warmth in my chest. Like, time has passed but maybe things haven't changed so much that we can't move past what's happened in the last few years. It gives me true hope for the first time since they came back, and I'm determined to hold on to the feeling for as long as possible.

I order mini-corn dogs, tots, and a large Diet Coke like I used to when we were kids, and once the guys order and we all have our food we find a table with enough seats for everyone to sit, eat, and chat. It's obvious they're feeling nostalgic too since they also got the same things they used to, all except Ryan.

"Woah, there. What happened to seventy-two slices of pizza, chicken wings, and a large Coke?" Ryan's bottle of water and chicken Caesar wrap are looking mighty sad in the face of our yummy fried food. Who knew they offered that here? And why?

Ryan shrugs nonchalantly and takes a bite of his wrap, wincing slightly as he chews and stares at it. "I don't eat like that anymore. I haven't for a few years."

Evan rolls his eyes and pops a huge onion ring into his mouth. A moment later he swallows and adds "Yeah, they don't allow this kind of food in the commune. Nothing processed, definitely nothing fried or with tons of sugar like soda. I used to sneak into town to McDonald's before I moved out so I could stay sane," he chuckles before taking another bite of his huge burger.

Ryan's head whips towards him, staring at him like he's been hiding all kinds of secrets. "You never told me that" he accuses. "Why didn't you tell me? Did you sneak out for other stuff too?"

Evan scoffs at him and shakes his head like he's disappointed in him. "Dude, I asked you once if you wanted to go with me and you freaked. You threatened to tell your dad! Why would I ask you again? It would just be a waste of time."

Ryan considers him for a moment and then asks "Is that where you always disappeared to? Dad and I thought you were sneaking off with a girl. He made me follow you once and I lost you in town. I figured you knew I was following you so you bolted."

Evan's face contorts with anger and disgust as he snarls "What the fuck, Ryan? Why would you do follow me? Are you really so wrapped up in him you agreed to do that?" He shakes his head in disappointment. "What does it matter what I was doing?"

Ryan lets his own anger loose before I can jump in. "Screw you! You know what he's like! I didn't have a choice and you know it." Brandon, Daniel, and I are all gaping at them, not sure what to do. Before it can escalate any further, I place my hand on Evan's forearm in an attempt to calm the situation. Ryan is across from me so I can't reach him, but I look from one of them to the other. Evan's arm is shaking with what I can only guess is rage, and Ryan's eyes flare when I touch him. He opens his mouth to start again and I point at him in warning.

"Stop! I have no idea what happened while you two were gone, but it sounds to me like it was rough. You both had to do what you could to survive it. We can talk about it later if you want but now is not the time, especially since there are kids around! We can either put this away and enjoy our evening, or you can both fuck off and I'll hang with Brandon and Daniel instead. It's your choice, but you will stick to your decision. If you stay, you'll let it go, and we'll have fun. If you leave, you fuck all the way off and don't talk to me for at least 24 hours." I glare at both of them and am satisfied to see the chagrin on their faces. Removing my hand from Evan's arm, I ask "So, what'll it be, boys?"

They share a glance, and right as I'm sure they're going to choose to leave, they nod at each other and Evan extends his arm out across the table. "Sorry, bro" he says. "We good? She's right. We both had to do what we could to stay sane."

"Yeah, man, we're good. I'm sorry too. I should have told you."

Thank goodness. To break the tension, I shove a mini corn dog in my mouth and chew noisily. The boys respond with a mixture of exasperation and fondness, and I give them a food filled smile. Swallowing, I ask "Ok, who gets what colored ball? I call dibs on black!"

Brandon instantly pipes up with "I call pink! I wore this shirt so I would match, I thought I'd have to fight you for it." Now that he mentions it, his polo is the exact same shade of hot pink as the golf balls, and now the outfit changes make sense.

The rest of dinner went smoothly, we reminisced on old stories from before they left and Brandon, Daniel and I filled Ryan and Evan in on what they'd missed in the last few years. It almost felt like they'd never left, we always had so much fun together and after I drew the line against fighting, it was like we slipped right back into our old dynamic. I think it healed me a bit, knowing my boys were here and safe with me, if only for a moment. I mourned nights like these for the last four years, and having it back could only be made better if my dad was still alive.

Mini golf was the same hilarious clusterfuck it always was. The guys all try to distract each other in an attempt to drive up their scores, and I have to keep score because everyone else tries to cheat, especially Brandon. I'm no expert, but I'm fairly certain Daniel wasn't 342 shots in after the second hole. Evan almost ended up in the water trap after Ryan and Daniel conspired to trip him, and I pocketed Brandon's ball for two holes. He was so upset he ran to grab a replacement ball, and when he wasn't looking I took that one too. I put them where he could easily find them on the next hole, and he threw me over his shoulder and ran around the course jostling me around for a solid five minutes until he tired out and let me down.

We are on the 18th hole when Daniel gets a phone call. "Hello?" looking at me he frowns while he listens. "Yeah, ok. I'm out right now. No, it's ok. Give me a few. Alright, be there soon. Bye." Hanging up, he puffs out a resigned breath. "Sorry, I have to go. Mom needs me to help her tonight."

"Are you coming back?" I'm disappointed he's leaving when we're all having such a good time, but I know she needs his help. She has MS and some of her days are worse than others.

"I'm not sure, probably not. I'll call if I can get away and see if you're still out." Handing me his yellow golf ball, he pulls me into a hug and kisses the top of my head. "Sorry I have to bail."

He says goodbye to the guys, and heads out without finishing his last hole. I stopped keeping score twenty minutes ago so it's not like it would have mattered, anyway. Once we've all finished the course, we decide to hit the bumper boats. I'm in luck they only seat one person each, so I don't have to worry about choosing a partner. Brandon would throw a tantrum if I didn't go with him, and I'm pretty sure Ryan might try to fight him for it. Each session is fifteen minutes long, and we're lucky enough that the only other group consists of four seventeen to eighteen year old guys. When the bell sounds for us to start, Brandon and Ryan immediately target Evan, so they it's clear they discussed this beforehand. I cackle like a madwoman as I drive straight for Brandon and knock him off course and into the corner of the pool wall. Evan goes after Ryan as if we planned our own attack and I keep Brandon jammed in his corner for at least five minutes while he curses me and my ancestors. I allow him out of his corner when I notice the other four guys have ganged up on Ryan and Evan. "Hey Bran!" I yell at him. He turns and glares at me until he sees me pointing over my shoulder. "Want to go help out?"

His eyes light up with glee and he nods eagerly. "Let's go fuck some kids up! I'll go right, you go left."

As I back off from Brandon and turn to rescue my guys, I channel my inner Dizzy from Starship Troopers and yell out "Flip six three hole, on one!" to warn the guys that I'm coming. I made them watch it with me 10,000 times growing up, so they are fully aware when I pull out that line they need to form up and put people on their butts. Together, the four of us circle the other guys and absolutely wreck them for the last five or so minutes of our time slot. They're a good group of guys and instead of getting butt hurt at their loss, they invite us to go again since no one else is waiting. I have to use the bathroom, so I tell the guys they can go ahead and I head to the restroom behind the ticket hut for the boats and batting cage.

With my business done, hands washed, and hair fluffed, I head back out to the walkway and almost walk right into Ryan. "Shit! Good lord Ryan, what are you doing here? I thought you were going another round?" Hand to my chest, I bend at the waist to breathe and calm my heart.

Rubbing my back, he laughs before apologizing. "I'm sorry, Jen. I didn't mean to scare you. I wanted to grab a minute with you. The guys are still at the boats, so I figured I'd come steal a minute." He guides me back into a standing position and draws me to him with his arm around my back. "I'm glad you wanted to do this, it's been fun hanging with everyone again. I didn't realize how much I'd missed it." His hand begins rubbing my back again, but this time in a slow, sensuous stroke from the small of my back up to the base of my neck. Looking up into his eyes, I smile as I enjoy the warmth of his hands on me.

"I did too. I want to spend time with you and find out where this goes, Ryan, but I still want to take things slow. I have to be able to trust you again, and I need to get to know you again first."

"I get it," he says, hand now cupping the back of my head. "I don't want to push you. But I need you to know I mean it, that I'm going to do whatever it takes."

And with that, he kisses me.

It's a possessive, dominating kiss from the moment his lips touch mine. It's nothing like the kiss we shared as children, that kiss was sweet and fumbling. With this kiss, his tongue almost immediately licks the seam of my lips to gain entry, and the moment I open for him he invades my mouth like he's searching for my secrets. His hands at my nape and back tighten to the edge of pain as he clutches me closer to him, and though I enjoy it, the small sting has me coming back to my senses and remembering where we are. Reluctantly, I try to pull back, and for a second he holds me tighter. I work my hands up to his chest and push against him to ensure he knows I need him to back off. He sucks my lower lip and pulls on it as he retreats before pressing his forehead to mine. Breathing heavy and eyelids still closed, he stays quiet for a moment. "Sorry," he whispers. "I couldn't help myself. I've wanted to do that since the moment I saw you sitting on the dock."

"I have too," I admit. "But this isn't the time or place." I stand on my toes and press a kiss to his cheek to soften the blow, and say "Come on, they're probably almost done."

The guys are climbing out of their boats when round the corner, and while Brandon gives me a knowing smirk, Evan's gaze is more pensive. We decide to head into the arcade for a few games before we call it a night, and I head straight to Whack-a-mole like I used to. I don't know what it is, but I am crazy talented at this game. The guys used to challenge me, and Evan got close to my high score once, but I am still the undefeated champ. It's nice to see my skills haven't rusted, because soon I am using my tickets to become the proud new owner of a kazoo, a rainbow slinky, and a pink plastic dinosaur. Ryan uses his tickets to win a stress relieving ball and Evan gifts me with a candy necklace like he used to. He always said there was nothing he wanted, so he'd get me either a candy necklace or something else he knew I would like. I still have some little toys he'd gotten for me stashed away with my other keepsakes.

After seeing Evan give me my gift Brandon decides he cannot be outdone, so in true Brandon Coleman fashion he uses his own tickets to purchase a ring pop and dramatically propose to me in front of everyone in attendance. Tearfully accepting, I throw my arms around him and smother his with face kisses until he's gagging and pushing me away. Looking up at Ryan and Evan, I'm a little bothered by Ryan's obvious irritation. These are normal shenanigans for us, so I'm not sure what the issue is. Hell, he used to be the main instigator! Evan is looking on with fondness, so I give him a dramatic wink that I can tell bothers Ryan even more.

He can stay mad all he wants, he's the one who left me. He wanted to be with me four years ago, and I haven't changed. I am still me, I'm just a better, stronger version of the me I was back then. I was good enough for him then, if I'm not good enough for him now it's his loss. I won't change myself for anyone, least of all someone who left me behind.

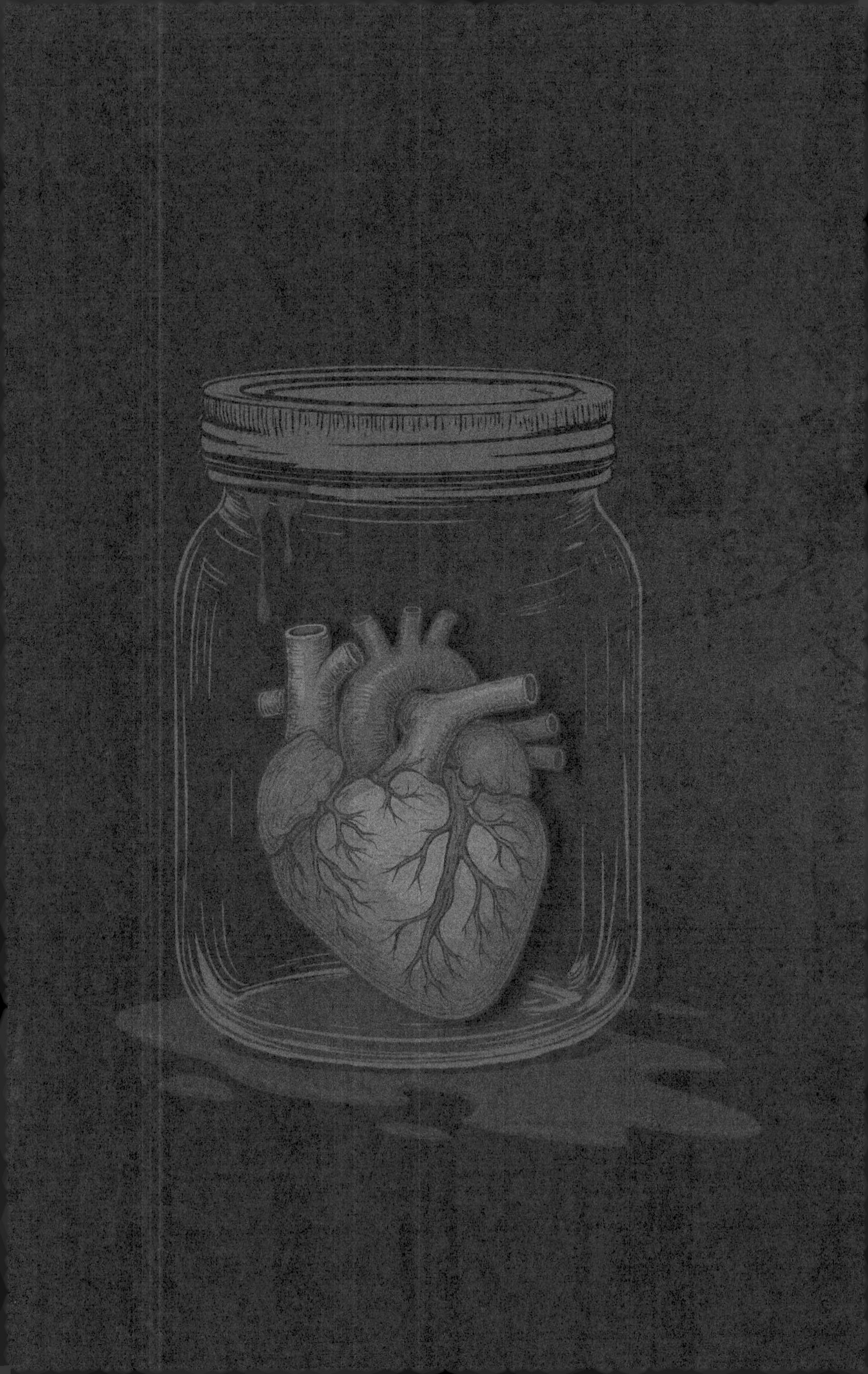

CHAPTER 13

Ryan was a little distant after Brandon's mock proposal and I could tell it was irritating Evan, so we called it a night not long after. Ryan asked if I wanted to go get dessert with him, but I declined because I didn't have the patience to deal with his moody bullshit. He was disappointed, but I'm not going to start off a relationship by catering to his domineering and possessive crap. It's hot in books and movies sometimes, but never in real life.

He's changed a lot, and I have to decide if it's for the better before I move any further with him. I'm a little irritated that he pushed a kiss on me after I told him I wanted to take things slow, and as I get ready for work the next day, I reminisce about the boy I used to know, and compare our first kiss to the one we shared last night.

Four Years Ago

Today is the day. I can't bear to see him with the other girls all over him anymore, so I'm going to do it. I'm going to tell him I love him and ask if he wants to be with me.

What's the worst that can happen? I ruin my friendship with him? If I keep going like this, it'll be ruined anyway.

"Hey Jen. What's up?" I startle at the sound of his voice, I was so lost in my thoughts I didn't hear him walking down the sidewalk. He looks so cute today. His hair is wet from his post gym shower, and his jeans and plain white t-shirt are fitting a little more snug than they used to. All the time spent in the weight room for football is making him bulk up.

"Me? Um, not much. Just... I'm waiting on Brandon. What are you doing?" I ask, trying to see if he's got anywhere he needs to be right away. I know I've got at least 20 minutes before Brandon shows because he had to meet with a teacher after school let out about a project.

"You ok?" he asks, face lined in concern. He's picking up on my nerves and because of that I decide to rip off the Band-aid.

"Yeah. Um, I actually needed to talk to you. Do you have a minute? Or are you expected somewhere?"

"No, Evan is finishing up practice so my mom will be here in about 30 minutes to pick us up. What's up? You're kind of worrying me." He takes a seat next to me on the half wall that separates the parking lot from the school and grabs my hand in his.

Screwing up my courage, I stare at our hands as I start to speak. "Look... I need to tell you something but I need you to understand it doesn't have to change anything. You don't even have to respond to me, but I need to get it off my chest. If you don't want to, we never have to talk about it again. I..."

"Jen... Jen!"

Startled, I peer up into his eyes. "Yeah?"

"Just tell me. We can figure it out, whatever it is. Spit it out, ok?" His patient smile gives me a little courage, and I take a deep breath as we stare into each other's eyes.

"I like you... ok?" Seeing surprise flash in his eyes, I drop my gaze back down to our entwined hands. "I have for a while now, but I've been too afraid to say anything. But that skank Melissa has been all over you lately and I just couldn't -- "

My words are cut off by Ryan's lips meeting mine. Shocked, I don't respond for a few seconds. Ryan is kissing me! ME!

His lips are so soft and gentle against mine, and because it's my first kiss I don't really have any idea of what to do. Desperate for more I lean towards him and we almost end up falling off the wall due to my enthusiasm. Ryan steadies us as he chuckles, and I can feel my cheeks and ears pinking up in embarrassment.

"Woah, there." he laughs. "We don't want to fall."

"Sorry," I say sheepishly. "I didn't mean to, you're just so tall. I was trying to reach you so you'd be more comfortable." My excuse is crap and I know it, but I'm already embarrassed enough, so maybe it'll help me save some face.

"I like you too Jen. I have for a long time. I've been trying to work up the courage to come to you, but I was worried I'd upset you."

"Upset me?" I ask, astounded. "Ryan, I've liked you for years. I think I maybe love you." No maybe, I totally do, but he doesn't need to know. "I... what does this mean? Do you want to like... be with me? Because I want to be with you."

Smiling wide, he squeezes my hand and pulls me in for another sweet, but brief, kiss. "Yeah. I want to be with you. I think I might love you too, I have for a long time." His smile turns a bit timid as he asks, "Do you want to be my girlfriend, Jen?"

"Hell yeah I do!" I say as I throw my arms around his neck and hug him tight. I've been waiting for this moment for years. I finally got up the courage to ask for what I wanted, and it was everything I could have dreamed of.

Until the next morning, when he's gone and my dream turns into a nightmare.

I haven't heard from Ryan all day today, but I'm fine with that because I need some time to sort myself out. Every time I think I know what's going on he throws some sort of twist at me. We have a discussion about boundaries, he crosses them with a crazy hot kiss. Then gets angry and possessive when I play around with our friend the same way we always have? It's not going to work for me. I told him he needed to make it work with all three of us, and I meant it. Either he gets his shit together or he doesn't. As much as a part of me hopes that he does, a bigger part of me knows I survived without him once, so I can do it again. It'll hurt like a bitch, but I'm strong and I have a fantastic support system.

Evan and I texted intermittently throughout the day, talking about the fun we had last night and making plans to meet for drinks or a movie soon. I'm looking forward to hanging out with him one on one, something I haven't gotten to do since they've been back. I've missed him and I'm excited about spending time with him without the tension existing between him and Ryan.

The day has gone by fast, and I'm happy to see Nick's boyfriend Travis shortly before closing time. He's still wearing his security uniform and his butt is fabulous in them so I can't help but cop a feel while Nick is watching, making the three of us laugh. We start talking about books and I remember I have a copy of an MM story two of my favorite authors put out together at home, so he decides to walk me home after my shift ends since Nick has to finish his inventory.

Once the deposit is counted and put away in the safe, I head to the cafe to find my escort. The guys have obvious tension between them, but they both smile at me as I approach.

"You ready, Travis? I can always bring it here and have Nick bring it home if you'd rather stay."

"And miss a chance to have you all to myself?" Giving me a wink, he kisses Nick's cheek before walking over to me and throwing an arm over my shoulder. "You ready, babe?"

"Yeah, I'm ready. You sure you don't want help with inventory Nick?"

He rolls his eyes and pushes us to the door so he can lock the internal deadbolt behind us. "Do I ever? You'll break my concentration. You two go be safe and catch up. If you're still together when I'm done I'll come join you." Unlocking the door, he smacks my ass as I walk by and cackles when I jump in surprise. Before I can get revenge, the door is shut and he's locked it back up.

The walk to my apartment is quiet. I can tell he's got something on his mind but can't decide if he should bring it up. When we reach my apartment, I use the app on my phone to unlock the door and turn to him. "What's wrong, Travis?"

His sad smile breaks my heart, and he moves to leave instead of telling me what's going on. Making the decision for him, I smile innocently as I step backwards into my apartment and yank him in after me by the fabric of his coat. His face shows his shock for a moment before it crumbles. I pull him over to my couch and push him to sit before grabbing my box of tissues and sitting next to him.

"Honey, what's wrong? Talk to me." Handing him a tissue in case he needs it, I grab his other hand and hold it tightly so he knows I'm here to listen.

"It's just... It's Nick. I think he's seeing someone else, or he's losing interest, or something. He's been weird the last week or so. Not... present, I guess. You know? I tried talking to him about it, but he only says he's got a lot going on."

I know exactly what's going on. He's going to propose and he's scared shitless so he's acting like a douche. Time to fix this by taking one for the team. I wasn't ready to talk about this yet, but if it keeps him from freaking out then it will be worth it.

"Oh, sweetheart. He's not seeing anyone, I promise. I think it's all my fault, honestly."

Sniffling, his eyes search mine. "Your fault? Why would it be your fault?"

"I asked him to keep a secret for me." At his frown, I rush to continue. "Not forever, especially not from you. I'm just dealing with something, and he only knows about it because he was there. I asked him to keep it to himself for a few days until I have the opportunity to figure things out since I'm not really ready to talk about it. I know he's worried about me."

"What happened? You don't have to talk about it if you're still not ready, but you know you can talk to me about anything."

Bracing myself, I pause before saying "Remember how Brandon and I had those friends who disappeared a few years ago? And how one of them was sort of my boyfriend?"

"Yeah? Ryan and Evan, right?"

"Right. Well, they're back."

"What? Sugar, that's great!" He pauses and studies me. "Wait, is it great?"

With a shrug, I give him a tired smile. "I'm not sure. We didn't hear from them for four years and all of a sudden they're back and want to act like everything can be like it was before. They had a lot of bad shit happen to them and it makes what happened understandable, but my problem is I don't know if I can forgive the fact that after they had the ability to find us and tell us they were ok, they didn't. Brandon and Daniel are hurting too, they're not sure what to think either. I'm pretty sure Brandon wants to welcome them back. Daniel is trying to hide wanting to write them off completely, but he won't admit it until we agree with him.

"I just don't know what to do. Ryan came to the store a few days ago, and last night we hung out as a group, and he kissed me. He said he wants to start where we left off, but he left me, Travis. How do I start over when he could leave again at any time?"

"There's no rule saying you have to make a decision right away. What does your heart tell you? Are you leaning either way?"

"I have no idea. I loved Ryan. He's the only guy I've ever loved, the only one who I ever considered being with. But for him to tell me he had the ability for the past few years to reach out to me, and he just... didn't? I don't know what to do with that."

"I think you should take it one day at a time. You've both grown up a lot since they left. What if you both start off trying to have a relationship right away and you realize you aren't compatible anymore? People change. Sixteen years old versus twenty is a huge difference. Maybe try being friends first. Try getting to know each other again, and then decide whether you want to try to be together. You're young, honey. You don't have to rush anything."

He's right. It's basically what I told Ryan, but coming from someone else who is outside looking in and hearing it put that way makes me sure I'm making the right decision.

"Thanks, Travis. That does help. It's just hard. I've been desperate to find out what happened to them for so long, and now that I have I don't think it's helped, you know? I feel selfish, but four years of pain and anger can't simply be wiped out in one day. He's so handsome. My heart still flutters when I see him, and I can tell he wants to make things up to me, but I honestly don't know if I can do it."

"Don't rush yourself to make a choice. Take all the time you need. You waited for him for four years, he can return the favor and wait until you make a decision you're comfortable with. You're worth the wait, always remember that."

I lean over and pull him into a tight hug. "Thank you, Travis. You remember that too, ok? Nick loves you. I'm sorry my drama is stressing him out, but don't worry ok? You two are perfect for each other. One day I'll find my match, like you two did. Whether it's Ryan or someone else, only time will tell, but I'm in no hurry. I'll get there."

"You sure will, sweetheart. If I rolled your way I'd snap you up in a second, but unfortunately, I prefer outies to innies." With a smirk and waggle of his eyebrows, he stands and pulls me into a proper hug. "ok," he sighs and gathers himself together. "I'm going to stop feeling sorry for myself and head back to the store and hang out with my man while he counts his coffee beans. Are you ok here tonight? Do you need to talk more, or want to come with me?"

"No, I'm fine. I've got a shower and a Netflix marathon calling my name. Thanks though." I turn to walk him out before remembering the whole reason he came by. "Oh! One sec." I run to my guest room and grab the book I promised. "You're going to love this. Spicy professor student angst."

"Yass! You know I like it dramatic, girl." Walking him to the door I open it for him and step aside for him to pass.

"Be safe, ok? I am fully aware you're a big, strong man, but keep an eye out for creepers."

"I'm always safe, Sugar." With a wink he leans down and gives me a kiss on the corner of my mouth. "I'll see you soon, ok? Call me if you want to talk some more, I won't let Nick know you told me what's going on."

"Thanks Travis. Let's do lunch this week, ok?"

With a nod and a wave, he takes off down the hall on the way back to the elevator.

The next morning, I wake to a text from Nick telling me he needs me to have someone to cover his shift because Travis was mugged and will be in the hospital for at least another day.

CHAPTER 14

Travis' wallet was taken, but not his watch, and he got the shit beat out of him. He had two cracked ribs and the doctors were worried about internal bleeding, so he had to stay a second day in the hospital to be safe. What terrified me is he was attacked after walking me home. Not only did I feel responsible, but his attack reminded me so much of my dad's it felt like they were related somehow. The only correlations may be the robbery and their relationships to me, but still.

I couldn't force these thoughts out of my head. As much as I was worried about Travis, if the two attacks were related, maybe the police could find new clues to my dad's death. After a few hours of debating with myself, I pick up the phone and call my dad's best friend.

"Hey, Johnny! To what do I owe the pleasure?" I can tell he's happy I called, but he and my dad were the only two people to call me Johnny, and hearing it takes my breath away for a second. For a few moments I'm unable to form a response as my grief comes crashing down around me.

"Shit, Jenevive, are you there? I'm sorry, I didn't think. I'm happy to hear from you, is all. You there, kid?"

"Yeah." I have to clear my throat to continue. "Yeah, sorry. I'm here. It just caught me off guard."

"I'm sorry, hon. What's up? Everything ok?" His tone is tinged with sadness, filling me with guilt.

"Eh. I'm ok. I'm calling because... well because I have a friend who was mugged last night."

"Damn, that's awful. Are they ok?"

"Yeah, he's fine. The thing is, he was walking back to the store from dropping me off at home. He walked me home from work and got attacked on his way back to the store. His boyfriend Nick works with me, and he was visiting him last night. I had a book for him to read so he came home with me to grab it. I just..."

I'm not sure how to bring this up with him. As much as he loved my dad, and he loves me, I don't think he wants to believe anyone could purposely hurt him specifically. Everyone loved my dad, and I think he doesn't want to believe it, so he simply ignores the possibility.

"What is it? Did something else happen?"

"It's just, I don't know. It seems too similar to me. If Travis' attack was a robbery, why wouldn't they take his watch? I know for a fact it was worth over $500, I was with Nick when he picked it out for him for Christmas last year. It doesn't make sense, just like dad's. What if neither of them were random? What if they're somehow connected? I'm the only common thread, Brian."

"Jen... it doesn't-"

"You cannot tell me that it's not a possibility. I'm not asking you to run with it, only consider it, please. Dad deserves for his case to be solved. He did so much for so many people, we need to do this for him. I have to find out what happened, he was all the family I had left, and he's gone."

The line is silent for a minute while he thinks over what I said. "Ok, kid. I don't want you to get your hopes up, but send me your friend's info and I'll check into it. No promises, though. ok?"

Hope flares in my chest for a moment before I force myself to tamp it down. "Thank you, Brian. I'll text you Travis' information right away. I'll text Brandon to check the parking lot video too, and send it over if we find anything."

"Sounds good. What else is going on, anything?"

I debate telling him about Ryan and Evan's return, but I'm not ready to delve into it with him yet. "Nope, same old, same old. You?"

"I'm good. Come over for dinner soon, huh? Melinda's been asking after you." Melinda, Brian's wife, is a sweet woman and an amazing cook. For the first two weeks after my dad died she made sure she prepared enough food for me and Brandon for every meal, so I wouldn't have to worry about it. She put it all together in covered dishes with index cards taped to the top with directions for heating and each one had a sweet note attached. She still does it once or twice a month. She said she doesn't want to intrude too much, but I always look forward to her cooking.

"I will, thanks. Talk to you soon."

I decided to visit Travis in the hospital before my evening shift, bringing goodies and trash magazines. While we chat, Nick heads down the hallway to grab himself a cup of coffee so we have a minute alone.

"So," I ask while holding his hand. "How are you really?" He likes to put on a front for Nick, neither of them like it when the other is sick or hurting, so they tend to downplay their symptoms.

"I'm fine, just sore as hell. Besides, Nick finally got his head out of his ass and stopped acting all weird. He's treating me like the king I am again." His grin is a little lopsided because the left side of his face is swollen, and the twinkle in his eyes is slightly dulled by the painkillers he's on, but seeing his smile eases a bit of my worry. He's going to be ok, physically and mentally. Nothing keeps this man down for long.

"I'm so glad you're ok. Rest up, alright? I have to head to work, but I'll be back tomorrow if you're still here. Once you're home and feeling better, you two can come out to the cabin for the night or weekend and we can relax. I've been thinking about getting a hot tub out there."

"That sounds like exactly what I need! You've got a deal. Now, give me a kiss and get your cute ass to work!"

Laughing, I gently kiss his less damaged cheek and give his hand a light squeeze before heading out. As I wait for the elevator, I notice Nick heading up the hall with a cup of coffee in his hand and a haunted shadow in his eyes. I step away from the elevator and walk to Nick with my arms held out.

He collapses against me, shaking with the effort to contain his sobs. Gruffly, he whispers "Jen, I thought I lost him."

"I know, honey. He's ok though, right? He's so strong, and you are too. Just spoil that boy as much as you can. He'll be fine in no time." I rub useless circles on his back while I hold him together, trying to soothe him as best as I can.

"Can I have the ring? I need to –"

"You need to do nothing. Not yet at least. Do you think he wants his engagement pictures to be ruined by a bunch of swelling and bruises? I know this scared you but Travis will never forgive you if you propose without him looking his best." Nick grunts and puffs out a laugh in acknowledgment. "Besides, I knew you'd want to so I've already planted the seed. I told him once he was on the mend you two can come out to the cabin for a night or the weekend. I even mentioned how I'm thinking about getting a hot tub. I simply didn't mention that I didn't need to be there the whole time."

He releases me and takes a step back. "You are a rock star. I'm sure we can delay him until his face heals up. Thank you so much, Jen. I'd never be able to make this work without you."

"Oh hush, you'd figure something out. Now, turn around, go back to the vending machine and bring that man of yours some M&;M's. Chocolate cures all."

Kissing my cheek, he grins and throws me a sassy salute. "Yes, ma'am!"

Chapter 15

Other than visiting Travis in the hospital again the next day, the rest of the week is quiet. Ryan and Evan text me every day. Evan and I are using the time to catch up on what we missed in each other's lives, and it's heartbreaking to learn what he went through for the first three years he was gone. Ryan's mom was even colder towards Evan once they moved, which I didn't think was possible, and his dad was delving further into the fire and brimstone belief system than he already was before they left. The members of the community were strict and devout, and because he wasn't like them he was practically shunned by the people his age. Getting a job with the construction company was his way out, and he loves the work. He's considering getting licensed as a general contractor and starting his own company in our area after getting a degree in business. We talk off and on all day every day, and it is amazing to have him back in my life.

Ryan is back to being flirty and suggestive without crossing any lines. He doesn't want to talk too much about his last few years, so he often steers the conversation to my life and memories of before they left. Each morning he asks to spent time with me, but I put him off for a few days because I want some time to figure out what I'm thinking. I know what he wants, but I'm not there yet.

When Friday rolls around, I decide I can't put him off any longer.

Ryan: Have dinner with me tonight.

Me: I have to work tonight until 9:30. Dessert instead?

Ryan: I guess I'll have to take what I can get. Where and when? Or do you want me to pick you up from the store?

Me: There's a frozen yogurt shop a few doors down from the store. Meet me at the store at 9:30. We can walk over.

Ryan: Ok. See you then.

Just because I'm not ready to jump back in where we left off doesn't mean I don't want to make a good impression, so I take my time getting ready for work. I leave my hair to the natural curls and pin a portion of it back with a silver clip to keep it out of my face. A bit of dark eye shadow is my attempt at a smokey eye and mascara completes my makeup, and I put on my favorite jeans and a lightweight long sleeve, scoop neck blouse in royal blue. Black ballet flats round out the outfit and I'm happy with my reflection in the mirror. More than anything, I am dressing this way for myself. Yes, I want to look good when I see Ryan, but looking good makes me feel good, which always boosts my confidence and makes me believe I can handle anything. I definitely need all the help I can get while figuring out what's going on with Ryan.

My shift passes by quickly and before I know it, it's time to start my closing tasks. As I'm counting out the final deposit, I hear a knock on the glass door. Carmen, the closing cafe manager, looks over to see me counting the cash, so she moves to open the door so I can finish. When she turns the corner and sees who I can only assume is Ryan at the door she whistles low and says "Damn girl, where can I get one of those? Please tell me you're taking that home tonight!"

I let out an amused snort, then curse. "Damnit, Carmen! I lost count. You suck!"

Carmen cackles like the evil witch she is while she unlocks the internal deadbolt on the front door. "Well, hello handsome. Please tell me you're the stripper-gram I ordered." There's a beat of silence before she throws her head back and laughs even harder. "I'm kidding. Come on in. I'm Carmen. Jen is over there counting the deposit."

"Uh, thanks. Nice to meet you?" He's obviously uncomfortable so the statement comes out more like a question. Carmen giggles as she locks the door back behind him and with a cheeky smile and wave heads to the cafe to finish up her own closing duties.

"Ignore her, she's perpetually in heat" I say, a fond smile tipping up the corners of my mouth. "I'll only be a minute. I have to recount the deposit since Carmen made me lose count."

"Honey if you could keep count with that man walking into the room, you have bigger problems!" Carmen hollers from across the room. "Hashtag just sayin'!"

Brows pinched in an incredulous look, Ryan leans closer to me and asks in a quiet voice "What in the fuck is a hashtag?"

"Don't worry about it," I snicker. "She's kind of a mess, but in a good way. Now hush, so I can finish counting and we can head out."

It only takes a few minutes to finish the deposit and tuck it away in the safe, and then I'm ready to go. "You ok if I head out, Carmen?"

"Hell yeah, girl! Get out of here. Don't do anything I wouldn't do!"

"Pretty sure that doesn't limit me at all, but thanks for the concern." I roll my eyes and blow her a sassy kiss. "See you tomorrow!"

Grabbing Ryan's arm, I tug him to the front door so we can head to the frozen yogurt shop. They're open until 10:30, so we'll have about an hour to hang out before they close. Carmen is there to lock the door behind us, and I jump when she smacks my ass as I walk by. She winks at my glower and I shake my head with an exasperated, but still affectionate, smile.

Once we're out on the sidewalk Ryan grabs my hand and waits for me to lead the way. "She's... different," he comments. "You two are friends?"

"Yeah, Carmen is great. She's a handful, but she's a great friend. Definitely never a dull moment with her around."

"Hmm. Sounds like it." he mumbles. "So how far of a walk is it?"

"It's up here. This place is great and usually relatively kid free by this time of night. I come here a few times a month on my way home from work." Ryan opens the door for me as we approach and follows me to the line. This place is a self serve shop, so we grab the medium-sized cups and step up to the machines. While Ryan walks down the line and searches for the flavor he wants, I head straight to the cake batter and fill up. He chooses sugar-free vanilla and I suppress a shudder. What's the point of froyo without sugar? Once his cup is full we head to the toppings bar. I add mini M&;M's, Reese pieces, and gummy bears, plus a wedge of waffle cone. Ryan goes straight for the fruit and loads up, but at my raised eyebrow he adds his own wedge of cone.

"You know, this is supposed to be dessert. Dessert should be sinful, not some sugar free bowl of sadness."

Ryan chuckles at me and shakes his head with a smile. "I'm not big on chocolate anymore. Besides, the fruit looked fresh. I couldn't pass it up." He pays for our food and we head outside to sit at one of the gazebos across the parking lot. I'm glad I wore a long sleeve shirt today, it's a bit chilly and with the frozen yogurt I'd probably freeze if I were in a t-shirt or tank top.

"So how's your grandmother doing? I haven't seen her in a while." I almost moan as I take my first bite of yogurty goodness. This stuff is the tits, but I learned my lesson with the cupcake.

"She's good. She's got a lot of doctors appointments and stuff so Evan and I are taking turns getting her to them. She's kind of pressuring me to declare a major, but I'm not sure what I want to do yet. I figure I can knock out all the general classes first, then move to the major classes. That will give me time, but she seems intent on me choosing now. It's incredibly frustrating, honestly."

"It sounds like it. Did she say why she wants you to declare?"

"Just that I need to decide what I want to do with my life. I'm only 20 though, I have plenty of time, right?" I've got a mouth full of delicious gummy bears so all I can do is chew and nod. "What about you? I know you want to take over the store, but what else? What's your plan?"

"I'm not sure. Graduate, obviously. I have probably two years left until I can. Eventually, Brandon's mom is going to sell me the store, but I'm not in any hurry for it to happen right away so it could be in two or in ten years. Other than that, I don't know. At some point I want to do some work on the cabin to update it and then move back in there, but I think it'll be awhile. I don't think I'm ready for that yet, plus I love my apartment. Being able to walk to work is so convenient, and I love this center. It's so full of life."

"You live here?" he asks, surprised.

"Yeah, just over there," I point to my building. "Brandon and I both live there."

"You live together? Why?" His face has lost all expression, like he's trying to cover his emotions. Why would he have a problem with that?

"No, not together. His apartment is a few doors down from mine though, so we're close enough. We both liked the building, and he liked the idea of being close enough to protect me." I roll my eyes. "As if I need his protection. I can, and do, kick his ass on the regular."

Ryan smiles and scrapes at the bottom of his bowl. "So what about family? You want kids and everything, right?"

"Not right now. It's not like I'm all 'I am woman, hear me roar! I don't need a man or children to complete me!' or anything, but probably one day. I definitely don't want any right now, though. I'm too young and I need to be settled first."

With a small frown, Ryan considers me for a moment before responding. "So you're not saying you don't want kids? You just don't want them in the immediate future?"

"No, I'm not saying I don't want at all, I'm simply not ready now. You're not looking to start having kids right away, are you? I don't think I can be on board with that."

"Oh, um, no." He stammers out a denial. "Sorry, I guess I'm used to the women from the community who are only concerned with getting married and having kids as soon as possible. I sometimes forget how different things are outside of there. It's an adjustment. I do want kids, but I have time. Almost everyone in the community gets married at 18 or 19 and start having kids practically right away, though."

"That's young to marry and have kids these days. Were you pressured to do it too?" My mind reels at the idea. I cannot imagine what my life would be like if I was married with kids. I'd rather be a 20-year-old virgin.

Oh! Wait. I am.

"Dad tried to convince me to, but I didn't click with anyone, so I've been able to escape that fate so far. The divorce rate is actually pretty non-existent in the community, which surprised me at first since everyone gets married so young."

"Are they all happy together? Like, are they staying together because they're actually happy and not because divorce isn't something that is accepted?" I hope the people are happy there. It already sounds to me like a freaking cult, finding out it's a cult that suppresses women or dictates the love lives of the people who live there would be even worse.

"They seem happy," he shrugs with indifference. "I haven't talked to the married couples about their satisfaction with their matches, so I'm not sure. It's a tight community, so my guess is we'd be aware if they weren't."

I want to ask him so many questions about the community. What beliefs do they have? What is the community like, is it like a commune? How many people live there? What is the day to day like? I almost start asking questions, but he seems like he doesn't want to talk about it. He always changes the subject when I bring up his past with them, so I'm surprised he's even talked about it this much.

We've both finished our bowls, so I gather them up to toss them in the trash can beside our table. Before I stand, I notice a drop of fruit juice on the corner of his mouth. Grabbing a napkin, I reach up and dab the spot to clean it off. When I start to pull away, Ryan's hand darts up to grab my wrist. Looking at me with hunger shining out of his blue gaze and still holding me, he uses his other hand to take the napkin from me. Using his grip to move me, he brings my hand to his mouth to kiss my palm. The heat in his eyes causes warmth to pool in my abdomen, which is a pretty new thing for me outside of books, and when he darts his tongue out to lick my skin my breath hitches in my chest.

What the hell was that? That was just my hand. I wonder what it would feel like on other....

Nope. Not going there. Not yet. I slowly pull my arm back and he reluctantly releases his hold.

"Sorry." But he's still looking at me like I'm a juicy steak, and let me tell you, I am here for it. In theory.

"It's ok. I think it's time I head home though. I've had a long day and I'm beat."

The heat leaves his eyes and he frowns. "Are you sure? We could go have a drink or something. Or we could hang at your place since it's not full of grandmothers and cousins."

"No, but maybe next time, ok?" I do not want to bring him to my apartment. I don't want to let this man convince me to move faster than I am comfortable with. I always wanted him to be my first, and I think I still do, but not this soon. Not after four years of uncertainty.

I can tell he's disappointed, but I refuse to compromise my decision. "Ok, when can we get together again?"

Getting up to throw our trash away, I turn from the can to find him right behind me. Close enough I almost jump out of my skin. "Shit, Ryan! You scared me to death." I put my hand to my chest and take a few deep breaths to settle my heart.

"I'm sorry," he says with his trademark smirk. That damn smirk turned me into putty when we were kids. Still does, apparently. "I didn't mean to scare you."

With that, he grabs my face in his hands and presses his lips to mine. It's another fierce and demanding kiss. I thought I'd made it clear I needed time, but even though I'm not really ready to move forward, I can't help responding. My gasp allows him to gain entrance to my mouth with his tongue and I lose myself in the moment. Soon enough, his hand squeezing my ass acts like a splash of cold water over my head. Again, even with me pushing at his chest, it takes him a minute to withdraw from me and let me go. His breaths are labored and his eyes are closed, and it takes him a few moments to gather himself. "Sorry... sorry, I couldn't help it."

"It's just, I need time. Remember? You need to be able to help it."

"I know. I'm sorry. I've just missed you and you look so beautiful tonight. Can I walk you home? I promise to behave." He tries to discreetly adjust himself, but there is no way to hide what he's doing. I pretend to ignore it while secretly being pleased that he has to do it in the first place.

"Sure, if you want. You don't have to though, I'm just right there."

"I insist." He walks me to my building, hand in hand. We're both silent not uncomfortable. As much as I want to kiss him again, I don't want to give him the wrong impression so when we arrive at the lobby door I turn to him.

"Hug?" I ask him.

"You don't want me to walk you up?" His eyebrows arch in surprise at my dismissal.

"No, I'm good. Thank you for dessert though. It's nice spending time with you again."

Smiling, he steps forward and wraps me in a tight hug. He's so much taller now, but his hug is still the all encompassing, warm embrace I remember. "Let's get together again soon, ok? I don't like having to wait a week to spend time with you."

Laughing, I extricate myself from him with a snort. "Dude, I waited four years to see you. A week is nothing."

With an eye roll, Ryan waves and turns to head back to his car. That wasn't too bad.

Now I have to figure out how to keep my pants on around him and everything will be fine. Right?

Seeing and texting with Jen over the last few days has been better than I could have hoped for. She's still somewhat hesitant, which I deserve, but I can feel our old relationship being rebuilt. She has turned into such an amazing woman, someone who surpassed my dreams of her for the past four years. I don't want to push her too fast, though I can't help testing my limits from time to time. I want to spend every moment I can with her and I try to think of excuses to spend time with her without looking desperate, but I can already tell that soon I won't care what it looks like anymore.

She's working at the barn this morning and agreed to hang out later, so once I pick up Gran's prescriptions and have her settled for a few hours I'm going to head out to the cabin. Walking in the door from the garage, I'm surprised by how quiet the house is. At this time in the morning Gran has the TV on full volume in her den. Depending on her mood, she's either watching a news talk show or court TV, but the house is eerily silent.

"Gran? Are you here?" Her car was here, so unless someone came to pick her up she should be. I make my way through the kitchen and living room and pass into her den but it's as if she's not here. "Gran?"

Turning to head back to the kitchen to drop off her prescriptions before I search any further, I catch a soft sound from the direction of the front of the house and veer that way to figure out what caused it. As I turn the corner, one of Gran's slippers lies in the middle of the walkway. What the hell?

Two more steps bring me around the bend and my heart stops as I finally catch sight of her. She's lying broken at the bottom of the staircase. Blood is seeping out of a cut in her hairline and more is trickling from her busted nose. The sound

I heard must have been her groaning, because it's obvious she's in excruciating pain. Her leg is broken so severely the bone is protruding through the skin and her breathing is shallow, and when I drop to my knees beside her and try to help her, a strangled cry escapes my lips before I can hold it back. "Gran, what the fuck? What happened?"

"La... language." She gasps out.

"Jesus, Gran, now is not the time for that! Hold on, I dropped my phone. I'm going to call 9-1-1. Wait here, ok? I'll call for help. Just... hold on, please!" My heart is beating out of my chest. I cannot lose her too. Not when I just got her back in my life after so long.

I move to rise, but still when her fingers brush my leg. "Hang on Gran, just one second, ok?" She moans and minutely shakes her head, but it's enough to stop me from moving away from her. "What? What do you need?"

She crooks her finger for me to come closer, and even though time is of the essence and I need to be calling the paramedics for her, I can't deny her anything. She got me out of that hellhole, away from those people. She's giving me a new start in life, and most importantly, she brought me back to Jen. I grab her small hand in my own, and she gives me a weak squeeze.

"Not..." she pauses and swallows before continuing slowly and quietly, "not an accident. He... pushed me."

"Who Gran? Who pushed you? What happened?"

Fear and anger are building in me with every labored breath she fights for. After another swallow and forced breath, she croaks "He's going for her now." She stops again, and this time the breath she takes rattles in her chest and some blood trickles out of her mouth. Pulling her hand from mine, she shakily raises her hand to cup my face. "Go, my boy... don't... let him hurt her." My stomach drops even further, knowing she could only be talking about Jen. Who is after her? Why?

Her hand drops as a wet cough wracks her body, and she struggles to breathe. I want to call for help. I want to run to Jen and make sure this mysterious person doesn't hurt her. I want to murder whoever hurt her. I can't leave her though, not in her last moments.

"Love... you. My sweet boy."

My heart shatters as she takes her last breath. Gran is the only woman who ever truly cared for me. My mother was cold and abusive, but though I didn't spend much time with Gran, and I was kept away from her for the last four years I know she loved me, and she tried to do her best by me. By both of us.

I don't want to leave her, but she's gone, and Jen could be in trouble. I dip down and press a kiss to her forehead and whisper "I love you too, Gran," before I run up the stairs to my bedroom to grab my gun. If someone is hurting or hunting Jen I need to be prepared for anything. I check the magazine and safety before grabbing my inner pants holster and a button down shirt to go over it all. As I run down the stairs I start working my holster onto my belt. My phone is on the floor in the middle of the hall leading back to the garage, so I scoop it up on my way out. Stuffing my phone in my pocket, I grab my old mountain bike from the garage wall and toss it in the bed of my truck. If I remember correctly, the track is too small to drive anything larger than a UTV out to the barn and I don't want to warn whoever may be there that I'm coming.

Whether "he" has touched Jen or not, he's dead. He's taken the only family that ever truly cared about me away from me, and that is unforgivable.

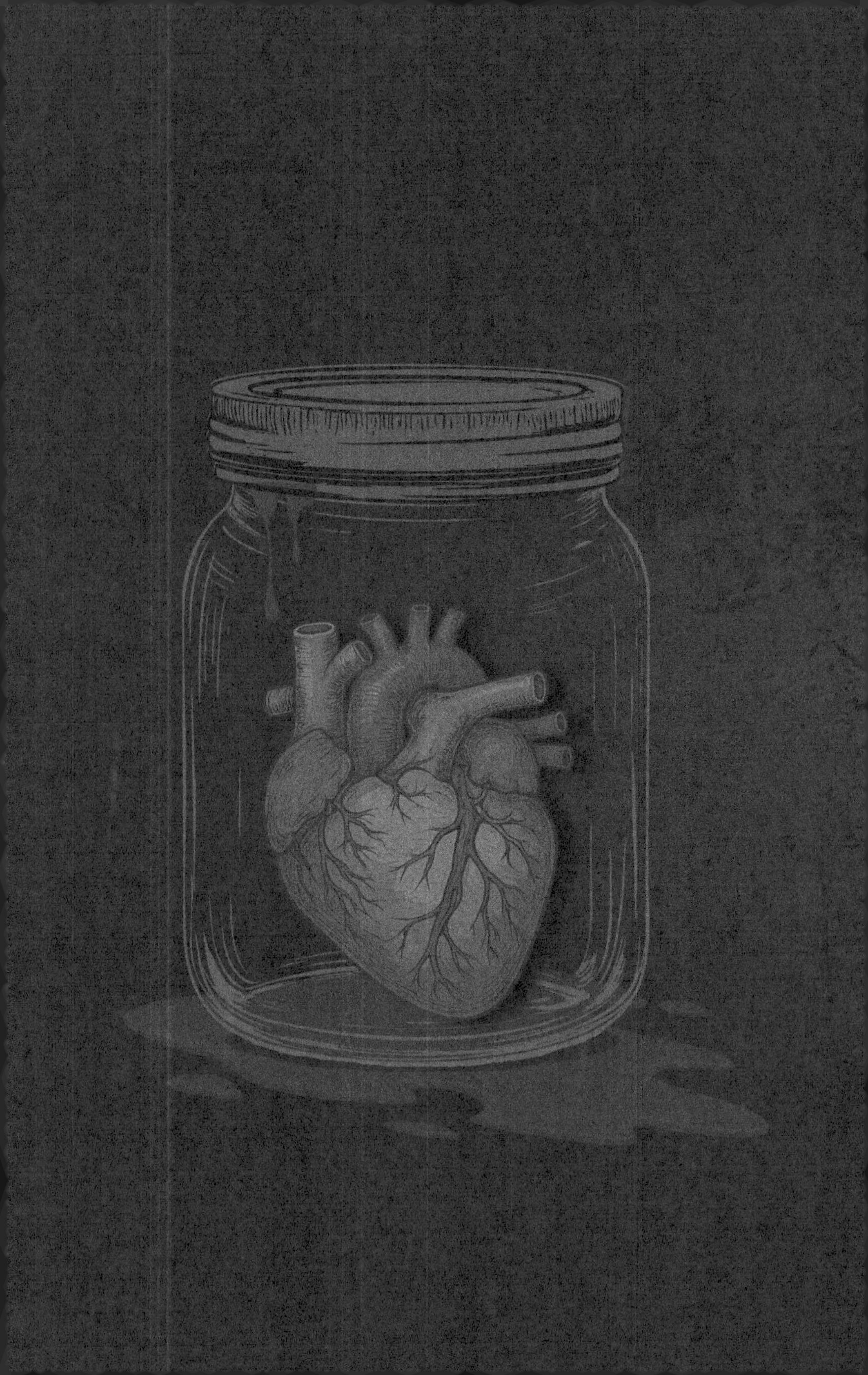

Chapter 16

Another morning free from my day job being taken over by my side hustle. As much as I love the extra cash, sometimes it would be nice to have a day to myself to do nothing except read a couple of books and eat my weight in candy. Ryan texted asking to hang out, so when I told him I had a job he offered to come out and hang out while I worked. He was never a hunter but didn't mind that I was, so I accepted the offer on the condition that he didn't mind when things got bloody and told him to meet me at the barn whenever he got a chance.

By the time he arrives I'm dressed in my coveralls and my station is set up and ready for me to start working. I open the door at his knock to find him watching the treeline to the left of the clearing that the barn is in with a frown of concentration. His profile is so handsome, and he's wearing the same cologne he used to when we were in high school. It's a fresh, clean smell and it brings me back to those days when we were all happy. He's wearing another button down shirt and slightly baggy jeans with heavy work boots, but his massive size makes it look like he's trying to detract from his stature with his clothing choice instead of being sloppy. As soon as he steps in the door he pulls me into a tight hug and puts his chin on the top of my head as he holds on to me. "Hey, Jen," he mumbles into my hair.

Pulling away, I give him a playful scowl. "I thought we talked about your use of that opening, asshole." Briefly, I think I see irritation in his eyes, but he gives me his trademark smirk so I'm not sure if I imagined it or not. Those lips that were the first I ever kissed are so full I find myself staring at them until his smirk turns into a full-blown grin.

I'm not ready to go down that road with him again yet, so I head to the workroom and leave him to follow me. I point to the wall across from my table where I've brought in a chair from the other room so he can sit and talk to me while I work. "Have a seat. I just finished getting set up so this'll take a while. What kind of music are you in the mood for? Music always helps me focus."

"I remember. I don't care, how about something relaxing? It's been a long day already and it's only 10:00am."

I give him a considering look, noticing for the first time the strain around his eyes and his tight jaw. "Sure. Alexa, play playlist 'Hardcore Jamz.'"

Ryan laughs and shakes his head when Return to Innocence by Enigma starts playing. "I had forgotten how weird your playlist names were. I see that's not something that changed."

"Nope, you know me. Or, at least, you did. I like to keep people on their toes. So, what's up? What's been going on today to make it so long?" I've started working on the deer at this point, so I can't focus on him too much, but his position across from me allows me to observe him periodically. Each time I glance up he's either staring hard at the deer and what I'm doing, or he's staring at me.

He's quiet for a few moments while he continues to watch me. Sighing, he shakes his head. "Just a rough morning. It's tough practically relearning how to live outside of the compound, and Gran isn't doing too well. I'm worried about my dad too. I have a lot on my mind, and some things happened this morning that I'm not ready to talk about yet."

"I'm sorry. Have you signed up for your general classes yet? I forgot to ask the other night." I'm still too raw to talk about his dad so maybe school is a safer subject. "I don't think it's that big of a deal for you to not know what you want yet. I'm lucky because I've loved the store since we were young and I have the opportunity to make it happen."

"Yeah, I remember how much you loved it. So, that's it? The store is 100% what you want? You don't think you might ever rather do something else instead?" There's a crease forming between his eyebrows like he's concerned for me.

"I've dreamed of the store being mine since I was ten. Mrs. C and I have been working together for years now and both of us want me to take over. She's training me to run the business, and we're using what I'm learning in business school to expand and improve things. Moving the store was my idea, and she let me drive a lot of the changes. It's worked out amazingly well, and we're both happy. I don't know what else I could ever do."

"There's always other options. Hopefully it stays your dream forever and you get what you want, though. You deserve to be happy, Jen."

I blush when I look up at him and he's staring at me. "Thanks. Obviously, the future isn't set in stone, but that's the plan. What about you? Do you have any idea what you might want?"

His eyes flash with heat this time, and I know I didn't imagine it. "I want a lot of things, Jen. As far as a career, I don't know yet. Right now, though? Right now,

I just want to spend time with you. Find out if we can pick things back up where we left off four years ago."

Oh, he thinks he's smooth, huh? That is so not going to work on me.

Ok. Maybe it's working a little, because I can my cheeks flush with embarrassment. "Yeah, well. We'll have to see about that. I'm happy to spend some time with you, but you told me you wanted to be with me, kissed me -- which was my first kiss ever, by the way -- and then disappeared without a word. It's going to take me some time to trust that you won't disappear again." He opens his mouth to object, but I hold up a blood covered hand. "I know. It wasn't your fault. That doesn't mean it stops hurting overnight. I finally worked up the courage to tell you how I felt after years of being afraid to and then you were just... gone. I've spent four years worrying about you and wondering if you left without a word because I did something wrong. All this time, I've thought either you were dead, or I ruined everything by admitting my feelings to you and you were happy to be away from me so you didn't have to deal with me."

At this point, I'm rambling and shaking so badly from the overload of emotions that I take a step back from the work table and take a deep breath. I've wanted to confront him for years. Tell him how his disappearance affected me. Rail at him for breaking my heart and making me worry. Making Brandon, Daniel, and my dad worry. Knowing what he's been through takes some of the wind out of my sails but I still need to tell him how I feel.

Ryan gets up from his seat and comes to stand in front of me. His hand reaches up to touch my face but I flinch away and take a step back. "Jen, what -"

"Sorry, one sec. I've got blood on me. Let me clean up a bit and we can talk. I can finish up after." Removing my gloves I walk over to the utility sink to wash my hands and face to make sure there isn't any blood on me. Looking down, I see some blood on the front of my coveralls, so I unzip it to my navel and tug my arms out so the top half can hang down around my waist. Towel in hand, I turn around to face Ryan and continue our conversation. "Look Ryan..."

The shock on his face has me stopping mid sentence. He's gone deathly pale, and the mixture of horror and fury in his dark blue eyes fills me with terror.

"Jen, what the fuck is that?"

CHAPTER 17

I look behind me, then down. Did I splash guts on my tank or something? The tank is black and doesn't feel wet, my bra isn't showing, and I'm not wearing any jewelry. I never do when I work out here, so what is freaking him out so bad?

"What is what? I don't see anything." I continue looking around before looking back to him. His face is no longer full of dread. It's full of fury.

What the hell?

"What? What's wrong? What are you talking about?" He's kind of freaking me out at this point because I have no clue what has happened. He starts stalking forward to me, his jaw clenched and eyes bright with anger. I try to step back away from him, but my back hits the utility sink and I have nowhere else to go.

Ryan roughly grabs both of my arms and holds them out so he can inspect them. He's squeezing my wrists hard enough that I can feel the bones grinding together and I wince at the pain. I try to pull them away from him, but he only grips them harder. "Ryan" I grit through clenched teeth, "Let me go. What is wrong with you?"

His eyes leave my arms and meet mine for the first time since I turned around. "What the fuck, Jenevive? What did you do to yourself? Why would you do this?"

I still have no idea what he's talking about. He went from zero to unhinged in less than a second, so I decide trying to deescalate the situation is my best option. "What is what, Ryan? What are you talking about? I can't give you answers if I don't know what you're talking about."

Shaking my arms with his grip he snarls at me "This, Jen! The tattoos! Why would you do this to your body? Why would you defile yourself like this? What were you thinking?"

I'm so shocked I can only stare at him for a second. My wrists are throbbing, but his reaction to my tattoos is something I never would have expected. "I... I don't understand. What's wrong with my tattoos? We talked about them all the time growing up. You knew what I wanted to do, you even helped me figure out the design!" When I told Ryan I wanted sleeves to depict the different parts of me, it was his idea to have them each represent one half of me. One light, full of life and bright colors, and one dark, filled with death and cooler jewel tones.

"I just can't believe you did it. Do you have any idea what you've done? You've ruined everything. He'll never agree now. He will never let me live this down! Fuck!"

He throws my arms away and stalks off, pacing back and forth while running his hands through his hair and tugging the ends. I rub my wrists while I watch him, trying to regain feeling in my fingers. He's muttering and cursing to himself, and I've never seen him this unbalanced. He's already hurt me once, and I have no idea what is going on so I slowly make my way over to my work station where all my tools are in case he tries to come at me again.

Although I'm anything but calm, being near my tools gives me more confidence in my ability to defend myself, so I try to gather more information. "What are you talking about, Ryan? What have I done? I don't understand, but maybe if you tell me what's happening we can figure it out together. Are you talking about your dad? I don't understand what my tattoos have to do with anything, or why anyone would even care."

Ryan spins to face me with complete and utter loathing. "He was right. You are a whore." His words hit me like a slap and my head jerks back like it was a physical blow. Tattoos make me a whore now? Obviously, he has no idea what he's talking about, but instead of junk punching him like I really want to, I want to figure out what he's talking about more, so I hold my tongue. For now. "It took me four fucking years Jen. Four years to convince my dad you were good enough. Four years to convince him you weren't the whore he thought you were, that you were exactly what our compound needed. Exactly what I needed! I defended you for four years even though he saw us kissing! I tried to make him understand I kissed you first and that was all that happened. I finally got him to agree, only to come back here to discover you were everything he ever said about you."

He laughs mirthlessly and shakes his head in disdain. "I came here to offer you everything, Jen. In a few years, Dad will retire and become an elder in the community and I will take his place. You were going to be my partner, my wife, and help me run the community. You ruined everything by desecrating your body. I was willing to deal with your hair, because that could be dyed back, but your arms can't be fixed! We can't hide that, Jen! Damnit!"

I think my brain has shut down. I spent four years pining after this nut job? Not only do I not give a single fuck what he or anyone else thinks of my tattoos, but under no circumstance would I ever agree to join his fucked up cult.

"First of all, what I do with my body is not now, nor has it ever been, your choice. Jesus, Ryan. What happened to you? You always hated how crazy your parents were. Are you telling me you buy into it all now? This is insane!"

His eyes narrow and I can tell I made things worse. "Do not talk about my father like that. I should have known you were a whore just like my mother. He warned me, but I didn't listen." Another mirthless chuckle escapes him, and then he releases a weary sigh. "I didn't want this to happen, Jen, but it looks like you're going to die the same as she did."

Shocked, I try to buy more time. "What? I thought your mom ran off with someone from the church?"

An evil smile tilts his mouth up at the corner. "She tried. My dad and I caught her before she could leave. Dad beat her lover to death while she watched, then I strangled her for trying to leave us and shaming him They were going to take Evan too, and Dad just couldn't let that happen."

What. The. Fuck.

"We tried to figure out a way to save face, but apparently her lover had told his friend they were running away together. Although it looked bad for my father, the fact that he told someone they were leaving worked in our favor. No one looked for them, and we were able to avoid any suspicion. My father was devastated by her betrayal and mortified she would dare embarrass him like this when the community relies on and looks up to him. It's almost time for me to take over his position, and it's taken me this long to convince him you wouldn't be like her, but I guess I was wrong." He sneers at me and starts walking in my direction. "Sorry, not sorry. You should have made better choices with your life, Jen."

I let him move a few steps closer before I whip my arm around with the heavy stainless steel tray gripped in my hand. His eyes widen in shock as the light glints off of the shined surface and the few pieces of meat I'd been able to harvest before taking a break go flying across the room. Less than a second later the edge of the tray connects with his temple, causing his eyes to roll to the back of his head before he drops to the ground, head slamming on the concrete and then stilling at an odd angle.

Chest heaving, I kick his fallen form in the stomach and growl out "How do you feel about that choice, you stupid mother fucker?" I turn to go grab some zip ties to tie him up, but the door to the workroom crashing open scares the crap out of me and I jump, moving into a batter's stance with my tray in preparation to take on whoever else has come into my space.

Ryan's car was at the cabin when I arrived, and as much as I want to believe Gran wasn't talking about him, I'm not naive. He changed after his mom disappeared. He became harder and started following his father's teachings more. He started buying into the superiority complex the whole community spouted and no matter what I tried, I couldn't get through to him. I hoped that leaving and coming back here with Gran and all our true friends would bring him back, that being near Jen would bring him back, but if he killed Gran there is no hope for him.

A bike was all I had for the entire time I lived at the compound, and for several months after I moved out on my own, so I make quick work of the two track road out to the barn and arrive in a few short minutes. It's felt like hours since Gran died next to me but in reality it has only been about thirty minutes. Hopefully Jen is safe and I'm worrying about nothing.

The front door to the barn is unlocked, so I quietly make my way in and to the door that I remember leads to the workroom. Not wanting to scare Jen or barge in like a fool, I place my ear against the door to attempt to hear something. I can make out a raised voice that sounds like Ryan, then a short pause before a loud bang and higher pitched yelling.

Fuck this, I'm going in there.

Throwing the door open, I'm shocked to find Ryan out cold on the floor and Jen standing over him and facing me with a metal tray held up like a bat. Her chest is heaving and her eyes are wide and angry. The fist around my heart loosens as I realize she's safe. I hold my hands up to signify to her that I'm not a threat and stay where I am, so I don't scare her.

"Evan?"

Chapter 18

Confusion hits me when I see Evan panting in the doorway. He quickly takes stock of the room -- Ryan out cold on the ground and me with my tray -- and puts his hands up to indicate he doesn't mean me harm.

"Evan? What are you doing here? What is going on? If you're going to attack me, so help me God I will kill you both and no one will ever find your bodies!"

Eyes wide, he shakes his head wildly and takes a second to catch his breath. "Thank God you're ok. No, shit, I would never hurt you Jenny! I got here as fast as I could. He's not dead, so can we please tie him up or something, so I can explain things?" I consider him for a moment, trying to gauge the sincerity in his eyes. His beautiful pain is closer to the surface than usual, and he's wearing his heart on his sleeve. "Please, Jen."

"Fine." I switch my tray for my knife and hold it out towards both of them, "but you tie him up. Stay over there. I'm going to throw you some zip ties. Do not move until I tell you to, ok?"

"Ok. I understand. Whatever you need." Proving to me he can take direction, he stays perfectly still with his hands still raised. I walk over to the tool cabinet and grab out some zip ties, keeping my eyes on him the whole time. I walk back over to him slowly, and stop about ten feet away from both of them. Tossing the zip ties at his feet, I step back across the room and nod at him to go ahead and bind Ryan.

Kneeling next to him. Evan is not gentle as he rolls Ryan into position so he can zip tie him. He's able to secure his feet together and moves to his hands when Ryan lets out a quiet moan. With a scowl, Evan cocks back and punches him across the face so hard spit flies out of Ryan's mouth before he goes quiet again. Standing up, Evan unknowingly copies me by kicking him in the stomach before turning back to me.

"Can we close him up somewhere? I can't stand looking at him right now and I don't want him interfering in our conversation if he wakes up while we're still talking."

He's being awfully calm for someone who has no idea why I beat the shit out of his cousin.

"Pick him up. We'll hang him from the hook by his hands. He won't be able to go anywhere, and we can go into the other room to talk where I know you won't have access to any weapons."

"Ok, I'll pick him up. Full disclosure, though, I do have a gun on me. I'm going to put my arms back up to prove I'm not moving towards it, and you can tell me what you want me to do with it. Whatever makes you feel safe, Jen."

Well, damn. That was unexpected. Chewing on my lower lip I ask "Where is the gun?"

"In an inner pants holster at the small of my back."

"Ok, turn around and walk towards the wall and stand flush to it. Hands stay up, press them against the wall above your head and out to the sides. Once you're in position I will take the gun and make sure you don't have anything else on you."

Slowly, he moves to follow my directions and makes no sudden movements. When he's against the walls with his hands up, I move to him and place the knife at his side. "Do not move."

A slight tremble shakes his body, but I'm not sure if it's from fear, anger, adrenaline, or something else. I pat him down first since I only have one hand to work with but I don't find anything else on him other than his phone, keys, and wallet. I grab the gun and step back from him. I switch the gun into my dominant hand and reluctantly say "Ok. You can turn around. Slowly. I'm going to lower the hook. Pick Ryan up and attach the ties to the hook, then wrap the strapping twice around his arms and slide the link over the tip of the hook so I can raise him."

Ryan is about 7,000 pounds of all dead weight muscle, but Evan is obviously as strong as I thought he is because as I walk over to the controls for the hook, he simply dips down and hauls Ryan up off the ground. As the hook lowers, I realize he picked him up in a way that will make it difficult to hook him up. When the hook lowers to where I want it, I meet Evan's eyes and hold up a warning finger.

"I'm going to come over there and hook his hands since you're holding him up. Do not make a move toward me. Once he's hooked, keep holding him until I raise him up enough to hang."

Evan nods silently and gulps. He holds completely still as I make my way over to him, watching me as I come closer. I grab Ryan's limp arms and feed the zip tie over the hook, then wrap the dangling strap around his wrists a few times before securing it on the hook as well. I walk backwards to the controls and press the button to raise it until Ryan is dangling with only his toes touching the ground.

He won't be able to break free even if he does wake up, so I'm not worried about him getting away while we talk.

Evan lets him go once I stop the lift. He steps back, putting his arms back up in the air. He's making a big effort to make me comfortable, like he always has, but after Ryan's outburst I'm afraid to trust him quite yet.

Gun again raised in his direction, I direct him to start moving. "Head over to the sitting room and go sit in the chair on the far side of the room. Keep your hands flat on the arms of the chair so I can see them at all times."

The Truth Will Set Me Free

Jen has nothing to worry about from me, but I will do whatever I can to make sure she feels as comfortable and safe as possible until she believes that again. I carefully make my way to the sitting room next to the bathroom and head straight to the chair across the room. Hands still raised the entire time, I wait until I'm seated to lower my palms to the arms of the chair and lean back in a slouch in the hopes that my body language will allow her to relax a bit.

Even through her fear, her beauty shines. She's so damned strong. I knew she didn't need me to save her, but even the best trained people can be taken by surprise by someone they trust. As much as it killed me growing up, she loved him. He was manipulative back then, and it's only gotten worse since we moved to the cult and his mom left him. If she let love cloud her judgement, he could have manipulated her into a situation she couldn't escape.

Sitting across from me, my gun in her lap, Jen examines me thoroughly. "I cannot stress this enough right now, Evan. I'm tired. I'm tired of being in the dark, and I'm tired of this bullshit already. Tell me what is going on, as quickly and concisely as possible, before I decide I don't care and kill you both."

"Ok, I'll tell you whatever you want. Where do you want me to start?"

"How about, what are you both really doing here?" Her narrowed eyes make it obvious she doesn't believe our story anymore.

"I wasn't lying, Jen. They took us away that night after destroying everything. They took our ability to contact anyone from the outside world and literally would not leave our sides until we were in the car on the way out, other than to let us use the bathroom. I thought this was all on Aunt Stacey, but when she left Uncle Patrick after the first year I realized he was probably the one driving it." Jen's eyes widen in surprise and pity at that, so I pause and ask "What?"

"It's just... Ryan sort of went crazy and did the whole evil villain monologue thing before I knocked him out. He said she didn't run away. Apparently he and his dad caught her before she could leave. The pastor beat the lover to death, and Ryan killed his mother after making her watch."

I close my eyes and release a deep sigh. I'm not surprised. Uncle Patrick has been getting more and more unstable since she "left," and Ryan started getting more and more zealous as time went on.

"I'm honestly not surprised. As much as I had no love for Aunt Stacey, she didn't deserve death at the hands of her own son. Charles was a great man, it's pretty devastating to learn that's what happened to him." Shaking my head in pity, I continue with my tale. "Anyway, I literally had nothing. They took everything from me. They took my money and sold my car, so I had no way of leaving them. The community was so unbelievably weird, no communication was allowed with the outside world except for internet usage while monitored by an elder. When I say monitored, I mean one of them literally sat next to you and watched everything you did online.

"It took me three years to save up enough money for first and last month's rent and a safety deposit for a room in a small duplex in the area. It was furnished, so luckily I had a bed to sleep on. The landlord was a construction foreman and when I told him I was a handyman and he heard my story, he gave me a job. I sort of became his right-hand man, and he taught me everything he could while I worked with him."

"I want to know the real reason you didn't get in contact with us sooner. First, though, I need to know why you came here like you did today." Pain fills her eyes again, though she tries to hide it. I've always known her better than anyone else; she can't hide from me.

"I will explain that too, I promise. Please believe me that I spent every day of the past four years wishing I could speak to you again. As far as today, though, I got home from the pharmacy to find Gran dying at the bottom of the stairs." Jen gasps and her hand covers her mouth. "I tried to call 9-1-1, but she motioned me over to her instead. She... she told me that 'he' pushed her, and that 'he' was coming for you next."

Their grandmother is dead? And Ryan pushed her? "Why would he hurt her? Didn't he love your grandmother?"

"I don't think Ryan loves anyone other than himself. Maybe you, in his own way. He's a lot like his dad now in that he believes women should be possessions, and my guess is he still wanted you. I heard him and Gran fighting last night though. She told him he needed to let the cult life go and move on. She wanted him to finish school and find a job away from his father, but he told her he would be taking over in the next few years. She begged him not to go back, but when that didn't work she threatened to take him out of her will, stop paying for his college, and kick him out of her house. Without that, he'd have no reason to stay here, so she told him to go back to his father if it was his ultimate plan anyway. He knew I was home last night, so my guess is he waited until I left to run errands for her this morning before taking action. I tried to save her, but she died before I could even call for help."

At this admission, a single tear tracks down his cheek. He lets it fall, refusing to move his hands from their position on the arms. At that moment, his heart is breaking for the grandmother he loved, but his priority is staying still so he doesn't scare me. My shield cracks, and I look at him, really look at him, for the first time today. Maybe even the first time ever.

I've always thought his pain was beautiful, because it matched my own. But now, in the middle of one of the most confusing and upsetting moments of my life it's like scales have been removed from my eyes.

I *see* Evan.

Since the day we met, he has always been there for me. He protected me as a child, he comforted me when I needed it, and he came for me even as he grieved for the grandmother that just died in his arms less than an hour ago.

We sit there in silence for a while, staring at each other and fighting through our own emotions. His grief (and who knows what else), my sorrow for his loss and the wonder of realizing this beautiful man loves me. He didn't say it out loud, but his actions scream it. They always have.

As I sit there in my shock, the silence allows me to hear the song change. I forgot to turn the music off, and "Blood Sport (from the room below)" by

Sleep Token begins. I firmly believe that sometimes music finds its way into the poignant moments of your life and provides the answers you didn't know you were looking for. The timing of this song speaks to my soul and affirms to me that I'm on the right track, and I slide the safety on the gun before rising from my seat and placing it on the cushion.

As I walk to Evan his brow furrows, but he doesn't move from the position I ordered him to take. Dropping to my knees in front of him, I gently tug on his knees to open his legs so I can slide closer to him. I raise my hand to his cheek and brush at the tear track with my thumb. His breath hitches and his eyes fall closed at my touch, and he tilts his head into my palm.

"I am so sorry, Evan. I cannot imagine what that was like." He turns his head and kisses my palm before turning back to me and opening his eyes. The pain of his loss is there, but for the first time, I find something else.

Love.

How have I missed this? He's always looked at me this way, but I never realized what it was. I can't say I love him, but now that I've discovered this new lens to view him with, I'm using it to examine at my own feelings. He's always been there for me. He's always treated me with respect, always made me laugh, always made me feel good about myself. I'd had a huge crush on him when he moved in with Ryan, but he never treated me like anything other than a friend and Ryan started flirting with me not long after he arrived, so I pushed it away thinking it would never amount to anything. He's so unbelievably handsome, so sweet. Unlike Ryan, he accepted and respected the boundaries I've set with him since they returned.

I wake from my musings to see he's staring at my mouth, and I'm being pulled into his beautiful orbit. I run my thumb across his bottom lip, and his eyes widen as they jump back to mine. Slowly, so he has time to back away, I lean in to him and brush his lips with my own so that I can find out if what I'm feeling is real. He trembles slightly with that small touch, so I lean back and study him. His eyes are closed again and his face is pulled into an expression of almost pain.

"I'm so sorry, I shouldn't have..." my words choke off when his eyes snap open, filled with fear.

"Please don't say that," he whispers. "Why did you stop?"

Instead of answering him, I lean back into him and press my lips more firmly against his, and he lets me take whatever I want from him even though I can tell he wants more. Breaking off again, I lean my head down on his shoulder. "What's wrong?" I ask. "Do you not like it? Should I stop? I should have asked first, I'm so sorry."

"Shhhh," he whispers into my hair and then sweetly kisses my head. "I never want you to stop. It's just... you asked me to stay still. I don't want to move until you're comfortable."

I blush and bury my face deeper in his chest for a moment. Lifting my head to meet his eyes, I ask him "Do you want to hurt me? If I let you move, will you make me regret it?" I'm fully aware I'm showing him how vulnerable I am right now, and after Ryan's revelation it may not be the best idea, but I've always been able to be vulnerable with Evan, and it feels right.

"Jenevive, I could never hurt you. If you allow me to move I will never let you regret it, and I'll spend the rest of my life proving to you that you can trust me."

Maintaining eye contact, I slide my hands over his and link our fingers together. "Ok."

"Ok?" he asks.

With a small smile, I nod and say, "Ok. You can move. Please don't let me regret this."

The smile he gives me is stunning. My breath catches in my chest as he releases one of my hands and slides his into the hair at the nape of my neck. He pulls me toward him and before he kisses me he whispers "I've waited for this for seven years. If you let me, I will never stop showing you that you never have to worry about me hurting you. You are everything, Jen. Let me prove it to you."

And with that, his lips fuse to my own in a kiss that rocks me to my core. Unlike Ryan with his battering-ram style, Evan tugs on my bottom lip, nibbling on it and then soothing away the slight sting with his tongue. I lick at the seam of his lips and he opens to me, our kisses languid and drugging. His hands hold me like I'm something precious and I have never felt so cherished or desired in my life.

Minutes pass as we explore each other, but eventually we separate. At some point, though I don't remember it happening, I somehow ended up in his lap. Not straddling him, but curled up against him. I tuck my head into the crook of his neck again, and he dips his head to place long, sweet kisses against my forehead. I don't want to ruin this moment, but I have to know.

"Why didn't you contact me when you were out of there, Evan? If you feel this way after all these years, why didn't you try to find me?"

He takes a deep breath and releases it slowly. I can tell he's trying to figure out how to answer, but I have no doubt whatever he says will be the truth.

"Jen, I've been in love with you since we met. I was too afraid back then to tell you, so terrified that you looked at me like a big brother and I didn't think I could bear the rejection. After we were taken away I tried everything I could think of to reach you but we were so closely monitored it was impossible. It took me three years to escape, and by then I was basically penniless and I didn't want to make my problems yours. I had been making plans though. I had just made enough money to buy my truck, and my boss was trying to use his contacts around here to find me a job with a company closer to here. He knew about you and wanted to help me make it back to you. He heard from someone a few days before Uncle Patrick told us about Gran's offer. I was suspicious of why he was suddenly ok with us coming back here, but I didn't care enough to not come. This is where I wanted to be, and it got me here, so I rolled with it. I was biding my time, trying to figure out how to approach you when we ran into Brandon at the store. I realized I couldn't wait any longer."

It's a lot to process, but I believe him. We stay seated in companionable silence for a few more minutes before we hear noise from the work room. "Sounds like he's awake" I say. "What are we going to do with him?"

Squeezing me tight for a moment, Evan quietly says "He killed my grandmother, and who knows what he was going to do to you. I can't let that go. She was the only person that ever tried for me. He doesn't deserve to take his chance with the court system."

"Ok."

Jerking back from me, he searches my face for something. "Ok?"

Giggling, I nod. "Ok. He was going to kill me. He killed his own mother and grandmother. This isn't my first rodeo, big guy. He shouldn't be allowed out to victimize anyone else. You do what you think is best, and I'll take care of the body for you."

The shock on his face is priceless, so I smack a kiss on to his parted lips, nip his chin, and hop up from his lap. I saunter over to the couch I had been sitting on before and grab the gun before turning back to him where he's still frozen in his chair. Rolling my eyes, I wave him towards me. "Come on, Ev. I'll explain later. For now, we have a predator to put down."

I didn't think he could make a more entertaining face, but I was wrong. After a moment he schools his features and shakes his head, clears his throat, and steps up to take my outstretched hand.

"Yeah, ok. But I'm going to need an explanation later."

Ryan's eyes find mine as soon as I open the door and walk back into my work room. His glower turns into a sneer when he notices Evan walk out behind me, his hand in mine.

"See? You're only proving me right. Were you fucking him the whole time when we were kids, or did you start today? I should have known you were when I saw you wearing that stupid necklace. He always was pathetic about you."

Startling at his words, I look to Evan to ask if he's telling the truth. His deep green eyes are full of panic and uncertainty, and he's obviously unsure of how I will react. Smiling at him, I reach my free hand up and grab the turtle pendant, rubbing the belly for luck. Knowing it came from Evan? The person who was always my safe space and my confidant? It makes it that much more special to me.

Chapter 19

Six Years Ago

Thankful today is Saturday, I head down to the lake behind my house to search for turtles and think of my mom. She's not here, but it's been three years since she died and I always feel closest to her down there.

We used to hunt for turtles when something important was coming up, so we could rub their bellies for luck. It was our private tradition. Dad never came because he said he thought it was silly, but I think he liked that it was our time together. I think that's why he still doesn't search with them for me, he knows it's my time to think of her and pretend she's still here.

Every year so far I've been able to find a turtle on the anniversary of her death. It feels a little silly, but I rub their belly and talk to them like my mom is there with me. I tell her all the things going on in my life and it helps me to feel close to her again.

Today, I spot one as soon as I reach the shoreline. He's massive, almost too big for me to pick up, but after I drop the lettuce I brought with me on the ground I'm able to lift it with both hands. Walking back to the dropped lettuce, I gently place him down so he can have a snack. I stare at him while he eats and try to think of what I want to say to my mom. Nothing comes this time. Three years is a long time to be without someone and her absence hurts like she left just yesterday.

I don't like to cry in front of my dad. He's hurting too and I don't want to make him feel worse, but he's not at home this morning so I don't have a reason to hold my tears back. They run silently down my cheeks as I sit and pet the turtle, watching him devour the lettuce like he hasn't eaten in days. Lost in my head, I jump when someone sits down next to me and our knees brush together. Evan settles in next to me, his sad eyes taking in my tears and the turtle in front of me.

He doesn't know what today is. I don't usually talk about it, but he's lost his mom too. She still may be alive but she left him too, so I feel like he'll understand what I'm going through. "Today is the anniversary of my mom's death today." I pause to take a deep breath and try to prevent myself from crying harder, "she was killed three years ago by a drunk driver."

Evan frowns and sits for a moment before reaching over and grabbing the hand I'm not using to pet the turtle. "I'm sorry. I'm sure you miss her a lot. What was she like? You never talk about her."

"She was amazing. She always made my costumes and volunteered at my school. She supported me no matter what -- encouraged me to be myself and like the music and books I liked no matter how 'weird' they were. She made this garlic pasta my dad and I can't make right no matter how hard we try to duplicate it, even using her recipe." Evan chuckles as I pout. "We used to hunt for turtles before something important was going to happen, or if we ever just felt like we needed a little luck in our life."

"Why turtles?" he asks.

"Mom believed they were lucky. She used to rub their bellies and say 'for luck,' like it was a rabbit foot or lucky penny. She said a lot of cultures believed turtles brought luck and good fortune, and she thought they were cute, so they kind of became her thing. Since we did it together as I grew up, it became our thing together. Sometimes when I miss her a lot I'll come and look for them. I always come down on the anniversary and feed at least one. I talk to them like she can hear me, and give them a belly rub before I take them back down to the water." I shrug my shoulders, blushing at how silly it sounds before I peek up at Evan. "It makes me feel close to her." His face is free of judgement, and that helps me feel better.

With a small smile, he squeezes my hand and says "You're lucky you had such a great mom, even if you only had her for a little while. I bet she's watching over you and sending you some luck whenever you need it."

I know he's right, but I can't help crying again. I miss her so much it hurts. So much that my body starts shaking and I'm fighting gasping sobs. Evan doesn't judge me, or get angry and remind me that his mom willingly abandoned him, or walk away. He simply picks me up, deposits me in his lap, and holds me while he rocks side to side until I tire myself out.

Exactly one year later I arrive home to a turtle pendant on my porch with no idea who left it, and I've worn it ever since.

For luck.

Stepping closer to Evan and placing my hand on his chest, I search his eyes before asking, "That was you, huh?"

He scratches the top of his head sheepishly before answering me, like he's trying to stall and think of what to say. "Yeah, I saw it in a store not too long before the anniversary. I thought, maybe, if you always had one with you, you'd feel closer to her."

If there was any shield left around my heart when it comes to Evan Holmes, he just busted through that shit like the Kool Aid man. Forgetting everything else around me, I reach up and pull him to me for a scorching kiss. There's a second of shocked hesitation in him, but he quickly responds by capturing my face in his hands and dominating me with his tongue, lips, and even teeth.

I haven't had a lot of experience with kissing, but kissing Evan is as natural as breathing. I meet his kiss with equal passion, nipping his lip and running my fingers through his messy hair. I must be doing something right though because he lets out a low groan and pulls me tighter against him with an arm around my back.

It takes a few moments to register, but the sound of hysterical laughter eventually draws me back to reality. Releasing Evan and stepping into his side, I take in Ryan's hanging form. He's crazed, blood is leaking out of his nose and matted in his hair and his eyes are wide with pupils blown. There's also a growing blood stain on his shirt sleeve, most likely from the zip ties cutting into his skin. Spit flies out of his mouth when he stops laughing and says "You didn't know? He was obsessed with you! He used to follow you around like a lost puppy when we were together. Always begging for a scrap of your attention. Fucking pathetic!"

I cock my head to the side and give him an overly contemplative face. "I don't know. I think I'd rather someone was actually in love with me and treated me with respect than want to control me and keep me like a possession." With a shrug, I dismiss Ryan and turn to Evan. "So, what's the play here?"

"The play is that you're going to let me the fuck go. I'll even let you live so you two pathetic lovebirds can be miserable with each other forever. I obviously misjudged you, Jen. You were always so sweet. So accommodating and pliant. Guess that's why you become a worthless slut."

"Shut the fuck up, Ryan! What is wrong with you?" Evan balls his fists like he's going to attack him again.

"What's wrong with me? You're the one who has something wrong. Dad always knew you were worthless, Evan, just like your whore mother. Why else do you think he would have killed her?"

Evan is sitting in the same chair I directed him into earlier. I grabbed some ice from the freezer and made him a compress for his knuckles to prevent them from swelling as much as possible. After Ryan dropped the bomb that his dad killed Evan's mom, we couldn't drag anything else out of him other than maniacal laughter. Evan finally had enough and punched him so hard he blacked out. He's currently hanging limp, and Evan is quietly seething.

Walking over to him, I kneel before him and gently pull up the compress to peek at his knuckles. They're not split, but they are a little red. I kiss them and press it back to his skin as I look up to find him staring at me while chewing at the corner of his bottom lip.

"What?" I ask him, suddenly self-conscious.

"It's just... I want to ask for something but I don't know how you'll react. I'm nervous about what you'll think of me, but I can't not ask, you know?"

"I just admitted I have experience in the disposal of human bodies. Do you honestly think whatever you're about to ask could phase me?"

He releases a huffing chuckle and shakes his head, fondness shining through his eyes. He grabs the hand I was using to hold the ice pack to his knuckles and brings my palm up to kiss it. "I want him dead."

"Right... I'm taking care of the disposal, remember?" I'm confused because I thought we already settled this.

"Yeah, I know. But I also need answers. About my mom, his mom and Charles, Gran, and you. I can't kill him without knowing what happened or why. What if his dad is behind all of this and there's a bigger plan? Knowing now what I do, so many pieces are falling into place, but they're only bringing up more questions. You're all I have left Jen. I can't kill him if not knowing those answers will put you in even more danger."

"So, what?" I climb into his lap and since kneeling isn't comfortable on this floor. "You're not letting him go right?"

"No. I can't risk him getting away."

"Then... keep him locked up? I mean, you can keep him here, the security is tight and no one comes out here. But keeping him locked up may not do anything.

He's obviously deranged at this point. You may have to take things further than that."

"You mean like torture?" he questions, surprise and unease on his face.

"I mean exactly like torture. Can you handle that?"

His shoulders sag and his head falls to rest his forehead on my collarbone. "Yes." He said. "I know we haven't talked too much about your story yet, but mine isn't as simple or pretty as we laid out the night we first saw you again. We can talk about it later, but yes. I can handle it if you can. I just didn't want you to be afraid of me."

I press a long kiss to the side of his head while I contemplate my answer. Laying my cheek against his head I tell him "I've told you. He killed your Gran, and he tried to kill me. I was all in before we learned he knew his piece of shit dad killed your mom. Whatever you need, I'm here."

"I'm not sure where to start" He admits quietly, like he's embarrassed that he's not a professional torturer. Luckily, I do. Pulling out my phone, I pull up my messaging app. "What are you doing?" Evan asks with a touch of panic in his tone.

"Relax. I'm calling in reinforcements."

> **Me:** 9-1-1. The Commies are in the fun house. Need something to stuff it up and lock it down at the barn asap.

> **Bran:** Roger that. Are you there alone? Any particular brand?

> **Me:** No brand, anything is fine as long as it's secure. Evan is with me.

> **Bran:** Evan huh? Can't wait to hear this story. Be there in 2 hours.

> **Me:** What part of 9-1-1 is confusing? I'm hemorrhaging here. 30 minutes.

> **Bran:** Use paper towels and duct tape. I'll get there when I get there, and I'll bring the good shit.

> **Me:** You suck. Hurry up!

"I just, I don't even know what to do with that conversation. Are you talking about Communists? What is he bringing? Why would he come here? Are we going to tell him?" His confusion is adorable.

I giggle and tell him "Brandon has known what I've been doing since around the time you left. He's got a weak stomach and often pukes at the sight of blood, but he's supportive and helps where he can. That was code telling him I need restraints and some kind of gag. I could use duct tape like he said, but I'd prefer something a little easier to take on and off."

"Have you done this before? Tortured someone?"

"Probably not like what we'll be doing with Ryan, but I have a little experience."

"When? What happened? Can you explain things to me while we wait for Brandon?"

"Sure." I climb up off of his lap and reach my hand out to him. "Brandon will be here in two hours though and I need to finish my job. Do you want to come out there with me so we can chat while I work?"

"Ok. Do you need help?" Taking my hand like before, he follows me back out to the workroom. Ryan is thankfully still passed out, so I don't have to listen to his bullshit while I work.

"Honestly, I know you probably don't want to touch him, but if you could clean the blood off of him and duct tape his mouth it would help more than anything. I already have enough to clean up, I don't want to have to clean up Bran's puke too. Plus, I'm tired of listening to his bullshit. He's not going to talk right now, or at least he won't say anything worth listening to."

"On it. Can't let the princess lose his lunch, can we?"

"Thanks. Cleaning supplies are in this cabinet." I grab a new pair of gloves from the cabinet and leave the doors open for Evan to grab what he needs. "Alexa, play playlist Rave Party."

Evan snorts when Bach starts playing while he's searching through the cabinet.

"What?" I say, gasping out with faux indignation. "I can be classy!"

"I never doubted it," he says. "Just surprised this is what you rave to."

"Well I figured this would be easier to talk over. I can surely put on gangster rap if you'd prefer."

"I'm good," he laughs. "So, can you tell me why you are experienced in the disposal of human remains? And why you're so calm about all of this?"

Much like he was nervous earlier to tell me what he needed, I'm a bit nervous to tell him my story. He seems ok with this situation, so maybe he won't freak out too much.

"Are you sure you want to know? It may change things." I hesitate for a second and chew on my lip. After what we've been through together today I don't think it will, but I've just found him and I'm concerned it will change how he thinks about me. Looking into his eyes, I think about how he kissed me earlier and told me how he felt, and I decide to lay it all out there. He waits patiently for me to continue. No pressure, no judgement.

"I have experience, and I'm so calm, because I've killed before. My Dad taught me how."

Chapter 20

Dad knocks on my bedroom door frame and watches me as I put my book down. "Ok Johnny, I think it's time for you to work with me on my side project. Are you ready?" His smile is a little strained around the edges, but there is hope in his eyes too. I've been waiting on this day for a long time, waiting for him to let me help him with his special projects. He's always told me I wasn't ready yet, but he has never explained why. I've been helping him in the cold room since I was old enough to hand him his tools, but there have been times he has refused to let me in to work with him. I've never known what goes on there during those times, and I've begged him so many times to let me in I thought it would never happen.

I jump up off of my bed and rush to follow him out to the barn. "What are we doing today? Am I helping with your tools or am I going to work too?" He waggles his head back and forth and purses his lips while thinking. I wait patiently for him to talk, afraid I'll ruin by saying something wrong. When we reach the barn door he hesitates.

"This is something your mom used to help me with. I need you to trust me and not be scared when you're in there. Can you do that for me?" He pauses and chews on the inside of his cheek while I nod at him, not sure what to say. That's what he does when he's nervous. What can he be doing in here that he's nervous about, especially if Mom helped him? "I'm serious Johnny. I need to believe you're ready for this and are going to give me the chance to explain everything to you. I'm trusting you're grown up enough to be able to do this work with me. If you think there's anything you can't handle, you need to tell me now. We can try again in a few years."

"I'm ready Daddy. I want to help you with whatever you need."

Taking a deep breath he stares at me for another minute before seeming to decide something for himself. He nods and unlocks the door, ushering me in ahead of him. "Alright now. This time I need you to suit up. I have a disposable suit for you here, this is just for one time wear. I need you to put your hair up and put this cap on, then these gloves and booties over your shoes. This is non-negotiable and if you want to keep helping me with these jobs you need to be used to wearing everything each time."

Too excited to care about the extra layers, I happily put on everything he sets out for me. He has to help me fit my fingers in the gloves right, but once they're on I look at him and smile. "Ready!" I chirp, excited to start.

"Ok Johnny girl. This is your last chance to back out. Once you go in there you won't have the opportunity to go back to how things were before you went in." His smile is earnest, but strained. It's almost like he can't decide if he truly wants my help or not. He's kind of scaring me, but I know no matter what, I want to help. Dad is my rock, and I want to be his too now since Mom is gone.

"I'm sure Dad. I want to help since Mom isn't here to help anymore."

Pulling me into a hug, Dad kisses my forehead and squeezes me tight. "You're the best kid a guy could ask for, you know that? I love you, Johnny. Your mom would be so proud of how you've grown up."

Without any more conversation or delay, Dad unlocks the deadbolts on the door to the cold room and lets me in, locking them back behind me. Once I cross the threshold I eye the sheet draped bundle on the table. We never cover the animals that are brought in here, so I can already tell something is different this time. Was it attacked by another animal? Is it torn up or partially eaten and someone has asked him to figure out what happened? I know he's done it before when the vet wasn't available our couldn't figure something out.

Dad walks over to the table and turns to me. "We've talked a lot about making sure nothing is wasted when we kill. We use every part we can, whether for eating, bait, trophy mounting, or sending what we can to the taxidermist and tanner to repurpose. If we can't leave the rest of the animal in the woods for others to feed off of, we dispose of it properly. I volunteer with the game meat donation programs so hunters that are either too lazy or unskilled to dress their own kills have a place to bring their animals. This way they're not left to waste and rot in the wild. We can help feed the hungry and keep disease from spreading through the rotting carcass.

"My dad taught me this, and I have taught both your mother and you. Sometimes, though, it's not enough. Sometimes the issue isn't animal waste, it's human." He pauses to make sure I'm following him, and maybe to pluck up a little more courage. His nerves are back in full force, and I still don't know what could be freaking him out so much. I wait until he's ready to tell me what's going on.

With one final, deep breath, Dad grabs on to the corner of the sheet covering the animal on the table and watches me as he pulls the sheet back, waiting for my reaction to the creature there.

The only issue is, it's not an animal.

It's a man.

My dad has a dead man on his cold room table. I don't understand what's happening, why he'd be here instead of at the hospital or the morgue. Speechless, I turn to him with my brow furrowed, trying to figure out what's going on.

"Sometimes, Johnny, humans are a waste of life. They lie, cheat, steal, and kill, and they give nothing back to those who live around them. Instead of being productive members of society or doing something that would possibly help others benefit, they are a drain instead. This man was a drug dealer and sex trafficker. He targeted kids your age, letting them try pot to develop a taste and then selling it to them when they got hooked. Eventually he'd sell them harder stuff. Sometimes, he'd even lace them with harder drugs to get them addicted faster. When the kids got hooked he'd let them work their debts off by selling their bodies, no matter how young they were. He's a woman beater and a general jackass. Somehow he never gets caught because he has minions doing all the work for him, and his girlfriend thinks he's misunderstood. She won't press charges when he beats her."

"How did he die?" I ask, hoping he's not about to say what I think he is.

"I killed him. I heard Brian complaining about him a few too many times, so I decided to go see for myself what he was up to. Last night I saw him get drunk, smack his girlfriend around a bit, and then head out to make a few deals with kids from your school. I waited until we were in a bad part of town when he was walking back to his car alone and took him down before he could get there. I knocked him out there and waited until he was back here to kill him. It's important to make sure you don't leave evidence behind for the police to find and tie you to a crime scene, Johnny. Killing him there is risky for a lot of reasons."

"I don't understand though. How could you kill a person? Why? Is this what you're doing every time you tell me you have a special project to work on?" I want to understand, I do. He has to have a good reason for this, especially if Mom was helping him. She always made sure to do the right thing, so this can't be too bad, right?

"When I've kept you away in the past it was because I didn't think you were ready to understand what I was doing yet. You're 12 now, so I think you're ready. I was 12 when my daddy brought me in on this, and I think you're more mature than I was at that age. We're accomplishing two things with this process. Not only are we helping remove someone from the streets who abuses and victimizes people, but we're giving back to the land and the animals on that live there. We'll butcher him as much as possible and save the meat for the traps, catfish bait, and to feed the snapping turtles in our pond. I'll even mix some in with the meat scraps I take to Jim's farm for his pigs. He'll be far more helpful in death than he ever was in life. The rest will be mixed with the animal parts in the Biohazard bags we take to the landfill."

I stare at the man's face. He can't be more than 25 years old. Did my Dad do the wrong thing? He always obeys the law. He helps whoever he can whenever they need it. He volunteers and always treats everyone with respect. I don't know if this changes how I feel about him, but if this man really is as horrible as he says? Maybe he was right to take him off the street. "Mom was really ok with this?" I ask him.

"Yeah, honey. She was. She even helped me decide when someone needed to be taken care of. She had hoped to teach you about all of this as you grew up, and I wish she'd have been here to ease you into this but she's not. I don't know if I've gone about this the right way or not, but I'm hoping you'll think about everything I've told you and make your own decision. It's also important you understand this isn't something we do to serve vengeance on those who have wronged us personally. We do this to ensure people who hurt and put a drain on society can do something to give back, even in such a small way." He gives me a half smile and continues on. "So, what do you think? Do you think you can help me with this? Or do you want to sit this one out?"

Nibbling on my lip, I make the decision to trust my dad. "I'd like to help. But, maybe this time I can just hand you the tools like I used to? So I can learn how first."

The smile he sends my way is full of relief and pride, which makes me think I made the right decision. "Absolutely. If you start to think you can't handle it, just tell me, ok?"

"Ok." I pause and work up my courage. "Um, do you think I could come with you the next time this happens? Or, help you decide like Mom did? I think it would help me understand better."

"I think you're still a bit too young to come with me, and more people means more chances for mistakes, but we'll keep working on your training and one day you can come. Until then, you can help me make the decisions before, and help me in here after. Sound good?"

"Sounds perfect. Where do we start?"

Chapter 21

Evan pauses for a moment, seemingly lost in thought. I'm worried it'll be too much for him, that knowing is so much worse than assuming or imagining, but once again he surprises me. "Can you tell me about it? Or is it too personal?"

I release a relieved laugh at his judgement free tone. "Um, yeah. I can tell you. It's probably a lot to take in. Just... just let me know if it gets to be too much or you have questions, ok?"

"You've agreed to let me torture information out of your ex boyfriend, and offered to dispose of the body for me when I'm done. I'll have questions, but I'm pretty sure I can handle what you have to say." He's none too gently cleaning the blood off of his cousin, taking my word for the fact that Brandon has a weak stomach, but not caring how careful he is. Makes sense, since we're only going to rough him up more later.

"You know my dad was some kind of special forces right? And he was a survivalist?" At his nod I continue. "You knew him. He was a great man. He had a strong moral code of his own that was passed down from his dad. My Grandpa was a police officer, but he got tired of people getting away with the horrible things they did. One night, a member of the local government beat his wife and children almost to death and walked away with no charges simply because of who he was. The woman was one of his wife's best friends, and they took her and the kids in and after hearing her story and learning how many times he'd hurt them and gotten away with it. They tried to ask for help but even the local sheriff and mayor were in his pocket so nothing happened to him. So, he decided to take justice into his own hands."

A puff of air leaves Evan and I risk glancing over at him. "Kind of like Dexter? I loved that show."

Smiling in relief at the acceptance I see in him, I laugh lightly and continue. "Yeah, I guess. Just not so high tech or meticulous. One night when he knew the wife and kids were safe at his house and the husband was home alone, he took her house keys. He went to the house, beat him like he beat his wife, then killed him and staged everything to look like a break in. This was before forensics was too advanced, so robbery was a decently easy sell. He probably saved her life and the lives of her children that night, and he finally felt like he was doing something to help the people around him. From then on, he went after the ones he could when their victims went unprotected. He brought my dad in when he was twelve because he walked in on him while he was killing someone out here in the barn. He explained things, and my dad wanted to help. So, he taught him everything he knew. My dad took what he learned, and instead of going into the police, he went into the armed forces. His best friend growing up, Brian Dobbs, became an officer and dad used his intel to choose his targets sometimes. People that Brian was frustrated about not being able to put away."

"Did Brian know?" Evan has finished cleaning up Ryan and is seated in the chair I had set up for Ryan. I continue dressing the deer and think about his question.

"I'm not sure. I think he has to, but at the same time, my dad never mentioned anything. My mom knew, and she helped him sometimes. And like his dad taught him starting when he was twelve, my dad brought me in. He kind of expanded on what my grandpa did though. He had to be more careful because of the advancements in forensics, so he decided to use his knowledge of hunting and butchering the animals to get rid of the bodies. At first, he only brought me in after they were dead. I'd been hunting for years by then and was proficient with guns, but then he started adding combat and other weapons training. After a few years, when he finally thought I was ready he let me plan my own project."

Two Years Ago

"You ready Johnny?" Dad smiles as I jump up from tying my boots and tosses me his keys. "You drive. This is your show tonight."

"Do I look ok? Trina said he likes girls who look like they're a little edgy and don't have a ton of money. He probably thinks they don't have the ability to fight back against him or make sure he's held responsible." I'm wearing a pair of tight, ripped black jeans with a royal purple racer back tank and combat boots with a low heel. My eye makeup is smoky and my newly highlighted hair (hot pink and purple strands) is braided so the colors are hidden for the most part. Don't want to be too noticeable by the rest of the bar patrons.

"You look great," Dad says. "Just remember, if he's not there tonight, or if you can't convince him to leave with you, don't push it. We can find another way. I'd rather delay than make a mistake."

"I understand, but I don't want to let him hurt anyone else either. He's always there on Thursday nights. He'll be there, and I'll get him."

Rob is at the bar like every other Thursday night. He's seated at the bar watching a basketball game on the big screen, so I head to the side opposite to him to order a Diet Coke in a lowball glass so I look like I'm drinking a Jack and Coke. An empty pool table stands directly across from where he's sitting, so I decide to claim it and play alone. I've been playing pool for years over at Brandon's house, so I'm pretty good, but knowing what I do of his personality I play down my skills in the hopes that he'll come over to try to "help" me.

Sure enough, I'm only there a few minutes before I see him walk up to the table. He's the kind of attractive that should make it easy for him to pull women. He's tall and fit, his black hair is long enough to fall over his light blue eyes and his stubble gives him a roguish appearance. His smile is cocky as he takes a pull of his beer before speaking.

"Hi. I'm Rob. Are you here alone? I'd love to join you if you're looking for an opponent. I don't often see one as pretty as you." Is that really his opening line? Like, does that work? Thank goodness I'm supposed to play a little hard to get, because I'd hate myself if I had to pretend to fall for that bullshit.

Giving him a dismissive once over and fake smile, I return to my game. "No thanks" I say. Can't be too easy, right?

"Don't be like that. I'm not trying to hit on you or anything, you just looked lonely. If you change your mind I'll be at the bar." He returns to the bar, but instead of going back to his original seat, he grabs the seat closest to me, only a few feet away.

Perfect.

I don't respond and continue playing my game. I make a point to bend over enough to be seductive, but not obvious, while playing. A few shots in, I send my dad a text.

> **Me:** Call in 5. I need to pretend I'm being stood up.

> **Dad:** Affirmative. Be careful.

I've cleared about half of the table when my phone rings. I walk around the table to face Rob as I answer with a smile on my face. "Hey. Yeah I'm here, getting in a game of pool while I wait for you." I pause while dad chuckles on the other end and screw my face into an irritated frown. "Seriously? Again? No. Fuck you Brad, you had enough chances. If you wanted to be with me you'd be here." Another pause for effect, more chuckling from my old man. "Don't bother. I'll be gone before you get here. Lose my number." I hang up in a huff and shove my phone in my back pocket. Bracing my hands against the pool table I dip my head and shake it slowly. After a moment I take in a deep breath and release it, picking the pool cue and returning to my game.

I start a mental countdown. Five.. four... three... two...

"Hey, I know you said no earlier, but we couldn't help overhearing your call. Being bailed on sucks. Are you sure you don't want company?" Oh, he's good. All concern and sweetness, no hint of darkness showing through his baby blues.

"I don't know. I'm kind of irritated right now. I probably won't be great company." I let a little embarrassment and shame shine through, and by the flare in his eyes I've caught him hook, line, and sinker.

"Look, no pressure, only company. If you go home you'll just dwell on everything."

I chew on my lip and pretend to consider his offer. "Ok." I say hesitantly. "You rack."

"Great! So, what's your name?"

"Jennifer." I tell him. Close enough, right? "I need another drink. Do you want anything?" I want to beat him to asking me. I'd rather be the one fetching drinks in order to keep up the ruse of drinking alcohol. Wouldn't do to dull my senses and reaction times.

"Why don't you let me get one for you instead to make up for butting in on your game?"

"No way. You're being kind enough to cheer me up after being ditched. My treat." I insist with a sweet smile.

"Sure, ok thanks. I'll take whatever you're having." He continues racking the balls while I head to the bar. Jack and Coke for him, another Diet Coke in a lowball for me.

We play two games. I slowly act more and more amenable to his advances, and by the end of the second game I'm allowing casual touches and responding to his flirting with some of my own. Right before I sink the eight ball I give him a seductive smirk. I let him win the first game and waited until halfway through the second to bury him. Quickly, I take my phone and shoot a text to my dad to be ready.

"Thanks Rob, but I think I'm going to head home."

"Are you sure? I thought we were having a nice time. I'd love to spend more with you."

Bait, meet trap.

"Well, like I said. I want to head home, but I don't have to go alone." I pause to let that sink in. "You interested in coming to keep me company?"

His eyes flare with interest and triumph. "Sure. I walked here though, my place isn't too far. We could go there if you want?"

"That's ok." I tell him. "You can ride with me to my place and then grab an Uber or I can take you home later."

"Sounds perfect, Beautiful. Lead the way." He places his arm around my waist as we head out, and I lead him to my dad's SUV with blacked out windows. "Sweet ride" he says, impressed when I unlock the doors for us.

"Thanks, it's my dad's. Mine is in the shop right now." Dad is actually hunkered down in the back of the truck. I could have left him at home, but he insisted on coming for my first time. He's hidden, but can be over the back of the seat and defending me in seconds.

I drive out to the cabin, and we make small talk. It's about a 30-minute drive, but he doesn't even bat an eye at the distance because he's focused on getting laid. "You live out here alone?" he asks.

"No." I say. "I live with my dad, but he's on a work trip right now. He'll be back in a few days."

"Wow, this place is amazing!" he tells me, checking out the lake behind the house. "Have you lived here long?"

"Yeah, we've been here for years. Come on in." I hop out and lead him inside. "You want a drink?" I ask. "We've got beer and a fully stocked bar."

"Sure, thanks. I'll take a beer."

"Why don't you head out to the back porch and I'll grab some and meet you out there." I watch as he heads outside and looks out over the water. Grabbing a beer, I pull the small baggie of crushed up sedative out of my back pocket and pour it into the beer, giving the bottle a little swirl to make sure everything mixes in and dissolves. I grab myself a hard cider in a dark bottle to hide how much I do or don't drink, and head out to him.

"Here you go," I say, handing him the bottle. "Have a seat." He takes a seat on the couch I point to in front of the gas fire pit, facing away from the house and out towards the water. I turn the fire on to let him think I'm setting the mood before sitting on the other end of the couch and turning to face him. "Let's play a game. Have you ever played never have I ever? Drink if you've done something the other person says they haven't. You game?"

Chuckling, he takes a deep pull of his beer. "Sure" he says, a predatory smile on his handsome face. I'll go first. "Never have I ever had a one night stand."

Taking the gloves off early, huh? ok, I'll play. He obviously thinks I'm that kind of girl, so I smirk and take a sip of my drink. My turn now. "Never have I ever... followed *a random girl home after a night of drinking." He gives me a wink and takes another deep pull. His bottle is almost empty and his eyes are starting to droop.*

Perfect.

"Hang on, let me get you another drink and grab a blanket. I'll be right back." I head inside and walk past the kitchen to see my dad in the hallway to the garage. "You ready? He's starting to go under."

"Ready. Are you sure you are?" I shoot him my worst glare and cause him to chuckle and back up with his hands up in surrender. "Just checking Johnny. This is your show, I'm only here as backup."

"I got this. He's not going to be allowed to hurt anyone else. Wait until I call you to come out, ok? I don't want him to turn and see you and freak out." He gives me a nod and stays put while I head back out to the kitchen to grab him another drink with a little more sedative. I've wasted a beer though, because Rob is out cold when I return. His head has fallen back, his mouth open wide with a slight snore coming from him. Just to be sure he's really out, I call his name loudly and tap his cheek. No response other than a little grunting. "Dad! He's out. Freaking lightweight. Let's grab him and go."

I've proven in the past I'm capable of securing and transporting both living and dead bodies, so dad helps me take him out to the work room in the barn. I would just kill him, but after what he put my friend and countless other women through I need him to understand what's happening to him and why. He took their choice away from them. Their choice about what to do with their body, and their choice on how to fight back. He deserves to experience some of those feelings of helplessness and fear, even if only for a few moments before he dies.

I don't think I'm God. I don't think I'm the be all, end all when it comes to determining what is right and wrong. What I do think, however, is someone who victimizes people weaker than them simply because they can will never stop. Not until there's someone more powerful who is willing to step in. In this situation, that person is me. I may not be physically stronger, or have more money or influence, but I have the training, the backing of my father, and most importantly, I have the absolute determination in me that he will never hurt another woman.

Rob is seated in an old wooden chair in the center of the workroom. We've moved the work table over to the side of the room and there is a ten-foot radius of blank space surrounding him. Dad and I sit in chairs we've pulled in from the attached sitting room and wait for him to wake. He's got a cup of coffee and a few different hunting and fishing magazines he's been meaning to catch up on. I've got a Diet Coke, a bag of gummy bears, and my Kindle.

After a few hours of comfortable silence, Rob starts to stir. I'm a little irritated because I just got to the start of a sexy part in my book, but now I can at least save it until I'm in the privacy of my own room later. I stash my Kindle, drink, and comfortable chair back in the other room and grab a handful of gummies and a folding chair and head back to plop myself down a few feet in front of Rob so I'll be the first thing he notices when he wakes. After a few minutes he finally opens his eyes and focuses on me, forehead creased in confusion as he takes in my change of clothes. I've gone from my cute outfit and braid to coveralls and a tight bun. My flirty smile has changed to a mask of indifference.

"What... what happened? Where am I?" he slurs out. Trying to move, he looks down and realizes he's tied securely to the chair by arms, legs, and torso. "What the fuck? What is this?"

"This? We're still playing our game Rob. It's my turn though, and I only have one more question." I purse my lips and cock my head like I'm curious what his response will be.

"Fuck you, you crazy bitch! Let me go right now. Do you have any idea who I am?" He's so angry spit is flying out of his mouth while he snarls at me.

"Oh, I know exactly who you are. That's why you're here. Now, how you answer will determine what happens next. Tell me the truth and I'll make things easy on you. Lie to me... well, let's just say you don't want to lie to me because I already know the answer to the question. It won't end well for you because I'm not feeling too patient tonight. I have to work tomorrow morning and don't want to be up too late." I pause, looking him over and knowing he's going to try to make this hard but betting he'll crack quickly. "Are you ready? Good. Ok, here goes. Never have I ever... forced myself on a woman after she told me no!"

His face pales immediately, but he tries to hide it with bravado. "Fuck you, you crazy bitch, I don't need to force myself on anyone! Have you seen me? They beg for it! Now let me the fuck go. You are going to regret this!"

"Wrong answer" I say calmly as I stand and make my way over to him. He's starting to sweat at his hairline and I can tell it's starting to sink in that he may not make it out of this room alive. Pulling my butterfly knife out of my coverall pocket, I flip it open and touch the tip of the blade to his pathetic little dick, hard enough he can feel it, but not yet hard enough to cut. He tries frantically to back away from the sharp blade but he's held fast so he has nowhere to move. "Try again. Never have I ever committed rape." I press the blade closer with each new sentence, and by the time I stop talking his pants have split and a small line of blood is trickling onto the chair. "Never have I ever forced myself on a woman who didn't want me. Never have I ever taken away a woman's choice. Never have I ever put my selfish needs ahead of a woman's right to decide if she wants to share her body. Never have I ever decided my own personal yes should outweigh someone else's no. Never have I ever raped a woman named Trina and threatened to kill her if she ever told anyone. And last but not least, never have I ever used my family's money and connections to sweep their reports under the rug."

He's crying now, a keening sound that's getting louder the harder I press my blade to him. "Ok, ok yes! Please stop! I'm sorry, ok? I couldn't help it! They started getting me all worked up, and then when it came time to follow through, the bitches tried to tell me no. ME! No one says no to me. Do you understand who I am? Do you see what I look like? They offered it whether they want to admit it or not, so I took what they offered!" Blood starts trickling where I have broken the skin and he yelps in fear. "Please, please I'll never do it again. Please let me go. I'll do whatever you want, and I swear I'll never do it again." At this point his tears are mixing with his snot and spit. He's already broken like the worthless child he is.

"You're sorry? So, you don't want to die?" I ask him, removing my blade from his dick and taking a step back.

"Yes! I'm so sorry." He begs between his hiccupping sobs. "I swear I won't ever do it again. Please don't kill me, my family will miss me. I'm going to medical school so I can help people. Please, I don't want to die."

"Yeah, well. Here's the thing. See, you got me all worked up about killing you, and now you're trying to back out." I shrug with an apologetic frown on my face, and then walk around him to stand at his back. I place a hand on his shaking shoulder, bending to whisper in his ear from behind. I lock eyes with my dad across the room as I say "Do you know who I am? No one says no to me."

And then I slit his throat.

Chapter 22

Evan listened to me tell the story of my first kill without judgement. A few minutes in, he came over to me and asked if he could help me work while I talked. It was kind of nice, having someone in here with me, so I had him glove up and hand me tools as I needed them. I explained what I was doing briefly, and he asked me to teach him everything so he can help again. Having someone to teach, like my dad taught me, fills me with a mixture of pride and sadness. Pride, because I can share this skill that my dad shared with me, and sadness because he's not here to witness this. He loved Evan, I think he actually preferred him over Ryan while we were growing up, and I think he'd be impressed with the man he's become and be comforted to know I may have found someone that can help me since he can't anymore.

So far, the only question Evan has asked is if anyone ever suspected me in Rob's disappearance, and as far as I am aware the answer is no. I have just finished up with the deer when my phone pings with an incoming text. Pulling my gloves off, I pull my phone out of my coverall pocket.

Bran: Daddy's here. Open the door, k?

I roll my eyes and huff a laugh. "Brandon's here. Let's go let him in. I want to get Ryan situated and go get some lunch."

Evan follows me out of the workroom and into the front room of the barn as I head to the door to let Brandon in. I stare in shock for a moment before I am laughing so hard I have to brace a hand on my knee to keep myself standing. What the fuck is wrong with my best friend? He has six black shopping bags with some kind of red script filled to the brim in his hands, and he's wearing my white oversized sunglasses that have been missing for months and a fucking feather boa. A black, pink, and silver feather boa, draped around his neck like some sort of high fashion scarf.

At my laugh, his smile falls and turns into a haughty scowl. "What? Don't laugh at me because you don't understand fashion!" At that, I'm laughing so hard I can't breathe.

All of a sudden, I'm going into a full on panic attack. Ever since my dad was murdered, I've been getting them. Weirdly enough, it happens most often when I'm laughing. I think my brain gets overstimulated and shuts down, and it was so bad at first I went to my family doctor to find out what was going on. My usual doctor wasn't there that day, so I saw his partner, and when I explained what was happening he looked me dead in the eyes and said "That's not a thing." Like... what? Because my body proves that it most certainly is. I never saw him again, and after seeing my regular doctor and telling him what happened he didn't last much longer at that practice. I now have Xanax for emergencies, but I try to avoid taking them if possible.

Brandon immediately drops his bags. "Shit, I'm sorry Killer. It's ok. You're ok, just breathe. There you go. You can do it. Deep breath in and out. Concentrate on me."

"What's wrong?" Evan sounds a little panicked. "What's happening to her?"

In a calm voice, Brandon responds while rubbing circles on my back. "She's fine. Just a little panic attack. They started happening after her dad died. No, no stop that. Deep breath. That's my girl. In... and out. Come on, you're ok Killer, I have you."

"Can I help? What should I do?" Evan is calmer but still sounds concerned. I want to comfort him but I'm not capable like this. Tears are streaming down my face and I cannot pull oxygen into my lungs, my heart is racing, and my chest is tightening even further. I'm dying, which totally sucks. The thought of dying a virgin makes me cry even harder.

Good job, brain, way to calm things down!

"If you want, come over here and help her breathe. Talk to her and take her mind off of it. This one is mild, so it shouldn't last too long."

Evan walks over and kneels in front of me. Reaching up, he places his hands on my cheeks and wipes my tears away with his thumbs, much like I did with him earlier. His beautiful green eyes are locked on mine and full of a strength I never knew he possessed. His voice is hypnotizing as he soothes me. "Breathe for me, baby girl. Match me. Come on. In... out. Copy me. There you go. Slow down. Deep breath in, slow breath out." Brandon's hand falters on my back for one brief second when Evan calls me 'baby girl,' but he recovers quickly and resumes his task. Staring into Evan's eyes gives me a focal point, and his exaggerated breathing gives me something to try to match my own to. I mimic his breaths until my heart rate slows and the grip around my chest loosens. A few minutes later, I'm breathing steadily again but feel drained.

With my breathing back to normal, I allow my eyes to fall closed. Because his hands are still cradling my face, I can feel Evan moving towards me and Brandon removes his hand as he steps back to give us a moment. Evan hesitates before reaching me, and his pause brings a small smile to my lips. Always looking for consent, this one. Silly boy, he doesn't realize it's already been given.

Eyes still closed and lips still smiling, I lean forward to close the distance and whisper "Thank you" against his lips before I place a sweet kiss there. Opening my eyes and leaning back, I notice Evan's cheeks and ears have pinked up. Freakin' adorable.

From behind me, I can hear an amused throat clearing and I smile at Evan while rolling my eyes.

"So, um. If I say that was kind of hot are you going to string me up too? Because... yeah."

"Shut up perv. Now, take that shit off and tell me what the fuck all of this is." Now that I'm not distracted by my favorite sunglasses and a giant feather boa, I notice the bags are all from his favorite sex shop.

No. Oh nononononononono. What the hell did he do? I asked for two things. Two! Why was a sex shop brought into this equation?

"Oh, this? Well you asked for restraints and a gag, so I got those. Hang on, let me grab those first." He spends like five minutes rifling through the bags without letting me see what's in them. Evan stands up and moves behind me to wrap his arms around me, holding me tight he nuzzles the side of his face against mine. "You ok, baby girl?" he whispers into my ear.

"Yeah, I'm fine. It happens sometimes, since... my dad. Brandon has banned me from watching funny compilation videos on TikTok because they set me off a lot. I'm drained, but fine. We'll figure out what the hell this crazy man is doing, get Ryan settled, then head back to the house for lunch and maybe a nap. Sound good?"

"Yeah, sounds good. I do need to go back for Gran at some point though. I hated leaving her there, but I was so afraid if I stayed I wouldn't reach you in time, and she was already gone."

"Wait, what?" Brandon asks, paused in his searching. "What's wrong with your Gran?"

I spin in his arms and wrap my arms around his neck. "I'm so sorry, Ev." I give him another sweet kiss before answering Brandon. "Ryan killed her. He pushed her down the stairs and Evan found her this morning. She was still alive when he got to her, she warned him he was coming after me next, and then she passed. Evan wanted to stay with her but was afraid Ryan would hurt me if I let my guard down." Evan's face is once again full of heartbreak, and I want to hold him to me until he doesn't hurt anymore.

"Shit, man. I'm so sorry." Brandon's teasing demeanor falls away and honest sympathy radiates from him. He may always be a total goofball, but he knows there is a time and place, and it isn't now.

"Why don't we clean up here and get Ryan situated, then have some lunch at the cabin and explain what's going on to Brandon. Together, we can figure out a story to explain where Ryan is when someone notices he's missing, like Daniel or his dad. Then, I'll go with you to your house so you can drive the Explorer back and I'll stay with you while we call and have her taken care of. I don't want you to have to go through that alone."

His small, sad smile breaks my heart all over again. "Ok. Sounds like a plan. Thank you. For all of this."

"Of course. I-"

My sentence is cut off by a maniacal "Aha!" behind me. I turn to see Brandon proudly holding up a pair of zebra print fuzzy handcuffs and a... rubber ball gag? Apparently adult time is over already. That may be a record.

Sputtering, I ask "What the fuck? Brandon I asked for restraints, not a good time!" I groan and hide my face against Evan's chest, shaking my head from side to side while his chest rumbles with laughter. "What did I do to deserve this?" I lament, though no one takes me seriously.

"Oh stop, you love me. I've been waiting on this moment for years and you know it. I had a feeling something was going on between you and Evan and as always it appears I was right. So, I came prepared." He smiles like a child proud of the lumpy ashtray he's made in art class for his parents who have never smoked a day in their lives. "Some of this is for him, some of this is for you" he says with an eyebrow wiggle. "Come on, let's go into the other room and I'll show you what I got."

Evan and I check on Ryan before we follow Brandon into the sitting room, and he's still out cold. I check his restraints and see he's as secure as he can be until I use those damned fuzzy cuffs. As I turn the corner in the sitting room to see everything Brandon is laying out on the couch and coffee table, it takes everything I have to not turn around and leave out of sheer embarrassment.

Or string him up next to Ryan.

The couch and coffee table are covered, I mean covered, in sex toys. I'm not sure why he's grouped them together the way he has, but he always has a method to his madness. The table holds the cuffs and ball gag, but also a bunch of other weird stuff that I never imagined I'd be seeing in person. Nipple clamps, a riding crop, a paddle, two cat-o-nine tails (one leather, one with strands made of chain), a penis cage, an electrical wand, and stuff that I can't even figure out. The couch is covered with things like the boa, a few dildos and vibrators or varying shapes and sizes, lubes, condoms, massage oils... is that... no. "Is that a strap on belt?!"

Brandon gives an over the top wink to Evan, whose face pales when he responds "Sure is, honey."

"Bran, what in the hell is all of this? Are you nuts?" I am so beyond confused right now.

"Listen, I may not be able to participate in whatever is about to go down because I am such a delicate flower, and I may not know what is happening yet. But what I do know is you always have a reason for what you do, even this kind of thing. So, if I can't help by participating, I sure as hell will participate by giving you whatever tools I think could help accomplish your task. My specialty is to make it entertaining while it's happening." He's pointing to the table while he speaks. He switches to his opposite hand to point at the couch. "That stuff is just because. If you and Evan are starting something up, you're going to need help"

"Wait." Evan stops him with a hand held up and a look of confusion and horror. "What is that thing?" He points at a cylindrical looking device with molded lips on the end laying on the couch.

"That? That's for you big guy. I wanted to make sure you were taken care of if our girl keeps holding out on you."

I sigh, head bowed in defeat. "I hate you sometimes."

"No you don't, Killer. You love me." He gives me a kiss on the cheek before heading to the door. "I'll head to the house and start lunch." He pauses at the threshold to the door and peers in Ryan's direction. Turning back to me he says "I think he's awake." I join him at the door and sure enough, he's glaring right at us. He's trying to say something but his mouth is duct taped shut, so his words comes out garbled.

Walking past him to the exit, Brandon gives him a bro nod. "Hey man. Sorry I can't stay and chat, but I'm starving and someone needs to cook for these crazy kids. Enjoy the gifts I left for you!"

And with that, my best friend saunters out and leaves us to our prisoner.

Because I don't have any other options, we have to use what Brandon brought. Part of me thinks its poetic justice. Ryan accuses me of being a whore, and part of his entrapment and torture will be facilitated with sex toys. I don't want the zip ties to cut much more into his wrist because we don't want him to bleed out, so instead of fighting him to stay still, Evan punches him across the face again to knock him out.

Brandon came through and brought padded nylon wrist and ankle restraints that will work better than the cuffs thank God. Leaving the zip ties on at first, I bind his wrists and feed a carabiner through a few of the chain links connecting each wrist cuff together. I attach the carabiner to a loop of metal connected at the top of the hook, and leave the chains already wrapped around his wrists in place before I take the pair of ankle cuffs and secure his feet together before snipping the zip ties off. I was going to put the ball gag on him now, but decide leaving it off will give him the false hope someone might hear him scream and come to his rescue.

Evan and I both step back and inspect him. I think he's about as secure as possible for now, so it's time to clean up the workroom and move on with the rest of our day.

"Ok, let's clean up and head to the house. My client doesn't need the meat until tomorrow, so I'll store it here for now. Alexa, play a random playlist." Raise Hell by Dorothy starts playing and I laugh at the perfection of the moment. Evan helps me stow the meat in the freezer and refrigerator and sort everything else into their respective bags and boxes. Once we move those to the front room, I grab my waders and hand him a pair of my dad's instructing him to put them on.

With the room clear of everything except Ryan, I grab the spray bottle of Cavicide and explain what I'm doing, in case he needs to clean up when I'm not here. "This stuff is amazing. It kills viruses, bacteria, and fungus. I always spray everything down to make sure there aren't any diseases or creepy crawlies that are blood borne or otherwise left behind. I spray it everywhere, leave it to sit for at least three minutes, then spray down the room with the hose. If my guest is human, I'll come back and wipe the room down with bleach too. I do that once a month anyway, but always after that."

Cleanup is done quickly, and we're both hungry, so we leave Brandon's gifts where he left them and head back to the cabin with Evan's bike thrown into the back of the UTV so he can ride up front with me.

Ok, so I took the penis gummies with me.

CHAPTER 23

When we arrive back at the cabin, we're greeted by the smell of grilled cheese and tomato soup. Brandon knows it's my comfort meal, and I appreciate the thought. Heading to the fridge, I grab myself a Diet Coke, and ask the boys what they want. Brandon has water, so I grab Evan a Dr. Pepper and help set up the island for us to eat. While Brandon pulls the sandwiches out of the oven where he left them to warm, I ladle soup into bowls for each of us and set them out as Brandon and Evan take their seats at the island. Walking past Brandon to sit in the space they left open between them, I kiss his cheek and whisper a thanks for making lunch.

All three of us are silent for a few moments while we eat and contemplate what's going on. Unsurprisingly, Brandon breaks the silence first. "So, care to explain why we have Ryan tied up in your barn? I'm not complaining or anything. He has seemed different since you guys came back, but this seems a little more serious than because he turned into an asshole."

Evan and I share a look, and it seems he's conflicted on where to start. I decide to take the burden off of him, swallowing my mouthful of cheesy goodness before saying "Long story short? Ryan pushed the Gran down the stairs this morning most likely because she threatened to kick him out of her will and send him back to his dad. Evan overheard them arguing about it last night, and he found her dying at the bottom of the stairs this morning. Then, when he came to hang out with me while I worked, we wanted to talk so I took off the top of my coveralls since I got some blood on them and he freaked when he saw my arms."

"What do you mean, when he saw your arms? What about them? Hasn't he seen them before?" Brandon and Evan are both confused, because I didn't explain this part to Evan either.

"Apparently he hadn't seen them since they've been back, because when I turned around after dropping the sleeves he went white as a ghost. He went crazy, saying I ruined everything and calling me a whore."

"What did you ruin?" Brandon asked, inspecting me. "What's wrong with your arms? I don't understand."

"He was talking about my tattoos. He said it had taken him four years to convince his dad I wasn't a whore because he saw us kissing the day before they took you away." I say, looking at Evan. "He said I was supposed to become his wife and help him take over running the community when his dad retires in a few years. Become the pliant and obedient wife." I scoff and take another bite of my sandwich before continuing. "He said my hair could be fixed, but we couldn't hide my arms. According to him, tattoos are a desecration of the body and can't be overlooked, unlike my hair. As if he didn't know I was planning on getting them. He helped me come up with the idea in the first place!" I'm seething all over again. Who does this asshole think he is? Did he really think he could come back here and make me into the perfect religious Stepford Wife?

"I'm so sorry Jen. I knew he'd gotten bad, but I didn't know it was this bad. Gran and I were both hoping he'd calm down once he was here and away from his dad, but obviously it didn't happen. I never dreamed he'd hurt her, or you, but then again I never could have imagined he'd kill his own mother either."

Brandon coughs on the water he drank and ends up spitting it all over the counter. "What? He killed his mom? I thought she ran off with someone!" He uses his napkin to clean up his mess while staring at Evan in shock.

"We thought she did too. Ryan told me he and his dad killed her and her lover when they were trying to run away together. He said they were trying to get Evan out too. Ryan's dad beat her lover to death while they made her watch, then Ryan strangled her for embarrassing his dad in front of the community."

"Charles was an amazing guy. I'm not sure what he saw in her, but he's the one that taught me my trade. He kind of took me under his wing when I got to the community, and he was the only support I had for the first year. He was better to me than Uncle Patrick ever was. He didn't deserve that kind of death." I lean over and rest my head on his shoulder to show him my support, and he kisses the top of my head in thanks.

"So, why didn't you just kill him?" Brandon asks.

"Because... I think there's a lot we don't know, and it's what Evan wants. He threatened to kill me before I knocked him out. Evan showed up because his Gran told him Ryan was coming for me, but we're not sure what he said to make her worry about that. It sounds like there's a lot going on with this cult of theirs and Evan is worried we may be in danger. Plus... Ryan told us his dad killed Evan's mom. She didn't run off." Head still on his shoulder, I grip his thigh in support. His mom was an absent mother at best, but it doesn't mean she deserved to die.

Brandon lets out a low whistle. "Shit man. This is so fucked up. What are we going to be doing with him? What are we going to do about your Gran?"

I press a kiss to Evan's shoulder before sitting up, but leave my hand resting on his thigh. "Evan is going to do whatever he wants with Ryan. He's secure enough for now, so he's not going anywhere. I was thinking we could head back to Gran's house, I'll drive the truck and you can drive the Explorer, and we'll act like we were out together and you brought me home to see her since it's been a while since I've seen her. I'll stay with you when you call the police, I don't want you to be alone for that."

"What do we say to them though? Do we tell them about Ryan?" Evan's tone is uncertain.

"I think we tell them as much of the truth as possible. We tell them you left to run errands this morning and then you came by the barn to hang out after dropping her prescription off. You have to be able to account for stopping at home this morning, so you can say you only ran in and dropped her prescription in the kitchen before heading out again and didn't see her. Then, if they ask, admit you heard them arguing last night and what it was about, say you haven't heard from him all day and speculate that he left on his own. To be safe, we should grab some gloves before we head over and move his clothes and mix them in with yours so it looks like some of his is gone. We don't want to waste time or get caught trying to get rid of anything. Brandon, do you think you could take his cell and head to the bus station? Keep the cell but remove the SIM card when you're there and destroy it before you leave in case they track his phone."

"Of course. Damn, I forget how well your dad trained you sometimes. Remind me not to piss you off bad enough" Brandon says with a chuckle. "Now, the most important question of all..."

I raise a single eyebrow at him at his pause. This is going to be something stupid, like we don't have enough to deal with right now.

"What is going on... here?" he asks, pointing his finger between me and Evan.

"Fuck off, Bran. Let it go. Now isn't the time, ok?" I give him my best scowl before turning to Evan with a smile. "You ready to go? I'm sure Brandon won't mind doing the dishes."

"Oh yeah, no, you two kids go ahead. I'll clean everything up after making this delicious and filling lunch for you, with little to no thanks for that or my shopping trip. No... no don't argue... I have this handled."

Yeah, I wasn't planning to argue. "Thanks, boo!" Grabbing a few pairs of black nitrile gloves from the pantry, I kiss Brandon's cheek before grabbing Evan's hand and pulling him out through the garage. I don't know how much more he can take, but I'm going to be there for him through it all, just like he always was for me.

In order to make everything work, I head upstairs while Evan calls the police. Ryan doesn't have much here, so I slip on my gloves and grab the majority of everything in his room and move it to Evan's, mixing their clothes and things together so it's not obvious they're different sizes. I mess with the remaining items a bit so it appears he packed in a hurry and left some things behind. Luckily, they share a bathroom and bath products, so there isn't much to be moved around in there. The whole process takes me maybe about ten minutes, so I make my way downstairs and make sure the prescription bag is in the kitchen where it's supposed to be.

Evan is sitting at the bottom of the stairs with his head in his hands, and his poor Gran is lying in front of him broken. Before sitting next to him I remove my gloves, stow them in my purse and open the front door to allow entry when the police arrive. He called Ryan's phone once after hanging up with the 9-1-1 and left a voicemail. I take his phone from him to call Ryan's phone again, then use my own phone to call him as well. We need to act like we're trying to reach him to tell him what happened. I text him as well, just in case they check, waiting a few minutes between each.

> **Me:** Hey, can you call me?

> **Me:** Please call me, or come home. We need to talk asap.

> **Me:** Ryan, please. It's your Gran, something happened. Please call Evan or me asap. It's important.

I didn't hear what he told dispatch when he called them, but he must have made it clear she's been gone for a while, because it takes about thirty minutes for them to arrive, and when they do it's without lights and sirens.

It takes a few hours, but the police and the coroner finally leave. We've both been questioned, but they seem satisfied with our answers. They are, however, concerned Ryan and his things aren't here and he isn't answering his phone. We give them all the information we have, like his dad's phone number and address, and they take Gran's body away. The officers inform Evan they will contact his uncle, and they haven't said anything about whether they believe if an accident or if foul play was involved, so I'll wait a few days and then call Brian to see if he can provide me with any information.

I send Evan upstairs to take a shower and pack an overnight bag before I start cleaning the foyer. The officers on site gave us the go ahead, and I don't want Evan to have to worry about dealing with this mess. I don't want him to see it more than he has to, and I definitely don't want him to have to clean up his own grandmother's blood.

"You didn't have to do that, Jen," he says, startling me as I finish drying the floor. "I could have done it."

"I know, but I wanted to. Besides, I have far more experience. Let's get out of here for the night, and we can deal with everything else tomorrow, ok?"

"Thank you," he says with a kiss. "Let's go."

CHAPTER 24

We decided to head to the cabin for the evening. On the way, he calls his new boss and explains what happened. He is a wonderful man who gives him a week off to make arrangements and grieve, and even though Brandon said he'd cover for me for the next few days I still call Mrs. C to tell her what's going on myself. She loved both Evan and Ryan growing up, and knew his Gran well, so knowing how Evan is all alone in this now she told me to take the week off with him to help him make arrangements.

I set him up in the guest room and show him where everything is before we head outside to relax with some drinks on the lounge chairs. I think we're both overwhelmed at this point, so we avoid talking about Ryan, his Gran, the cult, or anything else that may bring up negative emotions.

"Why aren't you living out here? This house is amazing, and sitting out here empty. It's not too far from town and work, so it seems perfect to me." Evan is looking out over the property with a smile. He always did love this place.

"Honestly? I don't think I'm ready to be here alone, not without my dad being here. I have a few months left on my lease, so I'm trying to decide if I want to stay there when it's up or not. I do have some plans for the house, a little updating to make it mine. My dad's room is so much bigger, and I would want to live in the master but I feel like it would be weird if I didn't make it my own space first. Like... I don't know, kind of like I'm living with a ghost."

"What kind of changes do you want to make? I could help, if you wanted. I'm not a licensed contractor yet, but I've done basically everything. I could do it for you, and you'd only have to pay for the supplies. I wouldn't charge you for labor, you know that."

"That would be amazing. There are a few things I want to do, but I don't even know where to start. Like, I want to put a hot tub out here, and I was thinking about adding on to the dock so I could build a covered area with seating. Inside, I want to do a few small things downstairs, but mostly I want to update the master. Dad built this house after my mom died, so the bathroom and closet in there is very masculine and utilitarian. I want to expand the closet and put an organization system in there, and then put a soaking tub in the bathroom and expand the shower, maybe add a double vanity. I want one of those two button toilets too. The bathroom would have to expand into his workout room, but I wanted to get rid of that stuff anyway. I was thinking about turning it into a reading room and adding built-in shelves to make it more like a personal library, so losing a small amount of space won't be a big deal. It's a lot to do, but if I'm going to live here without him, I need to make it my own."

"Understandable," he muses. "I'm comfortable doing everything you want, except maybe the dock footings. I may not be able to do all of it myself, but if I need help I'm sure we can rope Brandon or Daniel into lending me their muscle. If they can't, I'm sure I can get one or two of the guys at work to help on a weekend for free or cheap."

"That would be amazing!" I say, excitedly. "I would have to pay you though. It's too much work for you to do for free."

"Hell no. You're helping me with all of this, it's the least I can do. Besides, maybe you'll let me hang in the hot tub once it's here. Using it would go a long way to helping my sore muscles after a long day of free labor. Massages can help with that too, I've heard."

"I can probably make that happen. Hot tub snuggles and massages aren't too expensive, I suppose." I can feel my cheeks pinking up, slightly nervous he's staying the night tonight. I don't think he's going to try to pressure me to go too far too fast, but the temptation and proximity may get to us.

"Come here," he says, holding his hand out to me after lifting the back of his lounger to a more upright position.

"What? Why?" I ask."Because I want you to sit with me." He wiggles his fingers at me to coax me to take his hand. "Come here, Jen. Let's talk."

"We are talking," I huff as I rise from my chair to walk over to him. Taking my hand, he pulls me down to sit between his legs so he can wrap his arms around me and place his chin on my shoulder. Butterflies start rising in my stomach, something I don't think I've ever experienced on this level before.

"I know," he whispers behind my ear and then speaking softly into my skin, "but I want to talk about what happened earlier. With us."

Shit. "You know, the last time I had this conversation, you both disappeared for four years." I release a forced chuckle, but tense when I feel Evan still behind me. "What? What's wrong?"

"What do you mean the last time? Do you usually not have these conversa-tions? Should I not have brought it up? I don't know how this relationship stuff works. If that's what this even is, I mean. Shit, I'm sorry, forget it. Forget I said anything." He starts to lean back like he's embarrassed, but I grab his arm to hold him in place.

"No, it's ok. I meant, the last time I had this talk was with Ryan. I haven't... look, I've been on a few dates but I've never had a boyfriend or anything. I just never clicked with anyone. So, you should be aware before you decide you want to be involved with me. I have literally no experience with this." I shrug as much as his embrace will allow me to. "So, fair warning." I don't think it will make a difference to him, but it's important to me to share that piece of myself if he wants to try to start something.

Evan's body relaxes against me the more I speak and his forehead drops to press to the curve between my neck and shoulder. "Thank God" he chuckles.

"What do you mean? Thank God for what?"

"I don't have any experience either. You've been it for me since we were kids, Jen. I was trying to work up the courage to tell you before they moved us away. I wanted to make it back to you the whole time, even knowing you wanted Ryan. I thought if I could get to you, talk to you, I could make you see me. That I could make you mine."

"Yours? Is that what you want?" The butterflies that were flitting around in my stomach moments ago are turning into a full-blown hurricane.

"Fuck yes, it's what I want. I'll do whatever it takes to make you mine. I have to give you my own warning though," he pauses to press a kiss to my neck. "Once I have you," another kiss, higher this time, "I'm not going to let you go." He raises one of his hands and uses it to turn my face to his. He must be able to see the heat in my own gaze because he gives me a satisfied smirk before dipping his lips to mine.

I melt back into his body, and his tongue caresses mine in languid, teasing strokes for a few moments before his hand drops from my chin to my neck. With one arm banded tightly around my rib cage, and one hand gently squeezing around my throat, I can feel the coiled strength in him and his struggle to hold himself back from asking for more. I can also feel the moisture pooling between my legs, and I moan softly and squirm to try to ease the tension there. His erection is growing hard against my back, and when I accidentally-on-purpose roll my hips back to rub up against him, the arm around my chest drops to my waist and both his hand and arm tighten around me while he groans into my mouth.

"Don't," he growls. "I don't have much in the way of self-control right now. As much as I may want to, we shouldn't rush this."

I play pout up at him and press a kiss to his jaw. "Understood, sir. So, let me get this straight. If I say yes? If I say I want to be with you, I'm stuck? Like, forevzies?" I let out a giggle at the fake sternness he sends my way.

Pausing to think for a moment, he asks "Do I have to use that word?" with a dawning horror on his handsome face.

"Afraid so. It's forevzies or nothing."

Hanging his head in defeat for a moment, he gathers his courage before looking back into my eyes. "Forevzies it is then. I've waited for you for seven long years, Jen. If you're telling me I finally have you, though, I won't give you up. Think about it before you say yes. You don't have to answer me now, but I will not lose you again. If you say yes, you're mine. No going back, not after I've had the chance to be with you."

I lean back into him, my head laying back on his shoulder so I can stare up at the night sky. I want to say yes, based solely on the fact that being with him feels... right. But he's right. I don't want to make a rash decision and hurt him in the long run. The question is, am I ready to make this decision? I've never even been on a third date with someone. Am I really ready to commit to Evan so quickly?

It seems like it's happening so fast, yet I also know him so well. I've always been able to read him, just like he could me, and though four years undoubtedly changed both of us a great deal, I can still see his heart. He's still the same Evan underneath his new, harder exterior. His thoughts, first and foremost, are for others before himself. He was struggling with the death of his Gran at the hands of his cousin, and his first concern was my comfort. My feelings of safety. He's selfless, kind, generous, and beautiful. He's funny, sweet, and loyal. He could be mine if I trusted him enough to take the chance.

I come back to myself when Evan presses a kiss to my temple, and I realize the entire time I've been thinking, I've been rubbing the belly of my turtle pendant. Out of everyone I know, Evan was the one person who knew me well enough to provide what I needed most when I didn't even know what that was, and did it without expectation of validation or thanks.

"Ok," I whisper.

He stills against me as soon as I speak. "Ok?" he asks, just as quiet.

"Ok," I repeat, turning to press a kiss against his cheek. "forevzies."

Who knew such a stupid ass word could stop my heart and tilt my world on its axis? I told her the truth, if she agreed to be mine, there would be no turning back. I've waited years to claim her, after this small taste there is no way I'll ever be able to go back to the way things once were. Being around her for over a year after I kissed her the first time was hard enough, but I didn't have a choice. I was too uncertain of my place in her world then. She didn't remember it, so I had to wait until the time was right.

Five Years Ago

Jen was off yesterday in school, and no matter what I did she wouldn't tell me why. Ryan has practice this morning, so I thought I'd stop by and check on her. Most of the time if it's just the two of us she'll open up to me, so I'm hoping she will today too. It kills me when she's sad, and I can tell that's what this is. She's so bright, always so full of life, and yesterday it seemed as if all her light was snuffed out.

No one answers when I ring the doorbell, so I decide to check behind the house in case she's hanging out on the dock like she does when she needs to think. She's not on the dock, but she is in the yard, sitting facing the water with her back to me. Her posture is slumped and her body is slightly shaking, and I can see her arm is moving but I can't tell what she's doing. Walking up beside her, I finally notice she's petting a turtle eating a head of lettuce while silent tears fall into her lap.

I drop down to sit next to her and accidentally brush her knee with my own. She startles and looks up at me with heartbreak in her beautiful green eyes. "Hey, Jenny." I say. "What's wrong?" Whatever it is, I want to fix it for her. I never want to see this look in her eyes again.

I can't fix it though. I can only sit and listen as she tells me today is the anniversary of her mother's death. She tells me how wonderful her mother was, and how she feeds a turtle every year on this day to remember and feel close to her because her mother believed turtles were lucky, and about how they used to search for them together. I hold her hand as she tells me these things, and when she's done, I tell her "You're lucky you had such a great mom, even if you only had her for a little while. I bet she's watching over you and sending you some luck whenever you need it."

I wanted to make things better, but she starts crying harder. I can't stand seeing her like this, so I pick her up and pull her into my lap to rock her like my mom used to when I cried as a child, before her addiction got the better of her. I don't think of her like a child, but it's the only thing I can think to do and it gives me the opportunity to hold her.

It takes a long time for her to stop crying, but she finally tires herself out so much that she quiets and eventually falls asleep. Not wanting to let her go yet, I stay with her for about an hour until the turtle finishes his lettuce and my legs start to fall asleep. Carefully, so I don't wake her, I slowly rise with her still in my arms and I carry her up to the porch. I gently lay her down on one of the lounge chairs, and brush the hair out of her face that was stuck to her cheeks with her tears. Unable to help myself, I lean down and press a gentle kiss to her petal soft lips, and at that moment I am sure there could never be anyone else for me.

If I could, I would take all this pain from her, but since I can't I will make sure I am here for her whenever she needs someone to lean on, and I will make sure I'm here for her on this day every year going forward. I'll be there for her, so she knows she isn't alone.

Nine months later I'm browsing the jewelry cases in a department store while Uncle Patrick gets his watch fixed and I see a sterling silver turtle pendant necklace. An older woman comes over to ask me if I need help, and when she takes it out for me I know I have to buy it for her. The detail is amazing. The head, tail, arms, and legs all move independently of the shell, and the belly has the little shell grooves like a real turtle.

Not wanting Uncle Patrick to realize what I'm doing, I ask the woman if she can put it in a small box for me but hide the transaction from him. I tell her it's a surprise gift for my mom and my uncle can't keep a secret, so she's happy to play along.

As much as I want to run to her and give her the necklace right away, I hold on to it, so I can give it to her on the next anniversary. I know she's embarrassed about her breakdown last year, she's never talked to me about what happened, so I decide leaving it for her without fanfare would be the best course of action. Even if she doesn't realize it's from me, that's fine. Every time she wears it, she'll know she's not alone. For me, that's all that matters.

Everything I did for the last four years was done to return to her and make sure I was worthy. To make sure when we were together again, not only could I be the man she deserves, but I could be a man she would *see*. I didn't want to be the friend anymore, or the big brother. I want to be her confidant, her lover, and her equal partner.

Part of me wanted to celebrate when she told me she didn't have any experience in relationships, especially sexually, but it wouldn't have mattered. She never owed me anything, and I never expected or dreamed she wouldn't have been with other men. How could she not? Who wouldn't want her? Plenty of women had tried to entice me once I left the community, but I never found any of them appealing, they just weren't her. As embarrassing as it may be to most people to be a 22-year-old virgin, the only reason it matters to me is because if, or when, we ever reach that point in our relationship I don't want to fall short.

After kissing her out on the patio, though, with my hand around her throat and her squirming on my dick? I'm pretty sure we won't have any sort of problem. She seemed to like the pressure, so I'm less worried she won't be receptive to the things I want to do to her. I may not have any experience, but I certainly know what I've been dreaming about doing with her in my bed for years now. I have a feeling she'll enjoy every minute of it.

Chapter 25

Evan and I decide to move into the living room and turn on some horror movies after changing into more comfortable clothes once it gets a bit chilly outside. I had set the alarm and turned on the surveillance around the barn, so the system will alert me if anything happened there. I can check in to the camera at any time to ensure Ryan is still there. I brought my tablet to the couch and snuggled up against Evan with a fuzzy blanket. We chose one of our old favorite horror movies and checked on Ryan as we settled in.

Currently, he is screaming for help that will never come. No one will hear him. Not only because no one ever visits that part of my property except for me and people I invite, but because the inner wall of the barn is soundproofed. That was one of my favorite parts of the barn, someone could be standing right outside and never hear a thing.

This land has belonged to my family for years, the property has had several homes built and torn down, but the barn has always been there. When my dad decided to update the barn by adding the workroom, bathroom, and his man cave, he decided the barn needed to be basically replaced. The siding of the barn was all old, beautifully weathered wood, and he didn't want to lose that aesthetic because from the outside you'd never guess at the secrets that are hidden inside. He kept the footprint of the barn and carefully salvaged the siding before tearing down the rest of the structure. He then rebuilt the barn with the same outer dimensions, replaced the old siding, soundproofed the outer walls, and ran electricity, plumbing, and internet out there. A few years ago we added a high tech security and surveillance system. The system comes in handy for situations like this, allowing me to check on things there without having to make the trip. The sensors on the doors will also alert me if he was somehow able to escape.

Knowing he's buttoned up tight for the evening, Evan and I decide to do some online shopping and search Pinterest for ideas on the cabin updates. I start a new board to add all our choices to and help him create an account so he can share it with me. We decide he's going to start work on the master bathroom first, so after I text my friend who runs the local family owned home improvement store about opening a line of credit that can be used by both myself and Evan, we start picking out fixtures.

Although I would rather have my parents still living, I am lucky in they planned ahead in case anything ever happened to me. When my mom died, her full, and rather large, life insurance policy payout went straight into a trust for me that I gained access to on my twentieth birthday. I haven't touched it yet. When my dad died I then inherited everything he left behind which included the house, land, his equally large life insurance policy, and his sizable savings that he earned by investing in the right things. I never have to work another day in my life if I choose not to, but I love working at the store. I don't use the money I inherited for anything other than paying for the bills and upkeep for the cabin and the land, so it's an easy decision to use the money I have put aside to do this project right. Evan being willing to do the work for free allows me to feel a bit better about picking more expensive fixtures, especially since he has an idea about quality and what will work better in the space and for what I want.

Evan thinks he can have the master done in about two months, sooner if he can wrangle some help. My lease runs out in about five months, so if the master suite can be done in that amount of time I'll have plenty of time to decide if I want to extend my lease or not.

One thing I didn't have to wait to order was the hot tub. It's starting to turn cooler outside in the evenings, and if I'm going to be spending more time out here it will definitely be a bonus. Plus, Nick and Travis will love it when they come out to visit for their big night. Evan measured the area where I wanted to put it before we came inside, so I end up choosing a 7 person tub with lights, different settings, and Bluetooth speakers, and it will be delivered in a few days. It's more expensive than I anticipated but I think it's going to be worth the cost. I text Brandon and Daniel to let them know I've ordered one and invite them to come over for a barbecue the day after the delivery.

I also realized we forgot to tell Daniel about Gran's death and Ryan's supposed disappearance, so I decided to call and fill him in. He promises to keep an eye out for Ryan, and listen for any word on what they're thinking about Gran's case. He offers Evan a place to stay so I'm not put out, or to come over and stay if I'm worried about Ryan coming for me, but we decline on both accounts. Although he's worried about Ryan going missing in conjunction with Gran's death, he also sounds relieved that he's gone. He was the least excited of us when they came back, even though Ryan had been his best friend when we were kids.

When the first movie ends, we decide to start another and put away the tablet so we can relax and enjoy another. At some point I must fall asleep curled up against him, because the next thing I know I'm being lifted and carried up the stairs.

"What are you doing?" I mumble sleepily. "Put me down Evan. I'm too heavy to be carried like this."

He chuckles beneath me as he continues up the steps. "Hush. I've got you, and we're almost there." My bedroom door is open, so he carries me straight in and places me down on my bed, giving me a kiss before pulling back reluctantly. "Get some sleep. We can deal with my douche bag cousin tomorrow."

"Good night. I'll make breakfast in the morning and we can come up with a plan of attack. No pun intended," I giggle, waiting for him to leave so I can strip my pants off and climb under my covers. I considered asking him to stay with me, but I don't want to press things too fast. He's dealing with a lot after today, so I don't want him to feel pressured or obligated. He wants to take things slower, so I'm going to respect that.

I can't sleep, so instead of bothering Evan I decide to head down to the dock. I throw my hair up into a messy bun, put on some capri length yoga pants and one of my dad's oversized sweaters over my cami and panties, and grab one of the spare blankets from the hall closet before slipping my feet into flip-flops and heading down. The night is chilly, but calm and peaceful, and I wrap the blanket around me as I take my usual seat at the end of the dock.

So much has gone on in the last few weeks, today especially, and it's hard to wrap my head around everything. Ryan and Evan returning after four years of silence. Ryan pushing me to be with him and then turning on me the second he saw something he didn't like. Ryan admitting his father killed Evan's mom and his own mother's lover, and admitting to killing his mother and grandmother himself. Ryan trying to kill me. Realizing Evan has been in love with me for years. Learning Evan is ok with torturing his cousin, and admitting to him that I've killed before. Travis being attacked. Daniel being weird about the guys being back.

I wish my dad was here. He'd be able to help me sort this out, and if he couldn't, simply hearing his advice would be more helpful than anything else.

I allow my mind to drift while I stare at the ripples I'm making in the water by dragging my feet back and forth. The movement on the surface causes the stars to wink in and out of view and it's mesmerizing to watch. I don't know how long

I've been sitting out here, but as tiredness starts creeping back in I decide it's time to head back inside to bed.

"Jen?"

I like to think my training and life experiences have trained the possibility of a horror movie shriek escaping my lips, but I can only say that is the sound that left me. Hand to heart, I whip my head around to face whoever has come up behind me, fully expecting it to be Evan. Maybe he saw me sitting out here through one of the windows? He's standing in front of the light post so his face is shadowed, but I know it's not Evan because the build is all wrong.

"Daniel? What the fuck! You scared the shit out of me. What are you doing here? What time is it?" My heart is racing, and I'm part freaked out, part pissed. This is the second time he's shown up here without notice or explanation in the last few weeks. How often is he here?

"Shit, Jen. I didn't mean to scare you, I figured you heard me. What are you doing out here?"

"Of course I didn't hear you! Do you honestly think I would have let you sneak up on me? Jesus, dude. I can't sleep, but this is my house. I'll ask you again. What are you doing here?"

"Oh, um. I assumed you'd be staying at your apartment. I was worried about Ryan being gone and I just wanted to check here in case he tried to hide out or something. I can't think of any other places he'd go, unless he went back to his dad. I saw the truck in the driveway and thought I'd check to make sure it wasn't him."

"I only have one bed at my apartment. Plus, I thought I told you we were here. Evan's truck is here too. How often do you-"

"Daniel? What are you doing here? Jen? Are you ok? I thought I heard a scream." Evan's voice cuts me off mid-sentence as he runs from the house. Although I don't think Daniel would ever hurt me, knowing Evan is here too helps me to relax. I'm slightly on edge with him showing up here again, especially at this time of night.

"Yeah, I'm good." I tell him. "I didn't hear Daniel walk up behind me and I was just surprised. He thought we were at my apartment, so he came here to check for Ryan." Not wanting to stay on the ground with the guys towering over me, I place my blanket aside so I can stand. Evan walks to me and extends a hand to help me up, and I take it while looking at Daniel. A flash of anger and possibly jealousy flits through his eyes, so as soon as I'm upright I release his hand and move to put my shoes on and pick up and fold my blanket.

"I didn't mean to scare you," Daniel apologizes. "I got worried when I saw you sitting out here this late by yourself. If Ryan did kill Gran, we have no idea what else he's capable of."

"You're right, but I couldn't sleep and sometimes sitting out here helps." I shrug and give him a tired smile. "Now that I've had the crap scared out of me I'll either pass out as soon as my head hits the pillow, or I won't sleep until next Tuesday. Thanks for coming by to check on the house. We're going to be staying here all week since Evan can stay in the guest room."

We all start walking up to the house by silent agreement. "Yeah, I don't know if I'll be able to stay in Gran's house anymore. I'll probably figure out what I'm going to do over the next few days, but I don't think I can walk by the place where she died every day and stay sane."

"Yeah, man. That's rough. I have a guest room too if you need a place to stay for a while." Daniel offers.

I chew my lip for a second while I think. "Or, you could just stay here until you figure out what's next. The guest room isn't being used, and you're going to be doing all the work on the house. You won't let me pay you for labor, so the least I can do is give you room and board."

"What work?" Daniel asks. "What's wrong with the house?"

"Nothing is wrong. Jen wants to update some things for when she finally moves back here full time. I offered to do the work for her to help her save money. I may be calling on you and Brandon to lend a hand sometimes, so be prepared." Evan gives Daniel a tired smile.

"Sounds good. Let me know when, I'm happy to help."

"Thanks, D. Do you need to crash here? I know it's late."

"You don't mind? I worked a double and I'm exhausted. I can take the couch, if you're sure it's ok. I have to work again tomorrow and the idea of driving another 30 minutes home is a bit daunting."

"Of course. Do you have clothes to sleep in? I'm pretty sure Brandon has left some stuff if you don't."

"I've got a bag in the car. I'll be right back," he says, taking off around the side of the house at a jog. Evan and I share a look of concern and confusion as he turns the corner.

"Didn't we tell him we were staying here? And did you see how he looked at you when you offered me your hand?" I ask him with a whisper. "He's been weird lately, more so since you two have been back. I think we need to keep our relationship from him for now, until we can figure out what's going on. I don't understand why he came out here at this time of night. Do you think he expects something?"

"What he could expect to have happened? We'll keep things quiet and wait to discuss more or do anything until after he's left."

Our conversation is cut short by Daniel's reappearance. We head back inside and I get him situated with a blanket and pillow on the couch before Evan and I head back upstairs. As we turn the corner to where Daniel wouldn't be able to see us, Evan grabs me and pushes me up against the wall. He uses his hand to grip my throat and tilt my head up to meet his eyes, and all I find is heat and possession.

"I don't give a fuck if he is jealous, or if he wants you. He'd be stupid not to," he leans in to whisper into my ear. "But I'm telling you right now, Jen. It's too late for him. He can't have you." Pulling back he gives me a satisfied smile before claiming my lips in a possessive kiss. Forgetting Daniel is downstairs I release a moan that has him smiling against me before he pulls back to shush me. "Hush, baby girl. I thought we decided he can't know anything yet."

I push my bottom lip out in an exaggerated pout, but nod my agreement. "You're right. Let's go to bed. We'll deal with everything after he leaves in the morning."

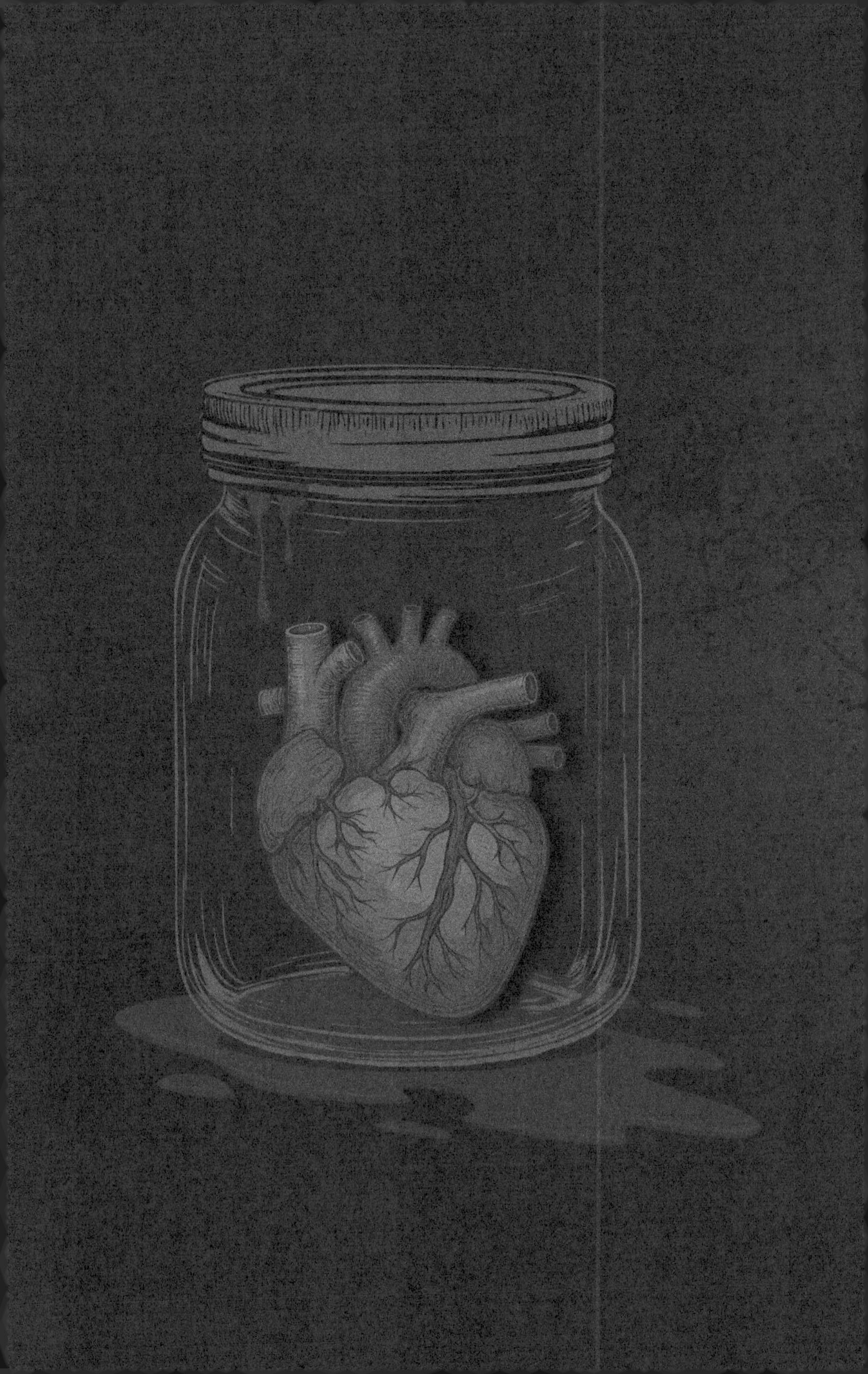

Chapter 26

I wake to the sound of rhythmic pounding. It's familiar, but in my tired state I can't place it, so I groggily climb out of bed to investigate. Entering the hall outside of my bedroom, I can tell it's coming from my dad's home gym. This close, grunts and the sound of something being hit filter through the door. Are the guys fighting?

Throwing the door open, I'm stopped in mid movement. Evan has hooked up my dad's old heavy bag and is punching and kicking it with impeccable form. He's shirtless, wearing only a pair of small shorts and wraps over his hands and feet. Sweat has matted his hair down to his head and is trailing down his muscles, highlighting all the curves and angles. My mouth is instantly dry, most likely because the majority of the moisture in my body has traveled somewhere south.

For a few years I worried something was wrong with me. I could get aroused when reading smutty books or if I watched the right kind of porn, but never with a real man. Brandon never had that problem with women or men, and I think even Daniel has dated a few women, though never long term. All my friends tried to convince me to date or have a one night stand, but I never felt anything. Looking at Evan Holmes at this moment, I finally understand what was wrong with me.

They weren't him.

Knowing Daniel is in the house is the only thing keeping me from walking over to Evan and dropping to my knees in front of him. Instead, in an effort at self-preservation I clear my throat to signal my arrival. He pauses and turns to face me, gloriously muscled chest heaving with labored breaths as he looks me up and down with fire in his eyes.

Shit! Am I naked? Looking down, I release a sigh when I realize I pulled on sleep shorts last night before crawling back into bed after using the bathroom. I always wear them when Daniel and Brandon sleep over, mostly because Brandon always ends up in bed with me. He's looking at me like I'm perfectly coiffed and wearing lingerie instead of in rumpled sleep clothes with what I am sure is epic bed head.

"Good morning, beautiful," Evan wears a hungry smile while he stalks towards me. He pokes his head past me to check down the hallway and make sure the coast is clear before pulling me inside and shutting and locking the door behind him. Backing me up against the wall, he dips his face to the crook of my neck while he slides his hands down my sides. "I dreamed of you last night. Knowing Daniel was here was the only thing keeping me from coming to you." I gasp as he picks me up without warning, pressing me against the wall and forcing me to wrap my legs around him or let them hang awkwardly. He begins pressing hot kisses to my neck, working his way from my collarbone to the special spot behind my ear before he coos "Do you think that's why he showed up? To play chaperone? Because I do."

I let out a low moan when his kisses turn to nips along my shoulder, and to show him I'm done with his teasing I grab his hair and draw him in for a deep kiss. For a moment, I almost draw back because I realize I haven't brushed my teeth yet, but fuck it. He doesn't seem to care. We have such a height difference that my core is brushing against his stomach instead of his dick, but I still take advantage of our position and grind myself against him like a brazen hussy. Evan groans and squeezes my ass as he presses against me harder for a moment before drawing back and putting his forehead to mine. "Fucking Daniel," he groans.

I giggle and smack an obnoxious kiss against his cheek. "Alright hot stuff, are you finished with your workout? I'm going to take a quick shower and then make breakfast. The sooner we eat, the sooner we can kick him out of here and figure out a plan of action for today."

With one last squeeze, he sets me back down on the ground. "Yeah, I'm done. I'll wash up and then come down and help." I turn to head back out of the room and yelp as he smacks my ass.

Evan and Daniel are both in the kitchen when I make my way downstairs. They've each made themselves some coffee and have started rummaging for breakfast. "Take a seat," Evan tells me, handing me a Diet Coke he pulled out of the fridge when he saw me. "Making breakfast is the least we can do after you let us stay last night."

I open my mouth to thank him but I'm interrupted by the front door opening and Brandon singing out "Good morning you crazy kids! Daddy's got breakfast for the masses. Good thing my mom always makes enough to feed an army, because we didn't expect Daniel to be here too, and I'm sure as fuck not sharing."

As he turns the corner, I can see he's not joking. He's got a cloth tote shaped like a big shopping basket overflowing in one arm and two casserole carriers balanced on the other. "Hey guys. Evan, mom sends her love and plenty of food. She doesn't want you two to worry about cooking while you're going through making arrangements and stuff, so she sent over breakfast, lunch, and dinner for today. She said she's organizing meal delivery with some other ladies in the area to make sure you're taken care of for the rest of the week."

"Thanks, man." I think he'd put his Gran out of his mind as much as possible, because he looks like he's been sucker punched. "Please give your mom a hug for me. I really appreciate this, and her letting Jen take off to help me. I have no idea what to do here." Brandon gives him a bear hug after placing the food on the counter and whispers something in his ear. Evan grips on to Brandon harder and buries his face into his neck for a moment. Daniel and I lock eyes while they share their moment, and by silent agreement we start unloading the tote and casserole dishes he brought.

Mrs. C is amazing. She's sent breakfast casserole, chocolate chip and blueberry muffins, sandwich fixings, pasta salad, three kinds of potato chips, her famous lasagna, garlic bread, and a dozen each of chocolate chip and peanut butter cookies. Not caring that I haven't eaten breakfast, I grab a peanut butter cookie before moving to the cabinets to grab plates and silverware out while Daniel puts everything away in the fridge. Daniel claps a hand against Evan's shoulder when he's done, and that seems to break the moment because Brandon and Evan separate. Tears shimmer in Evan's eyes, so I put down the plates and go to him, wrapping him up in a hug of my own.

Compartmentalization can be helpful or hurtful. It's often incredibly helpful when you're at the moment when it's needed. When you don't have any other choice but to keep moving forward. When those walls come down though? The release of what was held back can be soul shaking, and it's often much harder to build those walls back up. Evan's walls have cracked, and only time will tell if he lets them crumble or pieces them back together.

Either way, I'll be there to help.

Daniel left after breakfast. Knowing Ryan's dad won't bother himself with making arrangements for his mother, Evan, Brandon, and I divide and conquer the tasks that need to be completed. Mrs. C has offered to organize the celebration of life after the funeral with the help of some local women, so we only have to focus on the arrangements for the service and burial, as well as submitting an announcement to the local paper. Gran's body will be released on Wednesday, so the services have been scheduled for Thursday. To Evan's relief, he had searched through her small home office before we left her house yesterday and found her life insurance policy and burial plot information in a filing cabinet, along with a funeral plan, so most of the decisions had already been made and paid for. We contacted all the necessary people to start things rolling, and everything was done in a few hours.

One thing Evan did not find was her will, which we all found odd because she kept everything else together. Did Ryan find and destroy it before he left the house yesterday? Did she keep it somewhere else? Just one more question to ask Ryan before he dies.

Speaking of Ryan, "Ok, so what are we going to do with the fuckwit that created this mess?" I pull up the security app on my phone and check on him. He's hanging with his head drooped forward but I can tell he's alive because of the slight movement his breathing causes. "He's still secure, so we don't have to make a decision right now if you don't want to. He can hang a bit longer and have time to marinate in his bad decisions if you're not ready. It may do him some good to think we won't be coming back for him any time soon." I pause, thinking over our options. "Or, we could go and find out if he's ready to talk. If he's not, we have the option of beating the shit out of him until he does, or leaving him again. Your call, Ev. What do you want to do?"

"I want this to be over. Let's try to make him to talk now. If not, we can try beating it out of him, then leaving him again if that doesn't work. He can go a few days without food and water too. He didn't care if Gran died painfully when he pushed her down the stairs, so I don't care if he does either."

"That's my cue then," Brandon slaps his hands on his thighs and stands up to leave. "I'd love to stay and help, but I don't want vomit on my new shoes. Call me if I'm capable of doing something to help, ok?"

"Thanks, man," Evan chuckles. "I think running interference with Daniel going forward is what can help the most. He keeps popping up here and has been watching Jen very closely. Not only do we not want him to know we have Ryan, but we want to hold off on telling him about us. At least for now, until we can figure out what his deal is."

"I don't blame you. He has been a little weird lately. No worries, I'll do what I can."

I walk him to the door and give him a tight hug before he leaves. "Thanks for everything, Bran. Don't forget about dinner Thursday evening. I think relaxing in the new hot tub will be a perfect way to relax after the stress of the day."

"Fuck yes! Be prepared, I'm going to start bringing dates here. Sex parties at Killer's house!"

"Fuck off!" I laugh, pushing him out of my front door. Then, when he's far enough away, I whisper yell "Not until I have one first!" and slam the door in his shocked face.

I love messing with him.

I jump and spin, letting out a surprised shriek when Evan whispers "What was that about?" into my ear from behind me.

Hand to my chest, I whack him on his arm while I try to slow my racing heart. "You fucker! You scared the crap out of me. Brandon was being Brandon, excited about the hot tub. You know, planning orgies before it's even here. I swear, I'm going to have to make him pay to have it professionally cleaned every time he uses it without me here." Shuddering at the thought of the body fluids that would be swimming around my hot tub, I make a mental note to buy a locking cover. "Come on, let's go see what we can shake out of your cousin."

Chapter 27

Before we head out to the barn, I recommend we change into clothes that will fit easily and comfortably under coveralls. Although Evan is somewhat smaller than my dad, I think dad's will fit him fine, and the coveralls will protect his clothes from being stained with any evidence if things get messy. As an added layer of torture, I decide I'm going to dress to show off the tattoos Ryan hates so much. He thinks I'm a whore because of my tattoos? What will he think when I show up in a tank top that allows me to display my arms, my midsection with my belly button ring, and is low cut enough to show off my black lace bra and thin enough to show off my nipple piercings? Hopefully, it'll make him mad enough to start with his monologuing again, and if not, I'll still have fun pissing him off.

And seeing heat in Evan's eyes again.

Evan is waiting for me in the foyer wearing a plain gray t-shirt, basketball shorts, and tennis shoes, and he's holding a filled tote bag. I raise an eyebrow at him, asking "You ready? What's in the bag?"

Lazily running his gaze from my face to my toes, Evan smirks. "A few bottles of water. Vegetables. Cookies. None of which we will give Ryan, but all of which we will enjoy in front of him. It's been over 24 hours since he's had anything to eat or drink at this point. I may leave some out when we leave, so he has to see it but can't have it. It all depends on how he responds once we're there."

"I like it," I chuckle, shaking my head with a smile. "Let's go. I'll drive."

The drive is quick and peaceful. The leaves are starting to turn, so the canopy above has a slight rose gold tint as the sun filters through them and the path is still clear since they haven't yet started to fall. In a few weeks the two tracks will be almost impossible to follow and I'll only be able to reach the barn thanks to the gaps in the trees and my memory. We arrive at the barn and I park the UTV next to the front door, and Evan grabs his tote out of the back as I use my code to unlock the door. Locking it behind us once we're through, I unlock the inner door to the work room.

Thankfully, my dad had the forethought to install an amazing air filtration system, so the air still smells fresh, instead of smelling like a day old captive. Ryan is either asleep or passed out because he doesn't stir when the door opens. I press my finger to my lips to signal Evan to stay quiet and lead him to the bathroom where the coveralls are. Shutting the door behind us, I pull a pair for each of us out of the cabinet and hand him his while I slip my shoes off and step into my own. I leave them unzipped and hanging at the waist like I did yesterday and slide my socks and rubber boots on before turning around. When I do, and I take in Evan in my dad's coveralls, I'm thrown into a memory of my dad that hits me like a freight train.

Nine Years Ago

"Ok Johnny, are you ready to start?" My dad has a secret smile on his face, like he knows something I don't.

"Yep! I'm ready. Am I assisting today?" I love helping my dad out in the barn. I learn so much and it's fun to spend time with him. He's started letting me take the lead when we're butchering our own kills, but he hasn't let me work on the ones other people bring to us yet. I'm hopeful I'll be allowed to start helping with those someday soon too.

"Nope, today you're going to take point. Head into the bathroom, I left something for you in there."

Excited, but not knowing what to expect, I rush into the bathroom and find the cabinet doors open with a mechanic's style zip up coverall with "Johnny" embroidered over the left breast pocket. I hurry to put it on over my clothes and put my rubber boots on with it, since we'll be hosing down the room later. When I exit the bathroom, my dad is dressed in a matching set, with "John Sr." embroidered on his.

"Your mom always talked about getting these made for us," he says, sadly. "She loved the idea of us being a matching set, and I wanted to make that happen, even if she wasn't here to with us. I'm proud of you, Johnny, and I know your mom would be too. Are you ready to get started? This one is a donation, so it's not a paying customer we need to worry about, but we still need to be careful. You start, and I'll jump in if you need me, ok?"

"Jen? Baby girl, are you with me?" I jump, feeling his hand cup my cheek and pulling out of my memory to meet Evan's concerned gaze.

"Shit, yeah. Sorry. Thinking about my dad." I give him a rueful smile before shaking my head and pressing a finger to my lips to indicate I want him to be quiet. "Come on. Let's wake up our guest."

Arching a brow, he follows me quietly and without question. I shoot him a smirk as I silently open the cleaning cabinet and pull out the hose. Hooking it up to the faucet, I hand Evan the spray nozzle before whispering in his ear, "Wait until I'm seated on the table, then stand-off to the side and spray him in the face. I think seeing me like this will piss him off as much as the water."

I pull back and meet eyes with a wicked grin. Smiling back at me, he uses the hand not holding the hose to pull me against him and scorch me with his kiss. Leaning down to nuzzle my ear, he nips the lobe before responding to my directions. "You're lucky he's going to die soon, and because I know you wore that to drive him crazy. Because otherwise? I'd throw your ass over my shoulder and take you into the back room and show you who you belong to."

My whole body shivers at the promise in his words. "Oh yeah? Maybe we can arrange that later too. There's no reason we can't squeeze in both activities." Leaning back and planting a quick kiss on his lips, I wiggle my eyebrows and saunter over to my work table and hop up to face Ryan. I wink at Evan and whisper "show time."

Ryan jolts awake spluttering and coughing and the high pressure stream that's belting him in the face, but Evan doesn't let up for a good thirty seconds. I lean back on my hands, patiently waiting for Ryan to collect himself and focus on me. Evan walks over to me, dragging the hose with him and leaning against my side, happy to wait with me and let me take the lead this time.

"What the fuck? You stupid bi-" His words are cut off by a stream of water being shot directly into his mouth.

"Try again," Evan taunts smoothly.

"Fuck you! You-" more water, more sputtering and choking. This time, the stream lasts over a minute, and Ryan can't speak when the water stops because he's too busy coughing and trying to breathe.

"Now," I say, "third time's a charm, right? We have questions, you have answers. You can choose not to answer us, but that will only make things more difficult for you. No one knows you're here. Everyone thinks you killed your grandmother and then ran off like the coward you are. Even your father believes you did. No one is coming for you, and you can't escape, my dad made that impossible. So, what'll it be?"

"Fuck you," Ryan retorts through labored breaths. His chest is heaving and his eyes are filled with loathing. "I don't have to tell you shit, whore."

Evan walks over to Ryan, wrinkling his nose when he reaches his side. He probably smells pretty ripe after hanging for 24 hours. Without telegraphing his intentions, Evan lands a solid punch to Ryan's jaw, causing his head to snap back and a groan to escape him. "Do not," Evan growls menacingly, "ever speak to her like that again. She's not wrong. After what you've done, I have no problem doing this the hard way. You and your dad aren't the only ones in this family comfortable getting their hands dirty. Don't fucking test me."

Ryan forces a pained laugh and spits blood out on the ground at my feet. "You're so big and bad now, huh? Have to act all tough in front of Jen, so she'll finally think you're worth her time when she never did before? You're fucking pathetic. Have you told her how you couldn't get it up for any of the girls in the compound? They all told me they tried but you turned them all down. Are you gay? Is that the problem? Is that just one more reason you'll be burning in hell?"

Having heard enough, I hop down from the table and step up to Ryan with a sweet smile on my face. Pausing a step in front of him, I pull my leg back and kick him hard in the dick. The high-pitched keening wail coming from him is music to my ears, and I grab his hair to pull his head back from the hunched position he's trying to maintain so I have him looking into my eyes. "Don't ever say that shit in my hearing again, you get me? I will cut your worthless dick off and feed it to you without hesitation. Maybe then you'll realize homophobia is a refuge of the weak. I don't give a fuck what your father preached to you, he's not here to save you now. You'll either answer our questions, or suffer for refusing. I don't need the bullshit commentary." Smiling sweetly again I tighten my grip on his hair. "So, will you be answering our questions today, or no?"

"Fuck. Off."

"Wrong answer." Letting his hair go, I practically skip to the table and hop back up. "Evan, it's your play."

Evan circles Ryan like he's a shark scenting prey. I reach over to the tote sitting next to me and pull out a bottle of water, crack it open, and take a small sip. Ryan watches the bottle like it's the only thing in the room but doesn't say anything, so I cap it and place it on the table next to me. Next, I reach in and pull out a peanut butter cookie to start nibbling on. These were always his favorite when he was growing up, but who knows if he'd still want them since his body is a temple and blah blah blah. I can hear his stomach growling from my spot on the table, so I smirk as I continue to eat my cookie. He's still staring at the bottle of water though, so I finish the last bite and reach into the tote for the last container -- the veggies.

Pulling the Tupperware out, I scoot the water bottle back and place the opened container directly in his line of site. Pulling out a baby carrot, I bring it to my lips and watch him follow the movement. Hah! Evan is an evil genius for this. I crunch into the carrot and chew slowly, staring at Ryan while he frowns. Suddenly, I remember Evan is supposed to be making the next move, and my eyes jump over to him. He's smirking at me and my show, and I can feel my cheeks pinking up at his amusement. "Sorry," I mumble with a mouthful of carrot. Waving my hand in the most regal gesture I can muster while talking with food in my mouth, I mutter "your turn. My bad."

He throws his head back, laughing at my embarrassment and walking over to place a kiss on my cheek. Pausing by my ear he whispers, "Is it wrong that seeing you nail him in the balls and then taunt him turns me on?"

My eyes meet Ryan's over Evan's shoulder. He's looking at me with complete disgust, but Evan's words warm me and turn my embarrassment to pride and heat. Ryan's opinion doesn't phase me in the slightest. Instead, I lean forward and nip Evan's earlobe before he's able to pull back. "Go get 'em, Tiger," I whisper, leaning back against my hands on the table behind me.

He steps back and faces Ryan again. "Are you sure you don't want to answer my questions? It'll be a lot less painful, and we'll give you food, water, and a bathroom break if you need one. I'm not unreasonable, but there are things I need to know. I can't let you go until I have those answers."

"Fuck you, man. You aren't letting me go regardless. You could, though. I won't tell anyone you've kept me here, since you know I killed my mom and Gran. If you let me go, I'll tell you whatever you want, and then we can go our separate ways. I'll even leave Jen to you. She's damaged goods anyway."

Wham.

Another punch, this time to his left kidney. "I thought I told you not to talk about her like that. You're right though, we're not letting you go. But we can kill you quickly and painlessly. How you die is in your hands now. You killed Gran and your own mom, and tried to kill Jen. There's no telling what else you've done, so you can't be allowed to continue hurting people. Did you kill the girls from the community that disappeared? Did you hurt Jen's friend Travis? Why did your dad kill my mom?"

Girls were disappearing? What girls? He never told me girls were disappearing from there. That seems kind of important, especially now, knowing he killed his mom. And does he think he hurt Travis? Was it the gay comment? Or does he know something I don't? We're obviously going to have to talk about everything once we leave here.

"Bring it on." Ryan is pretty cocky for someone who is strung up like a fresh deer carcass. I'd probably admire him if I didn't find it so inconvenient and annoying. If he'd spit out the answers we want we'd be able to relax this week instead of dealing with him. Evan shakes his head in mock shame, and then attacks Ryan like he's another heavy bag in the gym. Punches, kicks, and combos fly and all Ryan can do is hang there and endure. The beating lasts for about five minutes before Evan steps back, chest heaving.

"Let's go," he says, heading to the bathroom. "He's not going to talk today. I say we give him another day to think about whether he'd like to change his mind."

I follow him into the bathroom and pull off my boots and coveralls while Evan does the same. "Are you sure you don't want to keep trying?" I ask him, confused as to why he's giving up so soon.

"Yeah, I'm sure. He's not going to talk today, probably not tomorrow either. He won't talk until he breaks and I think it'll take some time to get him there. We just need to keep him alive long enough for that to happen. I don't want to feed him or give him water, but he'll die without water, so I guess we have to at least give him that."

A slow smile curves my lips as an idea forms in my mind. One that will both keep him alive, and torture him in two more ways.

"Leave that to me," I tell him. "I've got the perfect plan."

We hose Ryan down one more time from head to toe on our way out. It's cold in the work room, but not cold enough to give him hypothermia, even with the wet clothes. I also finally place the ball gag in his mouth with Evan's help. It's a fight, but I figure if he's not going to talk, I'll give him a reason to stay quiet.

We lock everything back up tight and set the security systems before heading back to the UTV. "Do you want to drive back?" I ask. "I need to send a few texts."

"Sure, who are you texting?' he asks, grabbing the keys and jumping into the driver's seat like an excited 15-year-old boy.

"Brandon. He's got some connections I'm about to take advantage of." Settling into the passenger's seat, I pull my phone out and start texting.

> **Me:** Are you still hooking up with the doctor/nurse couple?

> **Bran:** Sometimes... why?

> **Me:** Think you can convince them to sell us another few bags of saline and IV supplies? I'd say four bags plus supplies. Tell them about Gran's death and say we plan to have a rager to help Evan forget. We'll need the bags for our inevitable hangovers.

> **Bran:** Let me see what I can do. I'll try to work my magic.

> **Me:** You always do, boo.

"I've asked Brandon to try to score me a few IVs worth of saline. I did a Medical Assisting course in high school and got my phlebotomy license too, which I keep up because it's a good skill to have. One time Bran got the norovirus, and he texted this male nurse he was seeing telling him he was dying after puking all night. He couldn't keep anything down, so the guy brought some saline bags over to hydrate him. The guy couldn't get a vein, but I could somehow. Since then when we go a little too far drinking, or when Brandon is so sick he can't keep anything down, we call the guy, or the doctor he works for who he's also seeing, and they give us some saline. I figure we can use the IVs instead of giving Ryan water. Unless something has changed he also hates needles so that'll be a fun bonus. Plus, it won't quench his thirst but it will keep him alive."

Evan grins and shakes his head in amusement. "Impressive. Are they aware he's seeing them both?"

"Oh, they know. They're a couple. The guy is a nurse in his mid twenties, and the woman is a doc about ten years older. They're not a true throuple, but he does date them every once in a while, always together though. They've asked him to think about a more permanent arrangement, but he's not sure yet."

"Um... what the fuck is a throuple?" The confusion on Evan's face is priceless.

Laughing, I answer "It's a relationship made up of three people. It can be any combination of men and women. Brandon happens to be bisexual, and so is the nurse, so it works for them. I think he'll end up with them eventually, he just needs to figure out it really is ok. More and more people are embracing the polyamourous lifestyle these days. I say, if you don't have to, why choose?"

"Is that why you kicked Ryan in the nuts? What he said about gays going to hell? I have to admit, I'm obviously not gay or anything, but more power to Brandon. If he's happy, who cares? I don't think I'm cut out for the polyamourous lifestyle though, just so you know."

"Don't worry about that, I don't think I am either. Brandon came out to me about a year after you guys left, though. He had a hard time with it for a while, but he's Brandon. He always gets back on his feet. I'm a little defensive over him, if you can't tell. We've been through a lot together."

Pulling up to the house, we park the UTV in the garage and head in to change. Neither Evan nor I are in the mood to be idle, so we decide to head to the local big box store to buy boxes for my dad's things, and then we hit the local hardware store to pick out some fixtures and start stocking up on what Evan will need to work on the master. Brandon texted to tell me he's getting the IV supplies today and will bring them over when he comes for dinner tonight, but he had to promise a double date and hot tub night within the next few weeks to make it happen. I'm ok with that since I know he really likes this couple, so maybe meeting them and showing him I approve instead of just telling him will help him figure out what he wants.

CHAPTER 28

We get home about an hour before Brandon is due to arrive, so we unload the supplies from Evan's truck into the garage and I show him what tools we have in there. Some of the more heavy-duty things are out in the barn, so we make a quick trip to grab the sledgehammers and protective gear.

We do not visit Ryan.

Evan had called the dumpster company earlier today and got that set up, so the first one will be delivered tomorrow. Tonight, we'll clear out my dad's bathroom and closet, sorting through everything to determine what I want to keep or donate, and if everything goes fast enough we'll start on the demolition.

Grief is odd. Everyone experiences and handles it differently, and no way is wrong or better than the other. My grief kept me from my dad's space for the last several months. I still don't want to go in there, but he wouldn't want that for me. He'd want me to stay in the home he built and loved so much, but I think the idea of going through his things and then staying here alone or paying some stranger to change things he chose was just too daunting. Having people who knew and cared for him help me through the process of taking the space and making it mine makes it feel not so scary. I know Brandon would have helped me sort through his things, it's something we've been discussing more and more recently, but he wouldn't have been able to help me with the construction. I think this is the push I've been needing.

I get started on heating up dinner while Evan takes the packing supplies and tools upstairs. Mrs. C's lasagna is the best I've ever had, and Evan has been talking about it all day, so I make sure everything is heated properly and that I bake the garlic bread she sent with it. Brandon arrives a few minutes before everything is ready, and Evan passes him on his way up with the last load of supplies, so we have a few minutes to chat before he gets back down here.

"Please tell me you're going to ride that pony tonight since Daniel isn't here to cock block!" he whisper shouts as he hugs me.

Snorting and pushing him away from me, I roll my eyes as I return to preparing our dinner. "Seriously? Do you really think it'll be that quick? We just kissed yesterday! Give us a little time to figure things out. This is all a little much, and all happening very fast. He literally watched his grandmother die at the hands of his cousin yesterday, who he then found knocked out after trying to attack the woman he loves. The same cousin who then admitted to killing his aunt, and informed him his uncle killed his mother and his mentor. I learned all of that plus the fact that the guy I thought I had been in love with since I was a child is some kind of psycho cult freak who wanted to own me and make me his cult leader wife, but now thinks I'm a whore because I have tattoos. I'm a little overwhelmed at the moment. I think sex can wait, don't you?"

When I turn back to face Brandon, waiting for a response, I stop short. "Why the fuck are you grinning at me like that?" I ask him.

"You just said he's in love with you."

"I am."

My body stills as Evan speaks close behind me, refusing to relax as he wraps his arms around my waist. "I wasn't... I didn't mean it like that."

"It's ok," he says, chuckling. "I told you that yesterday. I've been in love with you since we were kids. I'm not embarrassed, and I'm not afraid of people finding out. I won't push anything on you either. You're not there, and that's ok." He presses a kiss to my neck, right behind my ear and I shiver, relaxing back into him. Brandon's grin turns smug, and I narrow my eyes at him in warning before he opens his big fat mouth.

"Nope... no sex here. You can't cut the tension with a knife or anything."

I move forward to punch him, but Evan holds me back chuckling. "I think we can figure that out on our own, thanks though. How long until dinner is ready, baby girl?"

"About five minutes. Everything set upstairs?" I lean my head back and kiss his cheek, and this time he lets me pull away as he nods. "You guys find what you want to drink, I'll finish everything up."

The three of us work well in the kitchen together. They pull out drinks, plates, and utensils and set up while I pull the food out of the oven. Dinner is comfortable and relaxing. No talk of death, torture, sex, or anything that could ruin the mood. It's like old times, but a more adult version, and I can't help but think that if these are the kind of nights I can look forward to in my future, I will be a very lucky girl.

After dinner is cleaned up, we make our way to my dad's room. I pause when I get to the open door and take a deep breath. Part of me feels like it's wrong to be getting rid of his things and changing the design he chose. The majority of me believes this is the right thing to do, but that small part of me allows the doubt to seep in. Looking back at Brandon, I am sure he can see the uncertainty in my eyes. He pulls me into a tight hug and rests his cheek on the top of my head. "We don't have to do this, you know," he soothes. "But, I think, knowing your dad, he would want this for you. There is nothing that says we have to do it today, but if you're ready, we're here to help you."

I soak up his strength for a moment before I take a deep breath and nod. "Let's do it. He never liked dwelling on the past, and he'd kick my ass if he knew I was. I guess... let's start with the bathroom, then work our way to the closet?" My statement comes out as a question. I'm floundering and could use the guidance.

"Sounds like a plan." Evan kisses the back of my head and walks by, heading over to the moving boxes stacked up near the bathroom door. He starts folding and taping them so we can fill them. "I brought up a marker so we can write on the boxes too."

It takes maybe thirty minutes to clean out my dad's bathroom. There wasn't a lot in there other than toiletries, most of which we threw away, and grooming products. Evan and Brandon divide up things like his electric razors, beard trimmer, and other things they can use, and Brandon took his towels and bedding since they were "nicer than the shit I have at home." It felt good to know they would use them and it wouldn't all go to waste.

They made it so comfortable that I wasn't as nervous as I originally had been when came time to tackle the closet. I had come in right after he died and took the few pieces of clothing meant something to me, like the sweater I wore last night, so I told Evan and Ryan they could take whatever they wanted and the rest would be donated. Dad was bigger than both of them, but there were a few items they took like ties or comfort clothes, and we packed the rest up for Brandon to drop at the donation site on his way home this evening.

Things got a little tougher when I found the old photo albums and scrap books my mom had put together when I was a kid, and his watch box. My dad loved watches, so he had a collection of twelve. The majority were Invicta, and he chose the one he wore based on his mood or what he was wearing.

"You should keep these," Evan said.

Shaking my head, I pulled one from the box and stroked the surface with my fingers.

Nine Months Ago

"Merry Christmas Dad!" I smiled as I handed him the small box. I've already given him some gifts, but this is the one I'm most excited about.

"Johnny, you've already given me too much. This is getting ridiculous." He pretended to scold me as he snatched the box out of my hand like a naughty toddler. Ripping the paper off like an excited child, he stills when he sees the Invicta logo on the top of the box. "Please tell me you didn't," he accuses with narrowed eyes.

Shrugging, I smile and say "I didn't."

Opening the box, his eyes widen when he sees the watch nestled inside. "Johnny, this is too much!"

"Hush. I have a friend that got a seasonal job in the outlet. He cut me a deal and let me use his employee discount in exchange for some Christmas Crack. I knew you loved that one, so he hooked me up." Standing to kiss his cheek, I say "Merry Christmas Dad. If it doesn't fit we can take it to be sized, but I checked and I think I got it right."

Grinning and shaking his head, he replaces the watch he's currently wearing with the new one. The dark gunmetal band is offset by the matte black face and glossy black numbers and dials. It's one of their bigger watches, and it fits perfect on his large wrist. "I love it, hun. Thank you so much. This is going to be my new everyday watch."

It had become his everyday watch. He wore it most days, and he was wearing it the day he died. It's one of the reasons I don't think what happened was a robbery, that thing retails for over a thousand dollars, and whoever killed him didn't take it. Even pawned you could score a few hundred dollars, which was more than the cash he kept in his wallet.

"No," I say, my voice cracking on the word. I clear my throat and continue, my voice stronger again. "I want to keep this one, but you guys can take the rest if you want them. Maybe each pick a few then we can send Daniel a picture of what is left so he can have a few too." They share a glance, but after I assure them I'm serious they pick through what's there. After they've each chosen two, I send Daniel a picture message with the ones that are left.

Me: Would you like any of these? We're going through Dad's things tonight to prep for the remodel.

Daniel: You're not keeping them?

Me: I'm keeping one. You, Brandon, and Evan can have the rest. If you want any. Everything else will be donated.

Daniel: Are you sure? Which ones do the guys want?

Me: They already picked their favorites. You pick yours then you can work out the rest with them.

Daniel: Ok. I'll take the red and green ones. I always liked those on him. Thanks, Jen.

Me: Any others?

Daniel: I'll take what they don't want. I don't wear watches often so they can have top pick. Those were my favorite though.

Daniel: This means a lot to me, Jen. Thank you for thinking of me.

Daniel: I'm getting off work soon, do you want me to come and help?

I hate it when he sends multiple texts at once! I think he does it specifically to annoy me.

Me: No, thanks though. We're almost done here. I think I'm going to go to bed early tonight, it's been a long few days. I'll put the watches aside for you and give them to you Thursday, ok?

Daniel: Ok, let me know if you change your mind. Goodnight, Jen. Thanks again.

Me: Nite!

"Ok, Daniel wants these two." I pull them out of the case and set them aside. "You can divide up the rest and whatever the two of you don't want, if any, he'll take."

The closet is almost completely empty, only one box remains on the floor against the back wall, so I sit down next to it and pull it in front of me while the guys discuss their choices. Emotionally spent, I slump back to lean against the wall for a second. The second I put pressure against the wall, I hear a click and the wall behind me slides back, causing me to fall a bit and squeal embarrassingly.

"What the fuck?" Walls aren't supposed to move... right? Last time I checked, walls are *not* supposed to move.

"What's wrong?" Evan and Brandon ask at the same time, looking up from the watches in their hands.

"What the fuck?" Brandon asks.

"That's what I just said!" I lament, throwing my head back and groaning as I stare at the ceiling. "I really don't think I can take another shock today. Can we pretend we didn't find this?" I look at the guys with pleading eyes, hoping they'll give me permission to bury my head in the sand for the evening.

"Fuck no! You just found a secret door hidden in the back of a closet. This is some Scooby Doo shit right here, Jen! Besides, it's not like this is where he'd be hiding his dead bodies or anything," Brandon says with a chuckle.

Hanging my head in defeat, I know he's right. "Alright. We'll look. But I swear to God Brandon Coleman, if there is a rotting corpse or something equally horrific in there you're taking my closing shifts for a month."

"Deal. Let's do it, Shaggy!"

I pull in a deep breath and do my best to prepare myself before standing and pushing on the door. It pushes back another few inches before stopping, so I try to slide it to the side. The door slides to the right until there is another click and a light turns on, illuminating a small room I never would have imagined existed.

CHAPTER 29

There are no heads lining the walls. There are no bodies strung up. No feet or other questionable body parts nailed to the wall. No sexually deviant furniture, toys, or costumes.

Thank God. If my dad had been hiding a gimp suit and spanking bench in here I would have set the whole house on fire and never come back. *After* bleaching my eyes.

If it hadn't been behind a secret door hidden in the back of his closet, I'd think this was an ordinary room. There are bookshelves lining one wall filled with what look to be different journals, notebooks, and binders. One wall has glass front cabinets with different items displayed next to a large gun safe. There doesn't appear to be anything valuable in the display cabinet and I can't figure out a connection between the items. The final wall has an overstuffed lounge chair situated in front of dozens of framed photos covering the entire surface above a desk with three computer monitors. The photos obvious they're from a span of decades. There are photos of me, Dad, and Mom together, pictures of me growing up with my grandfather, pictures of my dad and grandfather while my dad grew up, and pictures of people I've never seen before. Some are so old they're in black and white, and I can tell that some of these people aren't my family because they're all different races. Who are they?

"I don't get it." Brandon's words jolt me out of my confused state and I turn back to both of them. 'Why is this room hidden? It looks like a sitting room or office or something. John wouldn't have hidden this."

"I don't know, Brandon. I can see exactly what you do." My response is a little snippy, but I'm completely overwhelmed and a little hurt. Why would he hide this from me? I turn on the left computer monitor to find feeds from our security system, both here and at the barn. Turning on the others reveals more of the same, except I also notice there's a view of the closet that I've never seen in our regular system coverage. Is this a panic room too? Looking back at the door I see a panel on the wall, so my guess is that's probably the case.

Sighing, I walk over to the bookshelves and pull one of the leather bound books from the middle shelf. "Shit." I exclaim, "I think these are my grandfather's journals. Listen to this. 'June 27, 1953. I'm becoming more certain that the sheriff is working for the Woolridge family. Each time we arrest one of them or one of their goons they get out on some technicality, or just disappear altogether. Tonight we brought in Jessie Woolridge for attacking a young woman and beating her date until he lost consciousness, all because he lost a game of darts and wanted to impress the girl. He was released within the hour with no explanation. I think Jessie is too dangerous to go after, but if things continue on this path I may have to figure out a way to take the sheriff out of the equation. There is no room for the corrupt in law enforcement. We are here to protect and serve. We take an oath, and Sheriff Watkins seems to be as corrupt as they come.'"

Evan releases a low, long whistle. "You know the Woolridge family is still around, right? Uncle Patrick used to be friends with Thompson Woolridge. I think he still talks to him, actually. He's Jessie's nephew."

I consider what I just read as I place the journal back where it belongs and walk over to the display cabinet. "Holy shit." I breathe. "Is that... a sheriff's badge? Do you think it belonged to Sheriff Watkins?"

Brandon and Evan come to look at the badge I'm pointing to. I don't want to touch anything, I want to figure out what's going on first. "It might be. We can do some research. We have a name, location, and timeline. We'll figure this out."

"Ok," I sigh. Looking around the room again. "I think I'm done for tonight. We know this is here now, and it's not going anywhere. You're welcome to stay and look around, but I'm out."

"Nah, let's head out. We can finish up later." Evan and Brandon turn to head back into the closet and I pause before following them, stopping to take a photo of my parents and me from the wall. Tracing my fingers down my dad's face, I whisper brokenly, "Why did you hide this from me?"

Looking up at the guys, I see Brandon clap a hand to Evan's shoulder and head out of the closet and back into the bedroom. Evan slowly walks to me with a sad smile and uses his thumbs to brush tears from my cheeks before cupping my face. "I don't think he would have hidden this from you forever. He trusted you with his biggest secret, but everyone needs their own space. Maybe that's all this was."

I smile as best as I can and pull him in for a kiss. "Come on," I say, pulling him out of the room with me. "I want cookies and ice cream." Examining the door I find the latch in the side, so I use that to try to pull the door shut. There's a little resistance at first, but as soon as I tug harder the door begins to slide itself shut and the light turns off automatically. As soon as the door clicks shut I realize how I never noticed there was a door here. The closet organization system my dad chose has metal channels running vertically that you slot shelves to at different heights, and he placed the door so one side is flush with the back corner, and the other is hidden by one of those metal pieces. "Smart. I think I'll keep it like this. It may not stay what it is, but you never know when a hidden room could come in handy. Especially a panic room."

Chapter 30

Dessert didn't help like I hoped. My ice cream melts into soup before I can finish and the cookies taste like ash in my mouth. Brandon and Evan try to cheer me up as much as possible, but a melancholy has settled over me that I can't seem to shake. I did better than I thought I would going through my dad's things, but the secret room has thrown me for a loop. I don't understand why he hid something like that from me. I knew what he was up to, but he was never one to keep trophies. He always said it was too dangerous, so were those his? Or were they all Grandpa's like the badge probably was, and he couldn't part with them?

I'm pulled out of my thoughts when Brandon stands to take his bowl to the sink. "You going to be ok tonight, Killer? I can stay if you want."

Giving him a strained smile, I shake my head and stand to join him at the sink after grabbing Evan's bowl and kissing him on the cheek. "No, go ahead. I'm fine, just overwhelmed. I'm sure I'll be able to find answers at some point, but I'm not ready to search for them tonight. I think I may watch some TV before heading to bed. Do you want help loading the donations in your car?"

"I'll help," Evan interjects. "Why don't you go take a bath and change into comfortable clothes. I'll help Brandon load the car and find something for us to watch."

"That sounds perfect, thanks." I give Evan a genuine smile and hug Brandon to me, thanking him for his help this evening before I head upstairs to relax in the tub.

It takes us two trips to load everything into Brandon's SUV. We're quiet while we work so Jen doesn't overhear us talking while we're still inside.

"Thanks, man," Brandon says when he closes his trunk.

"No problem. Thanks for dropping it all off." It's one less thing that Jen has to worry about right now, so it's definitely appreciated.

"That's not what I mean. Thanks for taking care of her." He turns, facing me with a serious look on his face and his hands in his pockets. "I know I joke around a lot, but I need you to understand something. That woman in there is everything to me. She is more than a sister. You two almost broke her when you left, but I'm lucky because she's stronger than that. Ryan wasn't the only one she missed, I think she actually missed you more but didn't want to admit it to herself or anyone else. This shit with Ryan is fucked up, but you're both handling everything well. She's hurt and angry, but I think she's more worried about you.

"I have never, and I literally mean never, seen her act with someone the way she's been acting with you the last few days. Even though this crazy shit is going on she seems truly happy. Do not fuck this up, and do not break her heart again, because I will forget how squeamish I am and string you right the fuck up next to Ryan. Get me?"

I stare at him for a moment, stunned. I've never heard Brandon speak like this, and it makes me feel better to know she had this fierce man on her side for the last few years. He's definitely grown up since we were kids.

"I get you. Trust me, I spent the last four years trying to work to make my way back to her. Trying to be worthy of her. The fact that she's even giving me a chance after everything that happened is more than I could have ever dreamed. I would, and will, kill or die for that woman. She's all I've ever wanted, and now that I have her I'm not letting her go. I will do everything in my power to take care of her, and protect her, even though she needs neither."

Brandon snorts a laugh. "Ain't that the fucking truth? She kicks my ass on the regular."

Grinning at him, I laugh because I know it's probably true, which is sexy as fuck. "Just do me a favor, ok?" I pause until he quirks an eyebrow in question. "Lay off the sex pressure. She's not ready, and I don't want to push this. I need to earn it, and her. We aren't in any hurry. I plan to keep her forever, so I don't need to rush things. I don't want her to be nervous or feel pressured around me."

He releases a put upon sigh before nodding. "I know. I'm just so used to teasing her that it's second nature. I'll do my best to stop, but I can't change who I am overnight. Just... be good to her and take care of her. I don't think it's me she needs right now, and as hard as that is for me to admit, I'm glad it's you. I always knew how you felt, and thought you were better for her than Ryan, but I had to let her make the decision for herself. As long as you're doing right by her, I'm on your side."

"Thanks, man. I have to admit, she's not the only one I missed. I'm glad to have you back too. Daniel seems a little fucking weird these days, but I'm guessing it's because he still has a crush on her?"

His scoff is all the answer I need. "I think crush isn't a strong enough word. He's been too chicken shit to say anything to her though, even after all this time. As much as he missed Ryan when you left I think he was glad too. He knew they were getting closer and I think it made him nervous. I think you both, but Ryan especially, being back makes him feel threatened -- which is funny when you think about it. I also think you two keeping things quiet for now is a smart idea. I don't think he would do anything crazy, but I do think it's be one more bit of drama that we can do without at the moment. I cannot fucking handle it when he's in Pouty Pete mode, dude."

"Noted," I say, chuckling. "Alright, I'm going to run in and change so I can put a movie on for us. Hopefully I can help her relax a bit before bed."

We share a quick hug before Brandon walks around to the driver's door. "I'm glad you're back, man," he tells me, looking over to me with a sad smile on his face. "Things weren't the same without you." With that, he ducks into the SUV and heads out.

I make my way upstairs and change into some clean basketball shorts and t-shirt. I grab a large, soft blanket from the linen closet on my way back downstairs and then grab a Diet Coke and water before heading to the couch. Instead of searching through her Amazon Prime account, I log her out and log into my own, quickly pulling up The Labyrinth and queuing it to start. This was always her "cheer up" movie when we were younger. Or her rainy day movie. Or her just because movie. She always said David Bowie in tight pants cures all that ails you.

I would be lying if I said I didn't purchase it and watch it myself the first chance I got once I moved out on my own.

I respond to a few emails and texts while I wait for her to come downstairs, mostly my boss and coworkers checking on me and giving their condolences, and one from the police checking to see if I'd heard from Ryan yet. When I hear her footsteps on the stairs I close my phone and put it on the coffee table before turning to face her.

She is so beautiful it takes my breath away every time I see her. I wasn't lying or exaggerating when I told Brandon I never could have dreamed that she'd give me this chance. As much as I planned and worked towards this, I never thought that she'd want this like I do. I thought for sure I'd have to fight for her, fight Ryan for her or some other guy who was lucky enough to have her affection. I saw Ryan pushing her, and I knew it wasn't the right thing to do. Jen is not a woman who accepts being pushed easily, she never has been. She needs to make her own decisions in her own time. When Ryan told me she'd said she wanted to take things slow, but that he was going to push her to "make her see" he was it for her, I wanted to beat the shit out of him. Just because he thinks he's hot shit on the compound doesn't mean he has the right to take the choice away from her. She's not one of those mild-mannered, obedient females that do what they're told and serve their father or husband blindly.

She's so much more than that. She deserves so much more than that, and I'm going to give it all to her.

Her eyes widen as they land on the paused opening credits, and she looks to me in surprise and something soft. "You remembered? We don't have to watch this, you've seen it enough times. We can find something else."

Holding my hand out to her, I patiently wait for her to grab it and then pull her down to my lap before dragging the blanket over us both. "Hush," I tell her, my lips to her temple. Fuck, I can't get enough of touching her. "We've watched your copy of it. This is my copy and it never felt right watching it without you, so I need to fix that."

I press play and we settle in, but before Sarah hits the screen I can feel her start shaking. Pausing the movie again I move my head back to her find her crying. Silent tears are running down her cheeks and the tip of her nose is turning pink. "Baby girl, what's wrong? Talk to me."

It takes her a few moments to answer, and when she does her voice is quiet and strained. "It's just... I don't know. I'm overwhelmed, I think. My heart is broken for you about Gran, and about your mom. As much as I'm mostly angry about Ryan, my heart is a little broken too. I thought I loved him when we were kids, but the more and more I think about it, the more I can see that he was manipulating me back then. I knew something was off with him when you came back, I think. I kept asking him to give me time to figure things out, and he kept pushing, kept kissing me even when I pushed back. I think I wanted him to be the right one since I spent the last four years not being able to connect with anyone. Learning he's some demented asshat has thrown me for a loop, I guess."

"I can see that. I knew something was wrong too, but I had no idea how bad it was. I think Gran felt it too." My breath catches in my chest as I mention Gran, and even in the middle of her own sadness she takes a moment to press a sweet kiss to my lips to comfort me. I can taste the salt of her tears, and my heart breaks and swells in the same moment. Who knew that was possible?

"It seems like it. I think the worst part is all this shit is bringing up thoughts of my dad. Travis's attack was so much like his, with the only difference is that Travis lived. We go through his things and find a room he kept hidden from me? I don't get it, Evan. We didn't have any secrets. Why would he keep it from me?" The pleading in her eyes is gut wrenching. She's not usually this vulnerable, but the fact that she's allowing herself to be this open with me makes pride surge in my chest and my need to protect her strengthen.

"I don't know, Jen. But I don't think he didn't trust you. I think some things are simply private. We won't know until we get back in there and do some more digging. Do you want to do it tonight? We can if you want to. Or, we can sit here and enjoy a movie together, and let it all go for the evening. We can pick it back up tomorrow, or whenever else you're ready. I promise I'll help. We'll figure it out."

Tucking her head into the crook of my neck, she takes a few deep breaths while thinking about what she wants to do. "Let's watch the movie. It'll all still be there tomorrow, right? I don't think I can take any more bombshells this evening."

"Absolutely. Is tonight going to be a sing along night, or are we just watching?"

Pulling her head back to give me a haughty glare, it takes all my considerable strength to not bust out a laugh at her outrage. "Have you met me? You don't watch The Labyrinth without singing along. Good Lord Evan, did you lose your mind when you left?"

I lose my battle and break out into a belly laugh. Fuck, I missed her. Pulling her in for a hard kiss, I smile when she pulls away and wiggles in excitement as soon as I push play and the music resumes.

Brandon is so worried about sex. When will we have it. What it'll be like. I'm not going to lie, I want that with her. I want to claim every part of her. But, shit. As long as I know she's mine, as long as she's in my arms, every night could be like this and I would die a happy man.

The Labyrinth is one of those movies that always soothes me, no matter what is going on in my life. The fact that Evan remembered and chose it for us to watch together tonight eases a bit of the ache in my heart, though it doesn't fully subside. We're about halfway through the movie before I realize I've been missing things because my eyes have been falling shut more and more frequently. I can't seem to stay awake after the madness of the last few days. Evan's breathing evened out a while ago too, so I'm not surprised when I lift my head to see he's fallen asleep too.

Kissing his cheek softly, I quietly say "Evan, honey, I think it's time for us to go to bed."

"What? Uh, no. I'm fine. Let's finish. I just closed my eyes for a second."

Giggling, I grab the edge of the blanket to pull it off and move to stand. "You may be fine, but I'm not. Come on, we can finish it tomorrow if you want."

"Are you sure?" Groggy, he takes my outstretched hand and stands up after me. I turn the TV off and pull him towards the stairs.

"Definitely, I was falling asleep. I'd rather stretch out and get some rest." When we reach his door I pause, nervously chewing on my lip.

"What is it?" he asks, forehead creased as he uses his thumb to pull my lip out from between my teeth. "Are you ok?"

"Yeah, I'm ok. I was wondering if you would want to sleep in my room tonight. With me, I mean." I pause, realizing how it sounded after I said it. "I didn't mean it like that!" I rush to get the words out after I see the surprise on his face. "I just meant... I have the feeling that I'll have nightmares tonight. Brandon usually stays with me when I get like this. I can call him back if you don't want to. I'd rather it be you tonight, though."

"Of course. Anything you need. Your room, or mine?" I don't see any discomfort or tension on his face, so I take it as a good sign and let out a sigh.

"My bed is bigger. It's a king, so we'll be more comfortable there." I tug him along with our still entwined hands and into my room. It hasn't changed all that much since he last saw it, and he looks around with a smile.

"Alright, hop on in," he instructs me with a slap to my ass. I jump and turn to scowl at him, but end up laughing and pulling him by his shirt to the foot of the bed. Two can play at this game.

Instead of walking around to the side and pulling back the covers to get in, I climb up on the bed at the foot and crawl slowly to the top, making sure I sway my ass as much as possible without looking like I'm having a seizure, or heaven forbid, twerking. I've never tried to be sexy before, so it's entirely possible I'm doing it wrong and it'll have the opposite effect. I refuse to turn and look back at him until I've pulled the blankets down and slid in under them, but when I do I can see it appears I did sexy just fine. Evan is unmoving at the foot of the bed and staring at me with hunger burning in his eyes. There's a sizable bulge tenting his athletic shorts and it takes a moment for him to shake himself out of whatever thoughts have him entranced. Shaking his head with a smirk, he reaches down to adjust himself without a hint of embarrassment as he walks around to the opposite side of the bed to pull back the covers and climb in.

"That wasn't very nice, you know," he growls as he reaches over to pull me to him. "Here I am, trying to be a gentleman, and you have to shake this in my face." Cupping my ass, he leans his head down and presses a kiss to the hollow of my throat before continuing. "You're lucky we're both exhausted tonight, because otherwise I'd be finding out."

"Finding out what?" What the hell is he talking about? When he trails a finger across my chest, I look down and let out what I can only describe as a chortle. I'd forgotten what sleep clothes I'd put on tonight. The bottoms are little black shorts with white and pink skull and crossbones covering the fabric with a white lace trim. My top is a black spaghetti strap with white letters across the front inviting the reader to "Fuck around and find out." Thank God I didn't put on the shorts that say "Ask me about Uranus!" I may need to start paying more attention to what I'm putting on from now on.

Before I can hold it back, I release a jaw cracking yawn that causes Evan to release a quiet chuckle. "See? Exhausted. We can leave everything else until tomorrow. Let's get some sleep, ok? If you have a nightmare, wake me up."

"Ok. Goodnight." I say, snuggling closer into him. I never understood books where the couples always sleep all curled up into each other. Brandon always sleeps on top of me and it drives me insane, even though I like knowing he's there. I often find myself pushing him away in the middle of the night so I can have some breathing room. Evan and I fit together perfectly, though. I stretch my neck up to give him a goodnight kiss, then lay my head on his chest. One of my legs has slid between both of his, and his arms are wrapped around me holding me close. His slow, even breaths lull me into a deep and peaceful sleep.

I don't wake until morning.

Chapter 31

I wake slowly, somewhat groggy from such a deep sleep. I haven't slept that well in a long time, and it always takes me a few minutes for my brain to come back online when I wake. As my senses fire up, I realize I'm really warm. Like back and under boob sweat warm. Gross. Most likely because I'm trapped underneath someone. My first thought is Brandon, but he never sleeps on top of me like this, and I've never felt the hard press of an erection up against me when we sleep together, either. Almost like even in sleep he knows we want to keep those pieces of ourselves apart.

I finally remember I asked Evan to stay with me last night. I switched from laying with my head on his chest to laying on my stomach like I usually do, so he must have followed me. He's still breathing deep and slow so I think he's still asleep, but I have to pee, and he's laying on my bladder. I try to slip out from under him without waking him up, but as soon as I move he groans and pulls me tighter, putting even more pressure on my poor bladder.

"Dude... if you don't let me up I'm going to pee myself. I don't think we want our relationship to start out with that kind of sharing."

He huffs out a tired laugh as he rolls off me and onto his back so stare up at the ceiling. "Sorry," he mumbles groggily as I head into my bathroom. I handle my business and wash my hands while I check myself out in the mirror. I'm rocking my usual bedhead, but finger combing it will at least tame it. I hate brushing my teeth before breakfast because it makes everything taste terrible, but I don't want to rock dragon breath on our first morning together, so I do a quick brush without toothpaste to at least freshen things up a bit.

I head back into the bedroom and he's sitting up and leaning back against the pillows. He lifts my side of the covers for me to slide back in and mumbles "come back here for a minute." When I climb back under the covers and curl up into his side, he pulls me close and kisses my head. He holds me close for a few minutes, and we soak up the early morning quiet. "So," he finally says, breaking the quiet. "What's on tap for today? Is there anything you need to do?"

"Well, we need to give Ryan fluids. We can do whatever else you want to do while we're there. I have no idea if he'll be willing to answer questions yet, but we can try if you want. I also need to make sure the area where the hot tub is going is ready to go for the delivery tonight. What about you?"

"I need to buy a suit today or tomorrow, I don't have one good enough for the funeral. Other than that, the dumpster is scheduled to be here at 10am, so I need to be here. Why don't you shower and get ready for the day, I'll do the same, and then I'll make us breakfast?"

"Sounds perfect," I tell him, and tilt my mouth up for a kiss.

Evan made pancakes, bacon, and hash browns for breakfast. It was all ready for me when I got downstairs after getting dressed for the day, and I cleaned up the dishes since he cooked. While I finished up in the kitchen, Evan's contact with the construction dumpster arrived and he went outside to show them where he wanted it. Luckily a portion of the driveway was under one of the windows in the master bedroom so it will be easy to simply throw most of the construction trash out of the window and into the dumpster instead of carting it through the house. It doesn't take long for them to situate everything outside so by the time I'm done and everything is put away Evan is ready to start our day. I load the IV supplies Brandon brought into a tote bag and we head out to the garage to jump in the UTV and make our way to the barn. I ask Evan to drive again because I can tell how much fun he has doing it.

We decide we're going to have to transfer him over to the table to secure him tightly enough to insert the catheter. He's terrified of needles he'll fight me if he's conscious, so strapping him down is the best option. We're hopeful he'll be out of it when we arrive, allowing us to get him situated where we need him without him fighting us. He's been in there without food or water for a while so he should be pretty drained of energy, but you never know what kind of fight is in a person until they're faced with a life and death situation.

I let us in through the locked doors, securing them shut behind us. Ryan is still hanging in place, his head drooping forward but no indication of whether he's awake or asleep. Quietly, I place the tote bag of supplies on the ground by the door. We each take a side of the table and unlock the wheels before rolling it over directly behind Ryan. He hasn't yet stirred, so I'm pretty sure he's out at this point. Before doing anything else, I head over to the cleaning closet and grab the straps we will use to secure him to the table at ankles, thigh, waist, elbow, shoulder, and forehead. Can't be too careful.

Once I have everything set up I grab the controller for the hook he's hanging from and step to the head of the table to slide it under Ryan as he lowers. Evan takes hold of the restraints keeping his feet together so he doesn't kick out and I push the button to begin to slowly lower the hook he's attached to as I push the table forward. I hear a low, dry groan emanating from Ryan but the only movement is his head rocking to the side. I mouth "Let's hurry" to Evan, who nods at me as he steps back with Ryan's ankle restraints still gripped in his hand. Lifting him from his feet makes it easier to slide the table underneath him and soon enough he's laid out on the table and secured tightly.

I head over to my tote bag and take it to the small rolling tray I use for my tools and start setting things out. Ryan's still unconscious so Evan uses the same hose he used last time to spray him directly in the face. He wakes up shouting as best he can behind his gag, but he's not able to move to turn his face away from the direct spray. After about thirty seconds Evan stops the stream and allows him to catch his breath.

The ball gag is still in place and his mumbled complaints are a continuous stream of nonsense. Finally opening his eyes, his struggle intensifies when he sees Evan and I standing to his side above him, and he realizes he's now laid down on a table and bound to it. His restraints are incredibly tight, though, so he can't move and inch. "Are you done yet?" Evan asks in a bored tone. When Ryan continues to try to fight against his bonds he's hit with another, longer stream of water. "How about now?"

Ryan blinks his eyes furiously in an attempt to clear the water from his lids and glares at Evan with hate.

"Great! Now, this is what's going to happen. Jen is going to start an IV in you so that you don't die of dehydration." He continues over the panicked groaning of Ryan at the news that I'll be coming at him with a needle. "You do have another choice. If you answer our questions we'll give you the food and water we brought in the bag over there, and maybe let you use the bathroom and clean yourself up." Pausing, he wrinkles his nose before continuing, "Although you stink like you didn't want to wait for a bathroom break."

He does smell pretty ripe, I can't lie. I'm just used to so many bad smells it doesn't really bother me anymore.

"So, do you want to talk, or do you want to go with the needle?" Handing me the hose, he reaches forward cautiously and unbuckles and removes the ball gag.

Ryan yelps as the ball is pulled out of his mouth and some small pieces of skin from his lips come off with it. He works his jaw for a few moments and then lets loose with a stream of vitriol so inventive that even I've never heard some of the words and phrases he's using.

I have no idea what thunderfucking is, but I'm totally stealing it for future use.

Deciding to join in on the fun I hit spray with the hose with a direct shot into his foul mouth. He gags and chokes since I aimed the stream right down his throat and Evan hits me with a playful wink when I look over to him.

"Tick tock, Ryan," I tell him. "I've got things to do today, I don't intend to be stuck here with your bratty ass."

"Fuck you!" he snarls at me.

"Ok! IV it is. You'll be happy to learn that I requested the largest needles so we could accomplish this done as quickly as possible for you. What do you think Evan, in the neck? Or I could use the thigh. I'd have to take his pants off for that though and no one here wants to find out what's under them... hmm." I tap my lip as I walk over to the prepared supplies and put my gloves on. I have no idea where he's been and I'm not taking a chance in getting anything from him. Grabbing the catheter, I unwrap it and hold it up, still capped, in Ryan's sight line.

His eyes widen and he grits his teeth to keep from saying anything and veins and muscles pop out on his neck from the tension. Even though he's a dick I'd never try his neck, so as much as I enjoy messing with him I'm not going to even try. I point to two spots on the arm closest to me and jerk my head to direct Evan where to hold the arm down. Thankfully, even though he's dehydrated he's got great veins, so I'm able to easily insert the catheter and add the tegaderm covering it in a few seconds.

"See? You big baby, it didn't even hurt as bad as everything else has in the last few days, I'm sure." Evan continues holding the arm in place as I hook up the IV bag and start the drip. "Okie doke" I chirp happily as I remove my gloves with a snap. "He's all yours, honey bun."

Evan raises an amused brow as Ryan scoffs at my pet name. Exactly why I used it. "Right," Evan begins. "So, do you feel like talking today, or no? We can keep you out here for as long as it takes. Personally, you being here is simply an inconvenience at this point, but I'm willing to put in the work if you are."

"I'm not telling you shit. You're too much of a pussy to do anything worse anyway."

Sighing in resignation since this project is going to be more drawn out than we hoped it would be, Evan moves forward to replace the ball gag in his mouth.

"Sounds good. Come on baby girl, let's go relax for a few minutes while he gets his fluids."

I take his outstretched hand and follow him into the sitting room and over to the chair he sat in only days ago. He sits and pulls me down on his lap, wrapping his arms around me and resting his chin on the top of my head. "I have a feeling it's going to take a while to break him. I was hoping I wouldn't have to get my hands too dirty, but I think I'll have to. I'm not opposed to it, I just wanted to be better than them, you know?"

"I know, I'm sorry. I can do it if you want?"

"No, I can do it. I was just hoping I wouldn't have to. I guess I forgot what a stubborn jackass he is. He'll hold out because he doesn't want me to have the information I need. He's always been like that. He knew I was in love with you when we were kids, and I think that's what pushed him even more to go after you. Everything I've ever loved, he's tarnished. He had to be better at it, or break it, or any number of things."

"Do you have any idea why?" Looking back, I can remember times when Ryan always had to outdo Evan. He had to win the game, or have better grades, or whatever it was that would make him come out on top. "I wonder if it's because of the pastor. He was always demanding Ryan was above reproach."

"I think that has a lot to do with it. I think a good bit of it was ego, too. They both have it. Why else would Uncle Patrick set himself up as the head of a cult? The community wasn't so bad when we got there. I mean, they were crazy devout and segregated themselves from society, but as time went on things started getting stricter and odd things would happen. People would go missing then either come back completely obedient or they wouldn't come back at all."

"How many people didn't come back? Do you think they ran away, or do you think something happened to them?"

"Well, I thought Aunt Stacey and Charles ran away, but we know that's not what happened now. I assumed most of the ones who didn't come back ran away too. They were mostly younger people, almost all girls around eighteen. I figured they'd had enough of the life and escaped, but what if they didn't? Ryan has to know. I need answers so I can figure out if I need to stop them."

"We'll make him talk. We won't stop until we do. In the meantime, we can torture him while we're not even here." I pull back and give him an evil smile.

Eyes narrowed in suspicion he asks, "What are you thinking?"

"I am a master at mental torture. Just ask Brandon." I wink and pop up from his lap and walk over to my dad's old sound docking system. It's wired into the whole building because he always preferred to use his iPod instead of streaming services. I head back to Evan and pull up the iTunes store, searching for Justin Bieber and buying his entire library. Next, Taylor Swift. Finally, I buy the hardest death metal songs I can think of. "Anything else you know he hates?" I ask Evan, grinning.

Laughing, he pauses to think for a minute before adding "He really hates techno."

We spend the next few minutes buying songs and making a playlist to leave on while we're gone. When we're done, I check on his IV. He's finished so I disconnect him, but I decide to leave him on the table since we'll just have to come back and do it again. After I dispose of the supplies and none too gently slap a Band-aid on his arm, I head back into the sitting room and hit shuffle on our new playlist. Justin Bieber begins playing and I cackle evilly before practically skipping back out to the workroom and up to Ryan.

Looking down at him I smirk as I tell him "I figured you're probably getting bored here all alone. We wanted to give you some entertainment to keep you occupied. We'll probably be here tomorrow, but I'm getting a new hot tub delivered so who knows if I'll be able to drag myself away. Oh, and don't worry, the iPod is plugged into a charger and set to shuffle so there's no risk of it shutting off any time soon. Enjoy!"

I stop by the door to turn the volume all the way up and snicker as Ryan starts yelling through the gag in his mouth. I'm pretty sure I heard a "fuck you" in there, but can't be bothered to find out.

Our day is spent running errands and getting the back porch ready for the hot tub delivery. We were able to find Evan a great suit on sale, and I found a dress as well. We also decided to stop for lunch and go furniture shopping for the updated master bedroom.

We ended up being lucky that we took Evan's truck because when we visited my favorite antique store we found the most beautiful king-sized wrought iron bed frame. It's currently painted a garish bright yellow, but I can paint it black and it'll fit perfectly with the look I'm going for in there. I found a few other pieces I think will work well at a furniture store but decided to wait on getting those. Finally, I ordered the wallpaper I wanted for the accent wall in the bedroom. Evan is a fantastic shopping partner. He gives his opinions freely, seems to understand and appreciate the aesthetic I'm going for, and actually pointed out some amazing pieces. He's the one that found the bed frame in the back of the store and recommended we refinish it, and I don't think I could have chosen better myself.

Once we arrive home we load the new bed frame into the garage and Evan heads upstairs to change into work clothes to pressure wash the patio where the hot tub will go. While he's changing I head outside and begin to move the items away from the area where the tub will go and start rearranging everything so it will still flow nicely. I don't want to lose anything out here, but there isn't enough room for everything with the hot tub taking up so much space, so I make the decision to put the table and chairs in storage in the barn for the time being. Noticing the remaining space is somewhat limited, Evan recommends extending the patio footprint and putting in an outdoor kitchen for me which I am so on board with. With that addition incoming, I decide to also add an outdoor TV so we can watch while we soak in the hot tub or relax in the new addition. The sound system is already wired out here, so adding the TV to that shouldn't be too much of a problem.

How did I go from not being sure if I was ready to live here to a serious home makeover?

I don't want to admit it, but it's absolutely Evan. Even though this is my house it almost feels like we're doing it as a couple, for our home that we will share, but I'm afraid to get ahead of myself. I never thought I'd be the girl who jumped headfirst into a relationship, but each moment passing with Evan feels more right. Maybe it's the shared trauma of what is happening, or maybe it's that he's not really a stranger. We may have spent the last few years apart, but I've known him since I was thirteen. While something made me wait and hold myself back from Ryan, I haven't felt that way for a single moment with Evan. He always made me so comfortable, and he still does. His first thought is always of me and I'm finding more and more that my first thoughts are of him too.

I'm happy with how everything is turning out, and I can't wait for the hot tub to be installed so we can start taking advantage of the cooling evenings out there. Hopefully Ryan will break soon so we don't have to keep going back to the barn every day. I don't mind it, but we have to go back to work in a few days and that will cause some scheduling problems.

After power washing the whole patio, because he's sweet like that, Evan decides he's going to put his grubby clothes to use and start the demo in the bathroom upstairs until the delivery guys arrive. I want a new bathing suit for our first time in the hot tub, so I leave him to it and run to the store. I am able to find a beautiful deep purple bikini that doesn't make me feel self-conscious in the least, which is a first for me in a bikini, and the confidence boost it gives me helps me decide I'm going to take the lead in stepping up our physical relationship. Evan and I are alone in the house together and I think he's being too respectful of me to make the first move, so I may have to do it. I make one more stop and pick up some additional supplies for tomorrow night.

If he doesn't start something, I will.

CHAPTER 32

I convince Evan to sleep in my room again, and again he's the perfect gentleman. I can tell he's exhausted since he worked on the bathroom until the delivery arrived and then for a few more hours after dinner, but I was hoping to at least get felt up a little! This time when I try to slide out from under him, he simply rolls over and away from me with a small grunt. I do my business and head downstairs for some sugary cereal to start my day. We don't have anything planned for today other than visiting Ryan, and he worked hard enough yesterday that he should be able to sleep in as long as he wants.

As I rinse my bowl I the sound of Evan tromping down the stairs reaches me. My breath catches when he walks around the corner with his shirt clutched in his hand and his jeans hanging low on his hips.

Dear, sweet, baby Jesus... *hello* abs.

He catches me staring and grins at me like a teasing shithead before slowly pulling his shirt on and giving me a hot kiss. He grabs my ass and pulls me tightly to him, pressing me up against his chiseled stomach. I need to lick those abs... like, stat.

"Good morning, baby girl. See something you like?"

Pulled out of my lustful musings, I immediately school my face to a look of thoughtful disgust as I walk away. "Eh, not really. I was distracted by how frail you look. Are you eating enough? You need to bulk up a bit. It's actually quite off-putting."

Smirking, he stalks up to me with a wicked gleam in his eyes. He leans down and whispers "I definitely need to eat something... but I'm not sure if it's breakfast." Licking the shell of my ear before taking a step back, he winks at me and turns to the fridge.

Freaking tease. He's talking a lot of big game for someone who isn't following through.

We head back to the barn after Evan eats, and we're determined to move things along. Gran's funeral is tomorrow, and we both go back to work a few days later. I also need to work on my classes. I was able to receive extensions on my schoolwork for the week, but I need to catch up. There are too many things going on and dealing with Ryan will make everything more difficult.

We pull up to the barn in the UTV and Evan follows me to the front door. Before I can unlock it, he spins me around and lifts me by my ass, slamming me against the door and taking my mouth in a hard, fierce kiss. The gasp I release at the suddenness of the action allows him to plunge his tongue into my mouth and tangle it with mine. He releases me on one side, still holding me up with one arm, and grips my hair at the nape of my neck in a tight fist and uses it to tilt my head back to exactly where he wants it. Fuck. Who knew I'd like to be dominated? I've always liked it in the books I read, the whole Alpha male dominates strong willed female and she still likes it because it lets her lose control and feel tiny and feminine trope, but in real life? Hell no. I'm too badass for that, right?

Wrong. I am so fucking here for this.

As soon as I start rolling my hips in an effort to relieve the tension is building between my legs, Evan pulls back from me and rests his forehead against my collarbone. "Sorry," he apologizes. "I needed to do that before heading into this clusterfuck. I'm not looking forward to this, but I'm tired of waiting and I want to move past everything. I want us to move forward without this hanging over our heads."

Sigh. "You're a cunt tease, Ev. But I get it. Let's make him talk."

As soon as the door opens, we're accosted by the tones of Taylor Swift at a deafening volume so the first thing I have to do is turn that shit off. Blissful silence settles over the room for a moment before Ryan realizes there's been a change, and he begins fighting against his restraints and screaming out through his gag. He's obviously weaker now than he was when we first locked him up, and I'm hopeful that means it will finally be easier to pull answers from him.

He smells terrible and looks worse, so I quickly go about getting his IV set up before anything else. I don't want him too weak to answer our questions when we start to break him. When the IV set up and going, Evan goes through my cabinets and tool boxes to pull out the instruments he wants.

"Alright, asshole. Today is going to be a little different," he announces, rolling the cart over next to the table. "I'm not fucking around with you anymore. We've got shit to do that doesn't involve you. Gran's funeral, thanks to you, is tomorrow. We also have to go back to work. I'd like to spend the rest of my spare time between those pretty thighs over there instead of in here fucking with you, so it's time to put up, or be shut up. Your choice, cuz."

I do my best to hide my shock at his comment of "being between my pretty thighs" because he hasn't tried anything yet. Part of me wonders if he's been waiting for this to be over before he makes a move, but the other part is wondering if he said it to fuck with him. Regardless, I play along and smirk over Ryan's head and wiggle my eyebrows at Evan to show we're a united front and help him situate things. While we wait for the IV to finish we retreat to the sitting room and make out like teenagers until my timer goes off. I set it for a few minutes early to give us time to change into the coveralls and boots since things are probably going to be a little messy.

Just to fuck with him a little more, I leave my sleeves off again and tie them around my waist so my tattoos are shown off by my low cut tank top. It's the little things in life, right?

"Time's up, buttercup!" I sing as I skip into the work room. "Let's get you disconnected so we can spend some quality time together, shall we?" I disconnect him quickly and roughly slap a Band-aid on him since we don't want him bleeding from areas that aren't intentional. As I'm disposing of the used IV supplies, Evan is getting the hose ready. I wasn't exaggerating about the smell, it's like an outhouse which isn't surprising since we haven't allowed him to use a bathroom in several days. We release the restraints holding him to the table and again maneuver him until he's hanging from the ceiling.

His angry screams are music to my ears as he gets another hose bath. I *may* even take the hose from Evan and shoot it at high power at his crotch for a minute until he's groaning in pain, but if I did, it was totally an accident.

I hose the table off while I let him drip and then head over and take his gag off. I busy myself sanitizing the table and drying it off while Evan stands in front of Ryan. He grabs the hair on the top of his head to use as leverage and forces him to look him in the eye. "What's the verdict? Because I woke up today and chose violence. You're not surviving this, so you can end things as they are, or with a lot more pain."

"Fuck... you..." Ryan rasps.

"You know," Evan says, "I was kind of hoping you'd say that. I missed my usual workout this morning after waking up next to that little vixen over there." He drops his head and walks over to the table of tools he'd laid out previously. For the first time I notice there are two small rolls of fabric on the table like fighters use to protect their hands, and I like where this is going. He quickly wraps up and I walk over to him and give him a quick kiss before hopping up on the work table and leaning back to watch. I have a feeling things are about to get fun.

Watching Jen fuck with Ryan in subtle, and not so subtle, ways turns me the fuck on. She is so absolutely beautiful, so sweet and caring, so fucking strong, and this is a side of her I never knew existed. I knew she was tough and had a little devil in her, but I never knew she had a dark side to match my own. Knowing that she can not only take care of herself, but that she would never run from me because of the things I have done, or will do, fills me with a sense of peace I couldn't have anticipated. Seeing her eye fuck me as I wrap my hands in preparation to beat the shit out of my asshole cousin?

That fills me with something else.

I reach down without shame and adjust my hard dick in my pants while I stare her down. Don't need it getting in the way of the ass beating I'm about to lay down, plus, the way she bites her bottom lip as she watches me is hot as hell. I think having this final proof that she's turned on by the violence is not only sexy as fuck, but it calms my fear that she would run if she saw this side of me. I've been putting off getting too intimate with her because I've been worried she'd run and I wouldn't be able to let her go. I never want to take her choice from her, but I need her to accept that she's mine. Watching her now though? I'm done stalling. That ass is going to be mine tonight.

Before turning my attention to my groaning cousin, I step up to Jen and widen her legs to stand between them. It was pretty obvious she liked it a little rough earlier, so I grip her hair and ass and pull her against me as I take her mouth. The delicious sounds she makes as I grind my cock into her make me wish we were back at the cabin, but I also kind of like that I'm making her wait for it. I pull back suddenly and nip her lip. "This ass is mine later," I whisper. "Let me know if you want in on the fun though, yeah?"

I chuckle as she takes a moment to focus before swallowing and nodding her head. Thank God I'm not the only one being affected like this, her pupils are blown and her breathing is hitching in her chest, and I know she wants me as much as I want her. I give her one last sweet kiss and step back, turning to face my cousin who is scowling at me through narrowed eyes.

"Ready, cuz?" His lip lifts in a sneer, but he doesn't say anything else. "First, I want to you to tell me about Gran. Second, your plans for Jen. Then, I want to know about my mom and Charles. I could honestly give a fuck about your bitch of a mother. Are you going to play ball? Or am I going to hurt you? I have to warn you, I'm starting to think the violence turns my girl on, so I have zero problems beating the shit out of you in front of her."

"Eat shit."

"Fair enough." I tell him. Without telegraphing my intentions, I start with a combo to his center. His grunts of pain are like music to my ears. He's caused so much suffering in his short life, it's time he suffers as well. I move around him, using him as I would if he were a heavy bag, and simply get my usual workout in. When I reach his back, I can't help but look up and meet Jen's eyes. Her lips are slightly parted and her perfect tits are heaving with her heavy breaths. I knew it! She's turned on.

I wink at her and circle back around to his face after hitting his kidneys. "How about now?"

He's breathing heavy and groaning, his head lolling in place. "I said... eat... shit."

"Ok then." I punch him across the face so hard his head snaps back on his neck and falls forward from the force. Blood is almost instantly dripping from his lips and a tooth falls to the floor at his feet. "You want in on this, baby girl?"

"Fuck yes! I thought you'd never ask." Jen hops down from the table and saunters up to Ryan, a look of concentration on her face. "Is it that you like the pain? Because we can give you that. Either way, I promise you we will figure out what it will take to break you." She quickly steps to the side as he spits blood in her direction, and I step right back up and pop him again.

This time, he falls unconscious. "Damn," she pouts. "I was going to kick him in the balls."

I smile at her and pull her to me. "Wanna make out for a few until he wakes up?" Her flirty eyes act as all the permission I need, so I pick her up and lay her down on the work table. "It's a shame I haven't fucked you yet, because I'd be bending this sweet ass over one of the chairs in the other room right now."

Her eyes widen in surprise, but I see the moment she decides to play things cool. "Not right here? The other room seems pretty far away."

"Fuck no. You're mine. No one else gets to see you naked. I don't care if he's about to die." I pause, realizing that if I'm not going to fuck her here, I can finally claim one small piece of her that I've been dying for since we were younger.

"Actually, you know what? Come on." I pick her back up and carry her into the sitting room anyway. I've been waiting too long, years, to touch her like I want to. I'm not going to fuck her now, but I'll be damned if I waste another minute without finding out what she tastes like.

She's grinding her pussy on my abs as we walk and I can feel the heat radiating off her, and it's only causing my dick to get harder. The little licks, sucks, and bites she's peppering my neck with are leaving a trail of cool moisture on my skin and sending shivers up my spine. I think I hear Ryan groan but I honestly could not care less about that fuck at this moment, so I speed up until I am able to stop in front of the chair she placed me in when we shared our first real kiss and place her on her feet. Looking into her eyes, the same heat and uncertainty I'm feeling is reflected back at me. Neither of us has ever gone this far before. I watched porn, only ever seeing her instead of the actresses to try to learn what to do if I ever got the chance to be with her. I felt like an idiot, but I even talked to my boss about it. He gave me advice that I'll never forget -- "Just do what feels right and listen to her body, not her words. Their words might lie, but their bodies never will."

I lean forward and catch her lips in a brief, sweet kiss. Pulling back, I smile and say "I want to taste you baby girl. Will you let me do that?"

Her beautiful cheeks pink up adorably and she looks down, chewing her plump bottom lip. "I, um... you don't have to. I haven't had that done before. I don't know what to do."

I chuckle as I kneel at her feet and take her boots off while she balances herself on my shoulders. I untie the sleeves from around her waist and slowly lower the zipper, revealing a pair of the sexiest tiny shorts I've ever seen under her coveralls, and I groan in appreciation. "Then we'll have to figure it out together, because I haven't either. I just have to try. Are you ready for this?"

"Fuck yes," she whispers, watching me undress her. I pull her feet out of the pants and throw them aside before sliding my hands up her thighs to the waistband of those tiny fucking shorts. Half of me wants to burn them, the other half wants her to wear nothing but them for the rest of her life. I pull them down, slowly exposing her milky skin to my eyes, but I pause when a flash of color catches my attention high up on her left thigh right below the crease at her hip. Shaking myself and continuing with my movement, I stare at that patch of colored skin as I reveal it instead of looking at my ultimate goal, but I can't help it. The tattoo itself is a rendering of her turtle pendant, shaded in a style similar to the water color sleeves on her arms, but in an exact match to the green of her eyes. I look up and catch those beautiful eyes with mine, seeing her blush still gracing her cheeks, and bend forward to place a kiss to the ink that acts as one more piece of proof that we're made to be together.

I can't wait until I show her my own surprise later.

Pushing thoughts of turtles from my mind, I press a gentle kiss to the junction of her thighs and have her step out of the shorts and panties before sitting on the chair. She's practically panting at this point, and if I'm honest with myself so am I. I press a hand to her chest and gently push her back so she is reclining and then begin licking, sucking, and biting my way up the inside of her thighs. So much of myself wants to dive in and make her scream, but this is our first time and I want to savor every moment of making her mine. Before I can stop myself, I grab her ass and pull her core to the edge of the seat and lick my way up the crease at her hip, biting gently when I reach the highest point. Her groan as she drops her legs further apart has me reaching down to adjust my dick again. I consider cupping myself, but I don't want to lose myself too quickly. I have a feeling if I do, I'll embarrass myself spectacularly.

I continue teasing her until she whimpers. "Evan, please!" I can't deny her anything, so I reach up and part her lips with my fingers and lick a long swipe from bottom to top, closing my eyes from a heady combination of her taste and the guttural sound that leaves her throat.

Perfection.

CHAPTER 33

H oly. Shit.

Holy shit! I'm pretty sure I'm losing my life force through my vagina right now.

I'm not a stranger to self stimulation. I have plenty of toys. My friend Jo is a sex toy party rep, and girlfriend has really hooked me up over the years, so I've brought on a bunch of solo O's. Shit, if I'm lazy but horny I can make it happen in 30 seconds or less sometimes. Nothing I've tried before feels close to this though.

His warm breath against my skin. His strong hands gripping me and pulling me tightly to him. His firm, wet tongue lapping at my clit. His blunt teeth nibbling on my lower lips.

Who the hell would have thought biting down there would be a thing? Not me, but fuck am I here for it.

My hands move to him of their own accord, one to the top of his head to pull him closer, the other to his shoulder to hold on tight. I'm so lost in the pleasure I don't realize he's released me with one hand until his finger slides under his tongue and dips slowly into my opening. "Oh, shit!" I cry out, pulling him to me harder.

His lips curl into a smile against my flesh, and I reluctantly allow him to pull his head back to look at me. "Do you like this, baby girl? Should I keep going?" An evil glint fills his eyes, and I narrow mine at him in irritation.

"You'd better not fucking stop. If you do, I'll kick you out to go play with your cousin and finish myself off!"

That wipes the smirk from his face. "Just for that, I'm going to fuck you with my fingers, and I'm not going to stop until you cum on my face. This orgasm is mine," he growls, diving back down and immediately starts sucking on my clit as he keeps his promise and starts fucking me with first one, then two strong fingers.

I can't even hold on to him at this point, I'm just grabbing on to whatever I can in a futile attempt to anchor myself. The boxing wraps he left on his hands are adding to the pleasure each time they caress my sensitive skin. I thought being with someone would be different, logically of course it would, but the overwhelming sensations I'm experiencing are more than I ever could have anticipated.

Before long, I can feel the tightening in my core that signals my impending orgasm, and I can't stop myself from reaching up to again grab the back of his head to pull him closer while grinding myself into him from below.

"Fuck, Ev. Please, don't stop! I'm so close!" My breathing is labored, my heartbeat is racing, and I am so close to the edge that my entire body is tensing up in anticipation. Suddenly, Evan sucks my clit into his mouth for one final time and bites down, and my entire body tenses as I shatter into a billion messy, sated pieces.

Did my soul leave my body? I'm pretty sure my soul just left my body.

That's ok though. I'll just lay here in a puddle of satisfaction until it comes back. It shouldn't take too long, right?

Slowing my breathing, I blink my eyes open, not remembering when I closed them, and I look down my body to find Evan smiling at me and licking his lips. "I told you I'd make you cum on my face." Groaning and rolling my eyes at his arrogance, I lean up and wrap my hand around the back of his neck and pull him in for a kiss. The taste is a little weird, but if he can deal with it, so can I.

As I reach my other hand down to pull down the zipper to his coveralls and return the favor, we both still as Ryan calls out from the work room. "Are you going to keep fucking your whore or do you want to talk about Gran?"

Evan's face turns from blissed out and aroused to enraged as soon as he hears the word whore. I grab his face between my hands and force him to look at me before he stands up to attack Ryan. Quiet enough so Ryan can't hear me, I say "We just shared something beautiful. Do not let him take that from us. If he wants to think I'm a whore because I have tattoos and because I'm with you, then let him. He's going to be dead in a few days anyways, and you know the opinions of limp-dicked fuckwads never bothered me."

That pulls a smile out of him, and he shakes his head with a fond look on his face. "I've always loved your elegant way with words. You're right though. It will drive him crazy if we don't show him his bullshit is working." Sighing, he pecks me on the lips one last time before standing up and gathering my clothes for me. "Thank you." He hands me my coveralls but withholds my panties and shorts. "I'm keeping these for now, though."

I shake my head and reluctantly get dressed. I hate going without panties, but if it makes him feel better, I'll suck it up. I redress and check myself in the mirror.

My lips are swollen, my skin is flushed, and my hair is all over the place. I might care if someone other than Ryan would be seeing me like this but I really, really fucking don't. He already thinks I'm a whore, and throwing it in his face that Evan is getting what he wanted for himself is fun. Coming up behind me, Evan wraps his arms around me and rests his chin on my shoulder. "Beautiful," he says, before kissing me behind my ear and reaching forward to grab my hand. "Let's go get some answers."

Ryan's head has fallen forward allowing a small of blood pool to collect at his feet, and his wet shirt is covered with thick red lines. It's my favorite look on him yet.

"Alright, we're here. Talk." Evan guides me back to the table so I can sit, and he hops up next to me. Ryan lifts his head and sneers at Evan before spitting more blood on the ground, and Evan smiles and sucks two of his fingers slowly into his mouth in a way that leaves no question as to where they've been. Why is that so hot? It shouldn't be hot, right?

"Sorry to be a cock block, bro." Ryan mumbles his answer through a swollen jaw. "Actually I'm not. Probably saved you from getting a disease."

"Oh, you mean you think my pussy isn't good enough for you now, after you just told me you begged your father to let you have me for four long years? Shame, shame, Ryan. Jealousy is not a good look."

"Fuck you, whore."

Evan moves to rise from the table, but I put a hand on his arm to still him. Looking down at me in question, his face smoothes into a smirk when I give him a saucy wink. I hop down and stride over to where Ryan is hanging, put my hands on my hips and look him up and down. With a disappointed shake of my head, I rear back and kick him in the dick as hard as I can. The scream he releases is filled with agony, and I soak it up as I practically skip back to table. I climb back up next to Evan and cross my legs while I wait for him to stop swinging on his chains and the new and pitiful keening to stop. Evan pulls me close and kisses the side of my head. Not bothering to lower his voice, he says "Damn, you're hot when you're fucking him up."

I wiggle my eyebrows as we wait for Ryan to quiet again. A few minutes pass before he calms, though it's obvious he's still in pain. "So, are you going to talk now, or are we going to have to keep convincing you?"

"Tell me what you want to know, and I'll tell you if I'll answer," Ryan replies, sounding braver than I can tell he really is at the moment.

"I want to know why. Why did you kill Gran when all she wanted to do was help us? She loved you, and you fucking killed her." Evan's tone is calm, his face seemingly unaffected, but his body is shaking with grief, anger, and tension. I am so proud of how strong he's being, but I need to hold back showing him until we're done here.

"Gran was a bitch," Ryan breathes. "She didn't love me. She loved you." More heavy breathing, more spitting blood. "She only invited me... to get to you."

"She did love you, idiot! She was trying to save you!" Evan obviously can't control himself anymore. The grief of losing his grandmother to the hands of his cousin is draining, and I don't blame him. I place my hand on his thigh to remind him I'm there for support but otherwise stay silent.

"No... she only brought me because of you. She told Dad as much! Gran told me if I didn't get my shit together and start distancing myself from Dad and the community she'd cut me off and take me out of her will. When I still refused she told me to pack my stuff by the end of the week and leave. That didn't work for my plan, so while you were gone today I pushed her down the stairs." He tries for a nonchalant shrug while his arms are suspended over his head. "It works better for me this way. I don't have to listen to her shit anymore, and I get her money. I figured I could inherit before she had the chance to take me out of the will and at least take the money back to the community. To Dad."

"So, you killed her for money? Is that what you're saying?"

"If that's how you want to think about it. Besides, she was ridiculous. She had to buy our time to get us to come here. The only reason I came was because Dad said I had to be married to take over for him. You know there aren't any women in the community who were good enough, so I convinced him to let me have Jen. Which is moot now since I can't bring her home looking like that. No one will accept her!"

Evan squeezes my waist to draw my attention to him. "Do you have any questions about this? I think I'm done listening to him today."

"Nope, I think that's all we needed from him on this subject, unless you need more answers."

"Nope. You can get changed if you want. I'll just be a minute."

"Oh hell no. I'm going to sit right here and watch whatever happens."

Kissing my temple, Evan slides off the table, grabs the gag, and saunters over to Ryan. "Anything else you want to add today? Tomorrow is the funeral, so we won't probably won't be by. It's going to be a long 36 or so hours for you."

"I got nothin'." His attempted sneer is ruined by the lopsided nature of his face and the blood still trickling out of the corner of his mouth.

"Alright then," Evan responds before buckling the gag back into his mouth. I thought he was going to leave him like that so I start sliding off the table, but then Evan again begins using Ryan as a punching bag again and I happily retake my seat. Why don't I have popcorn? Next time I'll have to bring snacks. Oh, maybe some gummy bears!

He's staying away from his face, hopefully because he realizes another hit there may make him start bleeding enough that he'll choke on his own blood. Not that I'd be upset if he died that way, I can't imagine it's a fun way to go, and he absolutely deserves it. I only worry we won't get the rest of the answers Evan wants.

Instead of watching the blows land, I watch Evan's form. Since my dad was bigger the coveralls are baggy, but I can tell he's been training for a long time. His form is impeccable and his movements are liquid. I'd love to see him go against someone who could actually fight back, he looks like he'd demolish anyone who tried to take him on.

And... my panties are damp. Well, they would be if I had been allowed to wear them. Oopsies.

After about five minutes, Evan slows and stops. Ryan is obviously in pain, and blood is leaking out of the gag. Holding his hand out to me, Evan asks "Are you ready, baby girl?

"Sure. Let's change and head home. Oh, and don't let me forget to put his mood music back on before we leave!"

Ryan's more aggressive groan at that news brings a smile to my face.

We spend the day working upstairs in the master bathroom. Well, he spends the day in there. I help him for a while then busy myself cleaning the rest of the house. Brandon and Daniel are still planning on coming over for dinner tomorrow night, so I'd rather prep things today so I don't have to do it tomorrow after the service, or once I have to go back to work. The boys will want steaks, so I run to the grocery store to buy what we'll need for dinner. I make the pasta salad and start the steaks marinating. I thought about moving Evan's things from the guest room into mine, but we're still not ready to tell Daniel we're together yet, so if they stay over he will need to still have his stuff in there.

I don't know why we haven't told him about us yet. He's just been so off since the guys came back and I want to avoid any drama possible, especially with the funeral being tomorrow. We talked on the drive back from the barn this morning and agreed we'd tell him soon, just not yet. Something in my gut tells me it's the right choice.

Dinner is more leftovers from Mrs. C and her amazing friends. It's almost surprising how comfortable we are with each other after so long apart, but I think spending this time together is helping me to imagine what life could be like with him, and I'm finding myself considering asking him to stay with me past this week, not just allowing him to stay here while he does the work on the house. We could split time between here and my apartment until the master is finished, and then make this our home. Would he want that though? Do I want that?

"Jen?" Evan's voice breaks into my thoughts and causes me to jump in my seat.

"Shit!" I laugh out. "Sorry, I zoned out there for a second."

"No worries. What were you thinking about so hard?"

"Just thinking about what happens next. Do you have any plans yet? Things have been moving kind of fast paced since you came back."

"I have no idea." He pauses to look at me and shrugs. "I haven't really thought about it at all, though I probably should. I've just been focusing on you, Ryan, and Gran's funeral, you know? I guess that's probably not the brightest idea."

"No, it's fine," I assure him, covering his hand with mine. "There has been so much shit going on so it's totally understandable. Why don't we forget about everything for tonight and reevaluate after the funeral tomorrow. If you want input, we can talk it over just the two of us, or we can bounce ideas off the guys too. It's your decision, but I'm here no matter what."

"Sounds great. I would love your input." He stands up and leans forward to kiss me on my temple. "Why don't we clean up and then hit the hot tub? It should be ready now and I've been dying to get in there. I've been toiling away for you all day so you owe me a soak and a massage."

"I guess I can handle that, since I did agree to your terms. Though, I wonder if another contractor would agree to take the job under similar terms, but instead I'm the one getting the massages?"

Evan narrows his eyes at me and growls low. "Fuck that. You signed a contract, baby girl."

"Oh yeah? I don't remember doing that. When did that happen?"

Leaning in close, he whispers "It was around the time you were coming in my mouth." I don't even try to suppress my full body shudder and faint happy sigh escaping my lips. Evan chuckles and swats my ass, directing me to start moving again so we can relax.

We quickly clean up and I send him upstairs to take a shower before he changes into his bathing suit since he's been working upstairs. Knowing he doesn't take long to shower, I rush to put my plan into action. In order to save time, I put my new bikini on under my clothes earlier, so all I have to do now is set everything up. I bought a few dozen electrical candles, a few citronella candles in case the bugs bother us, and a nice white wine I've been chilling for tonight. I set up everything around the hot tub and run to the downstairs bathroom to strip out of my clothes and make sure my suit looks good. I twist my hair up into a clip with a few strategic tendrils hanging loose and grab the sheer black cover up I purchased to accentuate my suit. And my tits.

Looking in the mirror, I'm happy with how I look. My face is makeup free so nothing smears when I'm wet, my natural curl is on point today, my tits and ass look fabulous in this bikini, and the black and purple tones make my porcelain skin pop and bring out the highlights in my hair.

I can hear him moving around upstairs, so I hustle myself back to the porch, turn on a new playlist and hop up on the ledge of the tub to wait for him. Marilyn Manson's cover of Cry Little Sister is a perfect start to this moment. Watching through the open patio door, I see the moment Evan turns the corner and notices my hard work. He stops short and his mouth drops open in surprise as his eyes move from the candles to me. I'm doing the best I can to not perv out on him and drool over the completely lickable body that is emphasized by his simple black swim trunks, and I'm glad I did because looking at his face allowed me to catch him eye fucking me as he bites his bottom lip after swallowing hard.

Slowly, he makes his way out to the patio and stops a few feet away from me. "What's all this?" he asks with a smile.

I shrug with nonchalance and smirk when his eyes follow the way my wrap slides from my shoulder. "I figured we needed a night to ourselves. You were right earlier, you've started the work upstairs and I haven't lived up to my end of the deal yet." Reaching my hand out to beckon him closer, I smile as he comes to me and takes my hand. "Tomorrow is going to be a hard day, and we've got so much going on. Let's forget about everything else tonight and relax. It will all still be there tomorrow. I want tonight to be just about us."

Sighing, his shoulders drop as he steps forward and touches his forehead to mine. "That sounds great. I can't believe you did this."

Another shrug. "You deserve it. Come on, let's hop in." I step to the closest chair and slowly slip my wrap off. He groans behind me and before I can turn around I'm swept off my feet and into his strong arms.

"You're going to be the death of me," he mumbles into the skin at my neck. Still holding me, he lifts me over the edge of the hot tub so I don't have to climb in, and the hot water feels amazing in contrast to the slightly chilly evening air. He climbs in behind me and pulls me off the side and down to his lap, cradling me against him like I'm something precious. I curl against him happily, reveling in the feel of him and wondering how I lived without him for the last few years. "You are so beautiful, Jen. I don't know how I'm ever going to get used to the idea that I can reach out and touch you anytime I want. I'm afraid I'm going to blink and wake up and this will all have been a dream. Or, you'll realize how special you are and try to leave me."

"Only try?" I ask with a smirk.

"I told you, once you agreed to be mine you became mine forever. I've waited for you for seven years. I'm not giving you up now that I have you. You don't have a choice anymore. Contract, remember?"

"Good thing I'm happy right where I am," I tell him, letting the water hold me up while I turn in his lap, so I straddle his waist instead of sitting across his legs. I wrap my arms around his neck and lean in to kiss him. My breasts are pressed tightly against his chest and I can his erection grows hard beneath me while his hands slide up my sides and caress my back in a feather-light touch. The fire from earlier in the barn is still burning hot between us, but neither of us seem to be in a hurry. His touch is as languid as our kiss, and we simply enjoy each other for a few minutes. Eventually we break apart and I curl up against him, happy to simply be able to take some time to relax with him.

After a few minutes of silence, his body has gotten slightly tense beneath me, and he's tightened his grip on me enough that I can't move. "Ev? Honey, what's wrong?" I can't hide the worry in my tone, I don't understand where the relaxed Evan from a few minutes ago has gone. "Did I do something wrong?"

I pull back hard enough that he loosens his grip so I can look at him, and his cheeks and ears are red. It's so warm in the tub that I can't tell if it's from the heat or embarrassment, so I wait patiently for a response.

"Uh, yeah," he murmurs, causing me to jerk back in surprise. "I mean, no! No, you didn't do anything wrong. I was just thinking."

"About what?"

He hesitates, searching my face for something. He must have found whatever he was looking for because he quickly mumbles "Fuck it," and pulls me in for a swift, hard kiss. "I know what I want. For my future, I mean."

"Oh, ok." I study him with my brow furrowed. "Did you change your mind? Because I don't know if I can let you go either."

The look on his face is part offended, part amused. "Fuck no. I was trying to think about how to tell you I'm moving in. With you, I mean. Here. Or your apartment. Wherever." I can feel my eyes growing wider with every word. He wants to move in with me? I can't say I wasn't thinking the same thing, and I'm glad to know it isn't just me thinking this way, but damn.

"Isn't that... I don't know, too quick?" I ask him, chewing on my bottom lip.

"You don't want me to? I've already been here almost a week, and we work well together. I guess I can fin out what's going to happen to Gran's house and stay there for a while if it's an option for me, but I don't want to wait. I don't see a reason to put off the inevitable."

"No! No that's not it. I was actually going to talk to you about it too, but was going to wait until after tomorrow to bring it up. I just don't want to do this, get more attached to you, and then have you leave again." I grab his chin as tight as I can and force him to look into my eyes and understand how serious I am. "I will not survive it if you leave me again, Evan Holmes. And honestly? I would probably make sure you wouldn't survive it either. Not after all this. You are fucking mine. I'm sorry I didn't understand it when we were younger, but I do now, and I'm not letting you go."

A slow, satisfied smile graces his lips and his wet hands rise from the water to cup my face. "I'm not going anywhere, baby girl. Only death will get rid of me, and I don't plan on dying anytime soon now that you're mine. I love you, and I will never leave you again. If I can promise you anything, I can promise you that."

My breath hitches and my heart flutters in my chest in response to his words while tears well in my eyes. I desperately want to say the words back, but I'm afraid it's too soon to be sure this is love. I loved Ryan, I thought, but it was so different and nearly broke me when he left. Do I even know what love, other than familial love, is? I'm not sure, and I'm almost terrified this is what it feels like. Because I wasn't kidding, I'm not sure I'd survive losing him.

His lips meet mine almost like he was afraid I wouldn't respond and didn't want to face the rejection. I allow it for now but I need to figure out what is going on inside my head and heart as soon as possible, so I simply deepen our kiss and swallow the moan that escapes him. His dick had softened while we talked, but I noticed as soon as I started threatening him he began growing thick again. After a few purposeful hip rolls, his dick is fully hard, and he's holding me to him by my nape and my waist and grinding up into my core like he can fuck me through our bathing suits.

The sensation of his erection against my pussy is enough to make my head drop back and a low throaty moan to escape my lips. My eyes are closed and my hips are moving against him in an instinctual roll, my mind solely focused on the pressure between my legs. Evan's hand slides up my back until he reaches the tie of my bikini top, pulling on one of the strings until the bow is undone and my breasts are revealed to his hungry gaze. "Fuck," he croaks, bringing the hand he used to untie my top around to caress the skin around my taught nipple before gently tugging on the bars bisecting them. "Sometimes I can't believe you're real."

Using the hand at the nape of my neck, he pulls me back slowly so he can lick his way from the base of my cleavage to my collarbone before taking one peaked tip in his mouth. His mouth is so warm and wet, his tongue laving my nipple as he sucks and nibbles, causing me to cry out and grind down on him harder. Moments later his fingers sink below the water and find the edge of my bottoms just beside my clit. Pulling them to the side, he circles my clit with a finger before licking a trail across my chest to my other nipple. I let him play with me for a few minutes, enjoying the multitude of pleasurable sensations before I reach down and begin untying his trunks. I wasn't sure if these would have a fly like other shorts, but thankfully they do, because it only takes seconds for me to undo his shorts and reach in to grab his hard dick.

His actions falter the moment I wrap my fingers tightly around him and he drops his forehead to my chest. "Shit," he breathes. I've read enough dirty books and watched enough porn to have a general idea of what to do, so I free his erection and stroke him slowly from base to tip and rub my thumb around the thick head. I guessed before now that he wasn't lacking in the cock department, but my fingers can barely touch while wrapped around him, and I don't think both of my hands holding it would span the entire length, though it may be close. He's basically the size of my favorite toy, and I cannot wait to feel him inside of me. As I continue to explore him his finger resumes its dance over my clit causing my hips to chase his touch and my own fingers to tighten around him. He twists his wrist and plunges two fingers inside of me as soon as he finds my opening and it's almost like that is the catalyst causing both of us to lose all control. I match his pace, speeding up as he does and tightening my grip as he adds pressure to my clit.

"God damn," he finally breathes, slowing and then removing his fingers to grip my hips and pull me down on him. "Grind down on my cock, baby girl. I want to feel you against me."

I smile and lean into him, pressing my tits against his chest to have some much-needed friction against my nipples and using the hand still wrapped around him to hold his erection against my pussy as I rock back and forth against it. The sensation of his hard flesh against my skin is overwhelming, and he must feel it too because he groans in what sounds like pain.

"I'm going to cum, Jen. Shit, you feel so good I don't think I can hold back."

"Good. Let go, please." Hearing, seeing, and experiencing him let go is the hottest thing I've ever experienced. I build towards my own climax and I hold his face to ensure we're looking into each other's eyes as we both climb to our own peaks.

It's taking everything I have to not impale her on my cock. I'm close enough I'd probably lose it the second I had her wrapped around me, so my potential embarrassment is all that holds me back. I've been dreaming of this moment for seven years, and nothing I imagined comes close to this.

I reach up and take her lips with my own as I pull her down on me harder and faster in hopes that I can make her cum before I do. She pulls back, still cupping my face and staring straight into my soul with beautiful, hooded green eyes. Reaching down and around her I slide my fingers far enough forward to reach her opening, thanks to the angle she's using to grind against me. Just like back at the barn, I first slide one, then two fingers inside her and stroke her tight walls in hopes of helping her cum first. Instead of allowing me to control the pace she starts riding my fingers in a frenzy, arching her back and using one hand on my shoulder to steady herself while her other still squeezes my cock and holds me against her pussy so I can hit her clit with every pass. Her moans are music to my ears and her perfect tits are bouncing so close to my face that I can't help but bend down to take one tight nipple into my mouth.

"Fuck!" she groans. "Are you close, Ev? I'm so close and I want you to come with me."

Am I close? It took an act of god not to cum the second she wrapped her hands around me, so yeah. You could say that.

"Cum on me, baby girl. I'll be right there with you," I lean closer to her and whisper in her ear, "then I'm going to take you upstairs and lick your pussy until you come on my face again. And then I'm going to fuck you until you come on my cock."

Her pace falters while I whisper in her ear, but after I finish speaking she groans and redoubles her pace. Soon enough she's tightening around my fingers, and her groaned "Oh, fuck!" heralds her climax and finally forces my own. I may have blacked out for a second, that was the hardest and longest I've ever cum before, and watching her break apart on top of me is the sexiest thing I've ever seen.

Now I need her to cum while I'm inside her.

CHAPTER 34

It takes a few minutes for both of us to catch our breath and our bodies to calm. I run my hands over her skin in a soothing pattern as she lays curled against me, letting out a sweet and content sigh. As much as I want to take her upstairs and show her how completely she's mine, I would also be satisfied to stay here all night with her like this if that's what she wants.

"This was a good purchase," she giggles quietly.

I laugh and kiss the top of her head. "Absolutely. Just don't tell Brandon what we did in here. He'll bitch about the fluids."

"Nah. He'll either pretend to be angry he didn't get to watch, or claim it means he has the green light for hot tub orgies. Neither of which will ever happen."

"Hell no, it won't. He doesn't get to see you like this, and the only hot tub sex will be ours." I don't care if they think of each other like siblings, that shit will never fucking happen.

"Sounds good to me," she says while leaning forward to tie her top. "Are you ready to get out? I'm starting to prune."

"Sure. You stay warm in here for a second while I take care of the candles."

I give her a kiss before tucking my dick back in my shorts and buttoning up so I can climb out. I towel off quickly before I turn each of the electronic candles off and blow out the citronellas. Once that's handled, I grab a towel and hold it out for her. "Let's head in and warm up," I tell her, drying her off.

She's still wearing a satisfied smile and she stands up on her toes to press a kiss to my lips before whispering against them. "Let's lock up and head to my room."

I follow behind her up the stairs and to her bedroom door, which is shut. When we reach the door she puts her hand on the knob but pauses and turns to me before opening the door.

"Please understand there is no pressure tonight. I wasn't sure if things would happen like they have, but I wanted to make things special just in case. I mean, I was hoping, but if you're not ready..."

I stop her words with a kiss, placing my hand over hers on the knob and guiding her to open the door and show me what she's done. The bedroom is set up with electric candles, like the patio was. They're covering every surface other than the bed and are providing the perfect amount of lighting. With a smile, I reach down and lift her into my arms. She squeaks and wraps her arms and legs around me but her shocked exclamation quickly morphs into a low moan as I use my tight grip on her ass to grind her pussy onto me.

"Not ready? Jen, I've been waiting for this since we were kids. I will never not be ready and eager to be with you."

Her cheeks pink at my words, and I can't help but lean forward to kiss her deeply. I knead her ass for a moment before I slide her back down my body so her feet can touch the floor. We maintain our kiss while I begin to remove her swimsuit. It's still somewhat wet so it does take a good amount of effort, but we laugh while she helps me enough that within seconds she's bare to my greedy eyes. Stepping back, I let my gaze roam over her perfect body and I'm forced to adjust my dick in my trunks because I've gotten painfully hard again already.

Her long curly hair is still up in a messy bun but some curls have fallen free and are laying wet against her neck, shoulders, and chest. Her beautiful face is free of makeup and I love that she didn't bother with it because she doesn't need any. An hourglass figure shows off full breasts with dainty nipple piercings, wide hips, thick thighs, and a narrow waist. I don't know how I got so lucky, but I do know I will do whatever I can to keep this stunning creature for the rest of my life.

I place a kiss on her collarbone and take a step towards the door. "I'll be right back," I tell her.

"Wait, where are you going?" She looks like she thinks I'm leaving her here.

"I need to get a condom," I tell her. "Unless you have some in here already?"

"Oh." Biting her lip, her gaze drops to the floor. "Um, well, I have an IUD. Neither of us has been with anyone, so... I mean, if you want to use one that's fine! I guess I'm just saying... I'm ok. If you don't, I mean."

And pass up an opportunity to be with her, skin to skin? Hell no. I take one more step back from her and a flash of disappointment crosses her features, but she'll realize soon enough I'm not refusing her offer. The moment of truth has come though, and as much as I believe she won't be bothered, I'm still kind of nervous to show her. My body tenses as I struggle to figure out what to say to her.

"What's wrong?" She asks me, beginning to cover herself in a nervous gesture. "Shit, I'm sorry. We can totally use a condom. I'm not trying to trap you or anything, I promise! Forget I mentioned it. I... wait, why are you laughing?"

"Because you're funny. You're fine. I just have something to show you and I'm... a bit nervous about it." Understatement. Worried she'll think I'm a total stalker, more likely.

"Oh." She pauses, looking me over as she takes a seat on the edge of the bed. "Do you have a tail or something? We could probably work with that. It might even be cute. Oh my God. Does it wag?" Her eyes are shining with humor, all worry about the condom discussion erased.

Narrowing my eyes at her in affront, I scowl in mock anger. "Funny girl. That mouth of yours won't be so smart once I fill it." I take a deep breath and prepare myself to show her what I've been hiding. "Just... if you have a problem or questions, talk to me first, ok?"

"Yeah, ok. I'm sure everything will be fine. Just show me." The sincerity in her eyes gives me enough courage to bare myself to her in more ways than one.

Another deep breath and I close my eyes to center myself as I undo the fly of my trunks. I thought my dick would softened during our conversation, but that is obviously an impossible feat with her sitting in front of me as she is. Screwing up my courage, I drop my trunks to the floor, ball my fists at my sides, and wait.

Her eyes immediately go to my dick and widen slightly when she takes in the size. I can tell she's aroused but also confused since there's nothing embarrassing about my dick, so I flex the fingers on my left hand to subtly draw her attention in that direction. The moment her eyes lock on my thigh, her mouth pops open and her gaze jerks to mine.

"But... what? How? When?"

On my left thigh, slightly lower than where hers is, is an almost exact replica of her turtle tattoo. The only difference is mine is larger and done in black and gray instead of color, and it covers some of my scars.

"I used to doodle it like this on my notes at school. You saw it once when we were studying together and told me you liked it. I figured you remembered since you basically got the same thing. I wanted to have a piece of you with me but couldn't have it anywhere Uncle Patrick might have seen it, so I got it there."

Leaning forward, she beckons me closer so she can run her fingers along the lines of the tattoo. "I do remember. I took one of the pages you'd drawn it on and saved it. It's what I used to get mine done. I guess I wanted a piece of you with me, too." Her brow furrows when her fingers brush against the ridges of one of the scars the ink covers. "What's this from?"

"That's a story for another time. Right now is about just you and me." I slide my fingers into her hair and grip her gently, tilting her face to mine as I bend down for a brief kiss. "These tattoos are one more sign that we're meant to be. I've always known you were mine, Jen. From the first time I saw you. Now it's time I prove it to you."

Her gaze turns heated and she scoots herself back onto the middle of the bed, leaning back on her elbows and pulling her knees up slightly, spreading her legs apart for me.

"Beautiful," I mumble as I lick my bottom lip. "Are you ready for me?"

Her only response is a smirk and a raised eyebrow, both of which disappear with a squeak when I grab her by the ankles and roughly pull her to me so her ass is on the edge of the bed. She gasps as I situate her but practically purrs as I drop to my knees in front of her and place her legs over my shoulders.

I place light kisses to her turtle tattoo and slide my hands up her thighs achingly slowly. When I reach her pussy I use my hands to spread her lower lips and almost come apart at the seams at how soaked she is. Inhaling her sweet, musky scent, I release a low growl and without warning lick a path from her opening to her clit and suck the bundle of nerves between my lips. Two of my fingers find her opening and I tease her with shallow motions as I continue to lick and suck at her clit.

Jen runs her fingers through my hair and grips it as I begin moving deeper with each thrust, her hips rolling up to meet my mouth in a hypnotizing rhythm. The throaty moans that escape her encourage me to keep going and I pull back and bite her hood as a distraction from the fact that I've added another finger.

"Oh, shit. What the actual fuck was that? Do it again!"

I chuckle into her skin as I tease her clit with the tip of my tongue. Speeding the movement of my fingers I groan as her grip tightens on my hair causing a slight sting of pain along my scalp. "You ready, baby?" I mumble against her thigh as I nibble the skin there.

"Fuck yes, please!" she pleads between low whimpers.

"Then cum for me." I bury my face in her once more and bite down a little harder than I did before and her body instantly responds. Her legs shake and tighten around my head as her back bows off the bed, her pussy squeezes my fingers so hard I can barely move them, and the combination of the shout of bliss and the flood of liquid she releases has me almost cumming along with her.

I don't stop my movements until she begs me to, giving her one last long lick as I pull my fingers out. I climb up her body and kiss her deeply before pulling back to look into her eyes.

"Are you ready? I know you said you are, but I want you to understand that we don't have to go any further tonight. I'm willing to wait."

"Fuck that!" she chuckles. "I believe you have a promise to keep, sir."

I adjust my position so I'm cradled between her thighs and slide my hand along her left leg to pull her thigh up so her leg is wrapped around my waist. The new position allows me to line my cock up with her pussy and I grind down into her a few times, coating myself in her juices.

If I ever deluded myself into thinking I could walk away from her if she wanted me to, tonight proves to me how wrong I was. I'm never letting this woman go.

"I was going to give you one more chance to back out. To walk away from me and live your life." I tell her, reaching down to grab on to my rock hard cock and line myself up with her opening. "I thought I could give you the option, but I can't. You're mine, baby girl. And I will never let you go."

My last words are proven as I thrust myself fully inside of her. I meant to be careful, to go slow in case I hurt her, but I couldn't contain myself. Luckily, the cry she releases is one of pleasure instead of pain, and she immediately grips me by my hair and ass, pulling me down to her harder. The combination of her warm, wet heat strangling my dick, her breasts pressing against my chest, her nails digging into my skin, and her hips rolling to meet mine are a dangerous combination.

This may be over too quickly.

I have never been so full. He's so incredibly thick, only slightly wider and longer than my favorite toy. I was worried it would hurt this first time, but all I feel is absolute bliss. The intimacy of this moment far exceeds my expectations, and Evan is everything I ever hoped for and more.

His thrusts are forceful but slow to start. The moment he slid inside of me our eyes locked, and as much as I want to close my own and simply experience everything, nothing could break my gaze from his at this moment. His beautiful green eyes are on fire and express to me more passion and love than words could ever articulate. He's told me he loves me, but I can *feel* it with every touch. Every press of his lips against mine. Every brush of his hands against my skin. A large part of me desperately wants to tell him I love him too, because I truly believe I do. The issue is the tiny kernel of fear I still harbor that he will leave again.

Each time he bottoms out he grinds against me to apply pressure to my clit and I grip his firm ass harder and pull him tighter against me. The bite of my nails makes him groan deep and quicken his pace as he leans down to kiss me forcefully. When he begins kissing his way down my neck to my breasts, I allow my eyes to finally fall closed and my head to tilt back so I can soak in the sensations. The moment his lips close around my nipple the heat intensifies low in my belly. He uses his teeth to tug on the metal of the piercing and his tongue laves the tip slowly in complete opposition to the motion of his hips. The juxtaposition drives me wild.

"Don't stop, please!" I whimper while wrapping my free arm around the top of his head to hold him to me. The added pressure burns the sensation of his smile into my skin and I honestly don't think anything could be more perfect than this moment.

He pulls back slightly to lick a path from between my breasts to my collarbone and then kisses me sweetly, slowing down with a smirk on his face.

"I said don't stop, you jerk!" I fuss at him.

"I know," he laughs. "But I was about to lose it. Just give me a second!" He hasn't stopped moving, but he has slowed his strokes considerably. "You feel so fucking good, baby girl, and I warned you I was going to make you cum around my cock. I can't break my promise, can I?"

His smile turns devilish as he slips the fingers of one hand into the hair at the nape of my neck and the other between us to circle my clit with gentle strokes. Using my hair as leverage he pulls my head up so he can whisper in my ear. "Brace yourself."

And with that -- I'm lost.

He bites down on my earlobe so hard it's just on the right side of pain while simultaneously pinching my clit and slamming his dick inside me so hard I'm almost pushed up the bed. The shout of pleasure that leaves my lips is instantly swallowed by his own hungry mouth, and we devour each other's sounds like they're the oxygen we need to breathe.

Evan adjusts the position of the hand between us and when he uses his thumb to push down on my clit my entire body explodes from the sensation. "Oh, fuck!" I cry out as my back bows and my pussy tightens from the onslaught of pleasure. His long, low groan as he buries his face in my neck is the sexiest sound I have ever heard, and my orgasm doesn't quiet until he stops moving inside me.

He takes several deep breaths before raising his head and staring into my eyes. We're both still breathing heavily, coming down from our shared high. I smile at him and crane my neck up to place a kiss on his lips. "That was better than I could have imagined. Thank you for making me feel so special," I tell him.

"Jen, I've been dreaming of this for years," he reminds me, rolling to the side and pulling me against his side. "Thank you. For giving me the chance to prove to you that I can make you happy."

"Oh, I didn't say I was happy. I said I was satisfied. Now that the first time is out of the way I should totally go sow my oats... hey!" My teasing is cut off by Evan flipping me over and onto my back again. His legs are trapping mine and his hands are holding my wrists over my head before I can start to fight him.

"Fuck that. Your ass is mine now, Jen. I warned you there was no going back and you agreed."

"Hmm... I guess you'll just have to remind me why I accepted your offer then," I say, looking down our bodies at his cock as it begins to harden again.

So he did.

Two more times.

Chapter 35

I wake refreshed in Evan's arms. My body is slightly sore in places I've never experienced before, but it's a sweet ache that will remind me all day of what we did together. Peeking over his shoulder at my clock, it shows thirty minutes before our alarm is set to go off so we can dress for the day, and when I look down I can see his morning wood tenting the fabric of the sheet we slept under.

In hopes of not waking him until I'm where I want to be, I slide my body so I'm straddling him. I can tell I'm already wet and ready and just thinking about taking him inside of me has me more awake than any caffeine could provide. Once I'm in place, I lean down to lick a path up his chest to his neck and grind my wet pussy down slowly on his dick. The low, sleepy groan he emits when I begin nibbling on his neck is accompanied by his hands sliding up my legs to my waist to pull me down harder onto him. Taking his reaction as permission, I reach down and guide him into me, my movements unhurried and languid. Evan grabs my hair in a tight fist and pulls my mouth to his, kissing me at a pace to match the rhythm of my hips.

We make slow, sleepy love for several minutes until I can feel the beginning of my orgasm start to take root. I pull back from his kiss and sit up straight so I can move above him more freely. His grip returns to my hips and he brings his knees up so he can brace his feet on the bed. Using his incredible strength he not only uses his hands on my waist to bring me down and over him, he also pistons up into me from below causing my head to fall back and a throaty groan to fall from my lips.

"Touch yourself for me Jen. Show me what's mine," he rasps.

I lean back further and let my hands roam my body, sliding both up my rib cage and over my breasts to pull at my nipple piercings and enjoy the slight sting, then dip one down to circle my clit. The sensations are overwhelming and it causes me to falter in my movements for a brief moment. Noticing my pause, Evan uses it as an opportunity to flip us so I'm underneath him, circling my throat with his hand as he holds the rest of his body above me. My eyelids flutter shut as I revel in the dominance shining from his gaze.

"I'm going to need you to turn over," he purrs in my ear. "Can you do that for me, Jen?"

I can only nod my head a fraction due to his grip, so I whisper "yes."

"Good girl" he says, pulling back from me to give me space to roll over. I can feel my cheeks turn pink and my pussy get wetter as I discovered a new domination and praise kink in the space of roughly thirteen seconds. Rolling over I lie flat on my stomach and await my next instructions. My breathing has sped and my face is buried in a pillow — for some reason I'm working overtime to keep him from finding out just how much his tone is affecting me.

The bed shifts behind me and he spreads my legs apart enough to fit his knees between mine.His hands slide from behind my knees to my ass where he grips me tight. "Now, on your knees." I continue to follow instructions, but when I rise on my hands as well as my knees his large hand pushes down between my shoulder blades so my ass is up, and my face is resting on the bed. "I said knees only. Do I need to stop? Or can you listen?"

"Please don't stop," I beg.

"Follow directions and I won't." He presses gently on my back to remind me to stay put, then hums in approval as slides his fingers into me from behind. "I've got a list of things that I've been dreaming about doing to you, Jen. It may take years to tick everything off my list. Would you like that? Will you let me take this pretty pussy however I want, whenever I want, like a good girl?"

"Fuck yes," I groan out. If he keeps this shit up I might slip and start calling him Daddy.

"Good. Now brace yourself on the headboard."

As I place my hands against the headboard his tongue runs up my slit briefly before he pulls back and presses the head of his cock to my opening. Hands once again around my hips he begins pounding into me from behind while simultaneously controlling my movements with his tight grip. The delicious sting from both his bruising hold and his forceful thrusts causes my previously building orgasm to flare back to life, and all I can do is keep my arms straight and beg him to fuck me harder. He takes me at my word and switches his hold so one hand is wrapped around my shoulder and the new position gives him added leverage and a slightly different angle causing my climax to speed towards me like a bullet train. With the sharp crack of his hand against my ass, my orgasmic cup runneth over and my entire body tightens so completely I can't even draw breath. My face buried in the mattress doesn't help either, so I turn my head to the side as soon as I can control my movements.

Evan's pace turns erratic as he fights against the stranglehold my body now has on him and within seconds. He continues pumping until my orgasm calms, and then collapses to my side and pulls me down to lie next to him.

"Good morning, beautiful," he says, kissing my forehead.

The day is overcast, but fortunately the forecast doesn't include rain. Knowing it was chilly outside, and we'd be attending the outdoor burial, I am glad the dress I purchased to wear was a simple knee-length black dress with long sleeves and a sweetheart neckline. I paired it with black ankle boots and sheer black hose, pinned a portion of my hair back to keep it out of my face in case it got windy, and applied minimal makeup, making sure to use waterproof mascara in case I cry.

Puttering around the kitchen to make a quick breakfast ready before we go, I almost jump out of my skin when Evan sneaks up behind me and wraps his arms around my waist. "You look gorgeous this morning," he says, placing a kiss on my shoulder above the neckline of my dress. "Thank you, for everything. For being here with me this past week, and giving me everything I need, even when I don't know I need it. I couldn't survive this without you."

Goosebumps pebble my skin at his soft touch and sweet words. "Of course," I respond as I turn in his arms and wrap my own around his neck. "You've always been there for me when I needed you, even when you weren't here." I pause to touch the turtle pendant before giving him a brief kiss. "The least I can do is reciprocate."

We eat our breakfast in comfortable silence and clean up together before we head out to the church Gran attended. She was a member of the local Lutheran church, but only attended a few times a year. Her infrequent attendance always made me wonder how Ryan's dad became so devout. He didn't learn it from her and my understanding is his father was the same way. Brandon and Daniel meet us in the foyer, and together we walk into the sanctuary a few minutes before the service is set to begin. Evan's Uncle Patrick is in the front row that has been reserved for family so Daniel, Brandon, and I scoot past him after giving him our condolences. He nods somberly without providing a response until Evan steps past him too. "Where is my son?" he snarls while grabbing a hold of Evan's arm to halt his progress.

Pulling his arm away and looking around to see if anyone has noticed their interaction, Evan continues to step past him. "I have no idea, are you saying he didn't go back to the compound? I haven't seen him since the day before I found Gran dead. Jen and I both have tried to contact him but he's not responding, which I'm sure the police have told you. He's not exactly my priority right now though, so I'm not trying very hard. The police will probably find him anyway."

"I don't believe you. He came back here for her," he snarls, pointing and sneering at me like I'm a bug he's stepped on but won't come off his shoe. "He wouldn't leave without her."

"Not that this is the appropriate time, or any of your business, but he didn't have a choice to leave with me. I wasn't interested in going anywhere with your son. Now, the service is about to start. You can either be quiet, and we can discuss this later like adults in an appropriate setting, or you can leave. Daniel here" I point in his direction in case he doesn't remember him, "will be happy to escort you out and issue a no-trespass order to ensure you don't disrupt the service. Gran deserves better than that."

Mr. Holmes' face and neck turn a brighter red the longer I talk. I'm not playing though. I will have Daniel escort him out faster than he can try to spit more vitriol, and I saw Brian back there too. My dad's best friend will back me up no matter what, so I'm not worried he'll be able to make a real scene. Just like I expected, though, he glares at me with hate and turns forward to face the front and sits without saying another word. Bullies always back down when they're confronted, and all Mr. Holmes has ever been is a bully in pastor's robes. Daniel, Brandon, Evan, and I all take our own seats and Evan takes my hand in both of his and holds it on his lap. He squeezes it and gives me a warm smile of thanks.

Being the best friend he is and keeping his head far better than Evan and I, Brandon grabs my other hand and gives it a warning squeeze. I don't think we're doing anything to make it obvious we're together but the reminder is appreciated. We don't want to make anyone suspicious about us, especially Ryan's dad since he knows he came here to take me back with him. I don't want him to start wondering if Evan or I did something to get Ryan out of the way. Questions can lead to snooping, which is the last thing we need.

The service begins after a few minutes, and the pastor is a kind man with many wonderful things to say about Evan's grandmother. When the time comes for the eulogy, Evan takes a deep breath before squeezing my hand again and rising. Although it's not the best time, I can't help but admire him in his suit. It's a simple, clean cut black suit with a white button down and his tie is one I bought for my dad a few years ago, black matte and satin paisley print. He made an effort to style his hair today with a bit of product, and his short beard is trimmed nicely. Even in his grief, even with the reminder of my dad staring back at me, he is breathtakingly handsome. His forest green eyes are bright with his pain, but even through his sadness his strength shines through.

His eulogy is short and sweet, honoring a woman who did her best for him whenever she could, tried for him when she couldn't, and loved him through it all. At the end, his words brought tears to my eyes. "She brought me back here because she knew I loved this place, that it is my true home. She wanted to give me the life I always dreamed of, and all she asked was to be a part of it. Gran lived through a lot of loss. First her husband, then her daughter, my mom. For years after my mom died we were separated, and she didn't for a second resent me for it. She invited me to come stay with her and welcomed me back with open arms, and I will never forget the wonderful time we spent together these last few weeks. Although I told her I loved her every day, I never really got to thank her for everything she's done for me. That is my only regret. Not telling her how much I appreciated her for everything she did, and who she was as a person. Hopefully, letting her know how much I loved her... well, hopefully it was enough."

Resting his hand on her coffin, he stares at the dark surface of the closed lid before coming back to join me on the pew. As the pastor asks if anyone else wants to speak, I take his hand again and lean over to kiss his cheek and whisper "It was enough."

Tears finally spill from his eyes, and I hand him a tissue to dry them if he wants to. Mr. Holmes looks over to see him crying and scoffs before attempting to stand and walk to the front. I snap my hand out to grab his arm and give him a warning glare before releasing him just as fast. Glaring at me, he continues to rise and makes his way up to face the congregation.

"Heaven is a place reserved for the righteous," he begins. "I don't rightly know if my mother would be included in those ranks, it's been many years since we've spent much time together. I tried to convince her to join me and my own congregation, but she declined and distanced herself from us as a result. She did take my son and his cousin in, at the end, and I know she cared for them just as well as they cared for her. I will pray God sees fit to enter her into his kingdom, for the power of Hell is mighty."

What. The. Fuck?

I scowl at him as he returns to his seat, and I can feel a subtle tremble starting in Evan's limbs. What was the point of that, other than being a dick when his mother recently died? No wonder Ryan's so fucked up, it appears that the apple didn't fall far from that rotten tree.

The remainder of the service and the burial go quietly. We don't speak to Mr. Holmes again. In fact, he doesn't speak with anyone other than in response to their condolences. Brandon rides with Evan and I to the community center where the celebration of life is being held, but Daniel has to miss it because he has to work. He was only able to find someone to cover the first half of his shift, so before leaving he gave Evan a hug and his condolences again, and promised to see us at the house tonight for dinner like we had originally planned.

We've been at the center for about thirty minutes when Mr. Holmes and another older gentleman approach our group. Mr. and Mrs. C are catching up with Evan while Brandon and I share a cheese plate, and their arrival interrupts our conversation.

"Evan? I'm Preston Talbert, your grandmother's attorney," he smiles sadly. "Well, more than her attorney, I was also a close friend. I want to express my condolences on your loss, and let you know how incredibly happy she was that you were back in her life. She missed you very much and spoke of you often."

"Thank you, sir," Evan says, standing to shake his hand. "I'm sorry for your loss too, as her friend. Gran was an awesome person."

"That she was. I wonder if you have a few moments to speak in private? I would have contacted you sooner, but I didn't know how to get in touch with you. Somehow, with all of her meticulous planning, she forgot to give me your phone number. I have your grandmother's will and would like to go over it with you and your uncle."

"Oh! Um, sure. Of course. Now? Or do we need to come to your office or something? I figured she didn't really have one since I searched the house when I was looking for her other paperwork and didn't come across one."

"That's very strange, there should have been a copy there in her files. No matter, since I helped her draw it up I kept a copy as well, so there's nothing to worry about. If you don't mind speaking now, there is a smaller meeting room down the hall." Mr. Talbert seems concerned the copy of the will was missing but works to hide it. I wonder if Ryan found it and destroyed it, hoping it was the only copy available?

"Sure, lead the way. I'd like my friends to come with me too, if that's ok?" Evan grabs my hand, silently asking if we mind coming with him.

"Of course they can't come. They're not family, Evan!" Mr. Holmes grits through clenched teeth.

Mr. Talbert clears his throat and smooths a hand down the front of his suit jacket before correcting Mr. Holmes. "That won't be a problem, Evan. This isn't a closed reading. If you'd like them to attend, they are welcome to join."

We follow after Mr. Talbert. Evan and I are confused about the missing copy of the will while Mr. Holmes fumes about being overruled. We're led into a small conference room with a credenza and white board on one wall and a table to seat eight in the center. Mr. Holmes takes a seat at the head of the table, no surprise there, and Mr. Talbert takes a seat on the far side of the table facing the seats Evan, Brandon, and I choose. Brandon and I have maneuvered Evan into the middle seat so we buffer him on each side, and I'm hopeful he doesn't notice we're trying to manage the situation for him. I grab his hand under the table in a silent show of support, and he gives me a quick squeeze in thanks.

"Now, this will was updated a few weeks ago. It was witnessed by myself and my paralegal at the time of the update, and there is an additional copy in her safe deposit box, to which I hold the only key. I have the key stored with the remainder of Evelyn's paperwork and will be able to provide it to you once all the necessary papers are signed. I won't bore you with the legalese contained within the document, I have a copy here for each of you to review at your convenience after our meeting if you choose. I was, however, directed to read to you the following section," he pauses, taking a deep breath and looking from Evan to Mr. Holmes. "'To my daughter, Angela. I know you left this Earth before me, but I leave you my love and the promise to take care of your son even after my death. I will see you on the other side, my darling daughter.'" Mr. Talbert pauses after reading this, and he braces himself to deliver the next part. "To my son Patrick, and my grandson Ryan. I leave you in my death what you gave me in life. Nothing. To put it in language you will no doubt understand, you reap what you sow.'"

The silence is deafening. Out of the corner of my eye I can see Mr. Holmes's neck turning red again, but otherwise he's holding himself together. Evan squeezes my hand as he studies his uncle, but his head snaps back to face Mr. Talbert when he continues reading.

"'To my grandson Evan. I leave you everything in my estate, to be outlined below. Just know, my sweet boy, that having you with me again has healed my heart, and I am so thankful for the care you are taking of me and the time we have spent together. You have had so many roadblocks in your life, and my hope is that bringing you back here will have been the beginning of a new start for you. Take chances, work hard, rise above what you witnessed as you grew up, and I do not doubt your dreams will come true. I love you, my boy.'"

The room is silent for a few moments, everyone staring at Mr. Talbert in shock. The quiet is broken by Mr. Holmes sliding his chair back and walking to the door. He pauses after opening the door and turns back at us to say, "If you know where my son is, and I find out something has happened to him, you'll regret it." His face is void of expression until he focuses on me, looking me up and down in a to denote he finds me lacking. "I know you're lying to me, little girl. He saw something in you that I've never been able to find, and he came back here for you. Against my advice. He wouldn't have left without you, no matter what."

"That sounds like a personal problem to me," I fire back. "He tried. He pushed himself on me multiple times, even after I asked him to back off. I turned him down. He was angry about it but didn't have any other choice because I wouldn't have gone anywhere with him willingly. We argued, he left. I haven't seen or heard from him since, and neither has Evan, though we've tried to get in touch with him to let him know about Gran's death. It wouldn't surprise me if he ran though, since it's looking more and more likely that he pushed your mother down the stairs. Otherwise, where is he? Why would he run and not check in with you if he hadn't done anything wrong?"

His face is contorted by rage at this point, and I don't care. We have an impartial witness in this room, someone who can both report what they saw and heard and step in if things get dicey. Mr. Holmes takes a step towards me with his hands balled into fists, opening his mouth to say something I can only assume will be scathing, but Mr. Talbert stands from his seat and clears his throat to interrupt. "This is very obviously a trying time for all of you. Here is a copy of the will for your review if you would like it, Mr. Holmes, and I think it best you leave now. Today is a celebration of your mother's life, and as her friend and attorney, it is my duty to ensure her memory isn't tarnished on today of all days. If you feel the need to discuss things further, please call me at my office at any time. My card is enclosed." He rounds the table and extends a large envelope to Mr. Holmes, who takes it and leaves without another word. "I am sorry about that, Evan. Your grandmother was worried about how he would take things but it can be normal in situations like these, I'm afraid. Do you have any questions or concerns for me?"

"I don't know what to say. I knew she talked about taking them out of the will, but I never expected she'd already done it and left everything to me. I don't even know how to start going through everything. Are there bills I will need to pay off? A mortgage? Papers I need to sign?" He looks to me and I can tell he's overwhelmed.

"Mr. Talbert and I will help. I've been through this once before, remember? We'll figure it out," I say, squeezing his hand.

"She's quite right. I do have paperwork but it can wait until tomorrow, or next week if you'd prefer. Your grandmother's house is paid off so there's no mortgage and her bills are automatically deducted from her accounts. She has provided a binder of the necessary accounts to make things easy for you. She was, by far, the most organized of my clients. All told, between the house, her rather substantial life insurance policy, and her other assets, you have inherited about 2.2 million dollars."

A cough sputters from Evan, and his hand tightens around mine to the point where it almost hurts. "You're joking. There's no way." His eyes plead with me to help him make sense of what's happening, or to tell him he's being played.

"I assure you, I'm not. The house accounts for about a third of that number, so if you choose to keep it the liquid assets would be less. She was ok with you selling the house though. It's rather large and old-fashioned, and she thought you may have something else in mind for your future. I have some Realtor connections you would like a reference."

Evan is frozen in his seat, staring at Mr. Talbert like he has six heads and holding on to my hand for dear life. Brandon places a hand on his shoulder in a show of support, and since I can tell he's not going to answer, I step in to help. "Thanks, Mr. Talbert," I say. "Do you have a copy of everything for him to take home today? We'll go through it and call your office to schedule some time to come by to sign the papers. We're both off work for only a few more days, so it'll most likely be tomorrow if you're free."

"Fine, fine. Call or come by anytime. This packet is for you, Evan. It contains your copy of the will and my business card. If you have any questions before you come by, don't hesitate to call, I've written my personal cell phone number on the back. Please know Evelyn meant a great deal to my wife and I, and I will do whatever I can to help you through this." Standing up, he places the packet of information on the table and slides it towards Evan. "Call me if your uncle becomes a problem as well, your grandmother worried he might and asked that I provide any legal help or guidance required when dealing with him."

"Thank you, Mr. Talbert. I appreciate your help with all this. I'm just kind of blown away. If it's ok with you, we'll come by in the morning to settle things. I'd like to get as many things taken care of as possible before I have to go back to work. My boss was generous enough to give me a week off, I don't want to push it by asking for more."

"Of course. I'll have everything ready for you in the morning, it should take about an hour. I'll see you then."

Mr. Talbert shakes each of our hands before leaving the room, closing the door behind him to give us a moment. "Shit, bro," Brandon huffs. "I did not see any of that coming. Are you ok?"

Groaning, Evan releases my hand so he can rub his face while he thinks. "I don't... know. I'm not surprised at Uncle Patrick being a dick, but leaving me everything? Millions? I had no idea she even had all that, and I definitely didn't think I'd be the sole beneficiary." He's quiet for a moment, staring at the envelope on the table in front of him. "Do you mind if I have a minute?"

"Absolutely," I say, moving to stand and leave the room but pausing when he grasps my wrist.

"Actually, Brandon, do you mind? I'd like to talk to Jen."

"Sure, man. I'll go check in on everything. Take whatever time you need." Brandon gives Evan's shoulder a final squeeze and deposits a kiss on the top of my head as he leaves the room, shutting the door behind him.

"Are you really ok?" I ask, frowning at him with concern.

"Not really," he admits with a pained smile, using his grip on my wrist to pull me into his lap. "This shit is all so overwhelming. She's just my Gran, I can't imagine what you went through with your dad."

Moving to tuck my head in against his neck, I let out a tired sigh. "It was hard. I was in a lot worse shape than you are, but I had Brandon and his parents to help me through it all. I don't know what I would have done without them. We'll be there for you, just like they were for me. And when you need space, let us know and you can have that, too, ok?"

Lips pressed against my forehead, he releases a slight chuckle. "I had years of space. I don't think you'll be able to get rid of me that quickly." I close my eyes and smile, soaking up the moment of quiet. "Thank you," he whispers, against my skin, "for giving me this chance. For the help you've been this week. For sticking by me, and supporting me without judgement on my decision with Ryan. For everything. I can never repay you."

"How about a massage after the boys leave this evening? We've already decided those are a viable form of currency." I grin at him, wiggling my eyebrows in a dorkily suggestive way.

"Deal," he says with a chuckle.

CHAPTER 36

After our late night and emotionally draining day, we decided to take a nap when we got home. The boys are supposed to arrive at 6:00, so we wake up around 5:00 to start getting ready for them to arrive. Evan wears his black swim trunks again with a gray t-shirt, and I grab my favorite navy blue polka dotted pin-up style bathing suit to wear under yoga pants and a slouchy, oversized t-shirt announcing "Give me smut or give me death." I throw my hair up in a messy bun and call it good.

I grab towels for everyone since the guys never bring their own, and a lighter for the grill and citronella candles. I hand the towels and lighter to Evan and then find a storage tub for the battery powered candles we left outside overnight. They're rated for outdoor use but I would rather not have them out there hinting at what happened last night. Daniel has been weird enough lately and Brandon will give us endless shit. It only takes a few minutes to get things cleaned up and situated on the patio and by the time we've pulled out the food I prepped yesterday Brandon and Daniel have both arrived and are checking out the hot tub while Evan gets the steaks started on the grill.

Dinner is relaxed and we avoid heavy subjects. Daniel is back to his old self, if not a little quiet. He seems tired but his attitude is better than it has been recently, so I'm glad to have things back to normal. They all pitch in cleaning up and then Evan and I hop in while Brandon and Daniel change into their swimsuits. In the span of a few minutes we're all relaxing in the hot tub with drinks and classic rock playing over the sound system.

"So, how did the gathering go?" Daniel asks as he takes a sip of his beer. "I'm sorry I couldn't make it, but no one could cover my shift."

"Fine for the most part," Evan hedges. "Uncle Patrick showed his ass during the will reading, but everything else seemed to go well."

"Oh shit, what happened?"

I sneak my foot over to rub against Evan's leg, reminding him I'm here. He gives me, then Brandon, strained smiles.

"Well, in a nutshell, he got pissed when he learned both he and Ryan had been written out of the will and I inherited everything. Like, a few million dollars worth of everything. Then, he basically accused us of knowing where Ryan is and threatened to 'get us' if he finds out we're responsible for him going missing."

"Wow," Daniel's eyebrows are so high they're almost lost in his hairline. "That is... a lot to take in."

My inelegant snort makes them all chuckle while I continue. "You think? I know how weird it feels to become a millionaire overnight. Add in being accused of doing something to his cousin? It was a weird few minutes."

"So no one has heard from him? I've tried calling him, and asked around at the station. No luck on my end. It's so weird that he'd come back and then run off again and not go back to his dad."

I shrug, looking at Evan and Brandon. "I tried calling and texting him for a few days but never got a response, Evan too. Did you, Brandon?"

"No, I let you two handle that. I figured if he didn't answer you he definitely wouldn't answer me."

"I think he was butt hurt I turned him down, and then angry with Gran. My guess is they got into a fight, and he ran after she got hurt." Daniel's brows furrow, but I'm not worried because nothing I've said is a lie. We did try calling and texting his phone and didn't receive a response. I did turn him down, and he did get into an argument with Gran.

"Can we talk about something else?" Evan cuts in. "I would rather not talk about him and what he did to her."

"Damn, of course. I'm sorry man. I guess, what are your plans now? Going forward, I mean?" Daniel turns and grabs two beers from the cooler the guys brought out for us, handing one to Evan after noticing his is empty too.

"I'm not sure. I like my job, but I also want to get licensed as a general contractor. Mr. Talbert doesn't think it'll take long for me to receive the inheritance, so maybe I'll use that to live on while I study to get my license. I know I want to put her house up for sale, I'll never live there, so that'll take some time to sort out too."

Brandon points behind Daniel for him to grab him another beer while he asks "So, are you going to live there in the meantime? Until it sells, I mean?"

Evan shakes his head. "No, I can't. I can't stay there where she died. I'm doing the work here so Jen has been gracious enough to grant me room and board since I won't let her pay for labor. I figure I can use the time it takes to get the work done to get things figured out. She's not in a hurry to get it done, and I think it'll take me some time to get my head on straight."

"You could stay with me if you wanted. I have a guest room and I'm closer to town so you wouldn't have as long of a commute. Plus you wouldn't be lonely when she goes back to her apartment."

"Thanks, man. I'll stay here for now since I'm doing most of the work at night, though. It'll be easier than having to drive to your place after, but I may take you up on it later."

"Sounds good. Oh! Speaking of remodeling, I'm doing some at home too. I'm trying to pick out some colors and tiles and stuff but I feel pretty hopeless with it all. Do you think you could come out over the next week or so and help me out, Jen?"

"Totally!" I chirp happily. "I love spending other people's money to decorate. And if you plan on doing it yourself we can all help out with it."

"Absolutely," Evan adds. "I'm happy to help. I'll probably grab you guys every once in a while to help with the heavy lifting here too, so it'll even out in the end."

"Sounds great, let me know when you're free. I'll make dinner since you've done it the past few times."

We talk, laugh, and drink in the hot tub for a few hours until we all admit how hot we are. Brandon, being himself, hoists me over his shoulder, runs down the yard, and launches me into the lake off the end of the dock. The shock of my entire body submerging under the cold water feels like it stops my heart for a second, but I quickly shoot up to the surface to take a breath. Luckily, I emerge in time to see him fighting off both Evan and Daniel as they wrestle with him to throw him in after me. They share an evil grin over his head and Evan counts to three before they both take off with Brandon between them.

We spend some more time splashing and fighting in the lake before I lean back and float for a while. I'm tired but I'm also too lazy to start the walk back to the house.

"Come on killer, let's get you to bed.," Brandon stands over me, pulling me into a standing position and turning to face away from me. "Hop on. I got you down here, I'll get you back up."

"Yes!" I cheer and jump on his back, happy I don't have to bully him into it. "Onward, my good steed! My bed awaits!"

Brandon neighs and starts making his way back up to the house so we can all dry off and get cleaned up and ready for bed. Everyone has had too much to drink so they're staying over again. I get the couches set up for Brandon and Daniel while they shower since Evan is supposed to be in the guest room and head up to shower and go to bed myself once they're done. "See you guys in the morning, we'll do breakfast if you're not gone before I'm up!"

Evan is heading into the bathroom when I walk up. I grab him by the waist of his trunks and hold a finger to my lips as I pull him into my room with me. The guest room door is shut in hopes of avoiding suspicion, but I'm getting to the point where I no longer care. Brandon is happy for us, and Daniel will have to suck it up if he's unhappy about it. Maybe we'll tell him when we go over to his house.

Evan follows me into my bathroom and helps me peel off my wet swimsuit. It's clumsy and awkward and hilarious and I'm trying insanely hard not to break out laughing loud enough for Brandon and Daniel to hear me downstairs. Evan removes his own suit while I get the water started in my shower, and once the steam starts rising we both step in. He hisses at the temperature and jumps back out of the spray, but if my shower isn't hot enough to feel like Satan himself is licking my back I don't want any part of it, so I smirk and stand in the path of the stream until he can get acclimated.

We don't speak. We take turns washing each other and it's so incredibly intimate, being in here like this together that I can't help but wrap my arms around his neck and lean up for a sweet kiss. He takes his time washing and conditioning my hair, giving me what is hands down the best scalp massage I have ever gotten and when it's my turn to wash him I repay the favor, both on his scalp and in his beard.

I swear to God he purrs as I work my fingers into the short hairs on his cheeks, and it's one of the sexiest sounds I've ever heard. We don't let things escalate though, we simply take care of each other in a way that surpasses anything I could have ever imagined.

Once we're both clean and dry, Evan reaches for the boxers he'd placed on my counter but I smirk and grab his hand and pull him out of the bathroom and over to my bed. I push him down onto his back and crawl up his body to whisper into his ear.

"How quiet can you be?" I ask him, starting to kiss and lick my way down his neck, chest, and abdomen.

"Um, if you're going to suck my dick, probably not very," he responds in a tight voice.

"Hmm. Too bad. If you make too much noise I'll have to stop. Wouldn't want to wake the sleeping beauties downstairs, would we?"

His groan is pained and I love the sound of it. Running my hands up his thighs I settle myself between his legs and lower my face to place a kiss on his tattoo. "Keep. Quiet. Make too much noise and I'll stop."

His head drops back and I hear a quiet thud against the bedding, so I smile to myself and focus back on my task. I use one hand to drag my nails down his thigh while I use the other to slide it up his shaft and angle him to my mouth. Licking a slow trail to his tip I am surprised that the taste is neither as unpleasant or salty as I expected. Obviously, I don't have a lot of practice at this, or actually any, but I've read plenty of books and watched my fair share of porn, so I'm just going to do the best I can.

My lips wrap around his tip and I lick at the underside for a moment, looking up his body to see his reaction. I can't see his face but I can see him gripping his hair with one hand, and the blankets with the other.

I want him to break.

I begin sucking and take him as far into my mouth as possible. I don't have an incredibly sensitive gag reflex but it's there, so I'm careful not to go too far. His choked "Shit!" is enough to let me know I'm doing something right, so I keep my pace and increase my pressure while bringing my other hand up to cup his balls. I can feel him shift as he leans up on an elbow and see him watching me with awe. His hand comes down on my head and he runs his fingers through my hair gently, but he doesn't apply any pressure to my head or try to control me. He simply watches and strokes me sweetly.

"Jesus, you are so beautiful," he whispers. "I need you to come up here though."

I raise an eyebrow at him and apply more suction as I take him in further than before, holding my position as long as possible. It feels strange, but watching his reaction is worth it. His head has dropped back and cords of muscle are standing out on his neck. When I finally pull myself off him, I climb up his body while kissing my way back to his mouth. He tries rolling us over so he can be on top, but I resist and push his shoulders back down onto the bed. "Nope," I tell him. "I'm in charge right now."

Sitting up, I reach back and grab his erection once more so I can guide him into my opening. The slow stretch feels incredible and I'm forced to bite my lip to keep quiet. This is my game, after all. It wouldn't do to lose it because I can't follow my own rules.

As I start to rock Evan slides his hands in a languid path from my knees, up my thighs and stomach, and finally to my breasts. I keep my pace slow and sensual, reveling in the feel of him being inside me. One of his hands dips to my clit and he starts circling it in slow motion, making me arch back and increase my speed until he growls and sits up to face me, grabbing me by the nape of my neck in a tight grip and sealing his mouth to mine in a bruising kiss.

"Are you sure you care if they hear us? Because I don't think I do."

"Hush!" I scold him. "Are you afraid you can't make me cum if things have to stay quiet?"

"Oh, that's how it is, huh?" he hisses at me while flipping us so I'm on my back looking up at him. "Be careful what you wish for, baby girl."

He pulls me over to the side of the bed by my ankles and stands and wrap my legs around his waist. Smirking, he lifts my ass into the air and slides back inside me. "I'm going to make you cum, but since you want to stay quiet I'll muzzle you if I have to. You started this game but I'm going to finish it."

With that, he slams his cock into me forcefully and without warning. I gasp loudly, causing him to keep his promise and cover my mouth with this hand while he fucks me. I can still breathe through my nose but my cries are muffled and since he's basically holding me in the air while he fucks me the bed isn't making much noise either. He removes his hand from my mouth and grabs one of my own to replace it while he continues to hold me up with one hand and uses the other to apply pressure to my clit.

I can feel the orgasm growing in my center, but all I can think about is how I want more. Harder. Faster. Just more.

"Is that all you've got?" I whisper to him, knowing if I try to speak any louder I'll lose myself and won't be able to stop.

He stops abruptly, the exact opposite of what I wanted from him. "Just remember you asked for this."

"Wha-?"

My words are cut off as he drops my legs and flips me over once more. This time my feet are on the floor and he uses my nape to push my head down towards the bed. He plays with my pussy from behind, sliding two fingers into me while he drapes his body over mine. "Same rules apply to you, baby girl. Stay quiet or I'll stop."

Goosebumps cover my body when he replaces his fingers with his dick, slowly moving in and out of me for a few moments. "Are you ready?" he whispers.

"Ready for what?"

"Brace yourself. And remember, Jen, stay quiet or I'll stop." He smiles against the skin at my neck, then he's adjusting his grip to my shoulder and hip. Using his hands to change the angle of my body, he rears back and starts fucking me harder than ever before. At this point, I don't care about the rhythmic slapping sound our skin makes each time we connect, but I am gripping the bedding next to my head and have buried my face in it in an attempt to keep quiet. I no longer care if the sounds reach Brandon and Daniel, but I sure as fuck don't want Evan to stop before I cum.

The orgasm begins gathering once again, so in an effort to make sure I don't lose this one I reach down and start circling my clit with my own fingers.

"Jesus, that's sexy," he grits out between thrusts. His pace falters for a second, showing me he's as close as I am.

It takes me a second to realize I'm whispering "Please, please!" over and over into the blanket. I turn my head to the side so he can hear me, but I have no idea what I'm asking for. My body is shaking, my pussy is clenching, and I am on the verge of exploding but something is keeping me from falling off the cliff.

"Fuck it," he mumbles a second before he pushes me harder into the bed by my shoulders.

Crack.

He spanks my ass so hard I'll have a mark on my cheek later, but apparently that was exactly what I'd needed to go over the ledge. Evan releases a deep grunt when I tighten around him, my entire body having gone rigid to the point where I don't have to worry about making a sound because I can't breathe to be able to make one. His grip on me tightens as his speed picks up and his thrusts lose their rhythm almost immediately. He buries his face in the crook of my neck and whispers a throaty "Fuuuuuuck" as I feel him pulsing inside of me with his own release.

Instead of collapsing on top of me, he pulls out and lifts me in his arms to place me on the bed. He climbs in after me and gathers me into his arms, catching his breath while he plays with my curls.

"Well," I pant. "That isn't what I had planned. I'm not mad about it though."

His chuckle is quiet. "You dared me into a game of sexual chicken. Did you really think that would work?"

"I mean, technically it worked out fine. I guess we'll find out if they heard anything."

"Would that be so bad?" he asks me. "I don't really want to hide this forever. He's going to find out eventually."

"No, but with as weird as he's been lately my gut tells me it's important to wait until after we're done with Ryan. We'll tell him after, I was thinking we could when we go to his house for dinner."

"Ok, sounds good. I'll follow you on this since you know him better than me now." He pauses to reach over to the nightstand when a text alerts and hands me my phone.

Brandon: I heard what you were doing when I came up for my toothbrush. Get it girl!

Me: Shit. Did Daniel hear?

Brandon: No, we have the tv on downstairs. Plus, I put my ear to the door to listen.

Me: You pervy fuck! Go to sleep.

Brandon: You love me. Nitey nite my little sex kitten! I'M SO PROUD.

"He's such a shit" I whine as I sit up to go to the bathroom and clean up.

"But he's right. You love him," Evan reminds me.

"Yeah. I guess I do."

Chapter 37

The next morning Evan heads downstairs and starts coffee while I prepare for the day. Brandon and Daniel are still there, and they've got breakfast in the works by the time I reach the kitchen. The meal is pleasant and I clean up while the guys get ready to go. We firm up plans to go to Daniel's house for dinner and decorating in a few days, and Evan and I leave at the same time they do so we can head to Mr. Talbert's office and handle the paperwork.

Mr. Talbert has everything ready when we arrive, just like he promised. After the papers are signed he reinforces his offer for help with anything Evan needs, especially if his Uncle Patrick tries to cause any problems. He also provides Evan with a list of several Realtors, cleaning companies, junk hauling companies, and appraisers to help with the sale of her home. Gran's bills are set to auto-draft from her account, and she has no debt so Evan doesn't have to worry about anything except transferring the accounts into his name and selling the house and her two cars.

I can tell he's still numb, but now that he's got the all clear we decide to go back to her house and pack up some things. We grab the rest of his stuff since he won't be staying here and things like her jewelry and files in case his Uncle Patrick decides he wants to try to take anything before we can go through it all. Mr. Talbert had an accounting of her valuables so we were able to verify everything was there and take it all with us in one trip thanks to his truck.

I'm craving a calzone, so we decide to stop for lunch on the way home at my favorite little Italian restaurant. Evan hasn't eaten here since we were kids so by the time his sub arrives he's practically drooling. Thankfully, it lives up to his memories.

We're walking out when he receives a text. "Hey, some guys from work are going out tomorrow night and want me to come. They always bring their girlfriends with them, and I'd like for you to meet them. Do you want to go?"

"Sure. I'd love to meet your friends. Let's do it."

Smiling, he leads me to his truck to open the door for me and help me in. We unload the truck when we get home, taking everything directly into my room so he can keep his clothes in there going forward. Over lunch, we officially decided to come clean to Daniel when we are at his house later this week, so there's no use in pretending any longer.

We work together to organize my room to fit both of our things in there. I make room in my closet and dressers so he has space for the things we brought today in addition to everything that was already here. Every once in a while I have the niggling thought that this is all happening too fast, but then I look at him and realize it doesn't matter. As long as we're happy, which we very much are, why does it matter? We have no family to step in, and I'm going to marry him tomorrow. The death of my dad and his Gran are two instances that prove you're never guaranteed tomorrow. I'd rather live my life enjoying and living for today than worrying about what people will think tomorrow.

I'm going to enjoy every day I have with Evan.

While getting our room straight, we decide today is the day. We're both tired of having to deal with Ryan and the fact that it takes up so much of our time, so he'll die today regardless of whether he talks or not. It's time to move on with our lives, and he's holding us back.

I've decided I'm not going to wear my coveralls to kill him. I pull on an old cropped tank and short exercise shorts so I can irritate him as he dies but pull a sweatshirt and yoga pants over it all to keep me warm on the trip out to the barn. My hair is up in a tight bun and I'm makeup and jewelry free. Evan has pulled on gray sweats over his basketball shorts and is wearing a t-shirt that appropriately reads "I never liked you anyway." The combination of women's kryptonite and a snarky t-shirt makes me consider keeping him in my bed all afternoon, but there will be time for that later, so I slap his ass as I pass by and race him to the garage.

He tosses a duffle bag in the back and winks as he slides into the driver's seat of the UTV and hits the button on the visor to open the garage door.

"You ready for this, Ev?" I ask him, taking his hand in mine. "Beating the shit out of someone is one thing. Taking a life is another. Trust me."

Signing, he squeezes my hand and brings it to his lips for a sweet kiss. "I have no doubt. I'm ready though. You're not doing this alone, and I owe it to a lot of people. He's hurt and killed so many, he can't be allowed to do that again."

"I know. He's your cousin, though, whether he's a piece of shit or not. This wouldn't be my first. I don't have any problem handling it so you don't have it on your conscience."

"I'll be fine. I think I need to do it. If I have trouble I don't have a problem asking for help."

The rest of the drive is quiet. The leaves are starting to turn beautiful fall colors and the crisp chill in the air fills me with excitement for the coming fall. As much as I love it out here, I'm hopeful this is the last time we'll have to come out here for a while.

The Enigma TNG is blasting through the sound system when we enter the cold room and I leave it on while we get situated since I like this song. Since Ryan is passed out with his head hanging forward we go about our usual setup routine of pulling out our tools and hose. I remove my hoodie and yoga pants and retake my place on the work table while Evan pulls on a clean pair of coveralls and wraps his hands in the boxing straps.

Once we're ready, Evan turns off the music and blasts the back of Ryan's head with a steady stream of water. Instead of his usual shouting, he groans and lets his head roll from side to side.

"Wakey wakey, Ry!" Evan goads, finally stopping the spray. "Ready to talk?"

"Can't... talk" Ryan croaks back.

"If I give you some water, will you? You have to be as tired of this as we are."

It takes a moment, but Ryan nods his head. Evan returns to the duffle bag he left by the door and retrieves a bottle of water. Cracking it open, he holds it to Ryan's lips and tips it up so he can drink. Normally I'd warn him not to drink too fast after not having anything for so long, but he's going to die soon, so I honestly don't care. His breathing is labored when he finishes the bottle, and Evan caps it and walks back to the bag and bends to grab another.

He pulls something else out of the bag and I squeal in delight when I realize it's a bag of gummy worms. I joked to him I'd need some next time and it looks like he remembered. He's such a good provider.

He opens the bag for me before handing it over with a kiss. I immediately pull one out of the bag and pop the end between my teeth, pulling the other end so it snaps in the middle. I swing my feet back and forth and chew happily as I watch the show unfold.

"So," Evan begins. "What information do you have for me? Because I have to tell you, I'm ready to move on. I don't want this to escalate, but I am prepared to do unto you as your father did unto me, if you catch my drift."

I furrow my brow, looking to Evan in confusion. His back is to me so I'm not sure what his face is showing, but I'm wondering if he's talking about the scars I felt under his tattoo. It sounds like we need to have a conversation.

"You... wouldn't" Ryan scoffs weakly.

"Oh, I would. And to a much worse extent too. Your dear old dad had to worry about leaving marks on my skin where people could see and judge. I have no such worries. That means you have two choices. Speak now and die easily, or suffer my pain."

"Fuck. You"

"Door number two it is!" Evan crows in dramatic game show fashion. He heads back to his duffle and brings it over to me at the table. He turns so his back is to Ryan and is

shielding what he's doing from him. Digging inside of the bag he pulls out a sealed pack of cigarettes and a cheap Bic lighter. "Don't worry, I brought gum and a toothbrush," he whispers with a strained grin.

I place my hand on his arm and force him to look at me. "Don't do this if it's going to hurt you more. There are other ways."

"No. I need this. An eye for an eye. Patrick took a lot from me, and I'm going to take it back from his son." He presses his lips to my forehead for a moment while he opens the pack of cigarettes then steps back and turns to Ryan whose eyes widen when they take in what is in his hands.

"So tell me, cousin. What were you planning on doing with Jen?" He lights the cigarette and blows the smoke in Ryan's face, causing him to cough weakly. Ryan's only response is to pinch his lips tightly together once he's stopped coughing. Holding the cigarette in place at the corner of his mouth Evan removes my switchblade from his pocket and slices Ryan's shirt open. Closing the blade and putting it back in his pocket, he takes a drag from the cigarette and exhales the smoke as he speaks. "I'll count down from six, giving you a break each time to change your mind. One to match each of my own. Are you ready?"

The hate in Ryan's eyes is a living thing. His jaw is clenched and his nostrils are flared with his heavy breaths. Evan's shoulders are blocking my view, but a moment after Ryan's head is thrown back and a pain filled groan emerges from between his clenched teeth I know he's been burned. The smell of charred flesh hits me and makes me wrinkle my nose, though it's not as bad as it could be. Thinking quickly, I grab another gummi worm and put it under my nose, holding it there with my lifted upper lip so it looks like I'm wearing a mustache and I smell sugary fruit instead of burned skin. I'm too involved in moving my lip around so the worm will wiggle to realize Evan has turned from Ryan and is staring at me with exasperated fondness.

"Oh. Um, sorry? Carry on! I'll behave." I grab my wormstache and take a bite to prove I'm done playing.

For now.

Evan shakes his head and turns back to Ryan as he takes another drag. "One down. Five to go. You can stop this any time." Ryan tries to twist his body away from Evan's reach, but he doesn't have enough leverage to do anything more than lean slightly away. Our captive stays silent until Evan once again places the burning tip of the cigarette against his chest while holding him still by his waist. His groan morphs into muffled curses as he spits them from behind clenched teeth, and this time it takes longer to complete. Another pause, another death glare from Ryan as he pants through the pain.

"Last chance, man. You know everything he did to me. You fucking watched it happen. You helped! Do you really want to go through what I did? Because I promise you, I won't leave anything out unless you tell me something to make me stop."

"I don't have to tell you anything. You're going to kill me anyway."

"True. But this way is much more painful." Evan shakes his head, takes one final drag, and then presses the lit tip to Ryan's chest once again. The volume of Ryan's cries increases the longer Evan is at work, and I'm almost certain he's about to break when Evan steps back and finally allows me to view his work.

There are six burns on Ryan's chest. Three are set horizontally, with the center point meeting with three other vertical lines. I can't be sure since he's moving around, but I think it's in the shape of a cross.

"Do you remember this, Ry? Do you remember how you held me down while your father burned the shape of the cross into my thigh as punishment for telling him I wanted to leave and move in with Gran after we moved to the new congregation? Because I do. I remember the smell of my burning flesh and the searing pain, and your absolute lack of empathy. Your willingness to do whatever he said like a good little soldier."

"I remember," Ryan rasps. "You disrespected him."

"He didn't deserve my respect! And he'll never have it. I bet you remember what happened next too. Do you want to save yourself from the same pain? Tell me what you planned to do with Jen. Tell me what bullshit your dad is getting up to at the compound. Tell me, and it all ends."

"I'm not telling you shit. I'm not betraying my father. Loyalty is something you've never understood."

Evan laughs at his ridiculous words and grinds his dropped cigarette under his boot as he pulls the switchblade back out of his pocket with one hand and the lighter with the other. Strolling back to my side at the table he bends for a bite of the gummi worm I hold up for him and pulls a large candle out of the duffle bag, lighting it next to me.

"Ambiance," he says with a chuckle. He opens his mouth for me to give him another worm as he holds the knife blade over the open flame. "Fair enough. You do remember though, don't you? What happens next?"

"Yes," Ryan hisses through gritted teeth.

"Wonderful," Evan mutters distractedly while watching the blade heat. "Because I realized a few days ago you didn't do it because your father forced you to. You did it because you wanted to." Turning and heading back over to him, Evan holds the heated blade in front of Ryan's eyes.

"I hope your God has mercy on you, cousin. Because I no longer will."

Ryan's screams fill the small space as Evan uses his blade like the ink pen on some macabre connect-the-dots drawing. He pauses to reheat his weapon after completing the horizontal line and I track the trails of blood that well up and slide down his exposed chest. Evan doesn't stop until he's completed the vertical line and Ryan has a completed cross burned into his skin.

His screams cut off abruptly when he passes out from the pain. Evan returns to the table and drops the knife before standing in front of me with an expression of insecurity he's trying very hard to hide. I spread my legs, place my bag of candy on the table beside me, and pull him close. The sign of relief he releases when I wrap myself around him breaks my heart a little, like he thought hearing about what happened to him would somehow change something for me.

"I am so sorry you went through that," I say into his neck. "You don't have to tell me about it, but I want you to know I'm always here to listen, no judgement. Not even for this, so don't worry about me watching and thinking less of you. You deserve this."

"Thank you," he replies, shoulders dropping from their raised position. "I know you've said it before, but I'm still getting used to having someone I can trust." I smile and pull him in for a kiss.

"What's next?" I ask him. "Do you think you can make him talk?"

"Probably not. His father did almost as much to him as he did to me, so he's used to the pain. There was only one time he didn't hold back from leaving marks, and that was on my leg where no one in the congregation would ever see it, even accidentally. Besides, Ryan is the most stubborn asshole I've ever met. He'd let me skin him alive just to say he bested me."

"I mean, I have a blade for it if you wanted to try," I tell him with a nonchalant shrug.

Evan chuckles and kisses my head, pulling away to dig back in his bag. "I almost forgot," he says, handing me a bottle of Diet Coke.

"My hero!" I cheer as I crack the seal. "Only you could know me well enough to feed and water me during torture. You totally get me."

I sip my drink and eat another gummi while Evan pulls a white extension cord out of his bag. He uses the switchblade to cut the metal tip from the end and drops it back in the bag. "Uncle Patrick used to use one of these with the ends cut off like this. The metal tips had a chance to break the skin, but he was good enough with the cord that he only ever left welts and bruises."

"Wait... are you telling me he whipped you with one of those?" I was already disgusted anyone could burn and cut a child, but whipping? "What else? Can you tell me?"

"Mostly fists and open-handed slaps. Starvation. Insults. If you can think of something that wouldn't leave scars or bring outside attention, he probably did it."

"I'm going to kill that motherfucker," I tell him, sincerely. "I'm going to strap him to this table and make his insides be his outsides. I'll shove his intestines in his fat, disgusting mouth and eat popcorn as he chokes to death and bleeds out simultaneously."

Evan is staring at me with his jaw dropped.

"What?" I ask, suddenly self-conscious. "I'm just sayin'."

His sudden smile hits me like a punch to the gut. "Nothing," he laughs, cupping my cheek. "No one has ever stood up for me or cared about what happened to me, except for Gran." He shrugs. "It means a lot to me."

My blush comes hard and fast, almost making me a little dizzy. I purse my lips and scrunch my nose, trying to seem unaffected. "Yeah, well. You deserve it." I'm coming back around to the L-word, but now is so not the time or place for it. Time to redirect!

"So like... want to finish up here so we can get some dinner? These gummi worms are the tits but I want Chinese."

"Yes ma'am," he responds with a knowing smile. "Want to do the honors with the hose this last time?"

"Hell yeah! Let's do it." I take one last sip of my drink before setting it down beside me and taking the hose Evan offers me. I wait until he's in position a few steps to the side behind Ryan and then blast him straight in the face. He once again wakes spluttering and coughing and I take my time moving the stream of water from his face to his open chest wounds, causing him to cry out in agony.

"Bitch!" he yells as soon as he can catch his breath.

Crack!

The first hit of the cord on Ryan's back sounds like a whip in the small room and Ryan screams out before he can grit his teeth to try to contain himself.

"I warned you not to talk to her like that." Evan pauses to walk around and face Ryan. "Your father's favorite number was twelve, right? Such a holy number loved by such a holy man. So, just like he did to me so many times, I'm going to give you a set of twelve lashes. The only difference is, I'm going to give you one set for each life you've taken, tried to take, or planned to take. By my count, that's at least four. Tell me what I want to hear, and it all stops."

"Not. Going to. Happen."

"Ok. Jen, if he passes out let me know so we can wait until he's awake."

"Yes, sir!" I tell him with a mock salute.

He takes his place again behind Ryan and begins whipping him with the cord. It must be less painful than the burning because while he grunts and strains his muscles he doesn't scream out like he did previously. He passes out once and I revive him with the hose after giving Evan a water and gummi break, and we're somewhere around the thirty lash mark when he starts laughing as hard as his weak body will allow. I hold my hand up to attract Evan's attention so he will stop and notice Ryan's off behavior.

"Something funny?" I ask him, tilting my head to the side.

"You think it matters if you kill me, but you won't have much time left." His breathing is labored and he's struggling to get his words out. "My father knows you have something to do with my disappearance, and he will come after you." He pauses to make eye contact with me. "You'll die just like your worthless father."

CHAPTER 38

"What the fuck did you just say?"

"You heard me, cunt. My father will see you dead, just like the other pathetic whores."

"No. What the fuck did you say about my dad?" I'm frozen in place, sure he's not telling me he knows something more about my father's death. Part of me realizes he's talking about his father killing other women, but they aren't what is important to me right now.

"Only that my dad told me he died like a spineless little bitch," he sneers.

I see red, then black. Then, red again, as I come back to myself staring at my blood covered hand. Evan's knife is lodged in Ryan's stomach, and my hand is wrapped around it.

I glance at Evan over Ryan's shoulder. His eyes are wide and filled with worry for me. He steps up to me and places his hand over the one I still have on the knife.

"Oops?"

"Do what you need to, baby girl. I'm satisfied." With a kiss, he walks to the table and takes my place and my bag of gummi worms with a wink.

"You fucking bitch!" Ryan grits out. "I can't wait until my father finds you alone. He's going to fuck your worthless body while you bleed out on his altar!"

"Sounds kinky."

And then I slit his throat.

One more and I'll have a Turkey. I do love being able to apply bowling terms to everyday life.

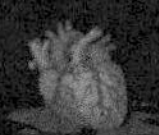

Though I am extremely accomplished at the disposal of animal remains, the disposal of a human body is a much more delicate and time-consuming affair. DNA sequencing makes it difficult to completely obliterate evidence unless you've got a giant vat of acid or something similar, but since I don't have access to such chemicals in large quantities, the destruction of identity will have to do.

Instead of simply removing the fingers and toes, I remove the pads of the fingers and toes so the prints aren't available should the body parts be found first. I will burn the small pieces of skin in the fire pit at the cabin, and spread the smaller pieces cut from the body between the lake for the turtles and fish, and the pieces I give to the local farmers for their stock. Teeth are removed to be scattered both in the woods and the lake behind my home, and the remainder of the body is dismembered and the pieces are mixed in with the parts left over from the last deer I butchered for disposal at the dump.

Though I do the majority of the work, Evan is a fantastic helper. He's not squeamish and isn't worried about getting bloody. In fact, the only negative reaction he had to me killing Ryan like I did was being upset for me that his blood sprayed my face and hair. He immediately retrieved and wet a dark rag to clean my face but left the rest of it covering me. His only comment was he didn't want it getting into my eyes or mouth, then he kissed me.

"Besides," he said with a sexy smirk and exaggerated eyebrow wiggle, "you've got that sexy warrior woman look going for you. Xena has nothing on you."

Since I decided to skip the coveralls I'm practically covered in blood by the time we're done. Between the spray from his throat and the butchering process I am covered head to toe. I'm used to the feeling of drying blood so it doesn't really bother me, but I can't go home like this in case someone randomly stops by, so I strip down in the bathroom and take a shower since Evan is determined to clean up for me. My clothes are ruined, so I've put them in a trash bag with the skin pieces and I will burn them all together this evening so that the evidence doesn't lie around forever.

I forgot to bring a change of clothes with me, so I throw on a pair of my coveralls and put my wet hair up in a messy bun for the ride back home. Just to fuck with Evan, I exit the bathroom with the zipper undone. It must effect him more than I expected because before I can blink I'm bent over the freshly cleaned work table and he's fucking me like it's his mission in life to make me cum.

Which is good, because I totally do.

It's dark by the time we leave the barn. I scatter a few teeth in the woods by tossing them out of the sides of the UTV like some creepy reverse tooth fairy and keep about half to toss into the lake. Evan showers while I change and order a pizza, then he gets the fire pit started while I make my way down to the water's edge. I walk a decent way along the shoreline and toss handfuls of meat and teeth into the water for the animals as I go. I often do this with scrap meat from the animals I butcher to keep them interested and well-fed, and it only takes a few minutes for my bag to be empty.

By the time I've washed my hands and gotten drinks for us the pizza arrives and we take it out to the patio to eat by the fire. It's only after we finish eating that I drop the pieces of skin and my bloody clothes into the flames so we can make sure all evidence is gone.

"Are you ok?" I ask Evan. Technically he didn't kill Ryan, but he was complicit and relived his own trauma while it happened.

"Me? I'm fine, I'm more worried about you and what he said about your dad." He grabs for my hand and uses it to pull me into his lap on the lounge chair he's seated on.

"I don't think I believe him. There will always be the niggling part of me that wonders, but there is no reason his dad would hurt mine. They had nothing to do with each other so it doesn't make sense." I've been thinking about it pretty much non-stop. Why? After four years, why would he even bother?

"The only reason I can think of is to isolate you. No protective father means you'd be an easier target in Patrick's mind."

"True. I don't want to think about it tonight, though. Ryan is gone, and it's finally just us. We both have to go back to work in a few days, so I want to enjoy the peace while we can."

"I can live with that. I'm looking forward to you meeting my friends tomorrow. I'd like to meet some of yours too. Maybe once the house is fixed and we officially live here we can have a housewarming party and bring them all together."

"I'd like that," I tell him, happy he wants to share and plan a life together.

Chapter 39

"I'm glad you wanted to come with me," Evan tells me, gripping my hand as we walk into the bar. "I don't want to stay too long, so let's make some kind of excuse in about an hour, ok?"

"Works for me," I respond, amused that he's already planning our escape. "You're the one that asked me to come. I'm just along for the ride."

Giving me a heated smirk, he releases my hand and wraps his strong arm around my waist to pull me in close to him. "Oh, you'll definitely be doing that later," he leers, giving me an exaggerated wink. "Did I tell you how sexy you look tonight?"

Throwing my head back with a laugh, I smack his ass. "That's why you don't want to stay long. You aren't fooling me, mister." I feel sexy tonight, to be honest. I want to make a good impression on Evan's friends, so I decided to go with a pair of black faux leather leggings, a plum silk off the shoulder t-shirt that drapes beautifully, and black studded ankle boots. My hair has cooperated and is perfectly curled for once, and I added a little drama to my makeup with eyeliner and a smokey eye that blends from plum to charcoal gray. I've even decided to wear some extra jewelry so in addition to my turtle pendant I'm wearing my mom's diamond stud earrings, a long multi-strand silver chain necklace, and several bangle bracelets that make me jingle as I walk.

He grins and wiggles his eyebrows at me before opening the bar's front door and leading me inside with pressure at the small of my back. A large group of people are gathered in the back corner of the bar around several pool tables, high tops, and dart boards, and that's where he leads me. When we arrive in their section Evan stays by my side as he offers up bro hugs and introductions to everyone there. It's mostly men, all of whom work with Evan, and a few girlfriends sprinkled in. Most are dressed similarly to me, making me glad I didn't wear the dress I had been eyeing in my closet.

The bar is a comfortable mix between a dive and something higher class. The wood is dark and the booths, chairs, and decor are all clean and well-kept, but not so pretentious that you can't enjoy a pitcher of beer and shoot pool while picking songs on the jukebox. His friends have a few pitchers of beer sitting out, but since Evan knows that I don't drink beer he heads to the bar while I take a seat at one of the high top tables surrounding our area to wait for him. I watch him walk over to the bar, loving the way that his jeans fit his ass and the black Henley he's wearing hints at his muscular frame beneath it. As soon as he starts speaking to the bartender my view is obstructed by a flannel shirt clad chest. Mark, I think his name is? He's standing in front of me and smiling like that's all it will take to make my panties melt.

Sadly for Mark, his mousey brown hair, muddy hazel eyes, and dimpled chin don't do anything for me. I prefer my man not to look like he's got an ass on his face. "Hey. Jen, right?" He already stinks of beer and his eyes have that drunken glossy sheen.

"Uh, yeah. You work with Evan, right?," Maybe if I remind him that I came with Evan, who he literally just talked to five minutes ago, he'll lose interest and move along.

"Yeah. Though he really hasn't been around as much lately. You the friend he grew up with before moving away? I remember him telling us about that."

"I am." Maybe short responses will do the trick.

"That's pretty cool. Do you want to have a drink with me?"

"Oh, no thanks. Evan is getting me one." Seriously?

"Come on, I'm sure I'll be better company than him. Why hang with a friend when we could be more than that?"

Is he for fucking real? "I came here with Evan, I'm leaving with Evan. Thanks, but no."

"What, are you a dyke or something? You too good for some dick?" His face turns red in anger, as if it's unacceptable that I have the audacity to turn him down even though I literally came here with someone else.

"Are you fucking serious? What I am is none of your business, you misogynistic prick. I came here with Evan because I'm with Evan. I'm not some piece of ass for your drunk ass to score with because you think you're better than you really are, so fuck off before this gets ugly."

"You bitch!" he starts, reaching for me like he's going to shake me into wanting to fuck him. I get ready to punch him in the dick before he puts his hand on me, but his arm is stopped within inches of mine. "What the fuck?" he yelps, jerking his head to the side to see an enraged Evan standing next to him.

"What the fuck did you just call her?" Evan asks him, his calm voice belying the rage in his eyes. "Because I'm pretty sure I heard you call her a bitch."

"He called me a dyke too!" I supply while reaching for the Old Fashioned that Evan is still holding and taking a big sip. Yum. Fuck this asshole, he deserves an ass beating. By this time everyone around us has stopped what they're doing and are watching the situation unfold. Evan couldn't care less if he has an audience because he grips Mark's arm tighter causing him to wince in pain.

"Shit... sorry man! I thought she was just your friend! I didn't know you two were together."

"Bullshit, asshat." I tell him. "I told you I came with Evan. I didn't stutter." Mark shoots me a glare of hate but I just smile and take another sip of my drink while I lean back and cross my legs. Is it wrong that his angry side is turning me on?

Better not overthink it.

"Here's what's going to happen." Evan tells him in a low, cold voice. "You're going to apologize to my girl, and then you're going to fuck right off. If you ever speak to her again, hell if you even look at her again, I will pull your teeth out one by one in front of your family."

Um, hello. According to the clock in my panties, it's time to head home.

"We cool?"

"Yeah... yeah man we're cool." He's nodding his head so fast he looks like a terrified bobblehead. "Sorry Jen, I didn't mean it. I think I've had too much to drink tonight. I won't bother you again."

Rolling my eyes at his crappy apology, I just flap my hand at him in dismissal. I'm too consumed by thoughts of Evan's alpha side to even care about him anymore.

"Good, now get the fuck out of here." Evan pushes him away and steps toward me, cupping my face gently with the same hand that was seconds ago gripping Mark in anger. "You ok baby girl?"

Biting my lip and looking into his eyes, I bat my lashes at him and say "I'm perfect. I was about to junk punch him, but you intervened before I could. I think I'm ready to head home though, if you are. We may not even make it that far after that though, so be prepared."

His eyes flash with lust for a moment before he grabs the back of my head and pulls me in for a scorching kiss. "Let's go home," he says before he places my half empty drink on the table beside me, bends down, throws me over his shoulder, and slaps my ass. After my surprised shriek dies, Evan turns to face his friends before saying "Sorry guys, but after that I think we're going to head out. Don't invite me again if Mark is going to be there, ok? I don't want to have to beat his ass."

He turns to leave and I'm able to brace my hands on his lower back so that I can look up and smile at his friends staring after us. Some are watching in shock, some in amusement, so I raise a hand to waive and call out "It was nice meeting you all! We'll have to have you out for a hot tub party soon!" before laughing and slapping his ass in reprisal. "You're in big trouble!" I tell him, pinching his side hard enough that he grunts and smacks me again.

The parking lot isn't well lit and lucky for me Evan chose a spot at the end of a row. He opens my door as he always does, giving me a kiss once I'm seated, and shuts the door for me before making his way around to the driver's side. While he's walking around, I take my shoes off so they won't be in my way, and as soon as he's seated in the driver's seat I slide down the bench next to him and turn to straddle his waist.

"What are you doing, baby girl?" Evan purrs at me. "I thought you wanted to go home." His arms instinctively wrap around me and grip my ass, pulling me down harder onto his growing erection.

Leaning in to trail my mouth from his collarbone to his ear, I suck his lobe into my mouth and admit "I did tell you that we may not make it home. It's not my fault that you threatening to beat that piece of shit's ass turned me on. I didn't even realize that was a real thing until it happened, so this is basically your fault." I shrug, as if it's just an unavoidable side effect and then bite his neck under his ear. "I need you, Ev," I whisper.

Shuddering, he grips my hair and pulls my head back before slamming his lips to mine. I open my mouth to invite him in and grind down on his hard dick. My moan escapes me, swallowed by Evan as he runs one of his hands under my shirt and up my side to cup my breast. I gasp as he pinches my nipple and he uses the opportunity to say "I'm not going to fuck you in this parking lot where anyone can see what's mine, but I'm not going to make you wait when you need me. I'm going to take care of you now, then fuck you right here when we get home."

The hand that was massaging my breast trails down my stomach and dips into my leggings and straight under my panties, his fingers slowly dipping down between my folds. Leaning his head back against his head rest, he closes his eyes for a moment before letting out a groan. "Fuck, baby girl. You weren't kidding. I'll threaten someone every day if it gets you this fucking wet."

I smirk and roll my hips, gasping out a moan when he slides two fingers deep into me. He isn't wrong, I'm wet enough that there's no resistance. The flat of his palm applies pressure to my clit as he starts moving faster and I can't help but ride his fingers like it's his cock, leaning in to kiss him again as I chase the orgasm that is building. I have no idea how long we are locked together, but as my climax nears I pull back from our kiss and lean against the steering wheel, my head thrown back in bliss. "Fuck!" I moan, "please don't stop!"

"Fuck no. Look at me Jen, let me watch your face as you cum on my fingers."

God damn. First threats get me hot and bothered, then possessive words make me almost cum? I don't know what's wrong with me, but I don't fucking care either.

Fisting my hair again, he tightens his grip and forces my head to sit at an angle where I'm forced to look into his eyes. He speeds up the movement of his fingers in my pussy and within seconds my climax crashes through me in a body shaking wave.

"Shit," I exhale as soon as my body calms. "Who knew I was such a freaky bitch?" Chuckling, I lean in and give him a sweet kiss. "Actually, I did. I read a lot of dirty books. I just didn't think they'd translate into real life."

"I know. I've asked Brandon what you read about and have checked out a few."

Is now the wrong time for a proposal? He read my books for God's sake!

My eyes widen and I shiver a little as he slides his fingers out of my pussy and his hand entirely out of my pants. I can't help that another moan escapes me as he sucks his fingers into his mouth before slapping my ass with his other hand. "Alright. Time for you to hop off so I can drive us home. I need to be inside you."

I give him another lingering kiss before sliding off his lap and back onto the bench seat. Deciding that I'm comfortable where I am, I buckle the middle seat belt and lean into his side. Evan adjusts his dick in his pants and buckles his own seat belt before kissing the side of my head as he starts the truck. He pulls out of the parking spot and turns us in the direction of home with his hand wrapped around my thigh, holding me close.

Our drive home is comfortable. I love the secure, warm feeling of his hand wrapped around my thigh. It's like he is afraid if he's not holding on to me I'll float away, but he doesn't realize that there's nowhere else I'd rather be. He's the missing part of my soul.

When we turn into my driveway his hand on my thigh begins a slow path higher, closer to the apex of my legs. Not wanting him to have to take his hand away, I reach my own hand up and press the button that will open the garage door and allow us entrance. When the truck comes to a complete stop, I unbuckle my seat belt and start sliding down the seat away from him. His hand snaps out and he wraps his fingers around my arm.

"Where do you think you're going? You're not leaving this truck until I say you can."

Smirking, I pry his fingers from my arm and continue scooting towards the passenger seat. "Patience, handsome. I just need a little space for a second." Once I can stretch my legs out, I lift my hips and slide my leggings off, watching Evan for his reaction. I'm not disappointed when I see him reach down and palm his still hard cock through his jeans. Once my pants are piled on the floor, I drag my shirt over my head leaving me in a matching black lace strapless bra and g-string.

Turning, I crawl my way back across the seat and slide my hand from his knee, up his thigh, over his bulge, and to the button on his fly. Eager for me to lead this time, Evan helps me undo the button and zipper and slides his pants down for me, taking his boxers with them. His erection stands proudly, a bead of precum dripping from the tip, and my mouth waters at the sight. I lean forward, staring up at him through hooded eyes before dropping down to press a kiss to his tip. His eyes are locked on my breasts as they almost spill out of my bra and I use that distraction to take him into my hand and squeeze his base. He hisses at the contact and his breath stutters in his chest. I lick my lips and lower myself so that I can lick him from base to tip, circling my tongue at the top and reveling in his salty flavor.

Using the hand wrapped around his base I angle him toward me and take him into my mouth slowly. His muscles tense beneath me as his hand slides into my hair. I begin to bob up and down, sucking on my way down and applying pressure with my tongue on the way back up. He allows me to set the pace for a while and I increase my pace as his grip tightens, causing me to rub my own thighs together as much as possible to provide a little friction to my needy pussy. His hold is almost to the point of pain when he uses his leverage to pull my head up and my mouth off him.

"That's enough," he pants. "I need you over here, now." He uses my hair as a handle and pulls me forward to straddle his lap. His cock presses against my core and I can't help but grind into him in an effort to soothe the need burning there. Tracing a hand up my side, he runs his finger under the band of my bra while he licks a path from my breast to my neck and then pulls the small knife I carry from the band. "I hope you don't care about these panties, because I'm cutting them the fuck off. I'll buy you another pair."

A shiver traces down my spine at his words and I lean back against the steering wheel so that I can watch him slide the warm metal tip of the opened blade lightly from the center of my bra down my stomach. My breath catches as he traces the line of my panties from the center over to the left side and slices the strap in two. I take good care of my knives, so it slides through like butter. Repeating the process on the right side, I help out by lifting my hips just enough for him to pull the panties out from under me and toss them aside. Licking the thumb of his opposite hand, he places it on my clit and starts rubbing it in agonizingly slow circles. I close my eyes and lean my head back, enjoying the caress, but they snap back open when the blade slides between the cups of my bra.

"Don't you fucking da-"

Slice.

This motherfucker just destroyed my favorite bra. "You asshole! I love this bra!"

"Bill me. I'll buy you a dozen more so I can cut those off too. I can afford it now." Closing the knife one handed, he tosses it to the side and firmly grips my ass, pulling me closer to his weeping dick. "Now, I believe I promised to fuck you before letting you out of this car. Climb up here, baby."

Still mad about the bra, I hesitate for a second and consider leaving him unsatisfied. He has no idea how hard it is to find the perfect strapless bra! I'd just be denying myself though, so I poke his nose and growl "No more cutting my bras without asking first. That thing was expensive and it takes forever to find a good one!"

Taking hold of my hand and nipping my finger, he gazes at me with serious eyes and promises "I swear. I'll only cut off clothes with your permission from now on. Or I'll buy them myself with the intent to destroy them." He holds up his pinky finger to seal the deal like we did when we were kids, and my heart swells as I link his with mine and lean in for a kiss. I sit up on my knees before dragging our entwined hands down between us and I use them to guide him into my opening. We both groan into our kiss as I drop down onto him. He grips my hips and uses them to drag me back and forth over his cock, and we quickly find a punishing rhythm together.

We may have started things off slow but neither of us want sweet tonight. We'd have moved inside and into bed if we didn't want fast and hot. I place my hands on his shoulders and brace my knees more firmly on the seat beneath us and use both points as leverage to lift myself up and down his length. His hands help me move and our pace increases to a fevered pitch. He breaks our kiss so that he can lean forward and take my aching nipple into his mouth. My body begins to stutter as my orgasm rises, and Evan takes my hesitation as a cue to take over. He starts pistoning his hips up into me while he slams me down to meet him and the sound of our skin slapping together echoes in the small space. "Oh, fuck!" I cry out, burying my face in his neck as my orgasm rips through me. Evan pumps up into me a few more times before crying out himself, pulsing inside of me, emptying himself as he joins me in release.

We're both silent for a few minutes other than our heavy breathing, basking in the moment and cradling each other. Once we've both caught our breath, he kisses my collarbone. "Let's go inside and clean up. I'll order dinner and we can watch a movie or something."

I slide off his lap and as I move I realize I forgot to shut the garage door behind us, so I reach up and press the button to close it. I gather my clothes, shoes, and knife before following Evan out of the driver's side door. He's pulled his pants up but left them undone, and he holds his hand out for me to precede him.

"I think delivery and a movie sounds like the perfect way to end the night."

CHAPTER 40

Monday morning comes too quickly. As much as I love the bookstore, I've loved this time off too. We had a lazy Sunday that was composed of a Game of Thrones marathon since I found out he'd never seen the show or read the books, and I promised I'd bring him a copy of the first book home from work so he could read it. I'm starting to run out of clothes at the cabin so Evan is going to meet me after work for dinner at my favorite Mexican restaurant in the shopping center, and then we're going to pack up some of my clothes and things in my apartment to take home with us.

Things have been crazy over the last week, so I have only talked to my work friends a few times over text. Carmen texted me to check in and make sure I was okay, and to give me shit about Ryan. I changed the subject every time because I didn't want to talk about it over text. She'll find out about Evan soon enough if Brandon hasn't already told her. I've talked to Nick and Travis a bit more frequently since Travis was hurt, but I haven't mentioned Evan to them either, so today when he comes to pick me up should be fun.

"Jen! You beautiful bitch, I missed you!" Carmen comes running to me when she arrives to open with me, wrapping me up in a tight hug.

Chuckling at her exuberance, I shake my head and hug her back. "I missed you too, girl. Glad to see things didn't burn down in my absence."

"Trust me, it was a close thing. Brandon is great, but I missed working with you. Let's open up so you can tell me all about that hot piece of ass I saw you with." She wiggles her eyebrows and rubs her hands together.

"Sorry to burst your bubble, hot stuff, but Ryan is so beyond out of the picture."

"Small dick?" she asks with a sympathetic frown.

"Oh my god, if it were only that simple. I'll need a Diet Coke and a muffin to make it through this story."

"On it, Captain!" she chips as she salutes me and runs off to open the café. Nick arrives a few moments later and gives me a kiss on the cheek in greeting before moving to the to help her. After the week I've had I decided to create a cozy mystery display to keep things a bit lighter, so after I catch up with my friends I'll work on that.

In less than an hour I'm seated at the table next to the café counter with my drink and a chocolate chip muffin, Carmen and Nick seated across from me since we haven't gotten busy yet.

"Alright chickie, spill the tea!" Carmen orders, taking a sip of her coffee. "What happened with Ryan, and who is this friend you were helping all week?"

"Well, long story sort of short... he pushed himself on me hard. I kept asking for him to back off and he wouldn't, so we got into a big fight. I basically told him to fuck off since he couldn't respect my boundaries, and that was the last time I saw him."

"What an asshole! I have to be honest, Jen. I'm kind of glad that didn't work out. Ryan gave me bad vibes," Nick adds, covering my hand with his.

"Understatement," I say, chuckling sadly. "Incidentally, the day after we got into our fight his cousin Evan found their grandmother dead at the bottom of their stairs. Ryan had disappeared at that point with no contact or information as to where he was going, so we think that he may have pushed her. I was with him when he found her and he has no other family left, so Mrs. C gave me the week to help him take care of things." By the time I finish talking both Carmen and Nick are staring at me with their mouths dropped open.

"Holy shit, are you ok?" Carmen asks. "Here I was just worrying about whether you got dicked down on your vacay and you found a freaking dead body!"

I knew this part was coming, but I still can't keep the blush from my cheeks. I try to hide it behind my cup but both of my friends catch it and squeal at the same time.

"Shut up!" Carmen shrieks. "Who was it? Why didn't you call me? Was it the cousin? Is he as hot as Ryan? I mean, Ryan is obviously a douchenozzle so that sort of ruins his hot level but you could bounce a quarter off that yummy ass."

"Down, girl!" I laugh. "Yeah, it happened really fast, but Evan and I are together. I had a huge crush on him when we were younger, and it turns out he felt the same for me." My hand goes to my turtle pendant and I rub the belly. "He's actually the one that left this for me on the anniversary of my mom's death years ago."

"No shit! Honey, that's amazing!" Nick looks truly happy for me. "When can we meet him?"

"Um, he's actually going to pick me up after my shift today. We're going to have dinner then grab some things from my apartment."

"Why do you need to grab things from your apartment? Are you staying with him tonight?" Carmen is smiling like the cat that ate the canary.

"No. He's staying with me out at the cabin. He isn't ready to stay in his gran's house after finding her body there, and since he's in construction he's doing the renovations for me that I've been wanting to do before I move in full time. I even bought a hot tub, which has been amazing."

"Oh my gosh, party at the cabin! Tell us about him, though," Carmen requests. Something in her expression has changed, she's become more serious and I'm not sure why.

"He's... Evan." I tell them, shrugging. "Growing up, before they left, he was always my best friend. My confidant. The person I went to when I needed someone and it couldn't be my dad. Ryan sort of gaslighted me into believing that Evan thought of me as a little sister back then, and I went for him instead. He's just amazing. Sweet, protective while knowing that I can also take care of myself, and so sexy," I finish, blushing.

"Oh my God," Nick gasps, jaw dropped. "You're in love with him."

I drop my head into my hands and groan. "I might be," I lament.

"What's wrong with that, honey?" Carmen asks. "Does he not feel the same way?"

"No, it's not that. He's told me that he's been in love with me since we were kids. It's just... isn't it too soon? We've only spent a week together as adults. Am I crazy?"

"Does it feel wrong?" There is no judgement in Nick's gaze or words. "I knew that Travis was it for me on our first date. That was the day after I met him, so we didn't have years of history to pull from like you do. Sometimes when you know, you know."

"No. It doesn't feel wrong. I'm not one hundred percent sure it's love, but... I feel like it is." I chew on my lip. "All I know is that I want to be with him," then, to fuck with them I cover my mouth with my cup before mumbling "and the sex is fucking amazing."

The chaos that ensues after that comment is everything I expected it to be.

It's nearing the end of my shift so I'm trying to finish up my cozy mystery display by the cafe. Carmen, Nick, and I chat between customers and I'm enjoying being surrounded by the books and energy that my store brings. I'm adding the finishing touches when I hear a low whistle coming from the cafe counter, then a gasp and squealed "Dibs!" from Carmen.

I turn to see what they're talking about, but both of them are staring at the front door. Following their line of sight I find Evan just inside the front door looking around.

"Sorry, babe," I tell her, smiling at Evan as he finally notices me and starts walking my way. "I licked it, so it's mine."

"Lucky bitch!" she hisses at me when Evan is only feet away. He turns his blinding smile on her for a moment causing her to release a quiet "Oofta!" in response while fanning herself.

His hair is mussed like he's been running his hands through it, and his clothes are dirty from working construction all day, but he looks as sexy as he always does. Today is the longest we've been apart since this whole thing started and I'm slightly surprised to realize that I missed him.

"Hi," I say, feeling shy for some reason and nibbling on the inside of my lip.

"Hi," he responds with a knowing smirk as he uses his thumb to rescue my lip before kissing me.

"Hashtag, swoon!" Carmen groans, draping herself over the counter and causing me to laugh.

Evan just laughs and kisses my forehead then turns in her direction. "You must be Carmen," he says, walking forward with his arm wrapped around me to shake her hand. "I'm Evan."

"I sure am, hot stuff!" she chirps while accepting his gesture and unashamedly looking him up and down. "This is Nick."

"Hey, man. Nice to meet you," Evan shakes his hand as well. "I am sorry about Travis, Jen told me what happened to him. She also said you'll both be coming over soon for dinner soon, so I look forward to meeting him too."

Ugh. Swoon is right! The difference between how Ryan and Evan interact with my friends is astounding, and it just reinforces that I've made the right choice.

Even more than the whole "he's an evil douchey murderer" thing.

"It's nice to meet you too. We've heard a lot about you today." Nick gives him a genuine smile. "Can I make you something? Jen has some time left on her shift, so you can hang with us if you want."

"Yeah, thanks. It's been a long day." I take a second to kiss his cheek and leave him with Nick and Carmen while I finish my display and tend to a few other things before Brandon comes in. It makes me happy that he's getting along with my friends and enjoying their company.

When Brandon comes in we chat as I collect my purse from the back. He walks with me over to the café to say hi to Evan before heading up front. They do their bro hug thing and catch up for a minute while I sidle up to Nick and Carmen.

"So... what do you think?" I ask them under my breath.

"Oh my God, Jen, he's perfect! I bet he's got a huge dick too, doesn't he? Ugh! Why can't I have your luck?"

I just laugh and shake my head at her in fond exasperation while looking to Nick.

"He's amazing, sweetheart," he says, grabbing my hand. "I'm so happy for you. I can't wait to get to know him better, and for Travis to meet him too. He invited us to come out for dinner in the next few weeks so that he can." His attention moving directly over my shoulder alerts me to the fact that someone has come up behind me, and I realize it's Evan when he wraps his arm around my waist.

"I know we've got the construction going on, but I thought we may be able to take a night off to have some friends over now that things have settled down." Evan shrugs, his ears tinged pink when I turn my smile on him.

"I love that idea. Maybe after we can invite some of your friends, minus the handsy jackass."

"Handsy jackass?" Brandon interjects.

"Yeah, we went to the bar to hang with some of his work friends the other night. There was this dude there who thought I'd want to be with him even though I was obviously with Evan. He didn't like my attitude when I turned him down, so he got mouthy and tried to touch me. Evan stopped him and threatened to remove his teeth for him." I have to grin at him because that shit still gets me hot just thinking about it, and he just winks at me.

"Um... like, I know you're not usually into girl parts, Jen, but... can I put in an application to make your couple into a throuple? Because damn." Carmen is fanning herself with the Men's Fitness magazine she keeps on the counter. For the articles.

I just snort and shake my head before doling out cheek kisses all around. "And that's my cue! Come on, Ev. I need queso."

"It was nice to meet you guys!" he calls over his shoulder as I pull him to the door. "Later, Bran!"

"Have fun, kids!" Brandon shoots back smiling.

"Uh, I'm so full!" I lament while patting my stomach. "It was so yummy though."

"Do you think they have any chips left? You may have eaten them all," Evan chuckles.

I narrow my eyes at him for a moment while using my phone to unlock the main entrance to my apartment building. "Do not stand between me and my love for their chips, Evan. It won't end well for you."

"I would never," he promises solemnly, pulling the door open when the lock clicks. Before we can walk through, we realize that my neighbor Mrs. Whitlock is on her way out with her mini Schnauzer Mister Pumpkins. Evan pulls the door wide for her to make her way through as I step back as well.

"Oh, hi Sugah," she says with a smile. Her voice is sweet and has a southern twang to it that I absolutely love.

"Hey Mrs. Whitlock! Hi there Mister P!" I bend to pet him as he jumps up looking for treats. "Sorry, I don't have anything for you today, but I will next time I promise." I scratch the spot behind his ear that he likes for a second, before I realize that I'm being kind of rude. "Oh! Sorry, Mrs. Whitlock, this is my boyfriend, Evan. He and Brandon are friends too, so he might be here every once in a while. Evan, this is Mrs. Whitlock, she makes the best macaroni and cheese I've ever had, and this handsome guy is Mister Pumpkins."

"Hello, ma'am. To hear that compliment from Jen means a heck of a lot since she's kind of obsessed with the stuff."

"Oh aren't you sweet! I haven't seen you lately Jen, have you been working too hard?"

"No, I had last week off. Evan is helping me do some renovations on the cabin so I've been staying there since I've been off work. I'm actually going back tonight, I just need to grab some things. You have my phone number in case you need anything, right? And Brandon's? I'm eventually going to move to the cabin full time but I'm always just a call away if you need me."

"You sweet girl! Yes, I have them both. I'm glad you're moving forward and able to take advantage of the beautiful home you have out there. Tell me before you move and I'll make you some macaroni, okay?"

"Sounds great," I laugh. "You know I can't pass that up! We have to get going, though, so have a good night! I'll see you again soon, and call if you need anything."

"I will, Sugah, thank you. Come on Mister Pumpkins, time to go poopies!" Evan pulls a face at the word "poopies," but I just laugh and grab his hand to pull him inside. "Oh, wait! Jen, there was a man here looking for you a few nights ago. He was knocking on your door when we got off the elevator after Mister Pumpkins had his evening potty break. I asked if I could help him, and told him I didn't think you were home, but he was very rude and pushed me aside to go to the elevator without speaking. He almost kicked poor Mister Pumpkins!"

Who in the hell could that have been? "I'm so sorry! What did he look like? I'm not sure who that could have been, I wasn't expecting anyone."

"He was older, but more like your daddy's age, God rest his soul. I was too worried about Mister Pumpkins that I didn't think to pay attention or remember anything else, I'm sorry."

"That's ok, I'm sorry he was so rude to you. Will you let me know if he comes again? Most of my friends know I'm staying at the cabin right now so hopefully he won't bother you again."

"Oh it's alright, Honey. You just stay safe, you hear? You two have a good night."

"You too!" Evan and I respond simultaneously, giving each other worried looks once we're through the door.

"Do you think it was your uncle? Ryan knew I lived here, he could have told him."

"Ryan knew? You brought him here?" Evan's eyes have darkened and his jaw is clenched as we enter the elevator. He's trying to hide his jealousy that Ryan had been here first, and I'd love to fuck with him, but he's just too cute.

"He knew my building, not my apartment. I never invited him in, I just let him walk me home from getting ice cream after work one night." His answering grumble as we walk down the hall to my door is adorable. I use my phone to unlock my front door and turn to face him. "You, sir, will be the first guy I've ever brought into my home, not including friends, of course."

His grin turns hungry as he steps up to me, and he places a scorching kiss on my lips. "Good." He backs up and slaps my ass, causing me to jump and glare at him. "Now get in there, I want to get home with enough time to enjoy the hot tub tonight."

CHAPTER 41

The next few days are more of the same. Evan and I both work, and when I have a closing shift he spends his evenings working on the master suite. Brandon joined him to help one evening and they were able to complete the demolition of the bathroom tile, meaning I have to hurry up and pick the new stuff soon.

Saturday arrives and I have the opening shift, so I leave Evan at home to spend his day however he wants and head in. Brandon has a date tonight so it'll just be Evan, Daniel and I at Daniel's house tonight to help him plan out his remodel. I head straight home from work to pick Evan up, and I lean over for a kiss once he's in the car before wiggling in my seat like an excited child.

"What's up, baby girl? Are you excited to spend Daniel's money?" His knowing smile makes me laugh.

"No! Well, yes, actually, but that's not what I'm excited about." I pause before grinning and singing out "I've got tea!"

"You have... tea? You don't like tea." The confusion on his face is priceless, especially when he looks down at my empty cup holders, and I'm glad I stopped at the end of the driveway because I lose it laughing for almost a full minute. "Oh my God, what?" he grouses. "You didn't like it when we were kids!"

"I'm sorry," I gasp between laughs. "It was just the look on your face!" I finally pull it together enough to stop laughing and explain myself to him. "No, having tea basically means you have gossip now. Carmen says it constantly, so I sort of unwillingly picked it up."

Rolling his eyes, Evan makes a "get on with it" gesture, and I pull out onto the road and head toward Daniel's house.

"I talked to Carmen today. She apparently ran into Daniel at the bar by the store last night. He was there with some of his cop buddies, and they talked for a while since she's met him through me. She really likes him! I'm going to talk to him to gauge his interest and maybe we can double date or something. He needs a girlfriend."

"Do you think he'll be interested? Carmen seems wild, but everything you've told me makes her seem like a great girl. I just wonder if she's too wild for Daniel. He seems to have lost his youthful exuberance as he got older."

"Youthful exuberance?" I chuckle. "I think she's exactly what he needs. She's fun, sweet, and absolutely wild. She'd be good for him, and he could probably be good for her too."

"Ok, let's make it happen then. Are we still telling him about us tonight?"

"Yeah, I think so. I haven't been hiding you or anything, it was just too much while dealing with Ryan. I don't want to run in shouting it, but we'll figure out the right time."

He grabs my hand from my thigh and kisses my knuckles. "I'll follow your lead. It's almost like we're strangers these days."

"Yeah, he's not exactly making a huge effort, is he? I'm hoping he's being cautious and will come around soon since you're not going anywhere."

"What's obvious, baby girl, is that he's in love with you. Which is too fucking bad for him because he can't have you."

"I think you're wrong, but I'm not going to argue. We'll see who's right when he and Carmen fall madly in love thanks to my meddling."

Daniel's face lights up when he opens the door and sees me in my "Sarcasm is my love language" shirt, but falls slightly when Evan shifts behind me. He tries to mask the momentary lapse by stepping back to let us in.

"Hey, guys. Come on in. I ordered pizza, I hope that's ok. I got stuck later than I anticipated at work today."

"As if you've ever known me to turn down pizza!" I scoff. "Now, give me Diet Coke and tell me my budget for spending your money before you show us what you want to do." My nose is in the air like I'm some pretentious decorator and it makes both men laugh.

"Right this way, your highness," Daniel says while sweeping his arm out in a grand gesture. We follow him to the kitchen and I hop up on the counter while he digs in the fridge. I squeal in happiness when he hands me one of the baby cans and cradle it to my chest in excitement. I'll need more than one, but these tiny cans make my heart happy.

"So, what are you looking to have done?" I ask as I crack my can open. Evan and I share a quick glance since he wasn't offered anything, but we stay quiet so we can see how things pan out.

"Well, I was thinking about a total kitchen overhaul, repainting most of the house, and then a few updates to the bathroom, though I think that's pretty good already."

Daniel's house is small but well-kept. He's got a tiny yard which he pays the neighbor kid monthly to keep up for him because he hates mowing his lawn. It has two bedrooms and one bathroom with an attic that has access via a hallway ladder.

"I think you could refinish these cabinets if you want to keep the same footprint, and it would save you a good bit of money," Evan notes. "They're in great shape, you could paint them and switch out the hardware. It would probably save you a few grand."

Daniel's jaw ticks and his shoulders tighten at Evan's comment. "I can afford new cabinets," he grates out.

Evan raises his hands in a placating gesture. "I don't doubt it. These are good quality already, though. If you don't refinish them you should donate them and your appliances to Habitat for Humanity, if you're getting rid of those too. Someone who needs them will have nice cabinets and you'll have a decent tax write off."

"Either way we can make the kitchen look great," I interject, trying to keep them from arguing. "These have a nice shape, and a gray or navy blue would look awesome in here unless you're set on new ones."

He looks around his kitchen like he's finally listening and nods his head slightly. "I guess you're right. I didn't think of that. Let's pull out my laptop and you can show me what you think I should do in here."

After only fifteen minutes, my head is throbbing. Daniel is acting like a fucking spoiled child. Every time Evan gives his opinion on something, he has to either counter it or pick the opposite of what he says. Things have devolved to the point where I can tell Evan is offering up shitty suggestions to fuck with him. Every time he thinks I'm not looking, he stares at me with this mix of anger and sullenness that, honestly, makes him look constipated. Our conversation, something that generally flows easily and comfortably, has been stilted and has been an exercise in patience on my end.

I escaped to the bathroom a few minutes ago so I could have a momentary break from the testosterone saturating the air and find something to take for this headache. Rifling through his drawers and cabinets, I come up empty. He always keeps his pain relievers in his bathroom, it's something we've always picked on each other about, so he must be out. I keep mine in the kitchen near the glasses and water, like a civilized person should, but he keeps his in the bathroom even though he never takes them there. In frustration, I examine myself in the mirror and take in the fatigue in my eyes. His shitty attitude is wearing on me, and we've only been here for half an hour. I have no idea how I'm going to survive dinner with him tonight.

There's no linen closet in here, but there is a new cabinet, so maybe he's moved his towels and pain killers there? Being the nosey bitch I am, I walk over to check it out. The handle sticks slightly, but I full harder and a ping sounds as the door jerks open and almost smacks me in the face. The new cabinet is completely empty except for three wire shelves on the floor that are leaning against the wall and a small piece of metal. Hmm... that looks awfully latch-like.

Oopsies.

The back is also not completely attached to the sides and a gap shows on the right side towards the bottom. Daniel is usually meticulous about his things, so keeping an improperly put together cabinet in his bathroom that already has limited space? It's one more thing not adding up about him today. The little piece of metal is partially poking out of the slightly open back of the cabinet, so in an effort to hide my misdeed I reach down to grab the broken piece so I can hide it in the bottom of the trashcan like the awesome friend I am. As my fingers connect with the back of the cabinet, the whole thing silently swings open on hidden hinges.

What in the actual fuck?

Something is back there! I've been in this bathroom a thousand times and there has never been a door here. To the best of my knowledge, there isn't a room on the other side of this wall either, it backs up to the garage. Pushing on the back of the cabinet further, it swings open to reveal a space between walls filled with dust, some tools, 2x4s, and a shiny new ladder.

He's got access to his attic directly from the ladder that pulls down in the hallway, so this isn't his attic access. I tugged on the cord as I walked by on my way to the bathroom like I always do because it irritates him. Why would he need a ladder in a hidden compartment to access the attic if he's already got an easily accessible location? Only weirdos and serial killers have hidden rooms and secret lairs, not people who need access to grandpa's old record collection. I should know, right?

He's a cop for God's sake, so maybe it's nothing nefarious. I've never seen him have a heated argument, let alone do anything to make me think he could do something as illegal or violent as killing someone. He's never even gotten a speeding ticket! Maybe he's decided to put a gun room in where someone wouldn't think to search for it? He is very passionate about gun safety.

I have to look. I have to find out what could be so special and private he would build his own secret attic access. Placing my hand on one of the rungs, I start to climb the creepy ass hidden ladder.

Knock knock!

Shit! I quickly pop back out of the cabinet and shut the door as quietly as possible. "Yeah?" I squeak. Nothing like getting busted trying to sneak in to somewhere you have no place being.

Evan's voice sounds on edge from the other side of the bathroom door. "You ok in there Jen? You didn't look too good."

What the fuck? What if I had to take a shit? "Yeah, I'm ok. My period started and I'm bleeding everywhere. Give me a few minutes and I'll be fine."

Snicker.

"Uh. ok, wow, sorry. You need anything? I finally moved my pain relievers to the kitchen like you always tell me to, so there aren't any in there." He coughs awkwardly, as if I've asked him to lick a dog turd or something. While a menstrual cycle may be a curse from Mother Nature, she definitely gave us the small perk of being able to freak most men out at the simple thought of it. Sucker!

"Nope, I'm good. I'll be out once I get myself together and clean up the mess."

"Um, yeah. ok then. Holler if you need anything."

Right, because after over 10 years of dealing with it, I'd need Daniel to save me from my own period.

I put my ear up to the door and listen for his footsteps to retreat down the hall before I tiptoe back to the cabinet and climb back inside. I test the ladder to make sure it's stable, and look up to the ceiling. It appears to be one piece of plywood, but I don't for a second think nothing is up there. Why else would there be a ladder in a newly built room, behind a false backed cabinet?

Climbing up the ladder, I gently push on the plywood directly above me to check it. Like the cabinet, the plywood on the ceiling swings up on hidden hinges. The opening above is filled with complete darkness, and my heart pounds in anticipation of what I could find up there. After taking a deep breath to brace myself, I pull my phone out of my back pocket and turn on my flashlight app so I can see what's up there. Another deep breath for courage, and peek my head up into the hole.

Holy. Shit.

It's a completely finished and furnished room! His attic spans the whole house though, and this is just a small space that has been walled in. Why would this be up there when he has two guest rooms? A table is in front of me blocking my view of the room, so I can't see what else is in there, other than the coffee table and a chair next to it, so I continue climbing and work on safely and silently pulling myself up and onto the floor before I look around. Once I stand and raise my flashlight to the rest of the room, my heart stops.

The breath leaves my lungs.

My body tenses. Time slows to a stop.

It's me.

Not in a mirror. Not on candid camera.

Everywhere.

CHAPTER 42

P hotos of me.

As a child. As a teen. Last. Fucking. Week.

There's a photo of me from the night Ryan and Evan came to my house and surprised us. It's an almost frontal view of me sitting on the end of the dock with my feet in the water. He would have had to either have a camera with a telephoto lens trained on the dock at all times, or he would have had to sneak into the woods to take it instead of going to the take a call like he claimed.

There's a picture of Ryan and I kissing behind the ticket booth the night we went to play mini golf and bumper boats. He said he had to leave to go help his mom! Did he stay and watch us the whole time, or did he wait and watch us before he left?

There's a picture of Ryan's dad messing with my apartment door. He seems frustrated because he has what appears to be a lock pick set in his hand. Since my lock is electronic he can't do anything to it. I guess that confirms my suspicions he was the person Mrs. Whitlock saw. I'm happy to have confirmation, but this is the worst possible way to receive it.

Elementary school art projects. My middle school diary. My prized A+ high school paper on archetypal analysis! Small items that were special to me, but have no reason to be in this room.

My hands are shaking and clammy, and I'm sick to my stomach. This isn't stuff he collected recently. This is stuff that has been missing for years! I never even got to show my dad the paper after I received it back from Mrs. MacDonald — it was missing from my book bag when I got home that night and tried to pull it out to show him. I was devastated because I was so fucking proud of that thing, and him hearing about it wasn't the same as seeing it. I can't believe he took that from me!

Most of the pictures and papers are stuck up on the wall with small pins. One section of wall has surveillance photos of every single one of the guys I've been out on a date with since high school. Each photo has a note next to it with his observations and a threat level listed in bullet point style. Next to Dragon Boy, the note says:

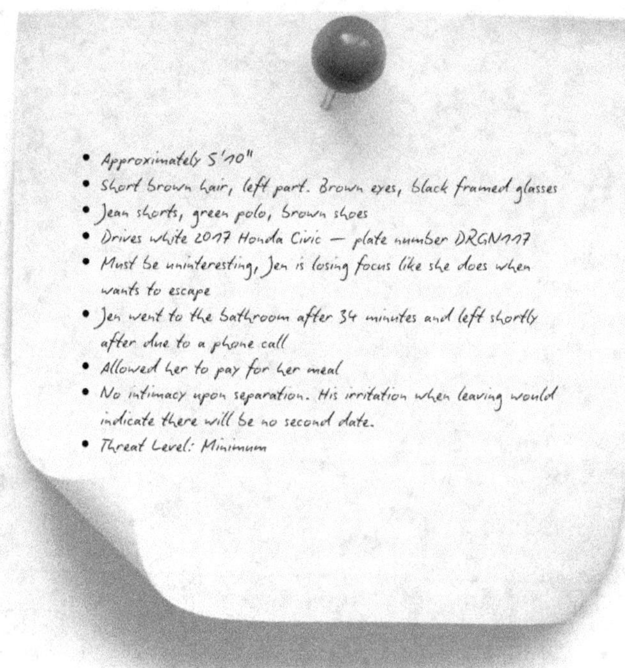

Each photo has these notes attached. Some with more details than others, but the highest threat level he assigned to any was medium. I assume he gave Caleb that designation because he's the only one I went out with twice, which only happened because our first date happened was to a Dorothy concert. There's not much potential for talking during shows, so I didn't realize he wasn't right for me until after our next date.

Slightly off to the left of the grouping of my past dates are two pictures of me and Travis from the night he walked me home to grab the book. In the first, my fist is clenched around the fabric on his jacket and his shocked face as I pull him into my apartment. In the second, I'm giving him a hug as he leaves. His stat sheet initially listed his threat level listed as "medium/high," but it has since been crossed out and replaced with "minimal." His driver's license has been taped to the bottom of it, and there's a bloody fingerprint dried on to the slick surface.

Is he the one who mugged Travis? He has to be if he's got his license here. What the hell? He's beating someone up because I hugged them?

How could he have been following me like this for so long without me noticing? Did my dad notice? He was in the Special Forces for goodness' sake! That man noticed everything. I can't imagine he would have allowed this to happen if he knew about it. He was so protective of me, and this level of obsession is terrifying. He would have protected me from this if he knew.

Below the photos of my old dates sits an old wooden desk with a few drawers with a computer set up on it. There's a single dying red rose laying across it, the stem obviously having been cut off under the flower itself by the rusty old pair of scissors next to it. I have no idea what that's from, since I haven't gotten flowers from anyone recently.

Not ready to check the computer yet, I pull out the thin top drawer and freeze with it halfway open. Carmex. Hundreds of open tubes of Carmex. Each with writing on them. I pick one tube up to read the writing. The note reads"9th grade homecoming" with the date.

I knew I brought some that night! And I knew something was always weird about how many of my tubes went missing regularly. He's been giving me tubes for years, sometimes singles, sometimes entire cases. Was he doing it so he could steal them after I'd used them?

Closing the door with disgust, I move on to the bottom drawer and rifle through the files contained there. The tabs are organized by year, one for each year of my life, and they grow thicker as the years pass. Some have photos, documents like papers and report cards or score sheets from my softball games, and the later ones have journals with his notes. I choose the file from my junior year of high school and my hands shake as I pull the journal out and open it to a random page.

thought once Ryan was gone she'd finally see me, see that I'm right here, but of course not. She can't see what's right in fucking front of her no matter how hard I try!

Today, she's wearing these short jean shorts that make her legs look a mile long with a ratty Avenged Sevenfold t-shirt and black Converse. Even with barely any makeup on and her hair thrown up in a messy bun, she's so hot it's difficult to keep my dick from getting hard around her.

During gym Kirk Hendricks started talking shit about trying to fuck her since Ryan's not here to cock block everyone.

I got so pissed I beat the shit out of him after school. NO ONE talks about my girl like that. I told him to spread the word that she's mine so no one else fucks with her and...

I slam the journal shut and close my eyes for a moment. I want to run downstairs and ask him what the fuck is going on, but I can't leave until I have all the facts — I may never have another opportunity to be in here. Placing the journal back where it belongs, I take yet another deep breath to center myself and wiggle the mouse to wake the screen and show me more secrets. Real-time footage of the hallway outside my apartment and the front door of my dad's cabin shines back at me. Back at my apartment, sweet Mrs. Whitlock opens her door and lets Mister Pumpkins off his leash to run inside. If my guess is correct, one camera is hidden in the hideous fake floral arrangement on the table next to the elevator in my hall, and the other is in shrubs across from the front of the house.

He's watching my fucking apartment, and he's watching the only place I've ever felt truly safe in real time. He's watching me come and go. He's watching who visits me. He's watching how long they stay!

Having had enough, I turn around to get the fuck out of this room. I feel sick and violated and angry. I don't know what I'm going to do yet, but I can't stay here. Before I can drop to the surprisingly clean floor to climb back down out of this hell, a simple metal shelf directly over the trap door that I missed during my first look around catches my eye. A hunting knife is embedded in the wall through the center of a printed 8×10 photo, the blade holding it there instead of pins like the rest of the pictures in the room. Because it's not being held up by the corners, the sides are curled down and I can't immediately see why this one is different from the others.

Hesitantly, I take two steps forward and lift the flashlight beam to shine on the picture. Using my sleeve wrapped fingers (why didn't I think of this while messing with the desk?) I lift the corner so I can inspect it.

The knife is stabbed directly through the middle of Evan's face, which has also been scratched out with a black marker. A face that just happens to be staring at me with hunger as I straddle his lap in my new hot tub. It's the night it came in because the candles I set up are lit all around us. Daniel not only watched it happen, but printed out a picture and stabbed a giant ass hunting knife through it! A hunting knife that looks an awful lot like... no.

No way. Just... no.

It can't be *that* knife. He can't have his knife in this room of horrors.

My focus on the photo meant I didn't register anything else on the shelf. Lightheaded, I adjust my stance and aim the flashlight, so I can closely examine the handle and blade of the knife. Even through the tears welling up in my eyes, I can't miss the JM etched into the side of the blade. It's right where it has been since I special ordered this knife for my father for his 50th birthday.

The knife he carried with him everywhere, but wasn't on his body when he was found.

The knife I've been scouring pawn shops and resale websites for in an attempt to find information to lead me to his killer.

The flashlight beam shakes as I will my tears to retreat. I bring the beam over to shine on the other items on the shelf and almost drop to my knees when I find my dad's well-worn wallet, meticulously repaired with duct tape. He insisted it still worked fine, but we both knew he was too lazy to go buy himself a new one, and too picky to let me pick one out for him instead. His truck keys sit next to the wallet, still connected to the key chain made out of the shell casing from the first buck I took down on my own. He was so damn proud of me that day, and said he wanted to always carry a reminder of it with him.

Checking to see if there is anything else I missed, I examine the other pictures pinned to the wall around the shelf, all with Evan's face crossed or scratched out. They're all photos of Evan and me together. Out shopping. In my yard at home. In my living room at home, through the glass. Me on top of him while he fingered me in the truck that night in the bar parking lot. Me on top of him while he fucked me in the truck in my garage.

This is too much. I'm no saint, but this is beyond anything I could imagine. Daniel has never outwardly shown any sort of romantic interest in me, has never treated me as anything other than a sister. He's had girlfriends, he upholds the law in everything, and he idolized my father.

Lungs aching and chest tight, I try to make sense of this, but know it will never be possible. This pain may be worse than the moment I learned he died, because I now know someone I trusted with my own life took my dad away from me. I think about how Dad took care of Daniel, how he taught him and made time for him and loved him, and I just get angry. My shaking turns from something born of shock and fear to a rage I've never before experienced.

It's one thing to stalk me. There are fucked up people in the world, but he should have had the balls to tell me how he felt. Hurting Travis though? Killing my Dad?

No.

This motherfucker will pay.

Before I head downstairs, I take pictures of everything in the room, so I can show Evan and Brandon later. I'm sure I haven't consciously registered half of what's in here thanks to my shock, so I'll have to comb through them to see what I missed, too. One day, I'll come back and take it all from him. Fuck him for taking all of this from me, and fuck him for thinking he has some claim over me!

Safely and quietly, I make my way back down the ladder and ensure the trap door is closed up like I found it. I pop back out of the cabinet and make sure the false back is exactly as it was before closing the door as tightly as I can. I take a few deep breaths and calm myself with the thoughts of what I'm going to do to him. I fan the flames of my need for pain, I whisper sweet nothings to my rage, and I give my imagination free rein to devise the perfect plan to trap and torture the man I thought was one of my best friends. My brother!

He can't have any idea that I found this. I need time to plan and I can't let him suspect anything has changed, so I flush the toilet and head over to the sink to splash some water on my face. Once I've calmed down enough to pretend I'm ok I head back to the living room where the TV is playing, but no conversation is happening. Turning the corner, both Evan and Daniel turn to see me. Daniel's face drains of color as he jumps out of his seat and practically runs to my side with worry on his face.

"Jen, holy shit you look awful. Are you sure you're ok?"

I guess I didn't collect myself as well as I thought I did. There goes my dream of an Oscar. "Yeah, I'm just having a *crazy* heavy flow. I hate to do this, but I think I need to go home and crawl in my bed with some meds and a heating pad."

"Shit, of course. Do you want to lay down here instead? I have a heating pad and I can set you up in the guest room. I can go to the store if you need anything else." He's desperate for me to say yes, to let him take care of me. How did I not notice the desperation in his eyes before? Now that my blinders have been removed, it honestly makes me nauseous. To see the complete obsession shining from the depths of his once familiar brown eyes, and know I've missed it completely for the last 15 plus years.

"No, I'm good. I always feel better in my own bed. Plus, I drove. I'm just going to head home and relax. Sorry to bail on you so early, but lady problems give zero fucks about previously made plans." I give a small, weak smile and shrug before I look over to Evan, who has been watching me with a furrowed brow on his handsome face. He rises from his seat and comes to stand next to me, gently placing his hand on my lower back to lead me to the door.

Noticing the touch, Daniel grits his teeth so hard I'm surprised he doesn't crack a tooth. Trying, and failing, to cover his irritation he gives me a sweet smile. "No worries. Go home and rest. Call or text me if you need me to bring you soup or anything. No matter what time, you know I don't mind."

The laugh I let out is completely forced, but I'm hoping he'll blame it on me not feeling well. "Jesus D, I'm vaginally hemorrhaging, I don't have the damn flu." His cheeks pink, and he chuckles as he rubs the back of his neck and follows me to the front door. Even though it takes everything I have and makes my skin crawl in a way nothing else ever has, I give him a quick hug, thank him for having us over, and promise to call if I need anything.

Evan and I are quiet as we walk to the car, and he ushers me to the passenger side so he can drive. He waits until we reach the stop sign at the end of the street before he turns to me.

"You and I both know you're not on your period. What the fuck happened?"

Chapter 43

All it takes is one look of concern from Evan for my shield to crack, and I can't hold in the anguish any longer. Shaking, my tears finally begin to fall and within moments my body is consumed with wracking sobs. I can't speak through the tears and my body unconsciously curls in on itself, making it harder for me to breathe.

"Shit! Breathe, baby girl. Hang on. I'm going to find somewhere to pull over. Just breathe for me, ok? I'm going to pull over here, stay with me Jen."

His words aren't registering over the deafening sound of my heart shattering. My dad was my world. He was the only biological family I had left. He was my true fucking best friend, my rock, my safe place, and he's gone forever. Taken from me by someone I loved. Someone he loved. How could Daniel do this? Why would he do it? Dad treated him like his own son. He was there for him when his own father abandoned him. Did that mean nothing to him?

I don't know how long I've been crying, but as I become aware of my surroundings I realize I'm in Evans arms, my legs and arms tightly wrapped around him and my face buried in his neck. Without my noticing it, he managed to take me out of my seat and bring me to the back cargo area of my SUV so we could sit comfortably without being squished in a seat together. He's running his fingers through my hair and speaking in a low soothing tone, telling me he will make sure everything is ok, because he will do anything to protect me. Even if that involves killing someone or risking his own life. He tells me he's here for me no matter what. He tells me he loves me. The broken pieces of my heart are scattered everywhere, but with each promise, each word, he begins the process of gathering them back up and fitting them back together.

It takes a few minutes, but I finally calm down enough to take a few deep breaths and speak.

"It was Daniel," I choke out in a broken voice.

"What was Daniel, baby? What happened?" He kisses my forehead and uses his fingers to lift my chin so he can look into my eyes.

"Daniel... he... he killed my dad." The tears begin again, but luckily this time they're silent.

"Fuck. Are you sure?" The anguish in his eyes matches my own, and having someone to share this agony with almost makes it a little easier to bear. I'm not the only one who loved him and the reminder helps.

"I'm sure. Can we go home? I need a few minutes to gather my thoughts, but I promise I'll tell you everything when we get there. I don't want him to catch us here."

"Of course," he says, climbing out of the car with a hand under my butt and me still wrapped around him like a monkey. He gets me deposited in the front passenger seat again and buckles my seat belt for me. He leans in to give me a kiss but I flinch back. "What's wrong?" he asks, worried.

"Nothing... I'm just all gross. I probably have snot face or something."

His smile and chuckle are sad, but sweet. "You're not gross, you're still beautiful. Even if you are covered in snot." Grinning to show me he's joking, he says "Give me a kiss, so I know you'll be alright. We'll get you home and you can tell me what happened, ok?"

I scowl at him and use my arm to wipe my nose just in case, and lean in to give him a kiss. "ok. Thank you." I lean my head back and close my eyes when he shuts my door, and keep them closed when he grabs my hand and holds it the whole way home.

I'm exhausted after my crying jag, so Evan guides me upstairs and sits me on the end of my bed. Proving yet again that he knows exactly what I need before I do, he heads to my closet and pulls out one of my dad's oversized sweaters. He then moves over to my dresser to pick out a cami and a pair of skull covered capri leggings.

He leans in to kiss my forehead as he places the clothes on the bed next to me. "Get changed, then come downstairs, ok? We'll get comfortable and you can tell me what happened when you're ready."

I nod slightly before he turns to leave, closing my door behind him softly. Rubbing my face, I lay back for a minute and stare at the ceiling while I try to gather my thoughts. I don't want to go through this again. I don't want to relive what I found, I don't want to talk about what I found, and I sure as fuck don't want to deal with another captive in my barn. I just want to live my fucking life, finding a new normal with Evan, Brandon, and absolutely without Daniel.

It takes me a few minutes, but I finally pluck up the courage to change my clothes. I head to the bathroom and throw my hair up into a messy bun and wash my face to clean the mascara smudges off. My skin is pale and there are dark circles under my eyes, making the green of my iris stand out in bright contrast. I look haunted, which isn't surprising since I feel that way.

I finally make my way downstairs and I want to start crying again the moment I turn the corner to the living room. Evan is seated at the corner of the couch in his own comfortable clothes with my favorite fuzzy blanket, a box of tissues and a trash can, and a big mug of hot chocolate. "Come here," he coaxes, holding a hand out. "I texted Brandon before we started on our way home. He'll be here in a few minutes. Let's relax for a bit before he gets here, ok?"

I'm frozen in place, my heart thumping for a very new, very different reason.

Is this what love feels like? Like... real love. Not that puppy love shit I thought I felt for Ryan. I think it has to be, because how else would he have the power to make me feel like everything is going to be ok when my world is crumbling around me? He's like a beacon of light in the middle of all the darkness I'm currently immersed in. A promise of hope for a better future.

I must have retreated into myself for a moment because I'm startled by Evan's gentle touch on my cheek. "Jen? Where did you go?"

"Sorry," I say. My cheeks flush in embarrassment as I reach my arms up to loop around his neck and pull him close. With my head pressed to his chest I tell him "I zoned out for a second. Thank you for calling Brandon, he needs to hear this too and I don't want to live through it more than once."

"I figured. Come on." Bending down he hoists me up with his hands under my butt, forcing me to wrap my legs around him again, and carries me to the couch. I'm getting used to his need to carry me, so I didn't even squeal when he lifted me this time. Progress!

He sets me down when we reach the couch and grabs my hot chocolate before sitting in the corner and extending his other hand to me again. This time I take it and allow him to pull me in against him and drape the blanket over both of us. Once we're settled he hands me my drink and I take a deep sip and almost spit it out as I cough.

"Holy shit!" I sputter, feeling his chest shake with a chuckle beneath me. "You didn't tell me you spiked it! Warn a girl next time."

"I figured you needed something a little stronger than chocolate. Sorry, I thought you would have smelled it." He grins like a shithead at my scowl.

"I've been crying, remember? My nose is all stuffy, so I can't smell anything!" I pout but take another deep pull since I know what to expect now. I wouldn't have guessed, but the whiskey pairs nicely with the chocolate and marshmallows. He even got it the perfect temperature — warm, not hot. I always burn my tongue too easily, which is another point in my book against coffee.

We sit in silence for about ten minutes before Brandon arrives. Me sipping on my hot chocolate, Evan tracing patterns on my thigh with his fingers. I'm not sure if he's trying to soothe me or himself, but either way it's kind of working. I hear Brandon barge in the front door and slam it shut before he runs toward us, entering the room like Kramer from Seinfeld.

"What happened?" he shouts, frantic. "Jen, what's wrong?" Knowing he's about to come for me, I quickly hand off my mug to Evan so when Brandon snatches me from him I won't spill the rest of my drink everywhere. Sure enough, he plucks me right out of Evan's lap and pulls me to him for a tight hug, dangling blanket and all. "Fuck, all Evan would say is you needed me immediately. You weren't physically hurt but something happened and you couldn't tell him yet. What's going on?"

He's squeezing me so tight I can't breathe, so I slap his back a few times to make him release me. "Shit, sorry," he winces. "What happened?"

"Sit down, ok? There's a lot I need to tell you both. I only want to say this once, so please let me get it all out before you ask any questions." I take a seat sideways on Evan's lap, leaning against the couch arm and extending my feet out to Brandon knowing I need contact with both of them to be able to survive telling this story. I pull the blanket back over us but poke my feet out and wiggle my toes at Brandon. Huffing a small, strained laugh he scoots closer and pulls my feet into his lap, wrapping his hands around them to keep them warm.

I grab my mug back from Evan and drain the rest in one go, needing the liquid courage. Then I tell them.

I tell them about the hidden door leading to a hidden room.

I tell them about the fact that he's been stalking me almost my whole life, taking pictures of me and stealing my things.

I tell them about the cameras he has set to record my doors.

I tell them he attacked Travis.

And finally, I tell them he killed my dad.

I'm crying again by the time I finish my story, but I'm not sobbing anymore. Tears are streaming silently down my face and it's almost like my mind is numb but my body hasn't gotten the memo.

Both Brandon and Evan are gripping me tighter now than when I first started my story, and Brandon is pale as a ghost with tears tracking down his face too. He gives my feet one final squeeze and then moves them off of his lap. He gets up from the couch and walks out the back door onto the porch, closing it softly behind him. Walking over to one of the chairs, I watch as he grips the back of the seat and bows his head. I try to go after him but Evan holds me back, saying "Just give him a minute. I think he needs to process. We can wait until he comes back."

I don't want to leave him out there alone, but Evan's right. He wouldn't have gone outside if he didn't need a moment by himself. So, instead of going to him like I want to, I curl up closer into Evan's warmth and wait for him to come back.

Brandon stays outside for a while, and the combination of my emotional exhaustion and Evan's warm embrace cause me to drift off until the sound of the sliding door rouses me. He walks to the kitchen and grabs a Diet Coke and two beers from the fridge, handing me the soda and Evan the second beer before sitting back down and grabbing my feet again.

"So, we're going to kill him, right?" he asks after taking a sip of his beer.

"Oh yeah," I respond. "He beat the shit out of my gay friend because he thought I was dating him! He's been stalking me my whole fucking life, tainting things that didn't involve him, and he fucking killed my dad! My children will never meet their grandfather. He'll never walk me down the aisle. That limp-dicked piece of shit stole the last biological family I had from me, and for fucking what? There is nothing he could possibly use to justify that. We're going to kill him, but we're going to make him pay first."

My guys are silent for a few minutes, taking in everything I've just said. Evan breaks the silence first, kissing the side of my head and telling me "I'm in. No matter what. Whatever you need, I'm in."

"Me too," Brandon says. "And this time, I don't give a shit about my weak stomach. I want my own pound of flesh from that asshole. We need a plan, and I want in too."

CHAPTER 44

We spend the rest of the evening trying to figure out the best plan of attack. I think the best way is to invite him here for one of our normal dinners, so we just need to figure out the finer details of when we want it to happen and what we want to do. I suggest drugging his drink since I've used that method before.

I only want to know one thing. Why? Why did he kill my dad? The only true father figure he's ever had? I don't care if I have to strip his skin off of him in layers to make him talk, I will do whatever it takes to avenge my dad and learn why he was taken from me. I don't care why he's stalked me basically my whole fucking life. He's obviously sick, and nothing he says could make me understand.

We're discussing the merits of stabbing and evisceration versus strangulation when Brandon's phone rings. "It's him," he says, looking at me uneasily.

"Shit! The fucking camera out front. He must have seen you rush in here." I bite my lip for a second before saying "Answer it. Make something up about you rushing here because I texted you for chocolate or tampons or something."

Taking a deep breath, he answers and puts it on speakerphone. "Hey man, what's up?"

"Not much, what are you up to tonight?"

"I'm out at the cabin. I was on a date and Jen texted me with a female supply emergency. I was able to use it as an excuse to bail early, which was convenient because the chick was a total psycho." He looks at me with wide eyes and mouths "She really was!" before continuing. "Her text was more dramatic than usual, so I rushed over here thinking she was bleeding to death or something, but it figures by the time I got here she'd be passed out. I ended up helping Evan with some heavy lifting in the master. What about you?"

Daniel's chuckle is strained as he replies. "Is she ok now? She looked rough earlier, I was worried about her."

"Yeah, man. She's good. Hopped up on pain killers and swaddled in heating pads like a burrito. She's been out for two hours at least, even with all the construction noise, so I wouldn't be surprised if she slept through the night at this rate."

"Good. Ok, well, do you two need any help? I was just calling to find out if you wanted to grab a beer or something. I could come out there if you'll be hanging for a while."

Faking a yawn, Brandon rolls his eyes. "I'm actually about to head to bed myself, we had a few drinks, so I'm going to crash on the couch. I was up early and those beers finished me off. Rain check?"

"Yeah, sure. I'll catch you later."

"Night." Hanging up the phone he tosses it onto the couch beside him and puts a hand to his stomach. "Talking to him like nothing is wrong is one of the most disgusting things I've ever done. I can't believe I thought of him as my brother." Sadness and revulsion war in his gaze and I can't help but crawl forward and draw him into a tight hug. He buries his face in my neck and the warmth of his tears slide against my skin. "I'm so fucking angry," he whispers. "How could he do this to you? To John? John fucking loved Daniel, Jen. How could he hurt him?"

"I don't know, B," I tell him. "But we're going to find out. I don't care what it takes, I don't care what we have to do. He's going to answer to me for what he's done, and I'm going to make what Ryan went through look like child's play."

"Good," Brandon sighs, leaning his head back against the couch. "Because I don't think I can keep this up for very long. I can't imagine how you're feeling if I feel like this. I'm so sorry, Killer."

"Me too. I'm sorry we trusted him, and that I feel like we failed him in some way."

"Fuck that," Evan growls. "You failed him about as much as I failed Ryan. Do not blame yourselves for him being a worthless human being." He kisses my temple and gives Brandon a stern glare.

"Now, what can I do to help? This is all your play. You let me do what I needed to with Ryan, now it's your turn."

"Honestly? I want my fucking knife. We need to figure out a way for me to have it, so I can kill his ass with it. Can you think of a way you could get it? I just don't want to take it before it's time because I don't want him to suspect anything, so I'm honestly not sure what to do."

Brandon looks thoughtful. "What if you invite him over to help with construction one night, say I have to work, and maybe at the last minute tell him Evan got called to an emergency at work, or Gran's lawyer's office or something? His guard will probably be down if it's just the two of you, and Evan and I can sneak into the house while Daniel is here to grab the knife."

Evan and I share a glace, gauging each other's response to the suggestion. "That could work," he says. "We can tell him I'm running behind to finish a job or something. You can drug his drink to knock him out, and I should be back in plenty of time to help."

I wiggle my head from side to side as I think over the possibilities. "It could work. My only worry is he'll think something is up."

"Not if you play it right. Invite him over as an apology for bailing early tonight. Tell him you felt bad that you couldn't help him more so you went and got some samples to go over with him."

Brandon's right, it could work. "I do need samples for here. Maybe we can go this week to pick up some for the house and I can grab a few things to make it look more legit when he comes. I'll call him to tell him you're running late, but also tell him to make up for bailing I grabbed physical samples to go through with him and we can do that over dinner while we wait for you."

"I hate the idea of you being here alone with him." Evan throws his hands up in defense when I scowl at him. "I know, I know! You can take care of yourself. I'm just saying, I don't think I want any of us alone with him right now. Crazy people are unpredictable."

"Obviously," I shudder. "I'll be careful, though. And we could always have Brandon sneak into the house from the back and hide upstairs instead of going with you."

"I like that better. I'm with Evan, I don't think anyone should be alone with him right now."

"Ok. I'll text him tomorrow or something to set everything up. You staying the night, Brandon? The guest room is all yours again, we moved Evan into my room."

"Yeah, I should since I told him I was. Can I grab my stuff from your room?"

"Actually, everything is in the guest room now. We needed to move it to make room." The smile I shoot Evan is small and tired, but genuine. I'm glad I have him, especially as a partner in Ryan and Daniel's destruction. I love Brandon, but he's not strong enough to be what I need right now. I need someone to walk through this with me and emerge bloody and victorious on the other side. Evan has already proven he's capable of doing that once. I know he'll be able to stand by me while it happens again.

Evan heads into our bedroom to get ready for bed while I make sure Brandon has everything he needs. Normally I'd leave him to himself, but I want to make sure I moved everything from my room and bathroom that he needs. He's somber, much quieter than usual and I can tell this whole thing is weighing on him as much as it is me.

Standing at the end of the bed I stop him as he walks past me with a hand on his arm. "I'm sorry," I whisper, looking into his pain filled eyes. "I wish things were different. And I know you say you want to be a part of this but-"

"Stop," he interrupts me. "I have to be part of this somehow. You can't always be the one. I need to step up too."

"The difference is this doesn't bother me like it does you."

"I'm going to help, Jen. I may not be able to draw blood or physically hurt him, but I sure as fuck will be a part of this. You are my sister, and John was a father to me. He betrayed us all in the worst way. I want him dead, so he can't hurt anyone else."

"Agreed," I sigh deeply. "Ok, I just want you to promise me you'll tell me if you need to back out, okay? There isn't any shame in it. "

"I promise," he says, leaning forward and kissing my forehead. "Now go climb in bed with your man. I was in his corner before, but after today... I know he's the one. I'm happy for you."

"Me, too. I love you, Brandon."

"I love you too, Killer. Now take that sweet ass to bed."

I head to my own room because I can tell he needs the time alone. He's always been like that, when he has a big shock he needs time alone to process, then he needs comfort. Turning back to him before I close the door I give him a small smile. "I'm too tired for sexy shenanigans tonight, so if you need me the door will be unlocked."

The laugh that follows me is a shadow of his usual, but I'll take it. "That's a shame. Sexy is my favorite kind of shenanigan."

I make a vomit sound as I finally close the door behind me and enter my own bedroom. Evan is stepping out of the bathroom when I enter, the boxers slung low on his hips and showing a peak of the bottom of the tattoo on his thigh. He's scrubbing his wet hair with a towel and looking at me with concern in his eyes, unaware that he's looking like a whole ass snack. I can tell the second he notices me checking him out because a heated warmth fills his eyes and a smile curves his lips. "That look makes me tempted to do very bad things to you, Jen. I thought you were tired."

"I am," I tell him with a grin, grabbing his hand and pulling him into the bathroom with me. "But you missed a spot in the shower. The Good Girlfriends Of America Club will revoke my membership if I let you go to sleep like that." With a shrug, I start getting undressed. "I don't make the rules, but I do have to follow them."

His chuckle as he turns and locks the door is decidedly dark. "I would never tell on you, but I'm also not one to break rules." He drops his boxers to the floor and steps out of them before turning the water on in the shower and holding his hand under the stream. As soon as steam begins rising he holds a hand out to me. "Come, Madam. Your hell water awaits."

"Aww, you do love me!" I chirp as I take his hand as we enter the shower stall together. The temperature is perfect, hot enough to almost scald but exactly what I need to help the tension release from my muscles. Evan directs me to stand under the spray so that I can wet my hair, and he starts massaging shampoo into my scalp moments later. The gentle massage relaxes me further and before long I'm even more putty like than usual in his hands. When he withdraws his hands I turn and drop my head back to rinse the shampoo out. I watch with lowered lids as he shampoos his own hair and my body warms further as I take in his tan skin and sharp angles. Once my hair is rinsed fully I guide him to switch positions with me and drop to my knees in front of him while his head is tilted back and eyes are closed. He's already half hard, but the moment I wrap my hands around him and angle his tip to my mouth his breath hisses between his teeth, and he stiffens in my grasp.

I lick and kiss his tip delicately, as if I'm planning on teasing him for a while. His groan makes me smile for a brief second before I take him into my mouth as far as I possibly can, hollowing out my cheeks with the force of my suction as I move up and down along his shaft. At first, his fingers in my hair are gentle, almost caressing, but as I increase my pace and pressure and skim my hands up along the back of his thighs to grip his tight ass his hold turns punishing. The slight sting along my scalp only spurs me on and I drop one hand between his legs to cup and roll his balls. His hips start moving to the point where he's practically fucking my face, and I gag slightly a few times when his thrusts push him further than I was expecting.

"Fuuuuck," he groans. "No. Nope, get up here." His words come out strained but his grip under my arms is firm as he pulls me up from my knees and turns me so my back is against the cool tile wall. His fingers instantly find my pussy, and he practically growls in my ear when he finds how wet I already am for him. "You've had an unbelievably fucked up day, so I was fine with waiting, but you started this." His kiss is slow and languid to match the pace of his fingers inside me, and the combination of his stern words and gentle caresses sets me on fire. He licks his way from my collarbone up to my earlobe and sucks it into his mouth while pulling my leg up to wrap around his waist.

"I will never give you up. You are mine, do you understand me? I will kill him before he ever puts a hand on you."

"Oh fuck!" He slams his cock into me hard and fast. He fucks me rough, and almost angry, and it's everything I need right now. I need to forget everything but us.

"Tell me" he snarls.

"Yes, I'm yours. Oh, God! Don't stop." Both of my legs are locked tight around his waist and one of his hands is holding me up by my ass while another is wrapped behind my back. He takes a step back so only my shoulders and head are touching the tile, and he bends down to take one of my nipples into his mouth. The combination of the hot water beating against my skin, cool tile against my shoulders, his warm mouth on my breast and the forceful thrusts of his cock inside me work together to force an unannounced orgasm out of me. No buildup, just bliss. My core convulses around him and causes him to stutter in his movements for a moment, but even though he falters he's obviously not done with me.

"Good girl," he coos in my ear in a husky voice. "Do you think you can give me one more? You're so fucking sexy when you come on my cock, baby."

I desperately want to give him what he's asking for, but I'm already so sensitive that I'm whimpering with each new thrust. "Please," I moan, not knowing what I'm asking him for. To stop? To never stop? Some combination of both, maybe.

"I've got you. Just stay with me baby. Give me one more and I'll take you to bed, ok? Damn, you're so beautiful." The addition of the pressure of his fingers on my already extremely sensitive clit is my ultimate undoing. This second orgasm was slow to build, spurred on by his sweet words and caresses, but the moment this thumb presses down I shatter. My entire body locks up and my nails dig into the skin of his back so hard I think I'm drawing blood, but I don't have the ability to release him. Evan releases a long, guttural moan with his face buried in my neck as he swells with release inside of me. He doesn't stop moving throughout my climax, instead rolling his hips and fingers against me, praising me for giving him what he asked for until my body finally calms.

I'm so beyond spent that my body is shaking, but it's that wonderful sort of exhaustion that signifies you're going to sleep hard and hopefully wake refreshed. Evan peppers my face and neck with kisses for a few moments, caressing my body as we both come down from the high of being together. When he finally lowers me to my feet he keeps hold of me for a bit to make sure I can stand on my own. I smile at him and stand on my toes to kiss his lips. "Thank you," I tell him as I reach for the body wash. He smiles brightly at me, and we finish our shower in silence.

As we dry off and he puts his boxers back on, I remember Brandon. "Oh, shit. Just FYI, there's a chance Brandon may come in tonight. He doesn't like sleeping alone when bad things happen. I'm sure since you're here he'll try to tough it out, but I'm guessing he'll be in sooner rather than later."

Evan laughs and pulls some basketball shorts on over his boxers while I slip into a tank top and cotton sleep shorts. "That's fine as long as he doesn't try to get fresh with me. I have a feeling I wouldn't be able to handle him."

I laugh as I climb into my bed and pull back the covers for him to join me. "You and me both, I'm sure."

Once he's in position in bed he pulls me to him, wrapping his arm around me and kissing my wet hair. I'm so happy here with him, regardless of everything else going on, and I realize I can't hold back any longer. I pull away from him and sit up, turning in place, so I'm facing him. His brow furrows with worry as I take his hand in mine and hold it in my lap examining it.

"What's wrong?" he asks, his voice filled with concern.

"Nothing," I tell him, biting my lip in nervousness. "I just... I need to tell you something."

"What could you possibly have to tell me that could make you nervous? We tortured and killed one man together, and are planning to do it again. I'm you're not a man, and unless you're about to kick me out-"

"I love you."

Evan is staring at me, mouth still hanging open in a perfect "o" from forming the words I interrupted. He's frozen in place, and I'm not sure he's breathing.

"Evan? Are you ok?" He just keeps blinking at me, examining my face in silence. He's starting to freak me out. "I swear to fuck, Evan. You'd better — eek!"

I let out a completely girly squeal of fright when he launches himself at me and slams me to my back on the bed, pressing a forceful kiss to my lips. "Say it again," he demands.

"I said, are you ok?" I know what he wants, but he needs to work for it since he made me squeal like a little bitch.

Scowling, he nips the tip of my nose playfully. "You know what I meant. Say. It. Again."

I meet his eyes and cup his cheeks, all playfulness leaving me for the moment. With a deep breath, I dive in. "I love you, Evan. I cannot imagine finding a partner who is more perfect for me than you. You accept all of me, even the dark parts, which is something I never thought would be possible. You take care of me better than anyone ever has, and yet you still step back and let me take care of myself. I think I've always loved you, I was just too afraid to admit it to myself. Especially when you were gone."

A slight sheen fills his eyes when I finish speaking, and a wide smile graces his beautiful lips. "I have loved you since we were kids, Jen. And you're right. I do accept every part of you, because all of your parts match my own, those dark ones included." He swipes his thumb through the single tear sliding down my cheek. "Maybe especially those parts. You never have to hide any part of yourself from me because I will back you every step of the way, and I'll even help clean up after you once you teach me how to do it properly."

My laugh is lighter now that I've admitted to him, and to myself, how I feel. "Now that we've got that covered, can I have some covers? I'm fucking cold."

He shakes his head while wearing a patient smile and dips down to kiss me slowly. "Of course. Since Brandon isn't currently here, you can tell me what your plans are for Daniel. I know you held back earlier." I curl into his side under the covers so he can wrap his arm tight around me. "I know you said you didn't want to have another Ryan situation, but I feel like you don't want this to be quick, either."

"I don't want to draw this out unless I have to. Meaning I don't want it to last days. I'm ok with hours though, and if he won't talk I can probably find answers in his creepy stalker lair. I've given him about fifteen years of my life, he doesn't deserve any more of it."

"Understandable," he says, running his fingers up and down my arm. "So what do you want to do?"

Biting my lip, I think carefully about my answer. "My dad always told me not to keep trophies. He'd always say that these days it's the surest way to get caught. I want something though. Some memento I can pull out on the darkest days when I miss my dad. Something that gives me comfort because it reminds me I used everything he taught me to avenge him. Does that make sense? Or is it going against what he believed?"

"I think he would understand. If you need it, you need it. We still need to go through John's closet room sometime, maybe there will be something in there to help you understand everything."

"I hope so. I guess what I do will depend on what happens between now and then. What I truly want is for him to die like my dad did — alone, in pain, and utterly betrayed, because I have no doubt he did." I sigh, my heart breaking once again for my dad, and for myself. "I want to use his knife. I want him to know that I know what he's done. I want him to know I know he's taken my father from me, and I want him to know that, obsession or not, he could have never had me, because he wasn't good enough.

"Dad died slowly, so Daniel will too. Evisceration will probably be too quick, and so will slitting his throat like I did to Ryan and the others. I'll probably just stab him in the gut once or twice and leave him there to bleed out. Alone, in pain, and betrayed by someone he loved."

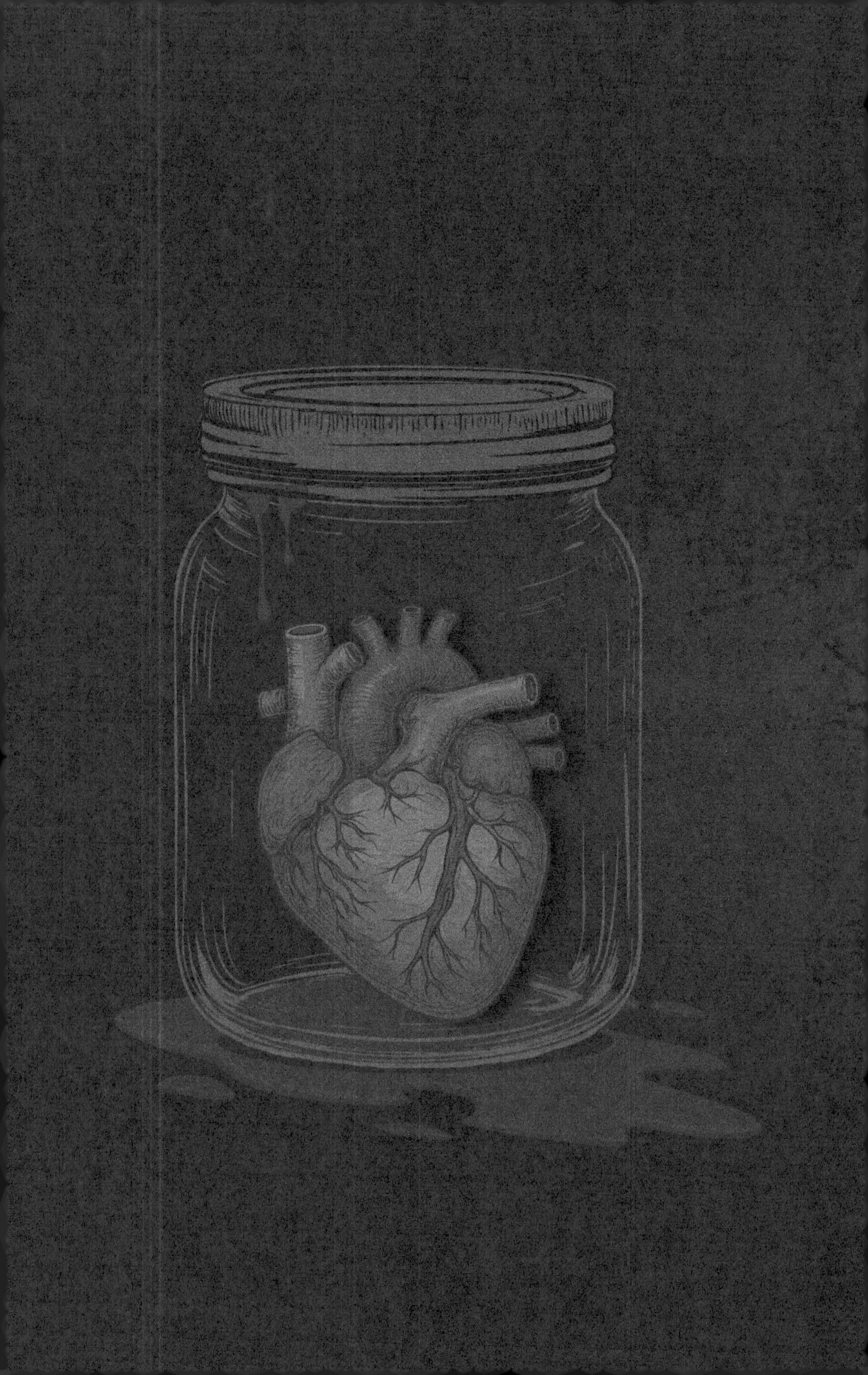

CHAPTER 45

I wake when the bed dips in front of me. I knew he'd need comfort tonight, so I'm glad I warned Evan ahead of time. He's spooned up behind me, his arm draped down my side and his forehead pressed against my shoulder as he breathes deeply. He grumbles a bit and pulls me closer when I lift my arm and the blanket enough for Brandon to scoot in and become the littlest spoon, but he quickly falls back to sleep.

"Sorry, Killer. I couldn't sleep," he whispers to me, bending his knees up so he can place his feet over mine like we used to when we were kids.

"It's ok," I whisper back, pressing a kiss to the back of his head. "Go to sleep, I've got you." I wiggle my toes to remind him I'm here for him and run my fingers through his hair until his body relaxes into sleep. He's such a strong and self-assured person that it always throws me when he struggles like this. It doesn't happen often, but when it does it takes a while for him to snap back out of it. That usually means a lot of time together, which I honestly don't mind, but I'm hoping this time having a plan will help him work through it faster.

I don't know if either of us will ever truly recover from this betrayal. My brain is fully aware that Daniel is an anomaly. I'm not so damaged from this to think one person dealing out this kind of crazy means everyone should be suspect from now on. It's just hard to reconcile the fact that Daniel was a part of my family, someone I grew up with, someone I saw and spoke to every week, sometimes every day, and I never had any inkling that he was hiding all of this. I never had any idea he even had the capacity for it.

Maybe it's all about perspective. I'm not innocent. I have several notches on my kill belt, and they're all justified to me. But does it make a difference why you're killing, if you're still doing it? The people I've killed have deserved it in my own opinion, they still have people who love them, people who will miss them. Am I like him?

No.

No, fuck that. Daniel killed my father for his own selfish reasons, I have no doubt. I have only killed people who hurt others for their own gain. People who spread pain, corruption, and misery to everyone they come into contact with. I have never killed someone out of anger, greed, or hate. I have never done it for any personal gain, other than ensuring my own safety in Ryan's case. But, again, that was about safety, not personal desire. I won't lie and say part of me didn't enjoy it and I'm not happy he's dead, but if he hadn't threatened my safety, killed his grandmother, and admitted to killing others I wouldn't have bothered with it. As it is, I don't think I would have ever felt safe with him walking around after finding out what he's really like. Daniel is the same. He's been stalking me practically my whole life, when will that not be enough? Was he content to wait only because I was alone before, or was he simply biding his time.

Half of me is desperate to know, and the other half simply doesn't care. What he's done is such an incredible violation and I can't trust that he won't escalate and hurt Evan, Brandon, and I in the future. Turning him in to the police won't do anything in the long run,. The evidence only leads to a few misdemeanor charges for petty theft, stalking, and possibly assault on Travis. Sure, I could probably file an order of protection but that isn't anything but a piece of paper which can be easily ignored.

God this is such bullshit. This can't be over soon enough.

It took me a long time to fall back to sleep. My mind kept replaying the last fifteen years looking for signs of what he's been doing, but I couldn't find any, so I kept getting more and more frustrated. Eventually, exhaustion and the warmth of the bodies surrounding me lulled me into a doze.

I wake up lying on my back and drenched in sweat. My legs had been pulled apart at some point during the night and both men covered one of them with their own. Hot breath tickles both sides of my neck and a weight on my stomach forces me to look down.

Evan and Brandon are curled into my sides with one arm across my stomach each, limp and heavy in sleep. Instead of cradling me, however, they're both gripping the arm of the other man, and Brandon is stroking Evan's arm with his fingers. They're so cute I don't want to wake them up, but the hilarity of the situation causes my body to shake with repressed laughter. They start petting each other's arms in an attempt to soothe me back to sleep and the sight of it strips me of my ability to keep silent. I release what can only be described as a chortle and it is so loud both men snap up to seated positions while gripping each other tightly. The combination of their simultaneous "Huh?" and "What the fuck?" and realization that they're holding onto one another is my final undoing and the panic attack hits full force.

"Shit, you're ok Jen. Evan, hold her. I'll be right back." In the back of my mind I understand Brandon has left the room, but I'm trying to place my focus on breathing and the hypnotizing sound of Evan's voice in my ear.

"Come on, Jen. Deep breath for me. Match mine, ok? Good girl. You can do this, everything is fine. I've got you, baby girl. You're doing so good. That's right, keep going." The sensation of his hand rubbing my back, him rocking my body from side to side, and the cadence of his voice and praise helps me crawl out of my head faster than I've ever been able to. As soon as I take my first sob free deep breath Brandon bolts back into the bedroom. He's got a cold Diet Coke, a cool wet rag, and a box of tissues.

"Sorry," I mutter, taking the tissues first, so I can blow my nose. Evan laughs softly at the sound of it, but my dad always told me that if it doesn't sound like a freight train when you blow your nose you're probably not doing it right. I reach for the cool rag next and wipe my face and neck with it before grabbing the opened drink and taking a sip. "I'm sorry I scared you both. You were just so cute I couldn't hold back my giggles."

"That wasn't a giggle, Killer. That was a fucking explosion." Brandon is worried, but I'm fine now, just extra tired.

"It's not my fault you were being so sweet to each other. I actually kind of felt like a third wheel. Should I step out and give you two some time alone?" The second I giggle Evan's grip around me loosens, and he sighs against my hair.

"I thought we discussed this last night. He's too much for me to handle."

"Fucking right I am!" Brandon states proudly. "If only you could be so lucky."

"Alright!" I laugh, "enough. Let's get this day started, shall we? Brandon and I have to work, and I'm craving waffles that I don't have to cook. Do either of you want to do it, or do we go out?"

"Out," Evan says, biting my shoulder gently before pushing me off of his lap. "We've earned it, and it's my treat today. I have take care of my woman and her other man."

"I could be your man too," Brandon coos, batting his eyelashes like Betty Boop before sauntering his way to the guest bathroom.

"Nope. I definitely couldn't handle him."

I laugh at his dejected frown and tug him to the bathroom to start the shower. "Me either."

We decided to go to my favorite diner for breakfast. It's one of the ones with older waitresses and classic movie and music posters all over the walls and great music plays every time you're there. They've added a cannoli waffle to the menu and I don't even care that I'll probably develop diabetes from it because it's totally going to be worth it. Neither of my boys say anything when I order which is good because I know they're both going to try to eat some of it.

We spend the time until our food arrives talking about the renovation, work, and what Evan's plans are with his Gran's house. Brandon suggests turning it into a rental property in order to bring in constant income instead of cash from the single purchase. We end up talking about buying and flipping homes together to use as rental and investment properties. The more we talk about it, the more Brandon's face lights up. The division of labor is cut and dry — Evan and I are the financial backers, Evan is the construction guy, I'm the designer, and Brandon will be the real estate agent and handle the rental aspect. He will eventually invest a portion of his cut back into the business. Obviously it won't be as easy as saying we're going to do it, but we can always test the waters with Gran's house while Evan finishes getting his general contractor's license, and we see if Brandon really does follow through with getting a real estate license.

The planning is a ray of light that breaks up the otherwise gloomy atmosphere hovering over us all since yesterday. I love the store. Working there and sharing my passion for books and music is something I want to do for the rest of my life, but I'm also excited at the prospect of working with the two people I love more than anything and doing something we're all good at. Seeing Brandon finally develop interest in a career path is icing on the cake, I want him to find something he loves as much as I love the store.

My waffle is everything I hoped for, but so filling I can only eat half. As I expected, Evan and Brandon split the rest between them. Brandon has about an hour before he has to open the store and Evan is off today, so we caravan back to our apartment building. Brandon needs to get ready for work, and Evan and plan to pack up a bit more of my stuff to take back to the cabin before my shift this evening.

Brandon and I open our apartment doors at almost the exact same moment, and as I stand frozen in my entryway, he comes running down the hall shouting for me. "Jen, holy shit, I think I was robbed!" I still can't speak when he mumbles "What the fuck?" from behind Evan.

"Shit!" I shout, startling Evan and Brandon as I turn and run out of my destroyed apartment. "Mrs. Whitlock!" I sprint to her door as fast as possible and knock loudly. Mr. Pumpkins immediately starts barking, and she shushes him from the small hallway to her front door. Thank God she sounds ok.

"Jen? Are you ok Sugah?" I don't want to scare her, but she's going to see the police here soon enough, so I'm not going to lie either.

"Hi Mrs. Whitlock. Yeah, I'm ok but someone broke into our apartments last night. I just wanted to check on you. No one bothered you, did they?"

"Oh dear! Both of you? Yours too Brandon?"

"Yes ma'am, it looks like it. I was at Jen's cabin last night so luckily I wasn't home for it. Did you hear anything?" Mr. Pumpkins jumps up on Brandon's leg, so he picks him up and gives him love and scratches.

"No, I'm so sorry Honey, I didn't hear anything at all! We were watching that handsome boy Henry on the new season of The Witcher and you know my Tommy just helped me with the new speakers so I can hear it better."

"That's ok! We were just worried something had happened to you too. I wanted to check on you and let you know we'll be calling the police so you won't be worried when they come. I'm going to talk to the front office about security too, but please just be more aware of what's going on around here, ok? Maybe tell Tommy so he can come around more often."

"Of course! Please be careful you two. I'm sorry I couldn't be more helpful."

"Don't worry about it, we're just glad you're ok," Brandon tells her as he hands over her dog. "You have our phone numbers. Jen is staying at the cabin, but I'll be around. You can call me anytime, ok? Day or night."

We say our goodbyes and walk over to Brandon's apartment together. His apartment is tossed too, but not as bad as mine. I call the police while Brandon calls the leasing office to tell them what happened. They're going to send some-one up to rekey and reprogram our door locks once the police leave so we'll have updated log in codes, which is doubly beneficial since Daniel has codes to both of our places in case of emergency, and the concierge is going to contact the other people on our floor to find out if they've checked their own apartments. The leasing manager is going to pull the logs from our locks to determine how and when the apartments were accessed and bring it up for the police immediately. Since Brandon is the opening manager today he heads over to open up. Nick agreed to come in for a few hours and cover for him so he can talk to the police, so he should be back in an hour or less.

Evan and I didn't want to disturb any evidence, so we sit in the hallway outside my door to wait for them. I text my dad's friend Brian to give him a head's up about what happened, then with my head leaning back against the wall and my face turned slightly away from the table where Daniel has his camera planted, I speak quietly in case it has sound capability. "This seems too brazen for Daniel, but who else it could be since they got both of our places. Do you?"

Evan, catching on easily to what I'm doing, acts like he's looking down at his cuticles to hide his own face. "The only person I can think of is Uncle Patrick."

"I guess it could be. I don't see Daniel being stupid enough to do this, do you?"

Evan's response is interrupted by the ringing of my phone. "Shit, it's Daniel. I can't hide this, or he'll suspect something is up." I answer the phone on speaker, though I usually hate when people do it in public. I want Evan to hear though. "Hey, D. What's up?"

"Good morning!" he says happily. "How are you feeling? I just wanted to check on you."

"Oh, that's sweet, thanks." I turn my face so the camera won't catch me rolling my eyes. "I'm much better. I must have slept fifteen hours and things are much calmer today. I'm no longer gushing like the elevators at The Overlook, so that's a plus." I snicker at the uncomfortable throat clearing on the other end of the line. "I'm fucking with you Daniel, relax."

"Hilarious, as always. What are you up to today? Do you have to work, or do you want to try helping me decorate again?" I may be looking for it, but he sounds like he's fishing.

"Actually, I'm at my apartment, waiting for the police to show up."

"What? Why? What happened?"

I can't tell if his voice is sincere or not, but it's definitely a bit panicked. "There was a break in last night. Both my place and Brandon's. We're not sure about the rest of the floor, but thankfully Mrs. Whitlock and Mr. Pumpkins weren't bothered."

"Oh, thank goodness. I always liked her. But why didn't you call me?" He sounds hurt. Could he have done this to encourage me to go running to him to protect and save me?

"It's not your jurisdiction, and we thought you were working. I was going to call you later to fill you in after they left."

"Look, I'm at Mom's, but she's having a good day, so I'm coming to you. Just hold tight, ok?"

"No!" I blurt accidentally. "I'm ok, really. Stay with your mom, she loves having you there with her, and she doesn't have many good days anymore. Evan is here now, and Brandon will be back from opening the store any minute." As if on cue, the elevator chimes and two officers getting off on our floor. "Hey, D. The officers are here. I'll call you later to fill you in and reschedule dinner, ok?"

Evan helps me stand before moving to greet the officers while I say goodbye to Daniel.

"Ok, call me if you change your mind. I can be there in no time, ok?"

"Sounds good. Thanks, D. Talk to you soon."

Evan and I greet the officers and indicate which apartments are the ones involved. Before we have a complete conversation they first enter my apartment, then head to Brandon's to clear them and make sure no one is still inside. Brandon returns while they're clearing his apartment, and we introduce him to the officers once they return to the hallway. They decide to divide and conquer since there are two of us, and one officer goes with Brandon while the other comes back to my apartment with me.

I didn't really look around earlier, and I honestly don't want to go through everything now. I feel violated, similar to how I felt in Daniel's attic, but on a much smaller scale. Nothing is where it should be. My kitchen cabinets are all hanging askew, my glasses and dishware all strewn across the ground, shattered. My couch cushions and pillows are thrown everywhere, pictures and paintings smashed and cut, TV shattered, curtains shredded, and so much more. If it could be damaged, it is. I move through the space carefully, grateful I decided to wear my sturdy leather boots with thick soles today to protect my feet.

I decide to check my bedroom first and more of the same is in there. Whoever it was even used a knife to shred my mattress before flipping it off of the bed frame. My clothes are all destroyed, so I'll have to search through them to find out if anything is salvageable, and the bathroom is possibly the messiest room so far since my bath products have been emptied and splashed everywhere.

Deciding I can't put it off any longer, I backtrack to my closed guest room door. It's the only closed door in the apartment, so my fear is the damage is worse in there. Even the guest bathroom door was left open, making it easy to see the mirror was shattered and the shower curtain was ripped from the hooks.

The officer speaks up when I move to open the door. "That door was shut when we entered, I closed it back so you'd see exactly how things were left. Did you leave it this way?"

"No," I sigh. "I always leave this door open. It's my favorite room and I like to look in when I walk past." Using my glove covered hand I grip the knob and take a deep breath and gather myself, then open the door.

Tears immediately prick the back of my eyes and in a moment of weakness I turn and bury my face in Evan's chest. My sanctuary has been completely demolished. My library, the pride and joy of both of my homes, has been completely ransacked. The oversized round swivel chair that took me a month to pick out has been gutted, the stuffing spread over the ground like snow and covering the mangled corpses of my cherished books. Covers and pages litter the ground like trash, separated from their bindings like wings from a butterfly. This collection took me years to cultivate, and more than half of them were signed by the authors. My skulls, crystals, and other keepsakes are all shattered and dust the ground like the dishes in my kitchen. The devastation is absolute, and I can't bear to look around any longer.

I've dealt with enough lately, and this is my last straw. If I find out this was Daniel, and he purposely destroyed what I love most, I will castrate him before he dies. I turn and flee my apartment, uninterested in spending another second in there. I close my eyes and lean my head against the wall in the hallway outside my door, breathing slow and trying to ease the hurt and sick feelings in the pit of my stomach while Evan rubs calming circles on my lower back.

"I know it's hard to tell right now," the officer says, "but could you tell if anything was missing?"

"Honestly, no. There wasn't anything too important in there anyway, other than in my library. Evan and I took some things to my cabin last week, so things like my computer, tablet, and jewelry were already gone, thank goodness. Honestly, the only things of value were the electronics I saw were smashed and my furniture. My books were valuable in that as a whole the cost added up, but they were really just valuable to me because most of them were signed. The books I have that are worth money are in my cabin in the safe there."

We speak a while longer and I answer more questions, mentally drained the whole time. While we're talking, Evan took it upon himself to call Mr. Talbert for the contact information for some companies he'd recommended to help clean Gran's house. With my heartfelt appreciation, he calls and lines up cleaning and junk hauling services to come out and salvage whatever possible for me, so I don't have to do it. Brandon's apartment wasn't gutted like mine, only a few areas were tossed and he didn't notice anything missing, so we're going to have the cleaning service straighten his place too. He's going to pack a bag with a few days worth of clothes and stay with us at the cabin.

The officers allow Brandon to return to work, and we finish things up with them. Before they leave, the leasing office manager and maintenance man show up to switch out our door locks and provide police with the log information for when the door was accessed last night.

"Here you go, officer," Mandy coos, handing the taller of the two a printed document while trying to give him a view down her shirt. "It says Jenevive's door was accessed twice last night, and Brandon's only once."

"Twice? What times?"

"Um... Brandon's was once at 8:36pm by key, and yours was once at 5:37 pm with the code, and 7:14pm with the key."

"But wait. How is that possible? We don't have physical keys, how would someone else?"

"Your dad came in and got them from the evening concierge. He didn't tell you? He never returned them either, so we'll need them back or you'll both be charged the replacement fee."

My heart stutters for a moment when she tells me my dad came in, followed quickly by rage. My voice comes out surprisingly calm when I tilt my head and say, "I wasn't aware that your office was in the business of giving out resident's keys without proof of identity."

"I beg your pardon. We do nothing of the sort! The concierge verified that your father was listed on both leases as a contact and able to access the key in emergency situations." She went from flirty to haughty in two seconds, and I don't have the time or the patience for her shit today.

"Officers, can you please make a note in your report that the leasing office provided a key to both of our apartments to someone without either of our permission? I'd like to be able to use that document as proof when I move to break my lease."

"How dare you! We have permission on file in writing! You're just trying to break your lease early because you don't want to be held responsible for the noise complaint from last night."

"My dad has been dead for almost a year, you dumb bitch. Please explain to me how you verified his identity before providing him entrance into our homes when he's six feet under? And what is this about a noise complaint? This is the first I'm hearing about it. Don't you think you should have contacted me last night or mentioned it to the police that are here about a fucking break in?" Jesus this woman is stupid.

Her face pales, and she turns to the officers in shock. "I... um, I don't know. My concierge swore they checked. I'll have to speak with them again."

"That won't be necessary, ma'am. You can provide us with their contact information, and we will handle that. But what is this about a noise complaint?" He looks about as done with her shit as I am.

"Oh, of course. I'll obtain that right away. And they told me there was a complaint around 7:30pm about loud music in Jenevive's apartment. It took some time for my staff to arrive to check it out, but when they got here it was quiet and no one came to the door."

"And what time was that?" the shorter officer asks.

"About 8:45?" She's chewing on her lip, obviously nervous since she's just given me ammo to sue her for my damages, which I will if they won't let me out of my lease without penalty.

Evan scoffs beside me. "Big surprise with prompt attention like that."

"What was the noise complaint about?"

"Loud music and thumping. Mr. Bevins from next door called it in. He's called in complaints before that have turned out to be frivolous and it wasn't during quiet hours so my staff didn't prioritize it. And, like I said, there wasn't any sound coming from the unit when they arrived so it was dismissed."

Done listening to her shit, I make sure she's looking at me. "I'm breaking my lease and you're not going to fight me on it. I don't feel safe here anymore because of your staff's failure to protect my privacy. If you give me a fight or try to charge me, I will involve my attorney and sue you for every fucking penny of damages that resulted from your negligence. The same goes for Brandon." I'm honestly not worried, but I was planning on moving out anyway so this helps my cause.

I can tell she's irritated but I don't care. I am done talking to her, so I step away with Evan. The officers ask her a few more questions and obtain some more information from her, then excuse her back to the office after she gives me our new door codes. We thank the officers and the maintenance man and leave, since I don't want to deal with my destroyed things again.

I also have the feeling we need to check on Gran's house.

Chapter 46

I would say that I hate being right all the time, but I would be lying.

In this situation, however, I am disappointed. The destruction is somewhere between my apartment and Brandon's. Some things look to be damaged for the simple sake of it, but the office and other places where Gran stored documents were looted the worst. I call the police while Evan calls Mr. Talbert for another copy of the list of valuables in the house, even though we already removed them, and he decides to personally bring it to be with us in case he is needed for legal help and advice. I provided dispatch with the information of our last call and the information of the officers that came out since I have no doubt everything is connected.

The same officers respond, and we repeat the same song and dance. Evan and I both suspect his Uncle Patrick, so we have no problems laying the possible blame at his feet. Mr. Talbert happily not only corroborates our story but provides them with additional information. We also mention Ryan and the fact that he's missing after the death of their grandmother to keep the ruse up.

By the time Mr. Talbert and the officers leave I have to go into work. Brandon stayed an extra hour for me so I could help Evan finish things up, but I can't call out again after missing a week. Neither Evan nor Brandon want to sit at home tonight, so they decide to hit the sports bar in the shopping center for a few hours then come back to the store and play video games on the big screen while they wait until I'm off, so we can all head home together. Evan gets along great with my friends and the night goes by quickly, though being surrounded by books makes me mourn what I've lost that much harder. I can always replace them, but some were gifts and the ones from my dad can never be replaced.

Daniel texted me several times throughout the day and evening to check on me, continuously offering to come and check things out or stay over if I feel unsafe. I had to tell him about Gran's house too in case he already knew or checks into the cases, and that seems to make him believe Ryan was the culprit. It takes the reminders that I have a high tech alarm system and that Brandon and Evan will both be at the cabin with me for him to relent, but he presses on scheduling dinner again. After speaking with the guys, we settle on two days from now. Brandon and I are both off for the evening, and Evan will be off of work at the same time I am, so the timing is perfect.

Now I'm just worried the anticipation will kill me before I can kill him.

Today is the day.

Not only is my apartment being cleaned out and my leasing agent is sending me documentation for the breaking of my lease with no penalty, but today is the day I have been waiting for, for almost a year.

My father's death will finally be avenged. My stalker, the man who I thought was as close as a brother, will die screaming by my hand. I honestly haven't decided if I want to drag it out or end it quickly. I think I've made a decision, but then change my mind just as quickly, so I've decided to play it by ear. There are so many parts of me that are conflicted about all of this. All of them want him dead, but it's the how that I'm struggling with.

One part wants to cut him apart or skin him alive, so he can experience a fraction of the pain I have.

One part wants to bind him, gag him, and tell him what I think about him and what he's done before I kill him.

One part wants to simply do it quickly, so he doesn't know what's coming and be done with it all.

Sometimes, one part almost doesn't even want to be bothered enough to do it myself so it can show him how little he means to me.

All I know for sure is that I will make sure he can never hurt anyone else, ever again.

I consider taking a half of a Xanax before Daniel arrives, especially after Brandon texted me to tell me he's going to be late, but I want to make sure I keep my head on straight. I don't know how long or how well I'll be able to pretend like everything is ok. Everything depends on it, so I have to do my best.

I've got the baggie of powder in my front pants pocket and I keep patting it to make sure it's still there, like it could have fallen out in the 30 seconds since the last time I checked. My phone vibrating in my back pocket causes me to jump, and I laugh at myself and how tightly I'm wound. Pulling it out of my pocket I check the screen, maybe Brandon is finally on his way?

Evan: You got this. Text me when he gets there if you can.

Me: I will.

The sound of a knock at the front door surprises me, since I usually hear vehicles on the gravel. I start towards the door and shoot Evan a quick text to tell him it's go time.

Me: He's here. Please be careful.

Evan: I will. You too. I love you.

Me: I love you too.

I shut down the screen and put the phone back in my pocket as I open the door, smiling as best I can at Daniel holding a case of beer.

"Hey, come on in," I direct him, stepping back so he can enter.

"Thanks. I brought this to replace everything we drank last time," he tells me with a small grin. The hand I didn't realize he was holding behind his back comes around, and he holds out a bottle of Orange flavored Diet Coke. "I saw this too, thought you may like to try it."

"Oh, wow, thanks." I'm kind of grossed out at the thought, but also kind of intrigued. I won't drink it since it came from him, but I may find another one to try later.

"Evan called. He's still not sure if work will be an all night thing or not. It depends on what the inspector tells them." I put the beer and Diet Coke in the fridge to cool and turn back to face him. "I actually went shopping for my choices for the renovation upstairs this week and saw some things I thought may work for your house, so I picked up samples for you too. Do you want to look at them outside?"

"That sounds great. Thanks, Jen. I really don't know what I'd do without your help. It would probably end up looking terrible." He chuckles and shakes his head in a self-deprecating manner, acting almost shy.

I force a laugh and wave him on. "Head on out, I'll grab everything. You want a drink?"

"I got the drinks. You grab your samples."

Shit.

"Oh, yeah ok. I'll be right out." I grab my totes of samples and bring them out to the patio with us, pulling everything out so we can go through them as he places our drinks on the table. He stands back for me to spread out what I've collected and thinking fast, I "accidentally" allow one of my bags to spill its contents and knock his bottle over.

"Damnit!" I curse, "quick, there are towels in there." I direct him to the new chest over by the hot tub and move my bags over to one of the empty chairs. I use the towel he tosses me to mop up the table and pick up his now empty bottle. "I'm sorry. I'll grab you a new one and throw these in the hamper, I'll be right back. You're welcome to take a look in the bags."

I make my way inside but pop my head back out of the door like I've just remembered something. "Oh, hey, D? I made some of the sweet tea you like. Would you rather have that or another beer? I forgot to ask earlier."

"Oh, yeah that sounds good actually. And I'm ok with waiting to order dinner if you want, so we can see if Evan is going to join us."

"Ok, perfect. I'll text him."

I head back inside, dropping the wet towels off in the laundry room before stopping in the kitchen for another drink. I pull out my phone and text Evan that Daniel is ok to wait for dinner and grab a glass for Daniel's tea. I think the sweetness will hide the drug better than beer will, so hopefully it works. He's not already drunk like the last time I tried this, so fingers crossed.

I've just finished stirring the powder in when Daniel opens the door to come inside. "I'm about done," I tell him, smiling. "I texted Evan to tell him we'd hold off dinner for a while but haven't heard back from him yet. I'm sure he's busy trying to finish up."

"Cool. You two seem to have gotten close in the past few weeks, and I haven't had much of a chance to talk to you alone in a while. Aren't you afraid he's going to leave again, like Ryan? It's like you've just... forgotten what he did. What he put you through." He shakes his head like he's disappointed. "Are you so sure he can be trusted?"

"Look... I understand. But he didn't want to leave, he was just a kid like we were and didn't have a choice. He's apologized, made amends, and he wants to make it up to us. I do trust him." I hold out his drink to him, so he'll come closer and take it. He draws closer and grabs the drink, taking a sip and scrunching his nose at it after tasting it. "Too much sugar?" I ask innocently.

"No, no. It's fine, thanks." He places it on the island counter beside him and leans back against it with his hands in his pockets. "I just don't want you to be hurt again. You were devastated the last time they left. I don't want you to go through that again."

Damnit, he needs to drink the tea. "I'm fine, Daniel, really. I'm grown up now. Friends come and go in life. Evan doesn't have to stay if he doesn't want to. I'm not forcing him to be here, and I'm surely not going to force anyone to stay in my life who doesn't want to be here. Everyone deserves a second chance though, D."

I head to the pantry, thinking that if I put a salty snack in front of him he'll drink more. I turn with a bag of pretzels in my hand and jump when I find him only inches away.

"Um, pretzels?" I ask, holding the bag up for him.

"You just don't get it," he snarls, anger starting to flare in his eyes. "But you will."

I wake slowly due to a combination of an aggressively throbbing headache and roiling nausea. What the fuck happened? I keep my eyes closed as I try to remember. Daniel got here. We were in the kitchen getting him another drink... wait. He was angry.

"I will what?" I ask him, suddenly extremely uncomfortable. "What will I get?"

"You'll get that Evan isn't right for you," he tells me, teeth and fists clenched.

"Wha- what do you mean?" Shit. If he's not hiding that he knows, things are probably about to go tits up. I check around me for anything I can use as a weapon, but nothing is within reach that I can use. If I make it out of this alive, I'm hiding weapons all over this fucking house like Dwight hides throwing stars and nunchucks.

"Don't lie to me!" he shouts in my face, spittle flying from his mouth and landing on my cheek. I'm too afraid to wipe it off in case the movement sets him off even more. But fuck, that's gross.

"I'm... I'm sorry we didn't tell you, ok? It's new. I wasn't sure if it would work out, so I didn't want to put too much stock in it yet. It's not serious or anything," I lie. "We're just sort of getting to know each other again."

"Stop lying!" he screams, lunging at me. I try to step back and out of the way so I can run around him and escape, but the second I twist a searing pain slams into me between my shoulder blades and my body locks up. My breath is forced out of my lungs and I'm falling straight into the shelf next to me. My last thought before my head slams against the wooden corner is that I need to fill the sugar jar.

It takes me a few minutes to work up the courage to open my eyes since the room is silent, giving me no hint as to where I am or who, if anyone, is nearby. I'm sluggish and it makes me worry I may have a concussion, so I experimentally crack one lid to see if I can stand it. The light is thankfully somewhat dim around me, so it only causes a slight amount of increased discomfort. Slowly, I open both eyes and realize the reason the light is so dim is because my fucking living room is covered with dozens of lit candles.

What the hell?

I try to lift my hand to check for a lump on the back of my head, but that brings my attention to the fact that my hands are tied behind my back. I close my eyes again for a second because my head injury has caused me to lose some of my concentration and ability to sense my surroundings. Maybe taking a moment to center myself will help my brain start functioning again. After a few deep breaths, I try opening my eyes again. First, I look around to see what is going on around me other than the candles. I'm in my own living room directly in front of the fireplace, facing my kitchen. The furniture has all been pushed back from me at least 6 feet in all directions and every surface is covered in different sized white candles. Soft jazz is playing through the stereo system, and I am alone.

Looking down to see what kind of chair I'm attached to and what type of restraints he used, my heart stops in my chest.

What. The. Fuck .

I'm in a fucking wedding gown.

A full on, poofy as hell, honest to fuck wedding gown.

I use the code Jen gave me to open Daniel's garage and pull my truck in, so I can close the door behind me. I don't want to bring too much attention to my visit, especially since he's about to go missing. Using her key, I gain access to the house and leave the lights off as I turn off the alarm and move through his space. The house is cool and quiet and takes me only seconds to arrive at the bathroom containing the secret door.

The moment I enter a thump and a muffled sound reaches me from inside the cabinet. Daniel isn't here, so what was that? I'm not leaving without her knife, so

I pull my gun and slowly make my way to the cabinet. Standing to the side, I raise my gun in one hand and swing the cabinet door open with the other.

"Shit. Brandon? What the hell?"

Brandon is hogtied on the floor of the small interior room with a gag in his mouth. The thump I heard must have been the ladder falling against the wall as he struggled to free himself from his restraints. As soon as he hears me, his head whips in my direction and he starts frantically yelling but I can't understand what he's saying.

I bend down and try to remove the gag, but the fabric is tied way too tight and I can't untie the knots there or around his wrists or ankles. "Hang on man, I don't have a knife on me, let me grab Mr. Martin's and I'll cut you loose. I can't untie them." His pouting groan and grumble of irritation bring a smile to my face in the middle of this shit storm, and I help scoot him out of the way so I can set up the ladder and climb up into the attic space.

Pulling up the flashlight app on my phone, I take a quick peek around the room before pulling the knife from the wall behind me and quickly heading back to Brandon's side. I carefully slide the knife between the gag and his skin, mumbling "Don't move" as I work. His eyes are huge and trained on what little he can see of the knife, but luckily Mr. Martin took excellent care of this thing because I'm able to quickly slice through the gag without cutting his skin.

"Fuck!" he shouts the second I remove it from his mouth. "That mother fucker! If I wasn't going to help kill him before, I sure as fuck am going to now."

"What happened? How did you get here?" I continue to work on getting him loose while he rants.

"The fucker surprised me in the parking lot at home. I parked there, so I could grab a few more days worth of clothes and was getting ready to head to Jen's when he just showed up. He fucking tased me and I woke up here a few minutes ago. I've been trying to wriggle loose but this shit is tight."

"Do you think you can stand up? If he attacked you, it means he doesn't care about hiding anymore, and he may hurt Jen. If you can't, I'll come back for you, but I have to go now."

"Fuck that, I'm coming if you have to carry me. Let's go."

Before I can do much to try to free myself Daniel steps around the corner from the hallway.

"Oh, good. You're awake. I'm sorry honey. I didn't mean for you to hit your head when you fell but I couldn't catch you in time. Are you ok?"

"What... what is this, Daniel? Why am I in a wedding gown? What is going on?"

"Do you like it? I've had it for two years, waiting until you were ready. The second I saw it I knew it was perfect for you, and I was right. You look like an angel in it, sweetheart. I've been trying to figure out how to tell you for so long, and I'm so glad our time is finally here."

Ok. So I already knew he was mental. The room in his attic and the fact that he killed my father and beat up my gay friend for being a "threat" proves it, among so many other things. But this? Does he expect me to jump into his arms and thank him for knocking me out and tying me up in this admittedly beautiful but absolutely ridiculous dress?

Damnit, focus. It doesn't matter if the dress is beautiful. It's fucking creepy.

"I don't understand, D. Tell me what? What is this about? What time is here?"

"It's time for us to be together, Jenevive. I've been waiting for years for you to come to me. It was just a matter of time." He's pacing in front of me, gripping his hair like he's going to pull it out. "We were so close, but then Ryan and Evan had to come back. I was so angry when I saw them. When I saw you see them! You fell right fucking back in to his trap, didn't you? I thought I'd have to eliminate Ryan somehow, but he shocked me by running off without you yet again. At first, I was so relieved because I figured I'd be there to pick up the pieces again. Except, this time you'd realize what's been in front of you all along." He stops in front of me, chest heaving. "But then fucking Evan stepped in! I never thought I'd have to worry about him, of all people, but he slid right the fuck in to my place." He slams his palm against his chest as he screams "My place!" The change in tone causes me to jump in my seat. "I knew how he felt about you when we were growing up, but he was always too afraid to say anything. Ryan used to make fun of him for it all the time, he had even found the turtle necklace Evan bought you before he ever gave it to you and told me about it. The only reason I let you keep it over the years is because I thought you only saw him as a big brother."

I look down and realize the comforting weight of the charm isn't resting against me, though I was wearing it when he arrived. "Where is it?" I ask him, furious that he's taken another thing from me that he has no right to.

"Don't worry about it. You don't need it, Jen. You have me. I'll buy you whatever you want. I'll buy you a better one, covered in diamonds if you want! Before I came here, I went to my mom's house. I staged a break in and killed her. Now, I'll have her life insurance policy and will be able to take care of you on more than a cop's salary!"

I broke every speed law on my way to the cabin. We don't want to alert him that we're here in case he's hurting her, so I park far enough back on the driveway he won't be able to detect us coming in. Sticking to the trees, we run as fast as we can to the clearing in front of the house and survey everything. The house seems dimly lit, but there is no movement in the windows. Brandon nudges me and points up to the master bedroom window. It's cracked open! I must not have closed it all the way the last time I was tossing trash into the dumpster, so it provides the perfect entry point. I can climb the gutter downspout and come at him from the stairs in case he's watching the doors. I point to the window, then myself, and then point to him and the back of the house. He nods and we take off to our assigned locations.

Climbing the downspout is difficult, but I am able to quickly and quietly make it to the window and peek in. The coast is clear, so I open it and slide inside. I have my gun and the hunting knife but nothing to subdue him with, so I stop in Jen's room and grab the tie from her robe and tuck it as best as I can in my back pocket. In a stroke of luck, I had tested the stairs this morning because a few of them were creaky and I made note of the ones I needed to fix, so I avoid those on my way down. Voices and a faint glow come from the living room, but I can't make out what they're saying until I reach the bottom of the stairs and the corner leading into where they are.

"Jesus, Daniel. Your mom?" Jen sounds horrified and heartbroken all at once. "Why? I don't need your money, I never have. My parents made sure I'll never need anything."

"I did it for us, Jen! The money is only a bonus. I want to be able to spoil you like you deserve, but I can't do that if I'm always having to drop whatever I'm doing to go take care of her." I hear a quiet thud and peek around the corner to find out what I'm dealing with.

My heart stops. He's on his knees in front of her, hands gripping her thighs tightly through the white gown she's wearing while blood drips slowly down the side of her face. I'm going to fucking kill him. Not only for hurting her, but he obviously touched her to change her clothes because she would never willingly wear that for him.

Actually, I'll let her kill him. I'm just going to take his filthy fucking hands first.

Daniel has dropped to his knees in front of me and is gripping my thighs like if he lets go I'll float away from him. He's suddenly like a completely different person and the gleam in his eyes is terrifying because it shows not only utter devotion, but also that his mind has broken from reality. "Now that we're together, I don't want to have to leave you to take care of her. How many times has she called me away from you lately?" While he's talking, movement catches my eye behind him and every ounce of tension drains from my body.

Evan is here. Somehow, he realized something was wrong, and he came for me in secret. Not wanting to draw attention to him I face Daniel once Evan places a finger to his mouth in a silencing motion and slowly steps into the living room with his gun drawn.

"So, you did all of this for me?" I ask him, watching Evan advance silently behind him out of the corner of my eye. "I don't understand though. You never told me how you felt. Why didn't you tell me sooner? All these years, and you never once hinted you felt something for me other than friendship."

"Guys throw themselves at you constantly, darling. I thought if I waited, if I was there for you and proved you could count on me that you would come to me eventually. Are you saying that if I'd told you earlier we could have been together all of this time?" The hope in his eyes is desperate, and it makes me nauseous.

"Not a damn chance," Evan says, placing the barrel of the gun against the back of his head. Daniel's eyes widen in first shock, and then fury. "Do not move, you creepy fuck."

My head snaps to the right when my patio door slides open. Brandon walks in, his face contorted in rage but my gaze is drawn back to Daniel when his grip tightens on my thighs. His face has gone ghostly white.

Evan steps to the side opposite Brandon and adjusts the position of the barrel so any shots fired would go outside, not through either of us. "Brandon, come around behind me and take the tie out of my back pocket. Daniel, take your fucking hands off of her and put them behind your back. I'm fairly certain you're familiar with the procedure." Daniel is gripping me tighter and shaking with fury at this point. "Do it slowly, or I will fucking end you right now."

Now that Evan and Brandon are here, I no longer have any fear. My breathing and heart rate have returned to normal, and the only thing out of the ordinary is the heat infusing my insides and rising up to my cheeks as Evan takes charge. Daniel detects the change and scowls, but slowly releases his hold on me and places his arms behind his back. I'm not stupid enough to take my eyes off of him yet, but I so desperately want to drown in the fire I know is in Evan's eyes right now.

"Brandon, tie his hands together as tightly as possible, and then move him the fuck away from her."

"My pleasure," Brandon snarls while jerking his hands back roughly and tying them together with the tie from my old robe. Once his hands are secure, Brandon pats him down and removes a black object from his back pocket.

Brandon presses the button causing the spark to jump and grins at Evan. "Mind taking a step back?"

Evan grunts a laugh and steps to my side as we all watch Brandon place the taser to Daniel's neck and power it up. His body goes rigid for a few moments before he falls to the ground, cracking his head against the floor and passing out cold.

CHAPTER 47

Evan kicks Daniel's limp form to the side and drops down in front of me. "Are you ok? We were so worried. Did he hurt you other than this place on your head? Did he touch you?" He pulls my dad's knife from his back pocket and hands it to Brandon who immediately moves behind me and starts working on cutting my bindings. The moment my hands are released I throw my arms around Evan and bury my face in his neck. I shake my head to show I'm fine, and hold him while the leftover adrenaline seeps out of my body. He holds me to him tightly and runs his hands up and down my back, soothing me and whispering reassurances as Brandon lifts the skirt of my dress to check for leg restraints. Finding them, he first cuts one, then moves to my other side to cut the other. Once I'm free Evan lifts me from the chair and carries me to the couch so he can sit me in his lap.

"I'm fine," I mumble into his skin before lifting my head. "Honestly, I'm just shocked and angry. Like, what the fuck was he thinking? On what planet would what he's done ever work as an effective form of courtship? And then telling me he killed his mom, so he could spoil me and not have to leave me to take care of her?"

"What?" Brandon interrupts, his face blanching. He often helped Daniel with Mrs. Schultz and was much closer to her than I was. I did care for her, but we weren't as close as Mrs. C and I. "He killed her too?"

"Yeah. He said he did it before coming over tonight and made it appear like a robbery. I guess he's got plenty of experience with it at this point, huh?" I shake my head with a mirthless laugh and lean further into Evan. "Let me change so we can head out to the barn."

"Wait, don't change yet, I have an idea." Brandon's got his devious face on, so I'll run with whatever he wants for now. "Just grab some clothes to change into later. I may not be able to torture him physically. Actually, I may after what happened today, but I sure as fuck can torture him mentally. We'll load him up, you meet us in the garage."

Evan and I share a look, shrug, and we each head off to accomplish our tasks after blowing out all the candles so my house doesn't burn down while we're gone. I'm not sure what Brandon has in mind but after being in this dress I will want comfort clothes, so I grab some yoga capris and a t-shirt. I'm feeling snarky and spiteful so my shirt reads "All of this cocaine in the world and your nose is still in my business." I throw my clothes in a bag and pop some Excedrin since my head is pounding before cleaning up a bit in the bathroom. Thankfully there's only a little blood and the cut is hidden in my hairline so no one should notice anything happened tomorrow.

The guys are waiting in the garage for me, both already seated in the UTV. Daniel is hogtied in the bed, Evan is driving, and Brandon is in the back seat. I hand Brandon my bag and round the vehicle to Daniel.

"What are you doing?" Brandon asks.

"He took my necklace, I almost forgot. Help me check his pockets."

Luckily, it is in the first pocket I check, so I don't have to keep touching him. Evan takes it and motions for me to turn around so he can put it on for me before kissing my neck. Relieved to have it back, I climb in the passenger seat, making sure to tuck the massive dress in so it doesn't catch on anything during the drive. Once we're on the way Evan grabs my hand and starts asking questions.

"What happened?"

"He snuck up on me while I was in the kitchen. First though, why are you two together? Brandon, I thought you got stuck at the store. That's what your text said."

"No. The fucker surprised me in the parking lot at home when I was on my way over here. He tased me and knocked me out. I woke up in the hidden room below the attic space tied up a few minutes before Evan found me. He must have texted you from my phone."

"He must have. I got a text from you saying there was an issue at the store so you would be a little late, but you would hurry. He showed up right on time but was acting weird. I had to spill his original drink because he got it himself, and when I went to grab him a replacement he followed me and cornered me in the pantry spouting shit about me figuring something out. The next thing I knew I woke up in this dress. He started talking about how we were meant to be together and Evan ruined it and blah blah. Fucking psycho."

"Yeah, the dress isn't making sense," Evan frowns. "Are you supposed to get married tonight or something?"

He said he bought it two years ago, and he wanted me in it since it's finally the 'right time.'" I use finger quotes when I say it, since those were his words. "I honestly think something in him snapped. My guess is it was seeing us together."

"Whatever happened, he's losing his hands before he dies for touching you." Evan squeezes my hand and brings it to his lips to press a kiss on my knuckles. Brandon chuckles when my cheeks turn pink.

"Speaking of, why am I still wearing this dress?" I turn to Brandon and see the evil grin on his face.

"What are your thoughts on PDA?"

Daniel is easily strung up the same way Ryan was. He's still unconscious, so we set about getting things ready for whatever we're going to do to him. My priority is to make him tell me about my dad. Then, I'm going to make him pay. I'm not sure if Evan is serious about taking his hands, but in case he is, I make sure to grab my bone cutter and add it to the tool tray. Knowing he touched me to change me into this dress makes my skin crawl since he also removed my bra to do it.

Evan and Brandon both put on a pair of my dad's coveralls in case things get messy, but I don't bother since I'll be burning this dress when I'm done. I have no doubt it will be covered in his blood before the night is over and I'm actually looking forward to it.

Brandon's plan is simple, in his mind at least. He wants Evan and I to have sex in front of Daniel while I'm wearing the dress he bought for me, or at the very least fool around a little. We're not sure we want to, but it's not like he hasn't watched us before, so I'm going to hold off on a decision. If he refuses to answer my questions I may have to take steps that I wouldn't usually take to make him talk. I will do whatever it takes to finally learn the truth of what happened to my dad, and if seeing me in the arms of Evan puts him over the edge so be it, even if the idea does squick me out.

Tired of waiting for him to wake up I pull the hose out and hand it to Evan while I center my work table directly in front of him and hop up, fluffing the skirt of my dress so it hangs nicely. Brandon handed me my dad's knife so can I hide it under the folds of the fabric at my side, and he hops up on the table on my other side to sit next to me. I crook my finger at Evan, calling him to me so I can kiss him before we begin. When he pulls away I smile up at him and say "I love you. Thank you for coming for me."

His smile is wide, and he presses another kiss to my lips while Brandon makes vomiting sounds next to me. "I love you too, and I will always come for you. Also, although I hate him for putting you in that dress, you do look stunning. I think all it needs to be perfect is his blood. Are you ready?"

"So ready," I reply, grin on my face. "Let's wake him up, shall we?"

Daniel wakes with a jolt, screaming through the ball gag stuffed in his mouth and jerking his body as much as his hanging position will allow. Evan continues blasting him for about a minute before stepping up and punching him in the stomach.

"Hi there, darling," I mock, using one of the names he called me tonight. "Did you have a nice nap?"

He stills at my voice and snaps his gaze to mine as best he can through the water droplets. I wait, relaxing where I sit and allowing him to take a moment to collect himself. His brow furrows when he finds Brandon sitting next to me on my left, and Evan back to standing at my right. His lids flutter shut for a moment while he shakes his head as if he needs to wake himself up, and then he looks up at his bound hands and the hook he's hanging from. His eyes are filled with betrayal, as if he believes he's the one being wronged.

"Don't you dare look at me like that. You're lucky you're not bleeding out on my fucking table!" He's not the fucking victim here. "I don't know what you could have possibly been thinking with what you pulled tonight, but it will be your last mistake."

He tries to talk to me but the gag prevents anything from coming out. I take a deep breath and shake my head sadly. Anger won't accomplish anything with him. I need to play on his feelings for me and manipulate him into getting the answers I want. Taking a deep breath, I soften my voice and facial expression and appeal to him as best as I can. "Listen, Daniel. I have questions, ok? If Evan removes the gag, will you talk to me? Please?" He pauses for a moment, assessing me before giving a stiff nod. Evan steps up and removes it before returning to my side.

"I don't understand, Jen. Why am I in here like this?"

What I don't understand is how he can ask that question with a straight face. The worst part is I can tell he actually means it.

"Brandon and Evan just want to make sure you don't hurt me again. We need to figure out what's going on, Daniel. Can you explain things to me? What happened earlier?"

"I would never hurt you, Jen! How could you guys even think that?" The incredulity in his tone would be Oscar worthy if he didn't believe himself.

"Daniel, you knocked me out and tied me up. You split my head open. You told me you killed your mom, and Brandon says you knocked him out and tied him up too. None of us understand what is happening right now. They're not going to be comfortable letting you down until they're sure I'm not in any danger."

"Jen, I love you. I didn't mean to hurt you, I just had to make you to listen! Please let me down so we can talk. You'll understand once we talk."

"I can't yet, Daniel. Talk to me now. Tell me what is going on and make me understand. I'm sure we can figure all of this out and move past this. Help me not be scared." Barf.

"How? You're with Evan now, and he's here. I thought tonight I'd be able to talk to you away from him and make you realize he's not right for you, but here he is just like he has been almost since the day they barged back into our lives! We never needed either of them, Jen, and we still don't! I'm the one who has always been by your side. He left you for four years, but he gets to slot right back into place and is given everything I've ever wanted? Everything I deserve?"

"Everything you deserve?" Brandon scoffs.

"Yes! I've done so much for you, Jen! Taken care of you and sacrificed for you. I saved you from them the first time around, and I can do it again if you give me the chance!"

"Wait." I take a step forward, away from Jen and towards Daniel. "What do you mean you saved her from us the first time?"

The sneer on his face is something I've never seen before and his disgust is evident when he responds. "How do you think Ryan's dad knew to move you two out of town? I ran into him about two weeks before you left and had to confess to him my concerns about the developing relationship between Ryan and Jen. Ryan had told me he was going to make a move on her soon, telling me all the filthy things he wanted to do to her, talking about her like she was just a piece of ass when she's so much more. So I told him I was worried about what kind of trouble they might get in if things turned sexual. How would it look if a pastor's son was seen all over town getting physical with a girl? If he got his teenage girlfriend pregnant?"

My body has locked down tight and I'm sure my face is devoid of expression. I'm barely even breathing. It takes every ounce of my energy to stand in place instead of slitting his throat right now. "So you're the reason I was taken from the only friends I've ever had. The only family that ever cared about me, and the only woman I have ever loved? The reason I was trapped and abused for three years until I was able to escape?"

"It was nothing personal to you, Evan. Not then at least. I had to get Ryan out of the picture. He was constantly gaslighting Jen, making her fall for him. She deserved so much better, so I had no choice. You just happened to be collateral. I am sorry if you suffered for it."

My head is filled with white noise and my body is trembling with rage. I turn to Jen and step up to her, bending to whisper "I'm not going to kill him," before kissing her on the temple. I try to turn, but she grabs my arm and pulls me back to face her. Using her left hand she cups my face and pulls me down for a kiss.

"Do what you need to," she whispers back. "I've waited this long, my answers can wait a few more minutes."

God damn, I love this woman. Her eyes show nothing but sincere understanding and acceptance and I have no doubt she will hold no resentment for what I'm about to do. Turning to Brandon, I ask "are you going to be good with a bit of blood?"

"Yeah, man. Do what you need to. If I have to, I'll step out." He seems like he's telling the truth, so I move to the tray of tools and quickly wrap my hands.

"What else, Daniel? What else have you done and sacrificed for me?" Jen questions, buying me some time.

It takes him a few moments to answer her because he's busy staring me down like I'm the Antichrist. "I already told you about my mom, but there have been so many men that weren't good enough for you, or tried to go after you that you never even notice. I took care of them for you. I scared them away or got rid of them completely so you didn't have to worry about them!" He's starting to foam at the mouth, making him look even crazier.

"None of that sounds like a sacrifice on your part, other than your mom. What have you sacrificed? Make me understand, Daniel. Please." I don't think she's faking the heartbreak in her voice. As angry as she is, I know this is more painful for her than anything.

"The FBI recruited me, did you know that? They wanted me to join up but I turned them down. I didn't want to be taken away from you. I knew you wouldn't want to leave the store, and I couldn't risk being put on assignment somewhere else, so I never even told you."

Wrapped up tight, I make my way over to him. "You should have taken the job, Danny-boy," I tell him before throwing a right hook at his jaw. His head snaps back and blood flows from his mouth as I begin beating the shit out of him. I stay away from his face after the first hit since I don't want to impede his ability to talk and I focus on his midsection. This beat down serves three purposes — I'm releasing some anger at the fact that he's the reason I was torn away from Jen for four years, I'm delivering some much deserved punishment, and it turns her on. Win-win-win, I'd say.

After a few minutes his groans turn into pained laughing and I stop and step back. Chest heaving, I look to Jen.

"What's so funny?" she asks him, her head cocked to the side in question.

"Is this... what it takes? Should I have told you... what I was doing all along? If all it took was violence, I would have shown you that side of me years ago."

Blood is trickling out of his mouth still, and his breathing is labored and gasping between words. Jen purses her lips in an adorable mockery of a thinking face and taps her chin for a second before dropping her bomb.

"I don't know, D. I do like the violence. Watching Evan beat the shit out of people does turn me on, and that big dick sure is a bonus. I think not murdering my dad is what really did it for me, though."

CHAPTER 48

All color drains from his face at my comment and his breathing stops.

"What... what do you mean? What are you talking about?"

Lifting the hand holding the knife from the folds of my skirt, I make sure the light reflects off of the blade, so he can see exactly what I'm holding.

"Jen, shit. Where... how did you get that? I can explain!" His voice has turned high-pitched in his panic, and his skin has blanched further than I've ever seen.

"Good. I was hoping you would be able to explain what I found in your attic. The years worth of photos, journals, and my belongings up there. The lists and photos and threat rankings of my admittedly few dates. The driver's license of my gay friend that you obviously attacked for spending time with me, even though you know his boyfriend. The photos of Evan and I together in intimate situations. The live feeds of my front fucking doors." I hop down from the table and walk towards him, lifting the knife to his throat and placing the tip against his Adam's apple. "This fucking knife. His wallet. His keys." I press harder with each sentence and my voice cracks at the end as a tear rolls down my cheek. "Please, Daniel. Please explain it all, so I can understand why you took my father away from me."

Normally, I'd prefer to do this without the tears, but he deserves to see exactly what he put me through. What he's still putting me through, so I hold nothing back.

"Fucking tell me!" I scream in his face, causing him to jump. "Start talking or I'm going to start cutting. At this point I don't think I will care which you choose, because it will be one or the other. Your choice."

"Ok... ok I'll explain. Please!" He leans his head back as far as he is able to try to move away from the tip of the knife, so I press it in harder and draw a drop of blood before removing it and returning to my seat on the table. "I've loved you since we were kids, Jen. You were over at my house one day playing and you left your hair tie in my room, and I thought you left it for me on purpose. I kept it in a special box I made out of one of my mom's old shoe boxes, and started a journal that night. I wanted to remember the day, and how special it was, forever.

I started collecting the things you'd leave around and documenting them after that. I was sure you loved me too and were afraid to say something, or you weren't ready, so I accepted your gifts and waited."

"They weren't gifts!" I snarl at him. "Those were my things. I always thought I was so fucking forgetful, losing things everywhere but it was just you, wasn't it?"

"I thought, if you were making me wait for you to be ready, that would be the next best thing."

"What about my dad? He loved you, Daniel. He took care of you! Why?"

My tears fall harder with his explanation. "I went to talk to him the day before he died. I told him how I felt and asked for his help in finally talking to you about being together." His face fills with rage before he continues. "He laughed at me, Jen. Laughed! He said I wasn't right for you and that we'd never make it as a couple. He told me you had already met your match, and he'd be back for you one day soon." Sneering at Evan, he shakes his head. "He told me he'd spoken to their grandmother, and she was working on getting Evan back here. That he'd always known you'd been waiting for him even though you didn't know it yourself yet."

My gasp is mirrored by Brandon's, and Evan jerks his gaze to mine. "He said that?"

"You love that, don't you? Mister Perfect being approved of by her father before you even got together. Well, he's not here to see it now, is he? I knew the second he told me Evan was coming back that I not only had to work faster, but he'd intervene if I tried to start something with you before it could happen. You always listened to whatever he said. So I followed him the next day and killed him, making it look like a robbery."

I close my eyes and my body shakes at his callous words. That statement killed any lingering feelings I had for him. Killed any remorse I have or would feel about making him hurt before he dies.

He should be very afraid right now.

"So, you killed him because he didn't think we would be a good couple? Because he didn't agree with you that we should be together? After a lifetime of treating you like his own son, you killed him. Just like that?"

"I had to, Jen! I did it for us! He was going to try to keep us apart! I'm sorry it hurt you, but I was there to pick up the pieces!"

"I don't give a fuck what you were there for, or that you're sorry." Deciding I've had enough, I turn away from him. "Evan, can you please put his gag back on? I don't want to hear anything else out of his worthless mouth."

"Of course," he tells me, leaning in for a sweet kiss. He whispers "I'm so sorry" into my ear before he pulls away and does as I asked.

"Jen, no. Please! We can work this out. I know you loved him but I ca-" His words are cut off by Evan slipping the gag over his mouth.

"Here's the thing, Daniel. Dad or no Dad, you never had a shred of a fucking chance with me. You're weak-minded, desperate, and pathetic." He tries fighting Evan but Brandon jumps up to help hold his head still while the gag is fastened. "You were nothing but a little brother to me. I have never been attracted to you in any way. I have never loved you as anything more than a friend. I have never thought any better of you than a purely platonic relationship." He's stopped fighting and is now staring at me in shock with tears running down his face. "You are nothing to me, Daniel Schulz, and you're about to experience all the pain you've inflicted on your victims."

I slide down off of the table again and step directly in front of him. Placing the knife to his cheek I drag the tip from his face to above his heart, leaving a thin slice that wells with blood in my wake before I lean up to whisper into his ear.

"You cut my heart out the second you killed my dad, Daniel, so I think I'll just keep yours instead. I hope it was worth it."

Evan, Brandon, and I head to the sitting room to gather ourselves for a few minutes. As much as I want to just kill him, after everything I've just heard I need to find out what they want as well. He attacked Brandon today and destroyed Evan's life for years. It's not just about me. It's about them too.

"Are you two ok?" Brandon asks after shutting the door behind him. Evan and I share a glance before he pulls me to him and holds me tight.

Speaking with my face pressed against his chest I revel in his deep rumble. "I'm so sorry about your dad. About all of it, Jen. I wish I'd seen it in both of them when we were younger, I feel like I missed so much. So many things could have been avoided."

"None of us saw it, not really." Brandon is pacing the room with his fists balled at his sides. "I always figured he had a crush on you, but he never said anything about it or acted like it was a big deal, so I let it ride. I knew nothing would ever come of it. He never even hinted that he was responsible for the pastor moving them away, and he sure as fuck never did anything to make me think he could be responsible for your dad. Never mind that he was capable of killing his own mom. Fuck, Jen. We missed all of it!"

I step away from Evan and stop Brandon in his path. Grabbing his hands, I make sure he's looking me in the eye before I start speaking. "We are not responsible for the fucked up behavior of that asshole. We loved him, we cared for him, and that wasn't good enough for him. We cannot, and I will not, carry that burden. What I will do is put him down like my dad trained me to." Waving Evan over to join us, I grab one of his hands too. "I can't think of a better way to honor my father than by using the skills he taught me to remove him and the threat he poses from society, can either of you?"

Both men shake their heads and squeeze my hands to show their support and approval. "So what's the plan here?" Evan asks. "Do we just kill him? Or is this going to be a Ryan type situation?"

"I don't know about you two," I reply while rolling my head on my shoulders, "but I don't think I have another week of torture in me. Honestly, I just want to inflict some pain and then get rid of him. Do either of you have a preference? I'll do it if you want or need it, but I'd prefer to spend my time elsewhere. It's more because he doesn't deserve any more of my time than anything else."

"I want to kill him myself for what he's done to all of you, but I can't." Brandon runs his hands over his face and grips his hair tightly. "I think I would best serve this whole thing as the cleanup crew. I feel like killing his mom upped our time table though. Once someone finds her they'll try to contact him, if someone doesn't look for him first because he doesn't show up for work. We can't risk anyone finding all of the shit in his attic and it bringing attention to you. I can go pack it all up, pack some of his stuff, then ditch his phone and car somewhere. I'll probably just need some help to get it down from the attic and loaded."

"You think you can do it by yourself? There's so much stuff in there." It's a lot of work to do by one person, but he does make a good point.

"Yeah, I got it. You two do what you need to here and I'll take care of the rest. I'll make sure it doesn't touch us."

"Thanks, Bran. Call if you need us, ok? He'll hold if he needs to, and if you're still there when we're done I'll send Evan to help while I clean up the mess."

We head back to the main room together. Evan is going to drive Brandon back in the UTV and give him the leftover boxes and packing materials we purchased to pack up my dad's things. Brandon puts on the pair of the gloves I hand him and searches Daniel's pockets, grabbing his car keys and phone. Once he has them he steps back and pulls the taser out of his own pocket.

"I just want you to know one thing." He pauses to take a deep breath and gather himself, but his voice still cracks when he continues and telling shimmer of tears fills his eyes. "I loved you like a brother. I would have killed or died for you. But knowing what you did, what you were trying to do? I will never forgive you, but only because after I leave this room and clean up your mess, you will be nothing to me, so my forgiveness won't matter. We will never waste another minute on the memory of you. More importantly, I will be by their side" he points at Evan and I while he gets closer into Daniel's face, "as their relationship develops. I will walk her down the aisle when they get married since her father is no longer there to. Because of you."

His tears fall free now, but he doesn't pause to wipe them away as he continues. "So fuck you Daniel. Fuck you for making us love you, and fuck you for thinking your selfish needs were more important than everyone else's. Fuck you for not fucking telling her how you feel and taking whatever happened like a man! Fuck you for believing your need for Jen was more important than her father being in her life.

"I'd tell you to have a nice life, but the little you have left is going to be decidedly the opposite. You deserve every single bit of it and more."

With those parting words Brandon turns to me, kisses me on my forehead, hands me the taser, and walks out to the UTV. Evan pulls me into his arms and looks down into my eyes. "Are you sure you'll be ok here for alone?"

"Yeah, I'm good. I may play a bit, I'm not sure yet." His chuckle brings a small smile to my face, which he kisses sweetly.

"Alright, I'll be back as quick as I can. I love you."

"I love you, too," I respond easily. Daniel's grunt of pain at hearing me say those words brings me unspeakable joy in the middle of this devastation. "Go. We'll be just fine, won't we sweetheart?"

I watch Evan follow Brandon out and smile as the lock clicks behind him. It'll probably take about 20 minutes to make it there and back, so I decide to start the party with a bit of mental torture and save the real fun for when Evan returns. Turning back to the table and retaking my seated position, I cross my legs and place my weapon filled hands in my lap. The blood from the cut I placed on him stains the white satin a lovely shade of crimson.

"Ryan didn't run away, you know." His brows lift in surprise and his gag muffled grunt sounds confused. "Evan and have I known where he is the whole time. Would you like to know? I'm surprised you didn't, to be honest. It's not like you weren't watching my every fucking move."

At his hesitant nod, I point to the freezer at the side of the room. "Some of him is still in there. The rest has probably already been eaten by the animals we fed him to. Gotta spread out the evidence, right?" At his violent head shake I giggle. "Oh, who am I talking to? Of course you know, officer. He's actually been dead for a few days now, but you were too stupid to notice, even though, again, you were watching my every fucking move. Evan and I kept him in here, exactly as you are, for about a week before killing him. He really did kill Gran, and he tried to attack me because of my tattoos." His brow creases in confusion. Funny how expressive he can be when his mouth is closed. "I know, right? They're fucking awesome! But apparently he'd been begging his father to 'let him have me' for years now, ever since they left. He came back for me but according to him my tattoos and piercings made me damaged goods. Evan came to try to save me when he found his Gran dying. She warned him Ryan was coming for me, and bam! Ryan The Deadbeat is out, and Evan is in. Literally." I waggle my eyebrows at him to drive home my crappy joke.

His head is shaking more and more, he obviously doesn't believe me, but if that's the case he isn't as good of a stalker as he thought he was. I decide to make myself more comfortable, so I quickly grab a chair from the sitting room and relax back into the cushions as I crack open the Diet Coke I grabbed and watch him.

"Wait. Did you think you were the only killer here?" Slurp. "I've been killing for years, D. Ryan wasn't my first, and you surely won't be my last. Evan and I work well together taking out the trash, just like my daddy taught me. I'd show you some pieces, but I've got enough clean up to do without having to rebag his body. It really is a shame, we could have all been a happy family together like we used to be."

At this point, he's pleading through his gag. I can tell he's begging me to let him speak, but I don't want to hear anything else from him. "I think that's why I never found anyone to be with, you know? No one was man enough to make me feel anything for them. Evan is sweet and respectful, but he also takes what he wants and has a violent and vindictive streak to match my own, and he is still practical about it all. And, I'm sure you noticed, he fucks like a jackhammer, which is a total plus, right? He's exactly what I need, not some pansy-assed fuckboy who can't admit his own feelings to the woman he loves because he's afraid of the inevitable and guaranteed rejection." I pause and take another obnoxious sip, shaking my head in mock sadness and noticing he's gone quiet. "Because, that's all you would have ever gotten. You understand that right? Rejected. There is no reality in which you and I would ever be together."

New tears are streaming down his cheeks, and his body is shaking with his muffled sobs. My attention moves away from him when I hear the door lock click once more and Evan enters. He notices Daniel's sad state and shakes his head with a smirk before placing an empty mason jar on the work table and then coming to stand at my side.

"Fuck's sake, Daniel. Man up. Play stupid games, win stupid prizes, right? That's what John always said. Actions have consequences and this is yours. Did you really think you could do this shit to Jen, and she'd just... what? Fall into your arms and embrace the crazy? Run off to Vegas and have a shotgun wedding because you put her in a white dress? Shit doesn't work that way, and Jen definitely doesn't.

Come on, baby girl. Let's go chat for a minute before we take care of him. I can't take the blubbering. At least Ryan was a man about things. I want to finish up here, so I can go back to working on our house."

I turn from Evan to Daniel as I stand and take Evan's hand. Daniel's sobs have stilled as he stares at me in shock.

"Oh, didn't I mention that?" I wince. "I guess I wasn't totally honest earlier. Evan and I have already moved in together. We also talked about getting engaged at the end of this year and plan to have a Halloween wedding in the clearing by the lake next year. I always wanted a Halloween wedding, so it's perfect. Guess we'll need to find you another groomsman, though, huh babe? Maybe your friend Mark from the other night can step in."

His agonized keening is music to my ears.

Chapter 49

Evan shuts the door behind us and pulls me into his arms. "Brandon is heading to Daniel's now. I told him not to worry about packing things nicely, just quickly, and to make sure he keeps the gloves on when he's past the bathroom door. Once he's done he'll call and I'll come out if I can. He also knows to wipe the ladder down from our previous visits."

"You think he's going to be ok? I'm not sure if he will be able to handle all of that."

"He's stronger than you think. He told me that even if it kills him, he's going to do it. He wants to pull his own weight." The heat from his body surrounding mine is a welcome addition since it's cold in here and I'm in a strapless dress.

"I don't doubt his strength, mental or otherwise. There's just a ton of shit up there, and I it's going to fuck with his head. He doesn't have the outlet I do though, so I worry."

"He can do it, and if he can't, we'll be able to help. Daniel can hang forever if we need to leave. I have no issue with him dying scared and alone, wondering if we'll ever come back for him."

"No, if I have my choice, I want him to slowly bleed out like Dad did. Scared and fully aware of the life leaving his body and knowing he can't do anything to stop it. Heart broken with the knowledge that his killer is someone he loves and trusted."

"Then that's what we'll do. I don't know if you noticed, but I brought you a mason jar." He smiles against my forehead when he mentions it.

"I did. What's it for?"

"His heart."

My body stills for a second before I pull back to look at him. "You heard that?" I blush slightly at his gesture, and I'm feeling like a total psycho, but come on! What other man would bring his girlfriend an empty mason jar so she can put the heart of her enemy inside? Without her having to ask for it first?

"Fuck yes I heard you. That shit made me hard enough that it was awkward driving Brandon back to the cabin. I didn't want you to go without a proper vessel for it. An empty Diet Coke can doesn't have the wow factor you really want."

Laughing, I step back and make my way to the door. "Let's get started. I told him about Ryan while you were gone. I want to fuck with him a bit more before we kill him. You're getting me all hot and bothered and it's making me petty since I still have to deal with him instead of tapping that ass." I laugh as I spank him lightly.

The moment we open the door and walk back into the cold room Daniel stops moving. He was trying to work his hands free, but he's secured so well it's impossible. "Nice try, but you won't get loose. Just ask Ryan. I was telling Evan that you didn't seem to believe me when I told you we killed him together."

"I'm not sure why you wouldn't. You know Jen's background and abilities, and obviously didn't have a problem stringing you up in here. Honestly, man, he was almost your ticket out of all of this. He told Jen something that made us assume his dad killed hers. We had no idea you were in any way involved."

"Guess you should have never moved your Tylenol," I say, shrugging. Daniel's brows furrow in confusion. "Funny how things work, huh?" I tilt my head to the side as I mock him. "I've been picking on you about moving that shit to your kitchen half our lives. You finally do it, and when I need it and I'm in your bathroom and it's not where it's always been? Of course, I'm going to go looking for it. We've never hidden things from each other so the new cabinet seemed a smart place to look."

My cell phone ringing interrupts my story, I head over to the table and see Brandon calling.

"What's wrong?" I ask.

Brandon hesitates in answering for a moment. "Um, well, nothing per se. It's just..."

"It's just what? What happened?" He's freaking me out, Evan comes over and rubs his hands along my arms to provide me with some warmth.

"I don't remember seeing it in the pictures you showed us... but, did you see a bunch of your panties up here?"

"Fucking excuse me?" I turn in place and glare at Daniel. "No! And how many is a bunch? And were they from my drawer or laundry?"

"Well, I'm not going to do a scent check or anything, Jesus!" Understandable. I still growl at him in irritation, though. "They may have been clean, but if they were, they aren't anymore. If you catch my meaning."

I turn away from Daniel and close my eyes, taking a deep breath to try to center myself. "Is that it? Is that the only thing that seems new?"

"I think this is some other shit from your apartment too, but yeah. I just wanted to fill you in, in case it changed your mind about what you wanted to do."

"Ok, thanks Brandon. Call if you need me. You're right, it does change things."

I hang up and turn back to Daniel after placing my phone gently on the table. "Daniel, I need you to answer a question for me. Can you do that?" His nod is hesitant, but it comes. "Did you, or did you not, destroy my apartment?"

He immediately begins shaking his head forcefully, trying to speak through the gag and pleading with his eyes for me to let him explain. "Evan? Please remove his gag. If he does anything other than explain to me how he has a new pile of my panties I didn't give him, after my apartment ironically happened to be broken into and destroyed within the last week, but not by him, feel free to beat the shit out of him again."

"Argh!" he groans once the gag is out of his mouth. "Jen, I swear, it wasn't me! You have to believe me!"

"I don't have to believe a fucking thing coming from your lying mouth, Daniel. Someone used my code to access my apartment. Only you, Brandon, Evan, and I have my code. Brandon and Evan were with me. So make me believe you. Tell me why I should." My hands are shaking. If I'm understanding Brandon correctly, and I have no doubt I am, this disgusting human hanging in front of me, begging for another chance, jacked off into a pile of my panties.

"I swear, I didn't! I mean, yes. I did go there the night you left my house sick once I knew Brandon was with you too. I just wanted to be surrounded by you for a little while because I was so worried about you. I grabbed a few pairs of your panties and some other things, but otherwise I left it in the exact same condition as when I got there, I swear!" Neither Evan nor I respond, we simply wait for him to continue. "Wait. There's footage! I can prove it! It was Ryan's dad, I have footage of him entering and exiting both of your apartments using a key. I can prove it!"

Well, at least we have proof our guess was correct. "And my panties? You thought... hey, Jen's not here. Might as well steal her panties since I'm already a giant fucking creeper? Take them home to my weird hidden room and beat off into them like the pathetic fuck I am?"

"It's not like that, Jen! Please, I'm so sorry. Let me go. I'll leave, I'll never bother you again! I understand now that you were never mine. I'll..."

His stream of pathetic begging is cut off by my phone ringing a second time. This time I decide to put it on speakerphone so everyone can hear. "Talk to me, Brandon. What now?"

"Two things. First, didn't you tell me some douchey friend of Evan's tried hitting on you when you went out with his friends? His name was Mark, right?"

"Yeah, he did. What about him?" Evan questions over my shoulder.

"Daniel pulled his wrap sheet, he's got some charges for possession and dealing."

"We all know that already. He was wild when he was younger but the boss knows about it. He's been clean for years." Daniel's head is hung in defeat. He's not even trying to fight, so there must be more coming.

"Well, according to his latest journal entry — what grown fucking man keeps a diary anyway? Seriously?"

"Brandon!" I snap, ready to be done with all of this.

"Right, sorry. According to this, Daniel had taken a stash of coke he pulled off of someone he arrested and pulled Mark for a traffic stop. He planted the coke on him and made a deal with him. Mark makes sure Evan has an accident on the job, and he not only goes free but gets to keep the drugs. If Evan dies, he gets a bonus, but it has to look like an accident. There's even an audio recording on one of those old handheld recorders in here. I'll keep it separate and bring it to you so you can have a chat with Mark."

I sigh and take a seat on the table again, exhausted and ready for this to be over. "And second?"

"Huh? Oh, yeah. So um, it looks like to get in the mood for the whole panty defiling thing, he watched a video."

"Of what?" Evan's voice is low and calm.

"Jen, in her bedroom at the cabin. During some... private time. She was alone and I think the camera was hidden on the bookshelf somewhere."

My body is shaking with rage, but my mind has reached an oddly calm state. "Anything else?" I ask, voice even.

"Not yet. Do you want me to keep calling, or should I stop?" He knows what the tone of my voice means better than anyone.

"I think we're good here. Thanks, Bran. Just call if you need help, I don't need any more updates."

I hang up and place the phone on the table next to me. "Daniel," I say in the same even tone. His head remains hung like a coward, so I snap. "Fucking look at me! Now." His eyes rise to meet mine and I can see the fear and anguish in them, and it does not move me. Evan is a silent sentinel beside me, letting me lead. "I'm not even going to address the two things I just learned. I'm simply going to ask you one thing, and if you ever cared about me you will answer me truthfully. Do you think you can do that?"

With tears streaming down his face, he nods slowly, still not speaking. "Is there anything you know, any information you've gathered while stalking me, that would be important for me to be aware of? Anything that impacts my life or safety. Like, was that the only time Ryan's dad came around? You're not leaving this room alive, but if you ever truly felt something that wasn't your own selfish need where I'm concerned, please tell me, so I can be prepared and keep myself safe."

After a deep breath, he nods again. "I've seen him outside of both of your places a few times. He couldn't get in until the other night when he somehow had keys. He did leave a rose once, I'm not sure why, but I took it so you wouldn't find it and freak out." My snort of disbelief makes him pause for a moment. "He also... he also came to me a few days after the funeral. He told me he knew I'd been in love with you since we were kids because Ryan had told him. He also said he thought Evan had done something to Ryan so he could have you instead, and if I could help him prove it you'd finally be mine. He doesn't believe Ryan would have run, since his taking over his position in the community depended on him bringing you back as his wife. I assured him you wouldn't have had anything to do with it, but he doesn't believe it. Which, I guess he was right anyway."

"Anything else? Anything you can warn me about as far as his plans?"

"No. Only that he won't stop until he finds Ryan. He's going to keep coming around."

"Thank you. Evan?" I turn to him and his face is void of expression. "Do you have any questions, or anything?"

"Nope. But I'd like to put him on the table, if that's ok with you."

"What? No! Why? Jen, please! I'm sorry. Just let me go. Please!" His pleas are high-pitched wails that grate on my ears and my already shredded nerves.

"Sure. Gag him first though. I don't want to hear anything else from him."

"Got it." Evan presses a kiss to my lips before moving to replace the gag. Daniel tries to resist but a swift left to the jaw dazes him long enough for Evan to secured it in place. We work quickly to position the table under him and his body secured so he can't fight us. I move back to the seat I brought in earlier and pick up my discarded drink. Evan calmly walks to my tool chest and grabs my largest mallet, then comes back to my side to hand me a bag of gummi bears he'd hidden in his back pocket. I squeal in excitement and tilt my head up for a kiss which he happily provides. Before standing up straight he whispers "I'm going to leave the killing for you, baby girl. I'm only going to maim him a little."

With a mouth full of delicious torture snacks, I tell Alexa to play my "Freak-nasty" playlist and sit back to relax while Evan works to the sound of calming instrumental music. Daniel's eyes are locked on mine, pleading with me to forgive him, or save him, or something, but I don't care. He dies today. He died the day he killed my dad, he just wasn't smart enough to realize it yet.

CHAPTER 50

Evan grabs Daniel by the jaw and forces him to meet his gaze. "The only reason I haven't gouged your eyes out with a rusty spoon is because I want you to see it when Jen slides her blade into you. That way, the last thing you will ever see is the woman you love leaving you for dead while she's in the arms of another man. The man you tried to remove from her life in more than one way."

He releases his jaw and flips the mallet in his hand, end over end. "In the meantime..."

Wham!

Evan gives no warning as he slams the mallet down on Daniel's hands. His scream is something I have never heard before. He waits until the screams turn to moans, then turns to face me. "I know I told you I wanted to take his hands, but I figured it would probably kill him before you were ready. This way I can destroy them for ever touching you, or thinking about touching you, or touching himself while thinking about you, and we don't have to rush. We don't want him to bleed out before you get to the good stuff."

I'm pretty sure the smile I give him is a completely lovesick one, because he smirks. "Thanks, handsome. You give the best presents." He winks at me, and I toss a bear up for him to catch with his mouth. He catches it expertly and in the same motion spins back around to bring the mallet down again.

Over the sound of Daniel's continued screams, Evan and I begin discussing some changes to the original plans I made to the master and other upstairs areas. With him moving in officially, we haven't talked about making it our space instead of just mine. Luckily, he likes my aesthetic, but he's started suggesting things I hadn't thought of, like a bench in the shower and a new upgraded closet system. He also has a coworker who does wiring for surround systems, so he can link the master to the house system easily. Dad never felt the need for it, but we'll use it frequently. Also, heated tile floors in the bathroom for those cold winter days?

After a few minutes Daniel's wailing has gotten on my nerves. "Can you finish up? I don't want to rush you or anything, but that noise is fucking annoying. Ryan at least took his licks like a man."

"Of course. We can finish this discussion later in the hot tub." He winks at me, turns, and completes his task with a few swift strikes. Daniels hands lay against the table bloody, swollen, and very obviously broken, and his screams finally stop when he passes out from the pain. I groan in a mix of relief and irritation, finish the last sip of my drink, and rise from my seat to make my way to the table.

"Let's open his shirt to make things easier. Bloody cloth is a pain in the ass during disposal." Grabbing the scissors on my tool tray, I begin cutting at the hem while Evan helps hold the fabric taught. Color catches my eye as I reach his chest, which is weird since there wasn't anything there a week ago. Once his shirt is cut open completely, I spread the fabric apart so I can see the addition clearly.

He has a new tattoo. It's so fresh it's still covered in the film tattoo artists put on it after it's done, and completely covers his chest.

It's my fucking name. With goddamned daisies all around it.

"Why daisies? I thought you never liked them."

"I have no clue," I sigh. "I don't like them, I never have. I don't hate them or anything," I clarify, "I just think they're boring. I have zero clue why he would do this. Between this and the dress, and tying me up, and hurting Brandon... he has to have broken with reality or something. I thought he'd know me better than to do all of this, but I guess it's pretty evident we lost him a while ago."

I trade my scissors for a scalpel and ask Evan to wake Daniel for me. Once his sputters turn to low moans I slap him across the face hard enough that my hand stings, causing him to startle and quiet as he stares at me.

"I was done, you know? I was simply going to kill you and move on, but in my preparation I discovered your new and very confusing artwork. Honestly, I'd ask why daises, but I don't fucking care. Unfortunately for you, the only part of me I plan on allowing you to take with you into the afterlife is going to be the memory of me sliding my father's blade into your gut and walking away. It means this" I tap my scalpel against the center of the tattoo, "has to go, I'm afraid."

His muffled "no, please" means nothing to me as I start cutting. Not even a minute in he passes out again, but I don't care. I want my name off of his body where he has no right to have it. My hands are slick with the blood and that is running down his chest in rivulets, spreading across the table and soaking into this mockery of a wedding dress. The irreverent thought that if I was before, I'm surely no longer pure enough for an actual white wedding dress slips through my mind and before I can stop myself I release a snort of laughter.

"What's so funny?"

"Nothing. Just laughing to myself about how a white wedding dress probably wasn't in the cards for me anyway."

He walks up to me as I make the final cut and peel the strip of skin from his body in one single piece. "Impressive," he compliments, turning me and pulling me to him. I place the scalpel and skin on my tool tray and smile as he wraps my bloody hands around his neck so he can hold me closer. "I don't give a fuck if you wear cheetah print, or something dyed red by the blood of your enemies, but I will be seeing you in a different wedding dress eventually. I'm going to fuck you in this one before we burn it, though. I have the feeling we'll be having an awful lot of bonfires this year, maybe I'll build you a big fire pit down by the water and it can be a weekly thing while we go through all of his stuff."

"I love that idea," I tell him, pulling him down to me for a scorching kiss. I love that I finally have someone who has good and bad pieces that fit my own. Someone who praises me for my ability to skin a living man, then touches me sweetly with that man's blood still on my hands.

"Let's finish up. No matter what he says, Brandon is going to need help." I pull him down for another kiss, then ask him to wake our guest one last time. I ready myself with my father's knife, once again tucked out of sight in the folds of the billowing skirt.

I feel like I have too much practice at waiting for men to stop whimpering after being woken up with a hose to the face at this point, I need new material. "Fucking shut up already!" I snap. His body is shaking with pain and sobs, and I genuinely cannot be fucked to deal with this dude anymore. At least Ryan had the balls to suffer with some grace. "I'm sure you can tell I have removed my name from you completely. I'll be burning it later on tonight with this disgusting dress."

"After I've fucked you in it," Evan growls, wrapping an arm around my stomach from behind me and licking a path from my shoulder to my ear.

"Right, after that, of course." I pause to examine Daniel one last time, and allow myself one small moment of pain. "I loved you," I confess in a broken whisper, a single tear slide down my cheek. "I loved you with my whole heart. You were my family, Daniel. I'm sorry that wasn't enough for you." I clear my throat and wipe my cheek against my shoulder to remove the errant tear.

"I thought I'd lost this forever, you know?" I hold the knife up to the light, letting it glint off of the deadly sharp blade. "He was so excited when he opened it that Christmas, and to think I'd lost both of them? It hurt so much more." I run my fingers along the edge of the blade, lightly enough not to cut myself, but enough to determine that it's still incredibly sharp.

"If for nothing else, thank you for keeping this safe for me."

I make eye contact with him and slam the blade straight down into his gut. This new scream is longer and louder than any he's released yet. "Goodbye, Daniel. For your sake, I hope you bleed out quicker than Dad did."

Removing the knife and watching the blood flow from his newest wound, I wipe the blade off on my dress and place it back on the tray. Extending my hand to Evan I say "Come on, Ev. You promised to fuck me out of this dress."

Chapter 51

Evan fittingly picks me up in a bridal hold and turns to take me back to the sitting room. Daniel's agonized howls are still muffled, and he's screaming my name but I don't care. Neither of us even acknowledge him, his fate has been sealed, and he is no longer our problem.

He kicks the door closed behind us when we reach the sitting room. "Part of me wants to fuck you in front of him, so he can see you're mine one last time. I'm not going to let him see you like that though. Not again. He's stolen that from you at least once, he won't have it on his last day." Placing me down in front of him he slips his fingers into my hair to hold me tight. "I don't think I've ever seen you look more beautiful. You're like some ancient warrior goddess, covered in the blood of your enemy. I need you to know that I am in awe of you, and no matter what has happened, and will ever happen, I love you. I am with you every step of the way, no matter what."

My eyes once again well with tears, but this time they're happy ones. "I love you too," I tell him simply.

"I know." His smirk is devastating and mischievous. "Now, take that dress off so I can erase his filthy touch from your skin. No one will ever touch you again, and if they try they'll end up like Daniel. Broken and bleeding. Possibly even dead."

"I love it when you talk sweet to me," I say, laughing and batting my eyelashes at him. Turning away from him, I peer back over my shoulder. "Unzip me?"

His gaze is hot as he runs it from my head to my toes. "Hands on the wall" he says quietly. "Face forward."

I consider resisting for about a half of a second, but honestly want to see where he's going with this so I comply. The warmth of his body pressing against mine as he steps up against me sends a quick shiver of anticipation through up my spine, and the shiver turns to heat when he licks up my neck and whispers "Good girl. Now, don't move" into my ear before biting the lobe gently.

I'm not sure I'll ever tire of hearing him say those words. Especially since I know what comes next.

He presses kisses along my shoulders and nibbles the base of my neck as his hands move to the zipper at my back. His mouth follows the path of his hands and every inch of revealed skin is pampered and loved. The moment the zipper is finally undone he pulls the fabric of the dress so it drops off of me and pools at my feet, leaving me only in my pair of dark blue lace cheeky panties. His hands caress my skin, starting at my fingertips and moving up my arms to my shoulders and then back down my spine to my waist. When he steps back up against me the skin of his chest meets my back. I have no idea when he took his shirt off, but his pants are still on and his erection presses hard and large against my ass.

His warm hands continue their languid path around my stomach and up to caress and fondle my breasts. My body is trembling in anticipation. The heat of his hands is a balm against my chilled skin and I'm aching for him to touch me more aggressively. I drop my head back against his shoulder, giving him better access to my neck and releasing a long, guttural moan when he pinches my nipples. His right hand rises to tighten around my throat and his left traces a slow path down my stomach and under my panties.

The combination of the tightening of his hand around my throat and his pleased rumble when his fingers find how wet I am makes me feel like I'm seconds away from orgasm, and he's barely even touched me. "Hmm. I knew you'd be ready for me, but you always are, aren't you?"

"Yes," I hiss when he pushes two fingers inside me.

"Remember what I said, baby girl. Don't. Move."

"Huh?" My question turns into a pout when he removes his hand from my panties and pulls away from me entirely. He places a hand between my shoulder blades and presses me towards the wall so my ass is sticking out slightly. Dropping to his knees behind me, he kneads my ass then slides my panties down to my feet, picking them up one at a time to remove both my panties and the pooled gown. I can hear the fabric hit the floor somewhere behind me.

"Oh, shit!"

My shout escapes me unbidden when I he bites my ass. I yelp when my other cheek stings from a slap.

"Hush, Jen. Let me work."

"Yes, sir," I pant. I'm pretty sure I would bark like a dog right now if it meant he didn't stop what he's doing. Maybe I'll try later to fuck with him.

Thoughts of sexy shenanigans flee the moment his lips close around my clit. My eyes roll back in my head and my forehead drops to rest against the wall in front of me. His fucking mouth is magic. His grip on my hips is tilting me and keeping me exactly where he wants me. I'm so close to coming that I whimper when he pulls away from me, but I shudder at the puff of air escaping him with his laugh.

"Turn around," he demands. "Hands behind you against the wall. One leg up on my shoulder."

I spin so fast I'm almost dizzy. Leaning my back against the wall I lift my left leg and place it on his shoulder, staring into his burning eyes. "You're going to cum on my tongue, then on my cock while I fuck you against this wall, do you understand me?"

"Yes, sir" I say.

"Good, then we're going to go clean up our mess, and start the rest of our lives together. You and me, Jen. forevzies." He smiles at my nod. "Now, where was I?"

His tongue traces a path from my opening to my clit and his fingers enter me once more. I was already on the brink of orgasm when he stopped, and it doesn't take long to climb back to that shining edge. Bracing my shoulders and hands against the wall and my foot against his back I'm able to roll my hips to meet his mouth and increase the pressure. One of my hand finds his hair without me realizing I've moved and the growl he releases tips me over the edge. The climax slams into me so hard that my leg on his shoulder and his hand on my ass are the only things keeping me upright. The additional vibrations that hit me with his rumbling laugh send me into overdrive and eventually I have to beg him to stop, pull back, anything before I fall completely apart.

Once I can stand on my own again, he gently removes my leg from his shoulder and rises to stand in front of me. My eyes are closed and my head is resting against the wall while I try to catch my breath and even though I'm wrung out, in the best way, the sound of the metal on his belt and his zipper releasing makes my heart speed in my chest again. I whimper and nibble my lip, worried I can't handle much more tonight.

"You can take it, Jen. Give me one more, ok baby? I need to be inside you after everything that's happened. I need to feel you around me to prove it to myself you're ok and this is over. I was so afraid I was going to lose you tonight, or I'd be too late, and he'd have done something horrible to you." He's cupping my face in both hands and by the time he's stopped speaking I'm looking into his brilliant green eyes. The tears rimming his green eyes almost breaks my heart, but we made it through all of this together and I'm going to remind him every day that I'm here, and I'm his.

"I love you," I tell him. "There is nothing on this Earth that could take me away from you. You and I will kill anything and anyone who tries. We already have, right?" I pull him into a deep kiss and raise my leg so my knee hooks around his trim hip. "Now, prove to both of us that I'm still alive, and I'm still yours."

"God damned right, you are," he snarls as he lines the tip of his cock up with my opening. I cry out when he slams home and bring both of my legs up to wrap around his waist. He's holding me up with his hands around my hips and using them to pick me up and slam me down on his cock with increasingly forceful thrusts. Each time he bottoms out his base comes into contact with my clit and since I'm already so swollen and sensitive it only takes a few strokes for my body to start tensing in preparation to cum again. The grunt he releases is almost pained when my body begins to stiffen and I tighten around him. His thrusts become less rhythmic and more forceful, and within a handful of strokes I'm pushed over the edge.

My fingernails drag roughly across the skin of his back, and before I can worry about whether I hurt him or drew blood his body shivers, and he begins pulsing inside of me with a growled "Fuuuuck!"

Fuck is right. I don't think I can feel my legs.

CHAPTER 52

Evan moves us over to the couch and we take a few minutes to catch our breath and collect ourselves. I'd love to stay here all day with him, but we do have a body to dispose of and it's getting late.

"Are you ready?" I ask him. "I want to wrap this up and relax tonight. We can get drunk and feel each other up later in the hot tub."

His laugh brings a smile to my face. "Sounds perfect. Did you bring your change of clothes back here?"

"No. I don't want to get anything else dirty. I'll take care of the body while wearing the dress. The bloodier it gets, the happier it makes me. Then, we'll burn it while we soak later. A nice romantic bonfire. With Brandon," I laugh.

"I'm not going to lie and say I like the idea of you putting it back on, but I get it." He walks over to where my panties and dress lay and brings them over to me. "Turn around, I'll zip you. I have to say, this dress is pretty, bit it is never in a million years something I would have picked for you. That asshole was delusional."

I snort. "You think? Come on, I want to finish this."

We emerge from the back room, expecting to find he'd died while we were busy entertaining ourselves.

"Fuck's sake," I growl. His chest is rising and falling in stops and stutters. The only other movement in the room are the tears tracking down the sides of his face and the blood dripping onto the floor and pooling in the drain beneath him. Muttering "I don't have time for this shit" to myself, I stride to my tool tray and pick up my knife once more.

"Sorry, D. I've got shit to do. Enjoy Hell, 'kay?"

His screams are weak and his eyes plead for me to stop, but I became numb to him and what he wanted days ago. He's lost so much blood already that when I slit his throat the usual geyser is more of a sad stream, and the silence that follows is bliss.

"Why don't you go ahead and clean up? I'm going to start getting this taken care of."

This, not him. He's not a him anymore. Evan leans in to give me a kiss before opening the mason jar and turning towards the bathroom to take a shower.

"Alexa, play playlist Warm Fuzzies." Evan huffs a laugh when the first notes of "Mein Herz Brennt" by Rammstein starts playing through the speakers.

"Appropriate," he calls over his shoulder as he walks into the bathroom and starts the shower.

Laughing, I sing along with Till as I begin my incision on Daniel's chest. I make quick work of opening his chest cavity with my bone saw and reaching his heart. Years of practice butchering animals means it takes only moments for me to remove his heart from his chest and drop it unceremoniously into its new home. My bloody hand leaves fingerprints on the glass and some of the cooling liquid drips on the rim and pools in the bottom of the jar. I leave the lid off until I can wipe the whole thing down.

"All done?" Evan asks, coming up behind me and kissing my bare shoulder.

"Yep," I chirp, turning to face him. "You heading out?"

"Are you sure you don't want me to stay here and help you? I don't want you to be alone in this." The concern on his face is heartwarming, but unnecessary.

"I'm good, I promise. He's just another animal that needs to be disposed of now. The most important thing is getting everything out of the attic and making sure we're in the clear. Brandon needs help. I'll call you if I need you, ok?" It's hard, but I'm keeping my bloody hands to myself so I don't contaminate anything on him before he leaves. More than anything at this moment, I want to be held by him, but it will have to wait.

"Ok. Promise me you'll call me when you're almost ready, so I can come back and pick you up?"

"Yes, sir!" I chirp with a mock salute.

Evan smiles and leans in for another scorching kiss, making sure not to touch my bloody dress or arms, but still cupping my face and dominating my mouth. "Good girl," he whispers with a sex smirk after pulling back. "Call if you need anything, even just to talk through this. I love you, Jen. I'm so sorry all of this was necessary."

"Me, too" I admit with a sad smile. "Go on, I got this."

Much like most of my other playlists, Warm Fuzzies is filled with songs that are pretty much the exact opposite of what the name suggests, which is what I need to keep me going right now. It's mostly songs about angst, darkness, and betrayal and includes mostly rock and pop. Things I can sing, dance, and scream to.

My mind is in turmoil. My thoughts vacillate between anger, sadness, numbness, relief, and denial. I'm both glad to be doing this alone, and desperate to call Evan and Brandon back to be with me while I work. There have been a few times when I've noticed teardrops falling from my face to land below, but I simply ignore them and continue working. Evan and Brandon have sent a few texts to check in with me, but I don't respond since I don't want to get my phone bloody.

It takes a few hours, but I finally have his body broken down properly. My dress and arms are coated in his blood, so I wash my hands and put gloves on, so I can sort everything into the proper containers without leaving bloody prints everywhere.

By the time I'm finished, I'm exhausted. Body and soul. Heart and mind. I want to take a long ass nap and an even longer vacation somewhere with a never ending supply of alcoholic beverages and a no pants rule, but I'll probably have to settle for pizza, Jack, and a hot tub. All in all, not a bad evening.

I decide to strip down in the middle of the cold room while "Your Woman" by White Town plays, and rinse off quickly with the hose before cleaning up. I've never cleaned in only my panties before so it feels weird, but I'm honestly just thankful he left them on me. If he'd taken my panties as well as my bra I'd have cheerfully cut his dick off, but I'm glad I didn't have to deal with that on top of everything else.

Mostly, because... ew.

I'm so used to the cleaning process that the dress is bagged, the body parts are stowed, and the surfaces are gleaming in no time. Evan and Brandon are done and will be on their way back to the cabin to unload everything within the hour, so I head to the bathroom to finally take a shower and make sure I remove every drop of his disgusting blood from my body.

The water is scorching hot, the steam rising to fill my lungs and chase the chill from the air. It takes the releasing of my tense muscles for me to realize my entire body has been shaking. I'm not sure if it's from the cold, grief, anger, or some combination of them all. As I let the water beat down on my skin and warm my bones it takes me a moment to realize the song has changed. Phil Collins' "In The Air Tonight" has started and the final crack that shatters the shield I've been building since the moment I started planning his death.

I fall to my knees since my legs no longer have the strength to keep me upright. The scream I let loose comes from the absolute depths of my soul. While I allowed myself to mourn my dad, it's almost like I couldn't fully accept he was stolen from me until he received justice. The rage, despair, and heartbreak I felt upon learning of his death has come back to me and has been made exponentially worse with the knowledge it was Daniel who did it.

I don't mourn Daniel.

I mourn the relationship I thought we had. The person I thought he was. The brother I grew up with, and the member of my family.

I mourn Brandon's loss of innocence at the hands of Daniel's crimes.

I mourn my father and the time we lost. The milestones we never got to experience together, and the heartbreak I do not doubt he suffered at the hands of a man he treated as his own son.

I mourn the fact that I am now without a single blood family member.

I mourn Daniel's mom and regret that she died because of his selfish desires.

I mourn Evan's Gran and the fact that she wasn't able to see the fruit of her efforts — her grandson being safe and happy, living the life he always wanted.

I even mourn Ryan a bit. Not that I lost him or had to kill him, but I mourn the years I convinced myself he was someone that he wasn't. I mourn the person he could have been if his father hadn't corrupted him.

I don't know how long I've been lying on the floor of my shower. The song has changed and the water is starting to cool when I slowly come back to myself and my surroundings. After a few deep breaths I have myself together enough to rise and start washing. Having showered here enough times I know I have about ten more minutes until the water gets cold. Each passing moment of self care and evidence removal allows me to rebuild my walls. I use a loofah cloth on my skin and a nail brush on my fingers and toes to make sure I clean blood out of any crevices I may have missed.

By the time I've finished my shower and gotten dressed, Evan is back and waiting for me on the work table.

"Everything go ok?" I ask him as I emerge from the bathroom.

"Yeah. Everything has been loaded into the room behind your dad's closet for now. We figured that was the safest place. Brandon also forged a note in Daniel's handwriting saying 'I'm sorry.' He left it with his mom's house keys, his gun, and his cell phone on his bed." I make an impressed sound as I step up between his legs and his face creases with concern as he cups my face. "You ok baby girl? I've been worried about you since I left."

I sigh and close my eyes, leaning into his comforting touch. "I'm ok. Just missing my dad and glad this is over, you know?"

"I know. We figured someone might have seen my truck, so we came up with a reason for me to be there, just in case. We're going with the remodel story. I'll say he asked me to come over so I could measure for kitchen cabinets. I did it while he wasn't there because we're putting in an order for the cabin tomorrow and my guy will give me a discount for more volume. I took the measurements and will order something simple for proof, then I'll donate them when they come in. Brandon left everything in the bedroom because I'd have no reason to go back there and see it."

"Smart," I say. "I can't believe I didn't think about your truck being seen. I'm sorry." I shake my head in frustration. That could have been the end of everything!

"Don't worry about it, we're a team, right?" I lean into him and put my chin on his shoulder, reveling in his warmth as he wraps his arms around me.

"Come on, we picked up Chinese and ice cream on the way home. Let's go relax for the rest of the evening. Everything else will still be here tomorrow."

Chapter 53

Two days later we are all in the kitchen making dinner when my doorbell rings. Brandon stops speaking mid sentence and I almost laugh at how comically terrified his face is.

"Chill. We got this, ok? We knew it was coming eventually." I pat him on the shoulder as I pass and head to get the door. "Keep making dinner, and stick as close to the truth as possible. Everything is fine."

I open the door to two officers, an older black male and younger white woman. "Ma'am, are you Jenevive Martin?" the older of the two asks.

"I am. Can I help you?" Brows furrowed, I look from one of them to the other.

"I'm Officer Caldwell, and this is Officer Dane," he says. "Could we come in and speak with you for a bit?"

"Um, can I ask what this is about first?" I make sure a healthy dose of confusion is the only thing showing on my face.

"I'm sorry to have to tell you this, Ms. Martin, but your friend Daniel's mother was found dead this morning, and we're trying to locate Daniel."

"Oh my gosh! Are you sure it's her? Yes, please, come in. My boyfriend and best friend are in the kitchen." I usher them to the kitchen where the guys are joking while they continue prepping dinner. Evan turns when I walk around the corner and startles when he sees my face and the two officers behind me.

"Jen? Baby what's wrong? What's happening?" He steps up to me wiping his hands with a dish towel. Brandon turns when Evan speaks and his face blanches at the sight of the officers.

"Thi is Officers Caldwell and Dane. I think... I guess they're looking for Daniel? His mom died yesterday and it sounds like they can't find him."

"Mrs. Shultz is dead? What happened?" Brandon circles the island and pulls out a stool to sit down. He's still devastated Daniel killed her, so it's not an act.

"Please, sit. How we can help?" I indicate the seats down the island from Brandon and head to the fridge. "Would either of you like something to drink? Water? Coffee?"

They both accept water and start asking questions once they're settled. According to them, Mrs. Schultz was the victim of a robbery. They've been trying to locate Daniel as he's her next of kin, but he hasn't been into work the last two days and he's not answering his phone or at his door at home.

"I haven't heard from him in the last few days either. We had a bit of a spat and I figured he was avoiding me."

"What was your fight about?" Officer Dane asks me.

I give Evan a sad, soft smile. "We were fighting about Evan. We grew up with him, and he left for a few years without saying goodbye due to no fault of his own. He and his cousin came back recently and we all reconnected. Brandon and I welcomed them once we knew what had happened, but Daniel wasn't so happy about it. When he came over the other night, I told him Evan and I are dating, and he kind of flipped out about it." I shrug and take a sip of my drink.

"Why was he angry?"

"I honestly don't know. He was spouting off about how we couldn't trust them, and what if he leaves again like Ryan."

"Who is Ryan?" Officer Caldwell asks.

"My cousin," Evan answers. "We moved back here together to live with my grandmother a few months ago. He's been gone for a few weeks now. Sadly, we think he pushed Gran down the stairs and fled. The police have been looking for him since she died, but we haven't heard from him and I don't think my uncle has either. Not that he'd tell me."

"So, when was the last time you all saw Daniel? Do you know where he could be?"

"No. Unless he was with us, his mom, or working he didn't do a lot. Sometimes he'd go out with other officers, but not often. He was here the other night looking at kitchen cabinet samples with me, but I was the only one who saw him. He left before Evan and Brandon arrived."

"And where were the two of you?" Officer Caldwell glances from Evan to Brandon.

Brandon answers this time. "We were at my place for a few after work, he was helping me fix a shelf since I'm hopeless with that shit. We stopped at Daniel's place on the way here to measure his kitchen for a cabinet order."

"You were there without him?" Officer Dane's asks, expression dubious.

"Yeah. Daniel, Jen, and I all have keys or codes to each other's places in case of emergency. I used my key since it was a last minute thing. That way he wouldn't have to drive back to his house from here to let us in."

"And why was it last minute?"

"I was going to put in an order with my cabinet guy the next day for the upstairs bathroom here. Daniel wanted to redo his kitchen and my guy gives me a volume discount, so I offered to add his order on to ours. That's why he was looking at samples with Jen. I can show you the receipt if you need to see it."

"Sure, thanks," Officer Caldwell nods. Evan pulls it up on his phone and shows it to them.

"I'm sorry," Brandon breaks in, "but what about Mrs. Schultz? What happened to her? And what will happen if you can't find Daniel? What about a funeral, or any other arrangements? They don't have any other family, and she deserves to be put to rest."

"Unfortunately, we don't have those details. You can call the medical examiner's office and speak with them there. If no one claims her, she will be buried by the state. I'm pretty sure if you claim her you have to pay the expenses."

I walk to Brandon and wrap an arm around him. "We'll call tomorrow, and I'll cover her expenses. If Daniel surfaces, and he wants to, he can pay me back. She's been good to us though, so I'll take care of it."

Brandon's shoulders droop in relief. "Thanks, Jen."

Kissing the top of his head, I turn to the officers. "So, how can we help? What do you need from us?"

Officer Dane examines me with distaste. I'm not sure why, but she seems to not like me. "We wanted to see if you knew where he could be. According to several of his coworkers the two of you were an item."

"Sorry, but no. Daniel was like a brother to me, has been since we were kids. We did spend a lot of time together. After Ryan and Evan moved away when we were kids it was just Daniel, Brandon, and I for the last four years. Then when Ryan and Evan came back, Ryan joined us for a time before leaving again. It's been the four of us for the last few weeks, though."

"I see. And you're sure you weren't seeing Daniel and then dropped him when Evan came back?"

This bitch.

Raising an eyebrow I meet her gaze. "I don't think I appreciate what you're accusing me of. Daniel was my friend, nothing more. He never has been. If you've got something to ask, ask."

"Fine," she sneers. "Do you know where Daniel is? Is he here? I want to know how and why you're offering to pay for funeral expenses for someone who isn't a family member."

I wonder if I should warn her that Bad Cop won't work on me. "No, he's not. And no, I don't. You're welcome to search my home because I have nothing to hide. I am offering to pay for her funeral expenses because Mrs. Schultz was a good woman, and she always welcomed us into her home. She was very sick, but she did everything she could to help me when my father died last year. I'm able to afford it because both of my parents are dead and left me a healthy inheritance. I still choose to work despite that, so I can easily afford it, and since Daniel was my family, I will take care of his if he can't." I dismiss Officer Caldwell and turn back to Officer Dane.

"You are welcome to search the house, my apartment, or any of my property you like. I can also show you my phone log of calls and texts sent to him the last two days that have gone unanswered. Since I have a key and his permission to enter, I'm also happy to go to his house with you and unlock it if you'd like to do a wellness check. If it would help your search, I can officially report him missing. I assume you think he's in danger?"

"We're not sure at this time. All of that would be good, though, thank you," he says.

I've decided I'm no longer dealing with Officer McBitchface. I pull my phone and show him the history of calls and texts that went unanswered, and so do Evan and Brandon. Taking them to search the house and show them he isn't here, I get side-eye from the skank when they realize Evan lives with me. She's not my mom though, so she can suck it.

Evan and Brandon put the dinner components away while I file a missing person's report. The officers follow us in my car to Daniel's house, and I give them the key and alarm code, and we wait in the car for them to do the wellness check. The three of us are silent as we wait, and it takes about ten minutes for them to come back outside. We exit the car and meet them at the edge of the driveway.

"Is he there? Did you see anything?"

Officer Caldwell gives me an apologetic wince. "He's not here, but we did find some concerning things. We're going to have to consider this a crime scene, so I need to have you go back home now. I'm going to have to keep the key too, I hope you don't mind."

"Of course," I respond woodenly. "But, is he hurt?" I ask as Brandon grabs my hand. "Was his house broken into too? The guys were just there, they can probably tell you if anything is different."

"No, ma'am. Nothing is damaged and he's not there. I'll call you if we have any updates, ok? Go on home, we'll take it from here." He hands me his card. "Please call me immediately if you hear from him."

"Sure, of course. You'll call if there's anything you need? Or if you find him?"

"Absolutely. Thank you for your help, Jenevive. And you guys too. We'll be in touch."

We shake hands with him and head back to the car. We're again silent until we turn into my long driveway.

"Masterful," Brandon says. "Also dinner was ruined so I ordered pizza. I'm starving."

A small lump sits on my front porch when we pull up to the house. "What is that?" I ask.

"No idea, I can't see it well enough." Evan jumps out of the car and walks up while I park in the garage. Brandon and I walk to join him, but he's standing in front of it blocking our view. His posture is rigid and his fists are clenched at his sides.

"Ev? What's wrong?" He spins to face us and the rage on his face shocks me so much I inadvertently take a step back. "Ev?" I repeat, unsure of what's going on.

"I'm going to fucking kill that man. I swear to God, Jen. I'm going to gut him like the fucking coward he is!"

Confused, I step up to his side. It's a single red rose, exactly like the one in Daniel's attic and it's covered in blood and holding down a torn piece of paper. The page has six words scrawled across it:

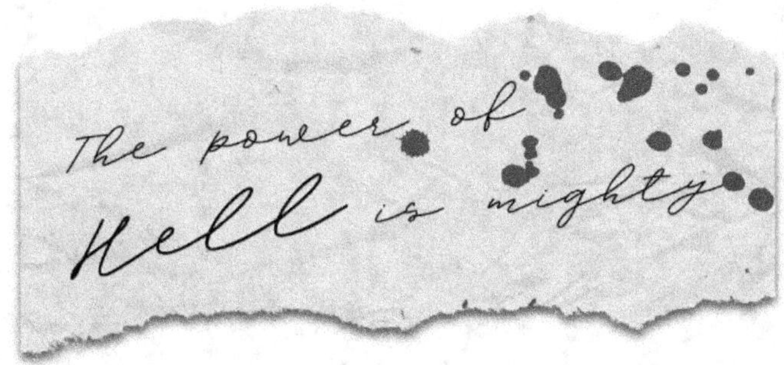

EPILOGUE

T he young woman stirs, consciousness slowly filtering into her mind. Groggy, she tries to shift her body into a more comfortable position, but she's met with resistance when she attempts to move her legs. Her eyes open slowly, heavy and sleep crusted, and it takes several moments for her to be able to focus her vision enough to see that her feet and hands are chained together by thick, dark links. Links that are tethered to an iron loop bolted into the cracked cement floor.

Where is she? When did she get here, and why is she here?

The last thing she remembers is being called downstairs by her mother while she was folding laundry. She could only remember turning the corner, seeing her mother's anguished face and stopping short in confusion, then... nothing.

Her head is throbbing in time with her heartbeats and her body aches all over from laying on the cold unforgiving ground. Looking around for something or someone to help her, it's obvious there is nothing she can use to take these chains off. The room is maybe fifteen square feet and lit by a single, bare bulb in the center of the water stained ceiling. It is completely bare except for her, her chain, one lone wooden chair bolted into the cement ground, and one long cement table that is eerily similar to an altar. One solid, seamless door is in the center of the wall across from her, and there are multiple deadbolts that require keys to unlock from the other side.

The air is moist and smells of mildew and rot, though nothing she can see accounts for the rotten smell. The floor is cold, bare, and stained in several spaces. She can't tell what created the stains, but the chains and smell indicate it's not from something innocent, like water.

Shaking from the cold and fear, she checks her pockets to see if she has anything on her that could help her, but they are completely empty. The manacles are so tightly bound onto her wrists and ankles that she can't slip a finger in between the metal and her skin, let alone even think about attempting to slide them off. The small padlocks hooked into the manacles give her a flash of hope, and she reaches up to her hair to remove her bobby pin so she can attempt to pick the locks. Her heart stutters when she realizes those have been taken from her too.

"Help!" she screams, unable to stay silent any longer. "Someone please, help me!"

Unsurprisingly, no one responds or runs to her rescue, and her screams ring out long enough for her to go hoarse with the effort. An undetermined amount of time later, after she collapsed in exhaustion and hopelessness, the click of lock tumblers crack through the small room like bullets. She sits up and curls into herself as much as the chains will allow in an attempt to protect herself as much as possible. Her long skirt covers her legs and she tucks the ends underneath her to protect her modesty from whoever is coming.

The door slowly swings open and the bright light behind it illuminates the shape of a large man while leaving his features in shadow.

"Please," she whispers brokenly. "Please let me go. I don't understand why I'm here. My father will come looking for me. Please." The first tears start streaming down her face against her will, and her shaking intensifies until her teeth are chattering. She's not afraid to beg if it could save her life.

The man doesn't move, but he does scoff at her tears. "Who do you think gave you to me, Mary?"

What? No. Her father loves her! He wouldn't give her to this man to be locked away.

"What... what do you mean? He wouldn't do that! My father loves me!"

The disappointed clicking of his tongue fills her with even more dread, though she didn't think it was possible. He takes two steps forward, allowing the light from the bare bulb in the room to reveal his identity. Mary gasps in shock, more confused now than before as she recognizes the man standing in front of her.

"What I mean, Mary, is that your father knows all about you and your sins. You're mine now, to save or condemn. What happens next is up to you."

Also By JS Mercier

The Secrets Duet

The Rooms We Hide
The Secrets They Keep

Connected Short Story

The Ghosts We Seek

Completed Duet

Secrets: The Complete Duet
Secrets: The Complete Duet includes both The Rooms We Hide and The Secrets They Keep, plus two exclusive bonus scenes!

The Void Prophecies

Exhale
Book 2 - Coming Soon
Book 3 - Coming Soon
Book 4 - Coming Soon

Connected Short Story

Radiant Poison
Radiant poison is my short story that was included in Sacrilege: a forbidden dark romance anthology

Standalones

Novella

Sweet Addiction

Short Story

The Jersey

Check Them Out On Amazon!

Stalk Me

I like it.

VISIT MY LINKTREE TO VIEW ALL
OF MY LINKS AND SOCIALS!

Acknowledgements

Leslie Anne - Thank you so much for creating a cover that inspired me from the moment that I saw it! I have loved working with you and getting to know you these past few months, I can't wait to continue working with you on the books to come.

Matt Dobbs - Thank you for dealing with my weird police questions - you're my hero! Can't wait until we can have another Tundra Party.

My parents, siblings, bestie, and husband - Thank you all for loving, encouraging, and enduring me throughout this process. I couldn't have finished this without you!

In Loving Memory

I would be remiss if I didn't add an acknowledgement of, and dedication to, my beautiful girl Sasha. She was in my lap when I had the inspiration for this story, she was with me many nights as I wrote, and if I'm honest, her snuggling up with me while I wrote sometimes made me sit and write longer so that she wasn't forced to move.

As one friend perfectly summed up for me, she was my soul kitty. From the moment I saw her as a three month old kitten, I knew we were meant to take care of each other. We had her for eleven wonderful years and she was taken from us too early, but I know that my BooCat will be waiting for me on the other side. This one is for you, Boo. Thank you for everything.

www.ingramcontent.com/pod-product-compliance
Lightning Source LLC
Chambersburg PA
CBHW070157310726
48976CB00001B/132